THE SIX SECRETS

THE SIX SECRETS

DANIEL SPRINGFIELD

ABOUT THE AUTHOR

Even though *The Six Secrets* is a fiction novel, Daniel Springfield spent thousands of hours of meticulous research to be as historically accurate as possible. Some of the characters are based on actual persons and some are fictional, yet the events, projects and organizations shaping the story are real. The upcoming saga is not only an adventure unfolding for the story's characters; it was a 'journey of revelations' for the author.

Daniel says, 'I write with belief; if I don't accept something as true or don't consider there are enough facts, I won't write it. During the research and writing process, I discovered astonishing truths – what I call 'wow moments' – regularly giving me chills. I trust you'll experience the same thrills and shocks I did.'

CONTENTS

CHAPTER ONE

Through the peephole, Frank Reiner sees the distinctive blank stare of a soulless man; ID raised, brow furrowed. Reiner must let the Agent in, unaware of three other men waiting in the wings. Door ajar – shoulders push – men barge in.

Before Frank can protest 'What the hell are you doing?' one of the burly men gags Reiner's mouth; the others thrust him onto one of the hotel room's twin beds. A sheet is wrenched from the other bed – dramatically whirled in the air – the tightly twisted material then slips around Frank Reiner's neck.

Tying a precision knot, they maneuver Reiner's thrashing body onto the balcony to secure the sheet to the railing.

In one swift motion, Reiner is thrown over the edge.

He scarcely has time to scream; his neck snapping, body jolting, dangling limply. Moments later the sheet rips, sending his already lifeless body plummeting eleven stories to the pavement below.

Frank Reiner's reported suicide came as a blow to work colleague and friend Max Stroheim. Max and Frank worked side-by-side for six years. Along with Bill Nedersham, they saw more life-defining moments in a day than most witness in a lifetime. Max knew Frank struggled with the remarkable information they'd been privy to. They all had.

But to take his own life?

It was a scenario Max did not envisage nor accept.

• • •

The NSA (National Security Agency) was officially formed by President Harry S. Truman and his Secretary of Defense, James Forrestal, in 1952 as an amalgamation of the AFSA (Armed Forces Security Agency) and NSCID (National Security Council Intelligence Directive). Yet, the seeds for the organization were planted years earlier.

Officially, the NSA was: 'A cryptologic intelligence agency of the United States Department of Defense responsible for the collection and analysis of foreign communications and foreign signals intelligence.'

In reality, the NSA was far larger and complex than even government officials knew. Truman and Forrestal gave the new agency sweeping powers – spreading well beyond the armed forces – extending further than the general public could dream to imagine.

Even before the official formation of the NSA, there were scores of secretive divisions, departments, and sub-departments. Even the President was only informed on a need-to-know basis, with the most secretive facility, initially referred to as S-4, requiring unprecedented clearances.

Few knew of S-4. And even fewer were allowed inside.

Nicknamed The Dark Side of the Moon, or sometimes dubbed Dreamland, S-4 was built deep underground within Nevada's Area 51. The Government denied the existence of Area 51 for almost 50 years, yet with the launch of Google Earth, Area 51's above-ground structures were seen by the public for the first time. But the network of its below-surface facilities remained unseen and unheard of – for a reason.

Two esteemed scientists, as well as the military's leading communications expert and code-breaker, Bill Nedersham, were employed to assist running the S-4 project and facilities. The two scientists were astrobiologist Dr. Max Stroheim and nuclear physicist Dr. Frank Reiner.

Max Stroheim and Frank Reiner were recruited from the NACA (National Advisory Committee for Aeronautics), being the forerunner of NASA, yet the two men had not previously met, nor encountered Bill Nedersham. Reiner and Nedersham were in their mid-thirties, being around ten years older than the youthful Max Stroheim, yet each man was single, dedicated, and career-driven.

Max Stroheim was handsome, softly spoken, thorough, and intellectually brilliant. A Harvard graduate holding several degrees, he was invited to be NACA's resident astrobiologist in 1947.

Astrobiology is the study of the origin, evolution, distribution, and future of life in the universe. This interdisciplinary field encompasses the search for habitable environments within our Solar System and habitable planets outside our Solar System, the search for evidence of prebiotic chemistry, the early evolution of life on Earth, and the potential for life to adapt on Earth and in outer space.

Max's astuteness was noted. When a sub-committee heading 'An important new government scientific project' requested an interview, he accepted without hesitation.

Dr. Stroheim was told little in the first meeting – no formal introductions – only enough information to arouse his curiosity.

Max Stroheim was not there to meet these men; they were there to meet him.

There was just one reference to what the job may entail: 'This is the most important position of learning power in the world but, for now, that is all we are at liberty to tell you.'

It was all the information an enthusiastic, young scientist would need.

Complex psych tests and evaluations were completed before Max attended his second interview. Only then was he addressed with these statements:

'You will have access to information and events only a select few have right of entry to. This material and the associated research will change your life forever. Because of that you'll need to dedicate your life to the cause. Your country demands it.

'You're only twenty-five, single, and live on your own. You don't drink; you don't smoke; you play golf. We know you are a dedicated and bright scientist. That must continue to be so.

'When the time is right, you'll become aware of the paramount importance for the secrecy of this operation and the subsequent meaning of the research.

'You'll be asked to move to a new location. You are allowed to live away from that location, however, you're never allowed to talk about any events or operations at the base or any another location you may work. Your research will be of the upmost secrecy. You're to tell no one – not family, not friends, no one. Ever. Do you understand?'

Max understood; the words delivered clearly and surely.

'If you're successful, you'll need to sign a confidentiality agreement. At that point, numeracy and work benefits will be discussed. Needless to say, you'll be handsomely rewarded. It is the price your country is prepared to pay for your involvement in something that may change the course of history.

'This is the most important decision you'll ever make. Your country needs you, but will only accept your involvement in such a groundbreaking assignment should you fully accept the significance and the conditions of the operation.

'You've twenty-four hours to make a decision. We hope you choose wisely.'

• • •

In the summer of 1948, Max Stroheim, Frank Reiner, and Bill Nedersham travel by convoy to Area 51. Each had individual training, yet this is their first time together. They are accompanied by forthright, assertive Colonel Ian Berkmeyer. Berkmeyer was not on the interview panels, yet he was described as 'The man in charge of special operations within Area 51.'

'I could give you the boloney name of the secret operation,' Berkmeyer barks in his Southern drawl, 'but that'll probably change later this week, anyhows.'

Berkmeyer is flippant with his words, yet the three men are not fooled by his manner. His guidance will be invaluable. They hang on his every word, especially when he begins sentences with 'You boys …'

'You boys have been told next to nothing. You must be dying to find out why all the secrecy, but just hold on a whiles. All will be revealed, but before we get to the base, there's some basic housekeeping rules, so listen carefully.'

He reels off a list of dos and don'ts with rapid precision. 'You boys are not military – you're classified as civilians working in a military environment. There is no need to salute anyone, talk, or even make eye-contact with anyone, unless I say so. Got it? If you're told to walk, you walk. If you're told to stop, you stop. If you're told to look straight ahead … you boys know the drill.'

Moving deeper underground, the four men pass numerous security checkpoints within the concealed complex. Berkmeyer enters push-button access codes, inserts keys, and punches in yet more access codes. He assists the men with their newly issued security clearances, scrutinizing each authorization at each checkpoint. They edge close to the inner sanctum to enter a sterilizing zone. Berkmeyer instructs the men to strip, before each takes an air shower, ensuring he and the men are dust-free. They then don sterilized protective clothing.

Berkmeyer has one more door to open.

He delivers direct instructions. 'Now, listen very carefully, you boys: This whole level is surrounded by a series of electromagnetic grids. One grid will turn off while we enter, individually, then you must quickly step inside on your own. Make sure you keep walking. There is another door that will shut behind you. The grid will shut down each time for four seconds only, then switch back on. Trust me when I say you don't want to get caught napping. When it turns back on we have another grid to shut down inside. Watch carefully as I will demonstrate the sequence just the once.'

Max Stroheim is the last to key-in the access codes. He quickly steps through the open doorway. He keeps walking, two steel doors closing behind him seconds later. He then joins Colonel Berkmeyer, Reiner, and Nedersham, standing outside yet another door.

'This is it,' Berkmeyer informs them. 'Now, you boys, Dr. Mendoza is inside. I'll do the talking.'

He then addresses Max. 'You'll be spending a lot of time with Mendoza, so I'll be bringing you back here later. I could tell you more, but hell, let's just go in.'

He presses a sequence of buttons on a keypad by the door.

The door opens.

The men step through the doorway into a dimly lit, large, sterile room, featuring medical-style equipment and monitors on the far wall. Also wearing a protective suit, Dr. Mendoza stands alongside a solitary hospital-style bed facing the doorway. On the bed is a body; a small body lying face-up – the head of the bed raised slightly, enabling the head of whatever it is to be propped up.

As the men walk inside the room, the door behind them closes. Their eyes adjust to the dim lighting. The figure on the bed moves ever so slightly, the head slowly turning to face the door.

Eyes blink – eyes focus – eyes blink again.

The three men cannot believe what they are seeing:

It is a LIVE ALIEN.

Ten minutes pass; the men stand in astonishment – staring at the most unusual living being they've ever seen. And it is staring back at them.

Colonel Berkmeyer steps forward. He formally introduces the men to Dr. Guillermo Mendoza, a quiet, unassuming man.

Initially shell-shocked, Max's mind is now racing – so many questions occupy his thoughts. His years and training as an astrobiologist were geared toward this very moment. Staring at what appears to be a live alien has surpassed any preconceived expectations he had.

A living creature from another planet? Max thinks to himself. *I'm guessing it IS from another planet? This is incredible.*

Before they can ask any questions, Colonel Berkmeyer speaks on Mendoza's behalf; addressing all, yet facing Max Stroheim.

'Stroheim, this will be your second home for the immediate future. You and Dr. Mendoza will be working together, so you'll have plenty of time to get to know each other,' he states, before addressing all. 'But for now, you boys have other facilities to see. Follow me.'

Berkmeyer ushers the three men from the room.

Dr. Stroheim turns to see the alien one more time.

'Wow' he mutters under his breath.

The four men return through three of the same checkpoints, remove their protective clothing, and don their original clothes. Berkmeyer leads them in a different direction.

'You boys will work together at times but, most of the time, you'll be in separate sections. Most people who work here, or at other facilities, are generally restricted to their area only. You have been briefed on the secrecy of these locations and projects. This confidentiality is more important than your individual research. Secrecy is everything.'

Colonel Berkmeyer continues to lecture 'the boys' on security issues, as they access a series of doors to continue deep inside another section of the complex.

Max Stroheim learns that when he was told *You're never allowed to talk about any events or operations at the base, or any another location you may work*, they meant it.

Colonel Berkmeyer continues, with an off-the-cuff remark. 'Remember the vows of secrecy you took? We have a saying around here: "If no one talks, then no one dies." I knew three people who disregarded that instruction.'

Max noted Berkmeyer didn't say *know three people*, he said the past tense, *knew*. Three people talked – and three died. *This is a clear message*, Max Stroheim recognizes. *The Colonel is not one to waste words.*

Max Stroheim and Bill Nedersham are quiet men, not intimidated by their surroundings. They choose to listen intently to Berkmeyer's words. Frank Reiner is more inquisitive.

Colonel Berkmeyer does not like being asked questions.

'You boys aren't here to ASK questions; you're here to ANSWER them. You don't question what goes on, especially in other divisions or departments. You trust the processes. If you don't trust the processes, you shouldn't be here.'

This comment was aimed at Frank Reiner – directly and forcefully.

They pass various sections, seeing men in lab coats busy behind the scenes. No one makes eye contact. No one talks.

Berkmeyer leads the men to a door. Outside the door is an interphone. He presses the button.

A reply comes through the interphone, 'Guten tag.'

With a hint of a smile, Berkmeyer barks, 'Speak English, you mad German bastard. I have the new team here.'

The door is opened by an elderly bespectacled man. He speaks English poorly, having a thick German accent, and introduces himself as physicist Dr. Dieter von Hoffenberg.

The men would later learn that hundreds of Germany's top scientists, before and after WWII, came to the USA. Many were involved in secret projects.

Von Hoffenberg ushers the men inside, noting fellow-physicist Frank Reiner. He will be spending much time in the future with him.

On a table in the center of the room is a large piece of metal.

'Lift it up,' von Hoffenberg instructs, looking at Dr. Reiner.

'What, all of us?' queries Frank Reiner. The piece of 'metal' is sizable, almost the size of a small car.

'No, just you,' instructs von Hoffenberg.

Frank Reiner steps forward, bemused, yet willing to attempt to lift the metallic-looking sheet.

'We've tried to cut it, burn it, weld it, shape it, bash it … but nothing,' says von Hoffenberg. He encourages Reiner to pick it up.

Frank runs his fingertips over the material, assessing the texture, before spreading his legs like a weightlifter and stretching his arms in preparation to lift with all his might. He grits his teeth. Yet he discovers he can lift the large 'metal' sheet with limited effort.

He lifts the whole piece into the air.

'It's as light as a feather,' Reiner gasps in shock.

The covering sheet is as thin as foil, yet solid in appearance and function. A dull grey metallic color, the material is wrapped over a purplish-colored I-beam. It appears to be some type of support structure. Clear markings are stamped within the assembly; symbols, like Egyptian hieroglyphics, featuring eight distinct images, aligned and evenly spaced. Bill Nedersham's eyes open wide. Clearly, he's never seen these encryptions before. He steps forward.

'We've found symbols on most of the craft we've found,' says Dr. von Hoffenberg.

'Most?' mutters Frank Reiner. 'So, there's more than one craft?'

'Many more. The symbols vary from craft to craft,' says Dr. von Hoffenberg, stepping forward to point at the outer skin of the craft. 'As you can see, there are no rivets, no seams, no weld marks, no lines whatsoever. This is like no other metalwork we have ever seen.' Frank Reiner, a physicist, is in awe of the unusual material of the craft's debris; Bill Nedersham, a cryptologist, is fascinated by the hieroglyphics; and Max Stroheim realizes this is the transport mode of a species possibly from another part of the universe. None of the men have seen anything like this before. They are looking at something of non-earthly nature, something beyond their scientific comprehension. They don't need to say a word.

Colonel Berkmeyer glances at his watch.

Moments later, a *buzz* on the interphone is attended to by Dr. von Hoffenberg. He opens the door to let in a tall, gaunt man around sixty years old. Max, Frank, and Bill recognize the man instantly. They'd met him during their interviews. He is Dr. Vannevar Bush, reputedly the most influential scientist and administrator in the United States. Dr. Bush was the instigator and organizer of the Manhattan Project, the top-secret research and development project that produced the first atomic bombs during World War II. It was Dr. Bush who persuaded the Government to fund such an ambitious project, and he who recruited Dr. Robert Oppenheimer and a team of renowned physicists to produce the world's first atom bomb. Dr. Bush was responsible for introducing a level of secrecy to projects unprecedented in America's history – now he is overseeing the projects at S-4.

Addressing Stroheim, Reiner, and Nedersham, Dr. Bush says, 'Hello, gentlemen – and welcome. I trust Colonel Berkmeyer has shown you some interesting things. I can't stay long so let me say that, although you have just arrived, you must already know that you are embarking on scientific research like no other. You will learn more in a few days than most would learn in a lifetime. And you now know the reason for the utmost secrecy. You are in a privileged position and you must know what you are about to embark on will have lifelong ramifications.'

He removes a pocket-watch from his vest pocket, checks the time, then places the watch back in his pocket. 'Over the coming days, I'll be seeing all of you individually in your sections, as well as in the communal area, so we'll have the chance to talk personally. But for now, welcome and understand that this is the first day of the rest of your lives.'

CHAPTER TWO

Max Stroheim spent thirty-four dedicated years as an employee of the NSA. It was his life. Not expecting any different, he somehow managed to meet and fall in love with a beautiful woman almost twenty years his junior.

Max married Mary Cole the day after he retired. For her to fall pregnant was an unexpected, yet pleasant shock.

After an uncomplicated labor, Cole Joseph Stroheim was born, taking Mary's maiden name and Joseph, the name of Max's only brother. Simply referred to as C.J., the baby boy was loved as much as any baby could be. The elderly Max Stroheim took to the role of fatherhood with the same passion and dedication as in his professional career. He moved the family to Pasadena, California, to be closer to Mary's family.

Young C.J. was a bright student and an excellent soccer player. As a teenager, he gained the reputation as one of the most powerful ball strikers in California. Max watched every game. C.J. and Max were from different generations, but they shared a mutual respect. C.J. had his father's academic problem-solving abilities, also being outgoing and creative like his mother.

Even failing health did not dull Mary's warmth and creativity. She mastered computer technology, embraced the Internet, and, had her health been better, she would have loved to write a book.

She suffered, yet never complained. Dignity was just one of the many valuable traits handed to her son.

Mary Stroheim passed away when C.J. was in his second year of university.

C.J. studied Journalism at the University of Southern California (USC) Annenberg School for Communication and Journalism. Max and Mary moved to Palm Springs, less than two hour's drive from LA and USC. Max chose a retirement home facility with the best medical care for Mary; money was never an issue.

Palm Springs was the perfect fit for the Stroheims; Max was an avid golfer and Mary enjoyed the social benefits of a similarly aged community. In Mary's final months, Max rarely played golf, spending every moment beside the woman he adored.

Mary had loved to travel. During the early stages of her deteriorating health, Max indulged Mary's passion: Atlantic and Pacific cruises, a tour of Europe, a two-month holiday in Australia, and visiting Max's brother, Joe, in Thailand. When it did not interfere with his schooling, C.J. accompanied his parents, including the trip to Thailand. After that trip, C.J. returned to his studies, while Max and Mary continued their holiday, traveling to Australia. It was the last time Mary was able to travel.

Australia was Max's destination of choice after Mary passed away. He stayed with his best friend, retired Air Force General Vince Pomerel, who'd left the US to live on Queensland's Gold Coast. Max then spent several weeks on his own at Mary's favorite destination; a small beachside hamlet in the island state of Tasmania.

Max learned how to play golf at early age. Although he never talks about the intricacies of his working career, he proudly recalls playing golf with Harry Truman, both during and after Truman's presidency. C.J. knows his father dealt with a number of presidents and influential people, yet little else. Max was a scientist of note; he is happy to impart scientific knowledge, discuss complex hypotheses, yet at no time does

Max divulge the secrets of his thirty-four years within the NSA.

Although he has physically aged, Max still hits an impressive golf ball. It is a calming influence on his life and Max can be found on the golf course most days.

C.J. has just turned thirty, exceptionally handsome and athletic. Quite the cheeky, partying womanizer in his college years, a long-term relationship has mellowed in C.J. That relationship has just ended; his life and professional career are at a crossroads.

C.J.'s journalistic career hasn't panned out as planned. Working for a regional newspaper based in Orange County, one of LA's southern counties, it is not the most challenging job, but it has given C.J. the convenience and flexibility to travel to Palm Springs and spend time with his aging father. Max Stroheim's health is of concern.

C.J. dabbles in book writing. Thanks to a contact through his best friend, Ellis Buckman, C.J. has a published an eBook. Entitled *Grains of Sand in the Universe*, it was based on an interesting article C.J. read in his second year as a journalist. After the death of his mother, it was a project to take his mind from the grief, as well as involve his father.

The article suggested that, if a single grain of sand represented a star in the sky (being a sun or a planet), and if you took every grain of sand from every beach on the entire planet, then there'd still be more than five times the number of stars in the universe than grains of sand on Earth. This statistic astonished C.J.; the sheer enormity of stars was almost beyond comprehension. C.J. knew his father was an astrobiologist, so the 'grains of sand' subject matter should be right up Max Stroheim's alley. Here was an opportunity for C.J. to share his father's wisdom. The two spent many hours discussing how the universe might work. Max agreed with the hypothesis that there are billions upon billions of other suns and planets, guiding C.J.'s research, and assisting where he could. C.J. began writing the fact-based book hoping to learn more about his father, as well as to fuel his fascination of the universe – and how little he really know about it. For C.J., it was a win-win situation.

With the help of his father, plus many hours of Internet research, C.J. wrote the book on the universe and how it possibly worked. It only sold one-thousand-or-so copies; however, C.J.'s proudest moment was when his father read the book … and gave it his approval.

Ellis Buckman and C.J. were in the same journalism class, becoming instant friends. Ellis is a journalist of distinction, working as a reporter for a prominent LA TV news network.

Today, C.J. is having a regular catch-up with Ellis over coffee. After coffee, C.J. will drive to Palm Springs. Although playing golf rarely (and poorly), he has agreed to accompany his father on the golf course.

Ellis Buckman is tall and lean, with slender, bony fingers; for someone appearing on nightly TV, he is not an attractive man. At best, he can be described as 'distinctive.' He is, however, always immaculately dressed, in designer suits and Italian leather shoes.

'So you're playing golf with your old man, hey,' says Ellis, sipping his coffee.

C.J. nods.

'What will you and old Maxi talk about for five hours around a golf course?' Ellis Buckman is an inquisitive man.

'I'm not sure.'

'Maybe your father might finally reveal what he did for all those years with the NSA?'

Ellis has asked this question many times over the years. Ellis Buckman knows Max Stroheim spent thirty-four years in the NSA and liaised with presidents and other famous scientists, yet C.J. has told Ellis little else. C.J. knows little himself.

Ellis Buckman is not fazed. 'Come on C.J. – I'm an investigative reporter; surely your father has hinted at what he did?'

C.J. shakes his head.

'So, out of the blue, the President of the United States happens to start playing golf with a scientist more than thirty years younger than himself – and they continue playing even after Truman retires. Surely you're curious to as why?'

'Of course I'm curious, but I've told you before, my father never talks about his career. I'm sure if he wanted to, or was able to, he would. Mum and I had to respect that. All I know is that he played golf with Harry Truman – and that both men loved golf.'

The Seven Lakes Country Club is Max Stroheim's local club. Although Max has health issues and is in his 90s, he still hits a straight ball. C.J. does not. There are few others on the course, with no golfers immediately behind them. C.J. has missed the fairway yet again, the ball rolling between trees. Max steps from the electric golf cart.

'I'll help you look for the ball,' he offers, following his son into the trees. He stops. 'Son, stop for a moment. I have some important things to tell you.'

'Tell me? What, here?'

'Here, now.' says Max seriously. He looks around to make sure no one is nearby. 'My whole life, I've been under surveillance. Every house we lived in was bugged – all the rooms, the phones, as well as the cars. Probably even the golf carts.'

'Bugged … how?' asks C.J., more startled by his father's sudden willingness to talk than the revelation itself.

'I found many devices over the years, particularly early on when bugging devices were bigger and less sophisticated, but they're still around to this day. I even found some in your room when you were a kid. I never touched them. What would be the point? They'd just replace them with another.'

'They?'

'The NSA, the secret bureaus, the CIA, the secret services, and God knows who else.' Max knows C.J. will ask 'Why?'

He does.

'That's what I want to talk to you about, son.' Max pauses briefly.

C.J. is fully attentive.

'I've never told a soul about my thirty-four years with the NSA; not even your mother. The risks were too great. Anyone who talked would talk no more – and anyone who listened mysteriously vanished. There was a saying behind closed doors: *If no one talks, then no one dies.*'

'So, are you saying that people who talked were killed by our own government?'

'No, I didn't say that,' Max pauses to choose his words carefully. 'At this stage, I cannot and will not tell you more. You are my son. I wouldn't risk your life for anything.'

'But Dad, I ...'

'Listen and listen very carefully, C.J. You know I haven't been well. I only have about a month to go. I think you knew, deep down. Don't say a word – it is what it is. I have secrets I'm prepared to take to the grave if need be. I'd prefer it wasn't the case but so be it. You're a journalist and you're inquisitive like your mother.

'Now, I've had access to information and events only a select few had access to. This information and the research associated with it changed my life forever.' Max takes a deep breath. 'If I were to share some of that information, it would change your life forever, too. It would also place you in great danger. As much as I think the world needs to know this information, I cannot ask that of you.'

With tears in his eyes, C.J. replies, 'Dad, can I be the one to make that decision?'

'This is not a game, son. I am serious.'

C.J. knows how serious his father is. 'Dad, I've always been prepared to take a risk – you know that. You know I'm not reckless. Whatever you're prepared to tell me, I'm equally prepared to accept the consequences.'

Max sees a rarely displayed maturity in his son.

'You would need to become a fugitive – leave your job, your home, your friends, and your girlfriend. You will have to move overseas – for a period of time at least. The research and the secrets revealed will enable you to write a book – an incredible book – one the world needs to read.'

Seeing the intense concentration on his son's face, Max continues. 'You will learn things that very few people have knowledge of. But that information will come at a price. You cannot tell anyone anything; not even Kelly.'

Kelly was C.J.'s girlfriend. He'd ended the relationship recently, but now is not the time to tell his father.

'I cannot stress enough that you can't tell a soul. Not Kelly – not your friend Ellis – not anyone,' warns Max.

'I can take that on,' C.J. attempts to convey his willingness to accept any conditions.

'It is not that simple, son. You must be fully aware of the responsibility that comes with such information. Also, understand that I took a vow never to divulge that information while I was alive.' Max pauses momentarily to change his tone. 'That doesn't mean I can't tell all after I'm gone.'

'What does that mean?'

'You'll see' replies Max, with a wry smile. 'Before I accepted the position at the NSA, I was given very little information, but I was asked for a commitment …'

'There's no need to ask, Dad. You already know I'll say "yes".'

Max never doubted what his son's answer would be. This day had taken much time in the planning.

'It will be no easy task, son. It will take time to learn the secrets. You will have a great deal to research. It will be like digging a hole in the sand: the more you dig, the more the walls will collapse. But you must keep digging. At some point, the end will be in sight. Then, and only then, will I give you the final information. You will learn of six secrets, six very important secrets. You will then be able to write a book. I already have a publisher organized for you.'

C.J. is confused. 'How will you give me these details if you are, um…?'

'I have everything planned. You'll see. When the time is right, you'll receive information to start researching. But, at that time you'll be in great danger. If they realize what you are doing, the risks will be extreme.'

C.J. has many questions to ask, but chooses to listen.

'When you have written the book and it is published, it will be too late for them. They will do everything in their power to stop the truth from coming out, but then they will go into damage control. Stay under the radar and you'll stay safe. Money will not be an issue, so write the book, tell the truth, and then say no more.'

Max has chosen every word carefully. He always does.

'I have organized for you to fly to Thailand. You'll receive the ticket when the time is right. Uncle Joe knows you'll be coming. He'll give you access to a safety deposit box, as well as a new passport, ID, and credit card. Again, money will not be an issue. There will be instructions to help your research.'

His father looks at him, expecting C.J. to say something. 'Research?'

'Yes, research, and a lot of it,' says Max on queue. 'I will guide you, but I want you to dig for yourself. I want you to come up with answers. It won't be easy. As I said, it will be like digging a hole in the sand, but don't give up. Eventually there will be structure; eventually everything will make sense. The six secrets are all connected. You'll see.

'When you were growing up, I always stressed for you to remain patient, to look at things from different perspectives. To embark on this journey will require more patience than you've ever had to show before.'

C.J. hangs on his father's every word.

'I know it all sounds like a big game, son, but trust me – it is for your own good. You will not be able to grasp the truth. Well, not initially. This will be the hardest thing you will ever do in your life. Not only will you discover things that'll be hard to comprehend, but you'll have to do it while traveling and moving.'

'Traveling and moving? So I go to Thailand then where?'

'Tasmania, Australia.'

C.J. is taken aback. 'Tasmania? I know you and Mum had a great holiday down there, but what's in Tasmania that is so important?'

'Nothing, specifically, but it's a long way away from America – and such a beautiful place. It was your mother's favorite place in the world.'

CHAPTER THREE

C.J. heard his parents talk of Boat Harbour Beach, telling how the sand is so white and fine it squeaks under your feet when you walk on it.

Ten years ago, Max and Mary Stroheim sat on the deck of a magnificent beach house, overlooking the crystal-clear waters of Boat Harbour Beach. Mary had seen late-night commercials advertising teeth-whitening products, and was certain the pristine sand must have somehow been bleached. When the sun shone on the shallow water lapping over the sand, the colors were breathtaking.

'Azure I think – or is it turquoise?' she asked.

Mary's friends had urged them to take a week out of their 'See all of Australia in three weeks tour' to come to a place they simply referred to as 'Paradise.' That week turned into a month.

Although both knew Mary's health would not allow her to return, Mary regularly commented it was the 'perfect location to write a book.'

That statement would become more profound than Mary ever envisaged.

Returning to Boat Harbour Beach after Mary's passing, Max contemplated life without his adoring wife. He should have been sad, yet thoughts of Mary's contentment when they walked along the beautiful beach curtailed his sorrow. It was Mary's favorite place in the world. It was now Max's, too.

Max Stroheim tells his son he's made arrangements made for a three-month stay at a beach house at Boat Harbour Beach.

'Three months?' C.J. asks.

'I know it's a long time. You'll need it – and it's a distraction-free environment to research. After Tasmania, you can take the next leg of the journey, but worry about that when the time comes. Be patient, move on step at a time.'

This is a lot of information for C.J. to digest. He knows he will be traveling halfway around the world to research for three months; that is massive in itself. And then he goes elsewhere?

Max elaborates. 'That is just the beginning, but you need to take time out to smell the roses.'

That adage was one of Mary Stroheim's favorite sayings.

Max and C.J. return to the golf cart. Without saying a word, Max removes from his golf bag a small tin box with a standard three-digit wheel combination lock. Max places a single finger to his lips. He places the box in C.J.'s golf bag, before carefully zipping the bag's compartment closed.

On the next hole, Max deliberately hits his ball into the rough. 'Damn slice,' he says, with unconvincing acting skills.

As they walk toward the ball, Max says, 'The box is not to be opened until instructed. You could easily force it open; however, the information inside will only be relevant once you've thoroughly researched.'

Max then hands C.J. a note.

C.J. studies it. 'What's this?'

'A riddle.'

The note reads: *The acronym for Krll in telephone numeric form.*

C.J. reads out loud, 'The acronym for K-R-L-L …'

Max interrupts. 'No, not K-R-L-L. It's one word: Krll.'

C.J. corrects himself to say 'So Krll – in telephone numeric form?'

Max acknowledges C.J. has no idea what the riddle means, although he will in time. Should he solve the riddle quickly, and Max expects him to do just that, then C.J. should still not open the box until he feels the time is right.

'How will I know the time is right?'

'You'll know. When you feel you have enough information to understand and accept the truth, open the box. The information inside the box will guide you to the next leg of your journey. Do not, under any circumstances, let anyone else see what's inside. Hide the box well.'

C.J. realizes his visit to Thailand is to pick up something. 'But what happens if I lose the box?'

'Then the journey ends. It was not meant to be.

'Son, you know I worked under the umbrella of the NSA. I'm sure you've read about whistleblower Edward Snowden, and you would no doubt know that, these days, the NSA has access to Internet information from pretty much every computer and cell phone. But I want you to realize this: In my thirty-four years with the NSA, there was no Internet and no global-roaming phones. Yet, by the late fifties and sixties, there were around ninety thousand people working for the NSA. Ninety thousand.

'The question you need to ask at some point is: "What did they all do?"

'With that said, now is not that time. I don't want you to look at the current NSA operations. Not yet, anyway. As I said, you need to be patient. If you get to the end of the challenges I have planned, you will learn everything. You will discover how and why America runs – and the global systems put in place that affect the whole planet. Important things that occur are rarely random events. This you will learn.'

C.J. has so many questions running through his mind. His father said he *worked under the umbrella of the NSA*, implying Max Stroheim did not work directly for the NSA. He also said that 90,000 people worked for the agency, at a time well before the computer and Internet era. *So what did the NSA do?*

Before he can ask any questions, his father declares 'I know you want to ask questions. As much as I would like to give you answers now, I can't, nor would it help you in your upcoming journey. What I will say is that I left the NSA in nineteen eighty-three; those processes that were developed, and expanded, in the nineteen forties, fifties, and beyond are still in existence today. Whether the president is a Bush, Clinton,

Obama, or even Trump, those systems will not change. This you will come to realize.'

C.J. recognizes why his father won't elaborate; however, he has one question he's always wanted to ask – and now seems the appropriate time.

'Dad, I know you met Mum while you were still with the NSA, or whoever it was you were working for. Mum was not a shy, accepting woman. I know she knew nothing about your work. What did you say when you first met, for her never to ask?'

Max recalls fondly how Mary did ask – repeatedly. 'Yes, son, your mother wasn't shy or accepting. I told her my work was very important and top-secret; to talk about it would jeopardize what I and others were working on. I vowed that, if she never asked me about my work, I would be open and honest about everything else in my life.'

'Everything?'

'Everything. She knew I was not an overly emotional person. She kept her promise and I kept mine. I think your mother ended up knowing me better than I knew myself.'

On the eighteenth hole, C.J. hits yet another wayward shot into trees. After leaving the golf cart to find the ball, C.J., with tears in his eyes, wraps his arms around his father.

'I love you Dad. I won't let you down.'

'I have always been proud of you, son. This journey is not just an expedition for you to find the truth; it is much larger than that. You will come to understand. The world needs to hear the truth. Harry Truman once said to me, "Sometimes, it is best to disregard what you *thought* was true until you *know* it is true."

'Son, you will need to know the truth for yourself before you can share that wisdom with others.'

C.J. has learnt more wisdom in eighteen holes of golf than most learn in eighteen years of life. He wills his father to keep talking.

'I wish I had the courage to come forward years ago but, when you were born, and being with your mother and all, well, I just wasn't prepared to take the risk,' Max tells with an air of self-disappointment. 'I have met with a publisher. I was going to write the book myself but, after your mother died, with all the surveillance and bugging, as well as my health failing, it became difficult. You are a journalist and a pretty good one at that, even though you haven't really had the chance to prove yourself. This could be your chance. It was actually your mother's idea for you to write the book.'

'Mum? But I didn't think Mum knew anything?'

'She didn't. She was a very smart woman, your mother. I'd been writing down a few notes here and there. She never once saw those notes – no one did – but somehow she put two-and-two together.'

Before they leave the security of the trees, Max hugs his son once more. He gives C.J. a last piece of advice.

'I love you, son. What you are about to undertake is important, but your well-being is more important. Not everything you find out will make sense. Much will, but not all. In many ways, you'll need to start from scratch. You have been part of the media. Disregard everything you have learned to date. Often, what is reported by others is not necessarily the truth. Remember that what appears to be the truth can be, and often is, manipulated. So take your time, do what you have to do and, most importantly, cover your tracks. I trust you, son. I know you'll do our family proud.'

• • •

In the following weeks, C.J. takes an extended leave of absence from his work to spend as much time as possible with his father. Max's health has deteriorated, but his mind is still sharp. Max does not talk further about what they talked about on the golf course, yet is philosophical and forthright about all other subjects. They spend more time talking than C.J. can ever recall. It is a special time for both men.

Max Stroheim was always a thorough, well-organized man. C.J. asks if there is anything to do regarding his father's affairs, and is not surprised to learn Max has planned everything already.

It is surreal for C.J. to be sitting at his father's side, knowing he will probably learn more about his father's working life after his death than while alive. He would so love the opportunity for his father to personally reveal what he knows, but respects the decisions his father has made. Max Stroheim is old school, an honest and good man. C.J. knows the decision for him to look into his father's past is one that would not have been made with haste. He must respect his father's wishes.

• • •

Max Stroheim's funeral is simple, yet dignified. Max was a private man, with few close friends. Most of his business colleagues and golfing buddies had passed away years earlier.

Reading the eulogy, C.J. tells 'I spent a lot of time with my father in recent times. He knew he was going to die – and he was okay with that. "I'll be joining your mother soon," he said. I have never seen a man love a woman as much as my father loved Mum. He always told me how lucky he was to have her in his life.

'Max Stroheim lived a long and fulfilling life, he had a successful career and a loving family. Most of you would know that, after Mum's passing ten years ago, apart from my father taking a few overseas holidays, he would play golf at Palm Springs almost daily. We played golf only a few weeks ago and, of course, he talked about Mum. But he also reminisced about his golfing days with former President Harry Truman. For those of you who are unaware, my father first played golf with Harry Truman in the early nineteen fifties, while Truman was President. They continued to play and be friends after Harry left politics and, from what I understand, they continued playing golf right through the fifties and most of the sixties.

'I'm sure Harry Truman and my father had some deep and meaningful conversations on the golf course, but my father was always more interested recalling their golf rivalry. For the record, my father told me that he won most of their golf games – to quote my father: "Harry had a wicked sense of humor, but he had an even more wicked slice!"

'Apart from myself, my father's only living relative is his younger brother, Joe, my Uncle Joe. Uncle Joe is in Thailand and unable to come today; however, we've talked on the phone. Uncle Joe recalled spending several glorious weeks with his brother just a few months earlier. Dad went over to Thailand several times in recent years and, although there is a twelve-year age gap with Uncle Joe, they were very close.

'Uncle Joe has sent me a business-class ticket to Bangkok with the understanding that I will visit when time permits. I think I'll go sooner than later.

'Thank you, all, for coming today. Max Stroheim was not just a great man; he was a great father and a doting husband. He'll be sadly missed, but his wisdom and understanding will never be forgotten. I love you Dad.'

Ellis Buckman stands alongside C.J., a hand on C.J.'s shoulder.

'Great speech, Stroheim. Old Maxi would've been proud.'

'Thanks, Ellis.'

'So, when are you going to Thailand?'

'I don't know. Soon, I guess. Uncle Joe is elderly, too. He's the only relative I have left.'

'Listen, Stroheim, if you want to talk about anything. You know, your last days with your father, or anything else, we can sit down over coffee or maybe nice glass of red. I'm free all day.'

'Not now, thanks Ellis. But thanks for the offer.'

• • •

A week later, C.J. and Ellis sip coffee and chat. Ellis is prying. Prying is not just a professional trait, it's in his nature.

'So, Stroheim, you're off to Bangkok tomorrow, hey. But why did you quit your job?'

'It was a dead-end job anyway,' C.J. answers, smiling. 'I didn't quite make the dizzy heights of a hotshot network reporter, like a certain someone I know.'

'Now, now – don't be like that.' Ellis leans in to ask, 'How long do you think you'll be gone for?'

'My mum passed ten years ago. Now I've lost my father. I broke up with my girlfriend of two and a half years only recently, and my job is meaningless. I've no major commitments and I'll probably get some inheritance money, so cash shouldn't an initial issue for a while.'

'You didn't answer the question,' forces Ellis.

'I might be gone a while.'

'What's a while? A week, a month, a year?'

'I don't know.'

'You'll keep me in the loop though?'

'I'll try.'

CHAPTER FOUR

Touching down in Bangkok, Thailand, the sixteen-hour flight was more tolerable sitting at the front of the plane. The other passengers relaxed, watched movies, or slept, but C.J. spent most of the flight in deep thought. His father's words resonated through his mind.

Now though, the grief for his father is tempered with curiosity and excitement.

C.J. often pondered about his father's role in the NSA. Years earlier, he researched the National Security Agency – and found little. This was before Edward Snowden copied and leaked classified information to reveal the NSA's global surveillance programs, and alliances with telecommunications companies and even European governments.

Back then, the average American had not heard of the NSA. C.J. read that the NSA was described as: 'a cryptologic intelligence agency of the United States Department of Defense, responsible for the collection and analysis of foreign communications and foreign signals intelligence ...'

C.J. found that classifying the exact role of the NSA was confusing, with much of the information about them contradictory. They were defined as being an intelligence organization of the United States Government, as being an offshoot of the Department of Defense, yet the NSA was also classified as 'independent.' Since 1957, the headquarters were at Fort Meade, Maryland, with more than 20,000 employees working at Fort Meade alone. To the best of C.J.'s knowledge, his father never worked in Maryland; he spent most of his working career in the states of New Mexico, Nevada, and California.

C.J. learned little information of use. As this was at a time when C.J.'s life revolved around parties, wine, and women, he did not further research the NSA.

Now his father revealed that by the late 1950s there were around 90,000 people working for the NSA in an era pre-Internet – and asked the question: *What did they all do?* This was merely a hint. Max Stroheim instructed his son to be patient – to wait for further instructions.

Hopefully those instructions will be in Thailand. C.J. thinks. *Still, before Edward Snowden's revelations, why was such a massive agency almost unheard of by the general public?*

Why was my father's work so secretive that it's still considered top-secret, more than 60 years after he began working there – and more than thirty years after he retired?

I know the NSA was supposedly set up as a 'cryptology agency' then, surely, a so-called 'foreign communications and foreign signals intelligence agency' from 1949, 1950 or even 1960 wouldn't be relevant today? The Korean and Vietnam wars are long gone, the Cold War is a thing of the past, and the military issues that plagued the United States fifty or sixty years ago are vastly different to what they are today. So why the secrecy?

Max Stroheim was an important man, with thirty-four years of working in a secretive world. Beyond that, C.J. knows nothing. To have the opportunity, and be given the trust, to possibly discover the truth behind his father's life is confrontational, yet stirring.

C.J. walks from the plane with a spring in his step.

Joe Stroheim is at the terminal to pick up his nephew. Max and Joe's age difference meant they were never close growing up; however, in later years that changed.

Joe moved to Bangkok in the 1980s due to his expanding import/export business, originally set up in Los Angeles. From humble beginnings Joe Stroheim (J.S.) Furnishings grew substantially. The company now incorporates manufacturing, as well as distribution, and exports globally.

Joe Stroheim never married, never had children, but was rumored to have a succession of Thai mistresses. While still the Managing Director of his firm, he is in semi-retirement and has managers run the day-to-day operations. Joe lives between two properties; a house in the heart of Bangkok's CBD and a beachfront condominium in Jomtien Beach, at the southern end of the popular tourist destination, Pattaya.

'I'd love to spend some time with you, C.J., but your father gave me specific instructions. I'm taking you to my house, which is near Siam Square – right in the heart of the city. You'll be staying there until tomorrow.'

'Tomorrow?'

'That's all. Your father has everything planned. You'll be picking something up from the bank just around the corner from my house. I won't be there. I'm going down to my apartment at Jomtien Beach, a few hours' drive away. Open the glove compartment, there's an envelope inside. This has all you'll need; keys to the house, your airline itinerary, a new credit card and passport, some business cards for Max and my lawyer here in Bangkok, as well as a publisher in England, and there's a note from your father for the code you'll need to access the security box at the bank. He said that you'd be the only one who would understand.'

C.J. opens the envelope to remove his father's note first.

The small, handwritten note reads: '*The number of goals, from each year in order, from the two years you won the Golden Boot awards.*'

This puzzle divulges a four-digit code. Joe was right, only C.J. would know the answer. C.J. is flabbergasted his father knew the answer; Max had remembered the number of goals his son kicked in the two most successful years of C.J.'s long forgotten junior soccer career.

When C.J. was nine, he kicked twenty-six goals for the year to win his inaugural golden boot award. At twelve, he kicked nineteen to claim his second.

The code must be: 2619.

C.J. then removes the airline itinerary, including business class e-tickets from Bangkok to Sydney, then a flight from Sydney to Launceston.

'Launceston?' he mutters.

Joe tells 'Launceston is in Tasmania. Max said you'd know all about this Boat Harbour Beach place. You'll also see that the bookings are under the name *Christopher Jones*. That's the name on the passport, as well as the credit card.'

C.J. removes the passport, focusing on the worn cover.

'Max carried the passport around in his back pocket for days. You know his attention to detail.'

On opening the passport, C.J. comments 'So how did he get this?'

'We did it; you can get almost anything copied at Khao San Road.'

'Where?'

'Khao San Road is here in Bangkok; only fifteen minutes by cab from my house. Max chose your new name; he cleverly worked it so you still had the initials C.J. He copied your handwriting for the signature, so you might want to practice the signature before flying out tomorrow.'

As C.J. inspects the credit card, Joe tells 'The password for the credit card is the same as the security box.'

C.J. then removes the two business cards, the Bangkok lawyer's card is the first card he inspects.

'Max said to contact Wichit only after you've written the book, so you'll have to return here at some stage. We'll have more time to talk then. Your father also instructed me to get you to handover your cell phone and any other traceable items, such as your current credit cards, passport, and driver's license. I'll give them to Witchit. The other card is for a publisher.'

'Mark Dalgleish, Dalgleish Publishing, Cambridge, England. Cambridge?'

'Cambridge is just north of London, I was told.'

Arriving outside Joe's house, C.J. leans across to hug his uncle. He then takes his small suitcase and his backpack, now containing the envelope contents, to the front door. Once C.J. opens the door, Joe waves goodbye, and drives away.

Anxious to go straight to the bank, C.J. looks only briefly at the magnificent furnishings inside, before placing his suitcase by the doorway. Then, with his backpack slung over his shoulder, he steps back outside, closing the door behind him.

C.J. enters the bank, handing over his new ID in the name of *Christopher Jones.*

C.J. presses the 2619 code into the security box. The box unlocks. Inside is a large sealed, padded envelope. His father's handwriting is on the front, instructing: *Open at Joe's.*

He can't get back to Joe's house quickly enough.

Inside the house, C.J. opens the envelope. Inside it is wad of cash, in US dollars and Thai baht, and a single sheet of paper. C.J. has little interest in the cash, pushing it aside to concentrate on the paper. This is why he is here – this is his father's life – this is his father's legacy.

With so much anticipation, he did not expect a single sheet.

He studies it carefully. It reads:

> OPC MJ-12, S-4
> PROJECTS: SIGN, GRUDGE, GRUDGE 13, REDLIGHT, SIGMA, POUNCE, PLUTO, MOONDUST & BLUE FLY
> CODE DREAMLAND
> IPU, AEC, AFOSI
> BOOKS YELLOW, <u>RED</u> & BLUE
> YY-II, DNI/27
> GREADA TREATY

What does it all mean?

Nothing rings a bell; nothing looks vaguely familiar.

At the bottom of the sheet, Max has written:

> Don't begin your research until you reach Boat Harbour Beach. For now, go and have a Thai massage. They do fantastic massages here – just around the corner, turn left, about 200 yards. Ask for Anong.

Max Stroheim knew the list of names, numbers, and letters will look unfamiliar to C.J. By instructing his son to 'go and have a Thai massage,' he is reminding his son to show patience. C.J. recognizes this, walking around the corner from Uncle Joe's home to find a luxurious massage house.

'Is Anong available?'

'Yes, sir.'

The massage was so good that C.J. returns the next morning, before returning to Joe's to pack.

C.J. boards his flight to Sydney, sleeping most of the way.

He then transfers to a domestic terminal to board a 90-minute flight to Launceston, Tasmania.

On arrival, he hires a car under the name of *Christopher Jones*. Awaiting his luggage at the baggage carousel, he uses the new credit card for the first time, reading the balance on the ATM with astonishment: more than $70,000 Australian dollars. In addition, he has US$8,000 and some Thai baht leftover from Bangkok. He knew his father was a reasonably wealthy man and his preparations for C.J.'s journey were thorough, but never expected this much money.

The two-hour drive to Boat Harbour Beach is picturesque; however, sightseeing is the last thing on C.J.'s mind. He is anxious to begin comprehending the letters, numbers, and words on his father's sheet. Even while being massaged, thinking about the list, C.J. drew a blank. There are numerous project names; none he has heard before. The list mentions three different-colored books, with RED underlined, and something called the *Greada Treaty*.

Greada Treaty? What on earth is that?

C.J. has studied wars of the modern era, yet can't recall any mention of a Greada Treaty. The more he thinks, the more intrigued he becomes. He knows the NSA is an intelligence-gathering agency, yet his father was a scientist, not a spy. The NSA is linked with the Department of Defense; however, he was sure his father worked in areas of little military strategic importance. He also knows his father 'worked under the umbrella of the NSA,' implying Max Stroheim did not work directly for the NSA.

C.J. has so many questions. Hopefully all will be revealed after beginning his research.

The road winds down through magnificent farmland to Boat

Harbour Beach – one way in and one way out. The hills fall to the cliff-side in lumpy rolls of lush green grass scattered with tall trees, tumbling downward to the sea, toward sharp rocky outcrops at the base of the hill. Beyond the ledge, the water is inviting, glistening like a glass full of diamonds.

'Wow, no wonder my parents loved this place. I totally get it.'

Pulling up outside the beach house, C.J. discovers the house is right on the beach, with a massive sundeck leading directly to pristine white sand.

C.J. again mutters 'Wow.'

It is late afternoon; if not for his desire to begin research, C.J. would spend more time admiring the natural beauty in front of him. Even so, he opens all the blinds and sliding doors to admire the splendid view, before plugging in his computer.

C.J. has studied his father's sheet with the numbers, letters, and words. He now knows the list almost by heart. The first series of letters and numbers on the list is: *OPC MJ-12.*

He nervously types *OPC MJ-12.* The very first Google search link is titled 'Majestic 12 and the Secret Government.'

C.J. reads the opening references to learn *Majestic 12 and the Secret Government* is the name of a series of lectures and speeches by William (Bill) Cooper. The C.J. of old would have impatiently skipped through the first references before going to the next.

One of the last things his father said before passing away was: 'Patience and time do more than strength or passion. Passion will dictate you want answers and want them instantly. Control your emotions, son. When researching, be methodical; take each step as it is presented to you. Should you need to read a book, then read a book. Should you need to read twenty books, so be it. The step-by-step journey will make you wiser than you ever dreamed.'

William Cooper was an American conspiracy theorist, radio broadcaster, and author. He served with the Air Force, before joining the Navy and becoming involved with Naval Intelligence, including a tour of duty during the Vietnam War. He was outspoken, yet knowledgeable and articulate.

Cooper talks of the OPC; however, C.J. firstly researches Wikipedia to see if information on OPC exists. It does:

> The Office of Policy Coordination (OPC) was 'a United States covert psychological operations and paramilitary action organization. Created as an independent office in 1948, it was merged with the Central Intelligence Agency (CIA) in 1951.'

According to Cooper, *MJ-12* is a separate organization, being the abbreviated form of a group known as the *Majestic 12*; an alleged secret committee of scientists, military leaders, and government officials formed in 1947 on executive order by US President Harry S. Truman.

C.J. is spellbound. He reads the line 'secret committee of SCIENTISTS, military leaders, and government officials' again.

Was his father in this secret committee?

Within *Majestic 12 and the Secret Government*, William Cooper claims seeing secret documents while serving in the Navy; documents describing governmental dealings with extraterrestrial aliens, with mention of a book he wrote called *Behold a Pale Horse*.

'Should you need to read a book then read the book. Should you need to read twenty books then so be it,' were his father's words.

C.J. finishes the Internet article then downloads the eBook version of William Cooper's book. C.J. has always loved reading. It was a major reason for becoming a journalist. One of the smarter investments in his intellectual development was completing two speed-reading courses. It was actually his mother's idea. This skill now serves him well.

The sun sets, the ocean shimmering with gold and crimson hues. C.J. admires the spectacular sunset only fleetingly, as he reads William Cooper's book. Cooper keeps mentioning the Majestic 12 as a collective, being 12 men. C.J. needs all his powers of patience not to deviate away from the book and simply Google *Who were the Majestic 12 members?*

C.J. anticipates his father's name to be in this group. But he must remain patient.

Cooper's book links the Illuminati with his beliefs that extraterrestrials were secretly involved with the US Government. C.J. has read articles on the Illuminati, understanding them to be an enlightenment-era secret society, wielding significant political power or influence. How much control is open to debate, although William Cooper is a firm believer they are exceptionally powerful.

C.J. views some of Cooper's claims as outrageous: He accused President Eisenhower of negotiating a treaty with extraterrestrials in 1954, then establishing an inner circle of Illuminati to manage relations with them to then keep the aliens presence a secret from the general public. He believed that aliens 'manipulated and/or ruled the human species through various secret societies, religions, magic, witchcraft, and the occult,' and that even the Illuminati were unknowingly being manipulated by them.

He described the Illuminati as:

> A secret international organization controlled by the Bilderberg Group, which conspired with a host of secret societies such as the Knights of Columbus, Masons, and Skull and Bones; to name a few. Its ultimate goal was the establishment of a New World Order.

According to Cooper, the Illuminati conspirators not only invented alien threats for their own gain, but actively conspired with extraterrestrials to take over the world.

Cooper believed that one of the key members of this Majestic 12, James Forrestal, was murdered. C.J. has heard James Forrestal's name. Cooper confirmed James Forrestal was President Truman's Secretary of Defense.

C.J. pauses in reflection.

Some of Cooper's claims are fantastical. This is the first research from his father's list and already secret societies, extraterrestrials, undisclosed treaties, and the murder of a US Secretary of Defense (an alleged MJ-12 member) are being mentioned.

CHAPTER FIVE

C.J. finishes William Cooper's *Behold a Pale Horse* sometime after midnight. He should be tired; he should be hungry; he is neither. He is desperate to find out if his father was a member of this Majestic 12 (or MJ-12), but first he takes his father's advice given repeatedly all through C.J.'s childhood: 'Always finish one job before you go to the next.'

After reading William Cooper's book and notes of Cooper's symposiums, C.J. decides to find out more about the author. He cannot believe what he discovers.

'What? No! Surely that can't be?' he mutters to himself.

After the release of *Beyond A Pale Horse* and a series of subsequent seminars, there are claims that the Majestic 12 used the IRS (Internal Revenue Service) to target Cooper. Whether this Majestic 12 could manipulate or use a massive government organization such as the IRS is beyond C.J.'s comprehension, yet the facts were Cooper was charged with the highest level of tax evasion – with little-to-no grounds. Cooper was not a rich man and, even if it were a legitimate charge, the procedure would be to send him a bill or a fine or, at worse, send him to court. Instead, the authorities bypassed normal protocol. Although they issued an arrest warrant, it was not executed. The result was Cooper being named *a major fugitive* by the US Marshals Service.

Cooper was not on the run; in fact, he stayed at his property the entire time. He had his own radio show and told listeners of this farcical 'major fugitive' implementation:

> Okay, last week I talked about Shadow Government and the alien and UFO cover-ups since the 1940s and 50s. I named names. Several people thought I might face some sort of backlash; well, they were right – it's happened folks. For those who know Bill Cooper, you would know I am not wealthy, and although I am critical of the Government, I pay my taxes and respect the law. Somehow, don't ask me how, the IRS says I owe them money – and a lot of it. Even though this is bull, the normal procedure for the IRS is to send me a bill or a notice telling me to pay up or it then goes to court. Did they do this? Of course not. I didn't even get a warrant to go to court. Folks, I am now considered a MAJOR FUGITIVE BY THE UNITED STATES MARSHALS SERVICE. They know where I work and they know where I live; yet I am somehow considered some sort of criminal on the run. Welcome to the age of the NEW WORLD ORDER folks. It has arrived. Be afraid … be VERY afraid.'

C.J. learns that Bill Cooper and his wife were asleep in his Arizona acreage hilltop home, when, just before midnight, Cooper was awoken by a ruckus and loud yelling at the base of the hill on the road leading to his house. He told his wife he was going to investigate, grabbing a bathrobe and a pistol from the wardrobe. He could see a car and two men at the bottom of the hill. He drove down to investigate. As he approached the car and the casually dressed men (who, unbeknown to Cooper, were undercover officers), a police car emerged from bushes to block Cooper's car in.

Cooper flung his car door open and fled, running past the police car and up the hill toward his house. The two undercover officers, as well as the uniformed policemen, began firing over Cooper's head. Cooper took the pistol from his robe pocket and returned fire. He was shot dead instantly.

C.J. is flabbergasted.

William Cooper had suggested MJ-12 member James Forrestal was murdered, the only member of the group or committee with specific references. C.J. discovers Forrestal was the last cabinet-level US Secretary of the Navy and the first United States Secretary of Defense. He was responsible for setting up the NSA (National Security Agency) and then the CIA (Central Intelligence Agency). This was a very, very important man.

Forrestal reportedly struggled with all the secret organizations and operations his government had undertaken. He believed the Government was losing control to private enterprise and non-government individuals. He felt his own government colleagues had the right to know some of the information relating to the MJ-12's knowledge of UFOs and alien activity. When he began to talk to other politicians about 'the alien problem' he was asked to resign by then President Harry S. Truman.

James Forrestal was taken to Bethesda, Maryland, to be placed in a naval rehab center – in a room on the sixteenth floor.

Not long after, James Forrestal was dead.

It is speculated that, sometime in the early morning of May 22, 1949, CIA agents tied a sheet around James Forrestal's neck, fastened the other end to a fixture in his room, and threw Forrestal out the window.

James Forrestal's secret diaries were confiscated – never to be seen again.

His death became the subject of a number of books and reports, with most agreeing there were major flaws in the official report of his death, inclusive of the evidence and circumstances surrounding it. Even so, the official report for the cause of death was 'suicide.'

The sun is about to rise, yet thoughts of sleep are far from C.J.'s mind. He's mesmerized by the information presenting itself.

Was my father a member of this Majestic 12?

C.J.'s curiosity cannot be subdued any longer. He Googles *Who were the Majestic 12 members?*

Their names and photos appear.

C.J. can barely contain his eagerness, as he scrolls down the page to reveal the names: *Dr. Vannevar Bush, Dr. Detlev Bronk, Dr. Lloyd Berkner,*

Sec. JAMES FORRESTAL, Gordon Gray, General Hoyt Vandenburg, Dr. Jerome Hunsaker, Dr. Donald Menzel, General Robert Montague, Sidney Souers, General Nathan Twining, and finally *Admiral Roscoe Hillenkoetter.*

There is no mention of *Dr. Max Stroheim*. Nothing.

After so many hours of traveling, then reading and researching, C.J. has finally succumbing to jetlag and fatigue. He turns off the computer, closes the blinds, and climbs into bed.

It is mid-afternoon when C.J. opens the blinds to unveil a glorious day. Small waves lap the shore near the steps leading from the beach house's deck. Being so deep in concentration researching, C.J. had scarcely appreciated how calming the sounds of the crashing waves were.

His parents mentioned a fantastic little café located along the beach. They would walk along the beach each morning for coffee and sometimes breakfast. It is well past breakfast time. C.J. is famished; a strong coffee sounds like an excellent idea. He still has a myriad of questions running through his mind, but for the first time since arriving, he realizes the pure beauty of the location.

He walks barefoot along the beach, by the water's edge. Shoes in hand, he carries his backpack, containing his computer, his father's list, and the tin box his father had given him that day on the golf course.

The café sign says *Open*, although no customers are inside. C.J. slips on his shoes to enter.

C.J. recalls his parents commenting that the people in the area were the friendliest they'd ever met.

His father said, 'It's a small community where everyone knows everyone. Each person we met shook my hand to introduce themselves by name. A nice, firm grip – not aggressive, but genuine and warm.'

There are two staff inside, a man in the kitchen and a woman behind the counter. Both are a similar age to C.J.

'Hi, my name is C.J.,' he says, with his hand outstretched to the woman behind the counter.

'Hi there C.J. Nice to meet you' she replies, reaching over the counter to shake C.J.'s hand. 'I'm Sarah.' Turning to the kitchen, she says, 'And this is my hubby, Rob, who also happens to be our resident chef.'

'Gidday, mate!' Rob yells from behind the kitchen benches.

Noting C.J.'s accent, Sarah asks, 'Are you an American?'

C.J. nods.

Rob chastises Sarah, saying, 'Leave the poor bugger alone Sair, he looks hungry.' He then talks directly to C.J. 'They've just dropped off fresh scallops and I'm getting them ready for tonight. You interested, mate?'

'Absolutely.'

C.J. has eaten scallops before, yet nothing remotely like these plump Tasmanian scallops, lightly cooked with the orange roe left on. He has no thoughts of conspiracy theories or secret organizations, focusing all his powers of concentration to enjoy each and every mouthful of the delicious seafood.

After savoring the last scallop, C.J. asks at what time the café closes?

'We're open tonight. The last orders are at seven-thirty.'

'Can I place an order for exactly what I just had for seven-thirty on the dot?'

'No worries,' is the reply.

C.J. walks back to the beach house carrying his backpack. He's reluctant to let it out of his sight. He knows he can't carry the tin box around forever so the next day he plans to drive into the nearest township, Wynyard, to stock up with some supplies. He has an idea of how and where to hide the tin box, as well as backed-up computer data on a USB memory stick.

For now he will do some more research.

Before going to the next set of codes on the sheet, C.J. heeds his father's advice to thoroughly rehash what he has already learnt. He is disappointed his father did not seem to be one of the Majestic 12, but after researching the twelve men thoroughly, it becomes obvious why: Max was just twenty-five when he joined the NSA, or what was to officially become the NSA. The men in the Majestic 12 or MJ-12 were much older – diplomats, military five-star generals, department heads, and well-known scientists of the era. Each had a successful career before their involvement in NSA secretive affairs and each were nearing the end of their careers. Max Stroheim's career was just beginning.

C.J. uses his journalistic know-how to ask questions.

If MJ-12 were meant to be such a secretive organization, why were each of the members so highly profiled?

What was my father's relationship with these men?

Why was their most influential member, James Forrestal, seemingly murdered?

C.J. searches for more information about the deaths of James Forrestal and William Cooper. At first glance, they appear unrelated. C.J. finds it uncanny, however, that the first two people he has researched both ended up dying prematurely.

Max Stroheim had told C.J. about the saying behind the scenes of the NSA: 'If no one talks, then no one dies.'

Both Forrestal and Cooper talked; both men died.

C.J. immerses himself on the Internet, yet is also mindful of the time. His mother instilled in him to always keep appointments – and never to be late.

It is nearing 7:30 p.m.

Sarah looks at her watch.

As C.J. walks into the café, she comments, 'Right on time. Rob has just started cooking your scallops.'

C.J. is amazed at the trust of the café owners. He'd said he would be there at 7:30 p.m. and they took his word. *This would not happen in LA.*

The café is quiet so Rob and Sarah chat with C.J. Sarah, in particular, loves to chat.

Sarah and Rob live nearby; their love of Boat Harbour Beach is apparent. While eating the tastiest seafood he can recall, C.J. can see why his father liked the location and the people so much.

Consuming his last scallop, C.J. jokes 'So do you serve scallops for breakfast?'

He walks along the moonlit, tranquil water's edge to return to the beach house. Refreshed and well fed, he continues his research.

The next code on his father's list is *S-4*. The first search result reveals S-4 is a product from the company Samsung. C.J. doesn't think it applicable, so scrolls through many pages before finding information more relevant to Max Stroheim's 'S-4'.

'This looks more promising.'

S-4 appears to be an installation within the military zone known as Area 51. Like most Americans, C.J. has heard of Area 51.

'Bingo!'

He excitedly clicks onto the site.

Area 51 is a remote detachment of Edwards Air Force Base. It is sometimes known as Dreamland or Groom Lake (being the dry lake bed). *Code Dreamland* is one of the references on his father's sheet. It is on its own line, not listed in the sequence of projects, codes, numerals, and letters his father wrote down. It makes C.J. wary, as his father was a methodical man.

Did he write everything down in order for a reason?

C.J. thinks he would; however, some of the information may indeed be interconnected. There is no way his father knew how the Internet would recall each and every event or project, nor how individuals would report it. C.J.'s mother was the computer brains in the family. Max Stroheim was from an era where everything was written down or typed. Even so, Max possessed an amazing memory. If he said Eisenhower was elected President in November 1952 and took office in January 1953, then it was right.

C.J. knows some of what he reads on the Internet will be true, some information will be distorted, and some will be false. He is confident his father knew the truth. That truth will reveal itself in time, as Max Stroheim predicted.

C.J. chooses to disregard the *Dreamland* reference at this point of his research, concentrating on the S-4 location at Nevada's Area 51. He learns of secret military installations, underground tunnel networks, technologically advanced aircraft production and testing, and even conspiracy theorists speculating alien visitations.

All information about Area 51 is classified 'top-secret.' From C.J.'s initial research, it is *not* operated by the NSA, but by the Air Force. This confuses C.J. until reading further articles, suggesting the CIA and NSA had continuous involvement, particularly in underground activities.

Area 51 was kept so secretive the US Government didn't even acknowledge its existence until 1995 – nearly fifty years after it began. What started as an axillary airfield during the early years of World War II morphed into the massive facility of today – and it is still shrouded in secrecy.

C.J. studies a map of the United States to ascertain Area 51's location. He also sees where other secret military-relevant installations are located. He instantly sees a trend.

Almost all secret bases, including Area 51, are clustered in the six south-western states. Most are in just three states: New Mexico, Nevada, and California; areas where Dr. Stroheim worked.

C.J. ponders the relevance of not only Area 51, but the vast majority of the secret base locations.

Why are they so close together?

He learns that many of these secret bases are located underground, often deep underground. The topography of the locations are all semi-arid-to-arid areas, away from major population centers.

C.J. researches the population densities of the states in question. There are many more states less densely populated than New Mexico, Nevada, and California, inclusive of the desert areas. This cannot be the sole reason.

Maybe it is to do with the soil?

He searches for maps of soil types in America; discovering a soil type known as *aridiols*. The areas of this soil type corresponds to the location of the secret military bases.

'This is weird?' he mutters, before placing two separate maps alongside each other.

They are a mirror image of each other.

'There seems to be a connection.'

C.J. investigates further.

Most of the land where these military installations are located is flat to accommodate airfields and runways, but some areas are surrounded by hills or mountains. C.J. has read that most of the bases are underground, learning aridiol soil is ideal for digging and tunneling.

'Surely this is no coincidence.'

It is now after midnight. C.J. lies in bed contemplating all this new information. The soothing sounds of the small waves crashing on the shoreline help him relax physically, even if his mind is still deep in thought. Between considerations of the MJ-12, S-4, Area 51, and the location of all these secret bases, C.J. nods off.

The next morning the sun rises over the ocean, with the rays streaming through the beach house's expansive glass doors and windows. He hadn't closed the window blinds.

'What a magnificent sunrise,' he murmurs, rubbing sleep from his eyes.

CHAPTER SIX

C.J. walks along the beach to the café. Even though it's only been open five minutes, there is already another customer. Seated facing the beach is a stunningly beautiful woman, mid-to-late twenties, immaculately dressed and groomed. She sips coffee and reads the paper, not noticing C.J. as he walks inside the café. He certainly notices her.

Sarah and Rob are not working this morning. Today's staff consists of a young girl at the front counter and a more mature lady in the kitchen.

The young girl welcomes C.J. energetically. 'Good morning.'

C.J. smiles to reply.

He outstretches his hand to shake hers, but she turns her back momentarily to face the kitchen.

'Better put the delivery of eggs in the fridge,' she instructs the lady in the kitchen, before turning to C.J. 'Sorry about that. Now, just a coffee or are you having breakfast?'

'Breakfast please, but I might start with a coffee.'

Hearing C.J. ordering coffee and breakfast, the beautiful girl's eyes momentarily look up from the newspaper.

She is Emma Burgess; born and raised locally, she left the area to study law in Melbourne, in the mainland state of Victoria. After graduating, she joined an inner-city law firm as a junior prosecuting lawyer. Her career looked promising, but family circumstances forced a reassessment of her priorities.

Emma's father is the local police sergeant in Wynyard, which is only fifteen minutes' drive from Boat Harbour Beach. Two years ago, Emma's mother was diagnosed with inoperable cancer and given only six to twelve months to live. Emma made the gut-wrenching decision to quit her job, returning to Tasmania to be with her family.

There are only two solicitors practicing law in Wynyard. One offered Emma a position, albeit part-time. The advantage of a small community like Wynyard, however, is people rally around those in need. Two years later, Emma is still at the same business, forgoing big city career advancement and financial rewards to be near her father. For a burly tough country policeman, he was markedly affected by the death of his wife.

Emma Burgess drives to Boat Harbour Beach most mornings, weather permitting. After walking along the beach, she sits at the café to enjoy a coffee and read the newspaper. To her, the beach is more than just one of the most beautiful places in the world, it is a part of her childhood. Her family holidayed there frequently.

After coffee, she drives to her office on the main street of Wynyard.

Barely making eye contact, Emma acknowledges C.J. with a brief reserved smile. C.J.'s good looks and confident manner escape her notice. Taking a seat facing the beach on the table next to Emma, C.J. can see her in his periphery, yet is conscious not to stare. Even so, he can see how attractive she is.

She lifts her eyes from the paper only intermittently, not to look at C.J. but to sip her coffee and look at the ocean.

On the third occasion of raising her eyes, C.J. comments, 'It's another beautiful day in paradise.'

'Sorry, what was that?'

Undeterred, C.J. repeats, 'I said, it's another beautiful day in paradise.'

Impassive, she politely replies, 'Oh, yes' before taking the last sip left in her coffee mug. She stands to fold the newspaper neatly, before offering it to C.J. He courteously declines. She returns the newspaper to the café counter, while the girl is making C.J.'s coffee. Emma places money alongside the newspaper.

'I'm off Tara – see you tomorrow.' She then talks louder in the direction of the kitchen, 'See you Deb.'

Both ladies respond 'See you Emma.'

After Emma leaves, C.J. introduces himself by name to the ladies in the café. Tara and Deb are friendly. C.J. asks Tara who the girl reading the newspaper was but, before she is able to answer, more customers enter the café.

After returning to the beach house, C.J. drives to Wynyard for supplies. Although only a small town, it is a shopping hub for surrounding farming districts. C.J. has no problem finding what he needs, as well as buying wine and fresh local seafood.

Only a fortnight before his father's death, Max said 'Son, you are like your mother in so many ways. She was outgoing and fun. It is one of the reasons I fell in love with her. As hard as I want you to work in the future, don't forget to stop and smell the roses. Douglas Adams wrote in *The Hitchhiker's Guide to the Galaxy*: "I'd far rather be happy than right any day."

'Take your time with the important things, but take just as much time with the unimportant. Son, above all things, be happy.'

They were such profound words from a man who spent his working life unconditionally focused. C.J. sometimes saw the playful side of his father in later years, particularly around his mother Mary, but Max Stroheim was by-and-large a serious man.

C.J. sits on the beach house deck while the sun sets. The dark clouds reflect the grandiose colors mirrored on the calm water. Overnight rain is predicted, but for now it is windless and the skies spectacular. C.J. sips his wine and eats the local seafood with immeasurable satisfaction.

When darkness falls, C.J. grabs his backpack to walk toward the beach. A storage area under the decking has basic garden tools. He removes a shovel to tread the few steps to the beach below. He takes one measured stride away from the last step then turns 90 degrees to take another measured stride to the west. He starts digging.

In Wynyard C.J. bought two sealable waterproof bags and several USB memory sticks. He has placed his father's tin box and one of the memory sticks containing a backup of his computer files to-date, his passport, and some US cash into the bag. He memorized the note attached to the tin box: *The acronym for KRLL in telephone numeric form*, before destroying the note.

He carefully sealed each bag, wrapped everything in a plastic garbage bag for additional waterproof-security, and now he buries it.

With the hole filled, he walks over the displaced sand repeatedly to remove any trace of his digging.

It'll probably rain tonight anyway, he thinks, which will further hide his footsteps and activity.

The sound of the rain rhythmically falling on the beach house's tin roof helps C.J. sleep through the night and into the next morning.

He intended to wake up with the sunrise; however, the overcast conditions filtered the impact of the early morning sun.

Realizing he has slept in, he leaps from bed. Only wearing his pajama shorts, he races to the deck to anxiously look over the edge. There is no evidence of his hole digging from the previous night; the usually fluffy sand is pitted from the earlier rain. It then dawns on him that he is bare-chested. Someone is walking along the beach – looking straight at him.

That someone is Emma Burgess.

The tides at Boat Harbour Beach are extreme; the beach has only a gentle slope, meaning the difference between high and low tides is measurable. Fortunately for C.J., Emma is walking along the water's edge with the tide low. Even so, she can see the shirtless and pale-chested man standing on the deck, with the red hues of embarrassment radiating from his face.

Although at a distance, she mischievously waves and shouts, 'Good morning!'

Reluctantly returning the wave, C.J.'s hand scarcely reaches above his bare waist as he scurries inside.

C.J. quickly showers, shaves, and dresses to walk along the beach.

Realizing the time, he hastens his stride to enter the café, but Emma has gone. He must have just missed her. He can see the folded newspaper and loose change on the counter, with Sarah standing behind.

'Good morning, C.J.' she says cheerfully, taking C.J. somewhat by surprise. He did not expect to see her in the mornings. He'd rationalized that Tara worked morning shifts and Sarah the evening.

Sarah explains that she and Rob mix their rosters to suit. 'It's one of the advantages of having your own business.'

C.J. asks about 'the girl who reads the newspaper.'

Sarah is only too willing to divulge, 'Oh, Emma, Emma Burgess? She certainly is pretty, isn't she?'

'That's not why I was asking. You see …'

'Don't worry C.J. She's single. You're not the first to mention her. Many of the local boys have asked about her. She lives in Wynyard; moved in with her father after she lost her mother only last year. Tragic – cancer – the poor thing. Emma comes in here nearly every morning – she's a lovely girl – and she's very, very smart. She's a solicitor, you know.'

Just then another customer enters the café.

C.J. finishes breakfast to return to the beach house to research, setting up his computer on the deck. His father wanted him to write a book, a factual book. He has barely scratched the surface.

C.J. licks his lips, preparing to tackle the next set of clues on his father's list: *PROJECTS: SIGN, GRUDGE, GRUDGE 13, REDLIGHT, SIGMA, POUNCE, PLUTO, MOONDUST*, and *BLUE FLY.*

He begins with Project Sign. He quickly discovers it was an official US Government study of UFOs (Unidentified Flying Objects) undertaken by the US Air Force in 1948.

'Whoa,' gasps C.J. The first project his father has asked him to research is a government study of UFOs.

C.J. learns that Project Sign was formed from the culmination of several years of Air Force reports and files of UFO sightings. The project was not initially classified as top-secret, but 'restricted' only, with speculation that some of the UFOs might have been technically advanced Russian aircraft. The personnel running Sign included some of the Air Force's top intelligence specialists. It took a little time to rule out some of the unidentified craft as being Russian, as the technology appeared to surpass anything the Russians, or the Americans, could produce. When the project team concluded that the UFOs were probably of extraterrestrial origin, Project Sign was quickly and 'officially' dissolved. It was replaced with Project Grudge. At this time, the project became more guarded – and changed direction.

The brief for Grudge was to disprove that UFOs were real, although some of the creditable reports of UFOs and human abductions were hidden within subprojects and reports, which included at least fourteen additional reports, named *Grudge 1* through to *Grudge 14*. Reports 1 to 12, as well as *Grudge 14* were generally innocuous, containing no classified or sensitive material. Only one report was not declassified: *Grudge 13*.

Grudge 13 had higher security clearances to access files, documenting a host of firsthand military encounters with UFOs, including: *Close Encounters of the 1st Kind, Sightings and Witnesses*; *Close Encounters of the 2nd Kind, UFO Sightings Witnessed within Close Proximity*; *Close Encounters of the 3rd Kind, UFO Encounters and extraterrestrial Life Forms Witnessed and Personal Encounters*; and *Military Reports Concerning Sightings on Radar and Electronic Surveillance of UFOs*. They also discussed the possible quantum mechanical processes of the craft, including Einstein's Theory of Relativity – and the potential relevance to the UFO's operations.

Projects Sign and Grudge were Air Force ventures. Max Stroheim did not work for the military. Working for the NSA – or at least 'under the NSA's umbrella' – he was obviously aware of these top-secret Air Force projects.

Dr. Stroheim was as an astrobiologist. C.J. knew his father's scientific background, although he looks up the official meaning of astrobiology to be sure:

> The study of the origin, evolution, distribution, and future of life in the universe: extraterrestrial life and life on Earth.

For C.J., the penny starts to drop. *The first two projects I've researched are about UFOs and extraterrestrials. My father was an astrobiologist. It's starting to make sense.*

He can't wait to learn more.

• • •

Four days of bad weather have seen C.J. walk along the beach each morning to be the only patron at the café. Emma Burgess has not shown. C.J. has enjoyed talking with the staff. Sarah, in particular, loves to chat.

Sarah asks the inevitable question of 'What are you doing at Boat Harbour Beach?'

He'd prepared an answer. 'I'm an author and I'm writing a book. I have to keep the subject matter a secret at this stage, but you have my word that, when it's finished and published, you'll be one of the first I'll send a copy to – and I promise I'll sign it for you. In fact, I love it so much down here, I'll give you a copy personally when I come back.'

For a nosey woman like Sarah, that response only fuels more questions. 'What is the book about?'

'I'm sorry, I can't say at the moment – you know, copyright laws, that kind of thing.'

She is like a dog with a bone, 'I won't tell anyone, promise. Can you at least tell me if it's fiction or non-fiction?'

C.J. shakes his head. 'Sorry Sarah, I have signed an agreement with my publisher. I legally can't talk about it until it comes out. You understand, don't you?'

'Well, if you legally can't talk about it …'

This, of course, is a lie. C.J. finds it difficult to lie. His mother had always told him to be truthful. Until now he hadn't lied.

With rain falling, C.J. sits inside the beach house to continue his research, with *Project Redlight.*

Later in the day the rain stops, the sun's rays reflecting from the wet white sand. C.J. stares at the sand.

Through researching his book *Grains of Sand in the Universe*, he felt the chances of other intelligent alien life existing in the universe were high. He knows of countless unofficial UFO reports and now, it seems, secret projects initiated by the US Government were investigating the possibilities – and his father may have been involved. Although making some headway into his father's list, C.J. has many questions running through his mind. He decides a walk along the beach is in order.

The café is to the left of the beach house. In the other direction are a series of small beaches interspersed with large boulder-like rocks, rock-pools, and rocky outcrops. C.J. turns right.

Beyond the last beach house is farmland with sweeping lush, grass hills sloping toward the seashore. Further beyond are steep bluffs featuring sheer cliff faces, with only rocks below. Cows graze on the lower inclines of the closer and less severe landscape, with several farmhouses perched on the slopes and ridges. It is magnificent countryside.

Walking past the last sandy beach, C.J. continues along the rocky shoreline. The rocks are difficult to walk on, but the backdrop is spectacular. It's worth the effort. He stops intermittently to take in the views, eventually coming to a large rocky outcrop jutting into the ocean. He sits on a flat rock facing back to Boat Harbour's main beach. The sun's glistening beads of light dance on the tranquil ocean and blue sky. Clouds reflect from the mirror-glass water of a nearby rock-pool. It is beautiful beyond words.

Over three hours pass. It is the perfect vantage point, not only for the magical view, but for personal reflection and thought.

CHAPTER SEVEN

The next morning, C.J. rolls out of bed. Seeing a sunny, cloudless day, he is about to step out on the deck, but pauses. He is only wearing pajama shorts again. He quickly checks to make sure no one is walking along the beach – with *no one* meaning Emma Burgess. The beach appears vacant, so he steps outside to yawn and stretch. At that very moment Emma appears from behind one of the large boulder rocks on the beach to the right of the beach house.

She has a wry smile, shaking her head in disbelief.

C.J. is caught out again, dashing inside and out of view. He knows she saw him and she knows he saw her. Too embarrassed to go straight to the café, he researches instead, choosing to walk to the café a little later.

The following morning C.J. awakes to discover another beautiful, cloudless day. Fully dressed, he steps onto the beach to turn left. He can see Emma Burgess walking further up the beach, heading toward the café.

Minutes later, he walks into the café.

'Good morning,' Emma says with cynicism, peering over her newspaper. 'It's nice to see you with your clothes on.' She smiles ever so smugly, lowering her eyes back to the daily news.

C.J. stutters and stammers, not expecting Emma Burgess to be so direct. 'Yes, sorry about that. Actually, sorry about that twice.'

C.J. thrusts his hand forward to shake hers. She accepts, lowering her newspaper, and talks first. 'Emma Burgess, resident coffee drinker.'

She is confident and feisty. He likes that.

'Pleased to meet you, Emma Burgess. I'm C.J., fellow resident coffee drinker.'

Had he more time to think, he may have come up with a more witty response.

She recognizes a mistake in his reply, 'So C.J., you *are* a resident?'

'Well no, not technically, but I'd like to be.'

He is impressed by his recovery. She is not, nonchalantly taking her last sip of coffee. She then stands up. 'Well, I must be off. Here's the paper, if you'd like it?'

C.J. declines, so Emma takes the paper over to the counter to leave it with her coffee money.

She yells 'Goodbye' to Tara and Deb, working behind the scenes.

Striding past C.J., she slyly comments 'You know, it's not illegal to walk around in pajama bottoms, but if you're contemplating becoming a local, might I suggest that you wear a top.'

Very few women get the better of C.J., yet Emma Burgess certainly did. He enjoyed their brief exchange, and made a conscious decision to go to the café five minutes earlier next time.

Returning to the beach house, he sits out on the deck researching Project Redlight. C.J. has already spent several days trying to determine exactly what Project Redlight was. Details are sketchy; however, it appears Redlight evolved from Project Grudge, sparked by the 1947 purported 'Roswell Incident.'

C.J., like most Americans, had heard of Roswell. It is alleged that, in July 1947, a military radar effected and took down an alien disk (UFO), which crashed near Roswell, New Mexico. Within the disk, scientists and military personnel found several dead alien beings. It is reported that nearby, wandering injured through the desert, was a live alien – and that alien was captured.

Reports suggest other crashed disks were recovered previously, however the Roswell crash allowed the retrieval of the least damaged wreckage to that date. It is also alleged, by William Cooper and others, that the captured alien remained alive and in captivity for several years.

William Cooper had briefly mentioned Project Redlight and Grudge in a series of lectures in the late 1980s. This was before he wrote *Behold a Pale Horse.* C.J. read a transcript from one of the forty-five-minute lectures.

Cooper suggests that, after the Roswell crash, new facilities to house the crashed UFO disk and dead alien bodies, plus the live alien, were built underground at Area 51. This was S-4. Cooper suggested it was under the guidance and control of the Majestic 12.

C.J. is learning that the more sensitive the information, the more secretive the projects became. With the formation of the MJ-12 (supposedly in 1947), they began controlling more and more projects, which were originally designated to the Air Force or the Navy. MJ-12 introduced a whole new level of security, building and using facilities deep underground. *Is it possible Max Stroheim worked at S-4? If the reports of a live alien are true, then would an esteemed astrobiologist, such as himself, be involved in such a project?*

C.J. has hardly left the serenity of Boat Harbour Beach since arriving. Being a beautiful day, he drives his rental car to ponder the connotations of his latest revelations, as well as to explore the local coastline. The view to the east of his beach house is a magnificent bluff, Table Cape.

Table Cape has glorious coastal views. He should be fully engrossed in the scenery, yet he can't stop thinking of his father's career, the reports of UFOs and extraterrestrials, and the location of the many secret bases, including S-4 within Area 51.

C.J. still has many questions to answer, but knows he must be patient. At one time, he entertained the notion that his father may have been a spy. Now he is jumping to the conclusion he may have been sifting through UFO wreckage. C.J. takes a deep breath to think rationally. He must be meticulous and methodical. *How would my father want me to handle this?*

C.J. will research the other projects and codes before drawing too many conclusions. C.J. also realizes he has yet to fully look at the timelines involved. This is important. It is an oversight Max Stroheim would not have made. He reflects on what he knows about his father's life.

Max Stroheim was educated at Harvard during World War II. He was then employed by NACA, which would later be known as NASA. He was recruited by the NSA, or the forerunner of the NSA, and was there for the next thirty-four years, retiring in 1982.

'Nineteen eighty-two?'

It dawns on C.J. that his father didn't join the NSA or its precursor until sometime in 1948. Even if he started in January or February of that year, the Roswell incident occurred in 1947.

'Nineteen forty-seven? That can't be,' a disappointed C.J. mutters.

Just when C.J. thought he was closing in on his father's secret or secrets, this insight comes as a major setback.

His father was not one of the MJ-12. He was not at Roswell in 1947. He was not part of Projects Sign or Grudge, and unlikely to be involved in Project Grudge 13. These all began before Max Stroheim joined the NSA, yet the information pertaining to these projects must be relevant for Max Stroheim to mention them. He obviously knew about them, even if he wasn't there at the time.

C.J. drives to Wynyard. For a small country town, it is a busy afternoon. He finds a car space a short walking distance from the supermarket, outside a solicitor's office. There would not be many legal firms in Wynyard so C.J. wonders if this is where Emma Burgess works. Not needing to contemplate for long, Emma steps out from the office at the same time as C.J. alights from the car.

'Well, well, if it isn't Emma Burgess' he says with a wry smile.

She replies without breaking stride. 'If it isn't our possible-future-resident coffee drinker. I have to run; I've a document to deliver. Bye.'

She runs across the road, jumps into her small, silver hatchback car, and waves to C.J. while driving away.

Driving back, C.J. stops at a viewing area about halfway down the main road overlooking his beach house, getting out of the car to admire the view. His father was very wise to send him to such a beautiful place. C.J. smiles to himself, knowing his parents really loved this place and the people. It is still early days in his research, yet already C.J. can envisage spending more time here in the future.

At the beach house C.J. delves into Project Redlight, discovering more ambiguity, with some reports claiming Redlight was also incorporated into another project, named *Aquarius*. At times the project had subdivisions, or was also called *Project Looking Glass, Project Gleem, Project Bando,* and *The Fairfield Project.*

'This is so confusing,' mutters C.J. 'Maybe it's meant to be that way?'

C.J. reads that only MJ-12 had access to Project Aquarius, which was a deliberate ploy to exclude all other government agencies, including the military. The files were presented to MJ-12 members and destroyed after each briefing. No notes, photographs, or audio recordings were made of these briefings, thus the information contained within Project Aquarius was truly confidential – and not traceable.

'It's no wonder that the information available today is disjointed and confusing.'

The next projects on Max Stroheim's list are: *SIGMA, POUNCE, PLUTO, MOONDUST & BLUE FLY.*

C.J. opens a bottle of wine in readiness to accompany more fresh Tasmanian seafood. As he sits on the deck to admire the tranquil view and sample the delicious food and wine, he mutters to himself, 'Dad did say to stop to smell the roses.'

After a restful sleep, C.J. awakens to the sun rising grandly over Table Cape, the rosy dawn shades reflecting from the high-tide water.

C.J. is in a particularly good mood. He's relaxed into the surrounds and achieved much in the way of research. His father's words about taking the time to have fun still resonate. After changing, C.J. takes a stroll barefoot along the water's edge. Tasmania is not renowned for its warm waters; however, he is pleasantly surprised by the water temperature. A number of swimmers without wetsuits have been entering the water in recent days.

C.J. packed minimally for his travels. A swimming costume was not a priority.

Being early in the morning, no one is around. C.J. has observed Emma Burgess walking along the beach between 7:30 and 7:45 a.m. He looks at his waterproof Tag Heuer watch. It is 7:10. He decides a quick swim is in order. The only shorts he has that remotely resemble swimming trunks are his pajama shorts. He puts them back on.

Racing across the fluffy sand, C.J. dives into the Bass Strait water. At first the cold takes his breathe away, yet after a few moments it is exhilarating – swimming a few strokes – and then more.

Bobbing his head out of the water, C.J. has swum some distance from shore. Just when deciding to swim back, he sees a figure on the beach at the other end of the beach, walking toward where he is swimming.

'Oh hell, not Emma again!'

With a flurry of rapid strokes heading toward the beach, C.J. can see Emma edging closer and closer.

When near enough to the shore, he plants his feet firmly in the sand to propel his body forward – wading through the shallow water – driving his knees high. She is not far away. He is committed. It is too obvious and too cold to turn around and swim back out. He must make a dash for it – hitting the beach running.

Emma laughs out loud as she watches the lily-white American, wearing only pajama bottoms, run up the sand at speed.

By the time C.J. arrives at the café, Emma is standing at the counter with money and paper. She and C.J. pass each other near the entry.

Emma has a smile from ear to ear. 'Nice running action you had there.'

C.J. is too embarrassed to comment. Emma walks away, sniggering.

Sarah is working today. She too can't help but tease C.J. Obviously Emma has relayed the news; 'I hear you are quite the swimmer – and quite the runner.'

C.J. bites back playfully. 'Does everyone know everything that goes on around here?'

'Pretty much. How's that book coming along?'

'Not bad.'

The next morning C.J. awakes even earlier for another swim. This time there is no Emma Burgess to witness his seaside dash – and swim.

Invigorated, he takes his time to shower and get ready. It is 8:15 a.m. when he steps out on the deck in readiness to walk along the beach. He sees Emma Burgess walking toward the café. She is a tad later than usual, he notes.

He enters the café to find Emma the only customer inside. 'Good morning, Emma Burgess.'

'Good morning, biathlon man.'

He breaks stride for a moment, half expecting Emma will invite him to sit with her. She doesn't. He politely nods to take a seat at his usual table.

She immerses herself in reading the newspaper. C.J. can hear smirks from behind the paper. She is obviously rehashing the image of him running out of the water wearing his pajama shorts. That's what C.J. thinks, anyway.

At one point Emma looks up to giggle out loud. C.J. has had enough.

He stands up to approach Emma, lamenting 'I know you think it's funny that you keep seeing me only in my pajama shorts, but it's not that funny. If I was wearing swimming trunks it wouldn't be such a big deal.'

'What on earth are you talking about?' she sternly replies.

'You've been sitting there laughing at the fact that I've been swimming in my pajama shorts.'

Emma coolly and calmly replies, 'I was laughing at the joke in the paper. Every day, there's a joke of the day. Normally it's not that funny, but today it just happens to be hilarious.' She takes a sip of coffee, before commenting, 'Boy, you're insecure, aren't you?'

'What do you mean, "insecure"?'

Emma remains calm, yet softens her tone. 'Look, I didn't mean to offend you. But you've got to admit that it's funny.'

'What, the joke in the paper?'

Emma has the biggest smile on her face in replying, 'No, not the joke. I have to be honest – I WAS laughing at you.'

She waits for a moment, before apologizing.

Sitting back down, C.J. replies, 'Apology accepted … I think.'

C.J. sits out on the sundrenched deck of the beach house. He is conscious of his pale skin when bare-chested, figuring he can work on a tan while researching. He sits facing the morning sun.

He has copied his father's list to his computer:

OPC MJ-12, S-4
PROJECTS: SIGN, GRUDGE, GRUDGE 13, REDLIGHT, SIGMA, POUNCE, PLUTO, MOONDUST & BLUE FLY
CODE DREAMLAND
IPU, AEC, AFOSI
BOOKS YELLOW, RED & BLUE
YY-II, DNI/27
GREADA TREATY

Having researched Projects Sigma, Pounce, and Pluto, today's research is directed at Projects Moondust and Blue Fly. Engrossed, he loses track of time.

Several hours in the sun with no shirt has taken its toll so, with no one around he decides to don his pajama shorts once more to cool off with a quick swim. Walking along the sand toward the water, he thinks two thoughts: 'I hope Emma doesn't see me again,' and 'I really must buy a pair of swimming trunks.'

Both thoughts become relative and quantified when Emma Burgess walks along the beach.

This time, close to shore, he sees her coming; prompting C.J. to immediately get out of the water. The only problem is the tide is low, meaning C.J. is almost as far from the beach house as Emma is to him. He sprints up the beach. She can clearly see his sunburnt face and front; a red and white blur racing up the steps, onto the decking, and then out of sight.

CHAPTER EIGHT

The next morning at the café, Emma enters at 8:00 a.m., anxious to tell Sarah of again catching C.J. in his pajama shorts, as well as being sunburnt. 'His front was all red, his back still lily white. He looked like a red-and-white candy cane!'

They have a good chuckle.

Sarah divulges 'He's an author, you know.'

Emma is surprised. Not overly impressed – just surprised.

Sarah gushes 'Yeah, he's down here writing a book.'

'What about?'

'I don't know. That's the weird thing – he won't talk about it. He said it was a secret or something. He reckoned that he signed an agreement with the publisher and wasn't allowed to talk about it. He's not even allowed to tell me if it's fiction or not.'

'That's odd. I've never heard of an agreement where the author cannot say a thing while writing. I'll look into it.'

'He's good looking, don't you think?' Sarah hopes to get a reaction.

'What?'

'He's a good-looking guy. Surely you've noticed?'

'Not really.'

'I think he likes you.'

'What?'

'He was asking about you the other day.'

Emma recognizes that this American, who claims to be a writer, will now know everything about her. When Sarah gossips, she omits few details. In fairness, it doesn't worry Emma. C.J. is a tourist. He probably won't be around for long anyway; however, in the meantime she can have a good laugh or two at his expense.

Emma takes her usual seat and starts reading the newspaper. C.J. walks in with a sunburnt face. She lifts her eyes from the paper momentarily, a devilish grin exposed.

Before she has the opportunity to open her mouth, C.J. remarks. 'Yes, yes – once again. I know, I know. So give me your best shot.'

'Firstly, hello and good morning – and what do you mean "my best shot"?'

'I know you want to say some condescending, pejorative, derogatory, or patronizing remark.'

'Wow, "condescending, pejorative, derogatory, patronizing" – they're big words,' she retorts sarcastically.

'So that's it – that's all you've got – you're only going to pick on my grammar?'

'Well, yes.' She pauses momentarily. 'And, by the way, you may want to put some vitamin E cream on your face and chest. The last time I saw skin that burnt it was on a roast chicken!'

C.J. laughs out loud.

C.J. drives into Wynyard to buy the largest bottles of vitamin E cream and sunscreen he can find. However, while Wynyard is a good shopping location for basic groceries (and wine), it is not exactly department store shopping as far as men's fashion-wear is concerned. He needs new clothes anyway, so drives to the next town, Burnie, some 20 minutes away.

Burnie has several larger menswear stores. The first purchase is a pair of board shorts – perfect for sitting on the deck and jumping straight into the ocean.

'That Emma Burgess won't ridicule me again!'

He returns to the rack to grab a further five pairs.

Back at Boat Harbour Beach, wearing new shorts, C.J. lathers his stinging chest and face lavishly with vitamin E cream, and then coats his back in sunscreen. Taking a seat on the deck, he deliberately faces away from the afternoon sun to work on tanning his back in what will be a futile attempt to achieve an even body tan.

C.J. learns that Project Sigma began under President Eisenhower's administration as a subdivision or offshoot from Project Aquarius – and like many of the other secrets projects of the era, had several other names and disinformation strategies to conceal its real objectives. Sigma purportedly dealt with alien cryptology, as well as the contact and communication with alien civilizations. Projects Pluto and Pounce also branched out from Aquarius. Project Pluto was possibly called Plato; however, it appears likely that Plato was a separate division under the Pluto umbrella.

Yet another ploy to confuse, thought C.J.

Pluto/Plato was allegedly a project designed to intercept alien radio communication and to form diplomatic relations with alien life forms.

Project Pounce was established around the same time as Sigma and Pluto to recover crashed craft and aliens – and to provide cover stories, disinformation, and to mask and cover up the real events.

Although Internet information on these projects is fragmented, C.J. notes that when these projects began, they coincided with his father's NSA career. *Maybe my father was involved with these projects?*

With the sun warming his back, C.J. researches Projects Moondust and Blue Fly. Internet information is disjointed and scarce.

'Moon Dust' was originally a nickname for any space debris, which did not appear to be of 'earthly' origin; in other words – UFOs. It seems the Air Force was incorporated into Project Moondust so if any flying craft were intercepted or debris located, the Air Force would forward that information, or evidence, through to Project Aquarius. This was not just UFOs, but 'any craft of interest.' This included Russian jet fighters or experimental craft, as at that point, the Cold War was of military concern. The Americans were trying to gain a technological edge, with Project Moondust one of the tools to exploit Soviet hardware if it landed in American hands. As Project Aquarius was under the control of MJ-12, any additional data or physical debris provided by the Air Force could be used for MJ-12's scientific advancement.

Project Blue Fly appears linked to Moondust. They may even be the same project, or Blue Fly may have been a subdivision of Moondust. What seems clear is that the projects were kept guarded by the Air Force, even when using Intelligence Agency resources globally to retrieve wreckage of interest from other countries.

C.J. notes that Moondust and Blue Fly began around 1960, marginally later than Projects Sigma, Pluto, and Pounce.

C.J.'s research has grown more complex by the day. Although learning much, for each answer there are many more questions.

His father's speech about 'digging a hole in the sand, where the walls continue to cave in' rings true.

A calming stroll along the beach might help to think clearer. He turns right to walk toward the rocky outcrops and cliffs.

When C.J. was younger, struggling with a school assignment, his father would tell him to think about the assignment and walk away.

'Sometimes, you can look at something all day long and just not see the solution. In those instances, it's best to leave it alone for a while. You can revisit it later when you are thinking clearly – then possibly look at the problem from a different angle or direction.'

'A different angle or direction,' C.J. mutters.

He changes direction – in thought and route – walking back along the beach toward the café. On arrival, much to his surprise, he sees Emma sitting at her usual table. The café is quite busy. C.J.'s usual table is occupied.

'Well, well, what have we here? Emma Burgess sitting at her usual location, but look at the time?' teases C.J., as he looks at his watch. 'It is three-thirty in the afternoon. I thought your resident coffee-drinking was only in the mornings?'

'I didn't realize you were keeping a diary.'

'And I see there is no newspaper; just a coffee,' he notes, before his eyes shift to the spare chair opposite her.

He gazes at the seat of the chair. Then placing his hand on the chair in readiness to pull it out.

Emma sarcastically snaps, 'Yes, certainly sit down unannounced. In America, you probably just pull chairs out and sit wherever you like, but here in Australia we have a little thing called *manners*! A simple "Please may I sit here?" or "Is it okay if I join you?" wouldn't be too much to expect, would it?'

Undeterred and unemotional, C.J. pulls the chair out from the table. He leans in to grab a man's wallet from the seat, then slides the chair back under the table. He then momentarily holds up the wallet to Emma's eye-level.

'I gather this is not yours?' he asks, with the hint of a smile.

With Emma lost for words, C.J. takes the wallet over to Tara, standing behind the counter.

'Hi Tara. I think this has fallen out of someone's back pocket. It was on the chair opposite where Emma Burgess is sitting.'

Tara knows instantly who the wallet belongs to. 'Thanks so much. That'll be Craig Hope's. He left just before Emma came in. I'll give him a call.'

'Does he live around here?'

'Craig's on the first farm at the end of the beach; not far away at all.'

'Would you like me to drop it off to him?'

Tara shakes her head. 'I'd doubt you'd find the entry to his farm. There are three or four entries up there and they go in all sorts of different directions. I'm sure he's close by. He'll come down, but thanks for the offer, anyway.'

Emma stands up to approach C.J., saying sheepishly, 'Looks like I owe you an apology.' Turning to Tara, she instructs 'Tara, I'll pay for Mr., um …' before realizing she doesn't know C.J.'s surname. She faces C.J. to ask 'By the way, what's your last name?'

C.J. hesitates for a moment. He's about to say 'Stroheim' but gathers his thoughts. 'Jones, um, Christopher Jones.'

'I'll pay for Mr. Jones's coffee,' announces Emma.

Tara acknowledges Emma then rings Craig Hope.

Emma's embarrassment for misreading the situation with C.J. is short lived. She invites him to 'officially' sit with her. C.J. is smug, thinking he had the better of Emma Burgess – but for how long?

As soon as he is seated, she looks him directly in the eye. 'You find it difficult to lie, don't you?'

C.J. is taken aback. 'Excuse me?'

'You heard me. You find it difficult to lie, don't you, *Christopher Jones*?'

C.J. is flustered, insisting, 'Please call me C.J. – and what do you mean "lie"?'

'When someone is asked for their last name, they don't hesitate, not for a millisecond. You hesitated.' She looks deeply into his eyes. 'Why?'

C.J.'s been put on the spot and they both know it.

He draws a deep breath to reply 'I am so used to everyone simply calling me *C.J.* that it comes as a shock when someone calls me Mr. Jones. No one calls me Mr. Jones.'

For someone who doesn't normally lie, C.J. thinks he has made a good recovery.

Emma thinks differently; 'You don't look Irish.'

'Why? Why don't I look Irish?'

'You have a common Irish name like *Jones*, yet you don't look Irish at all.'

'I am sure there are many of us Joneses …' C.J. uneasily replies. Even saying the plural of Jones makes C.J. feel uncomfortable, yet he ploughs on regardless. '… all around the world, even outside of Ireland – and I doubt we all look the same.'

Tara delivers C.J.'s coffee, allowing C.J. a brief respite from Emma's questioning.

Tara relays that Craig Hope will be coming to the café in an hour to retrieve his wallet and he's very appreciative. As much as C.J. would love for Tara to stay and chat, the café is busy. C.J. knows Emma Burgess is not done with him.

Emma leans over the table to whisper, 'You know, the name Jones is NOT Irish. It's *Welsh*.'

C.J. says nothing. *What can I say?*

She takes her last sip of coffee. C.J. still says nothing.

She pushes her chair out to leave. Before stepping away, she leans in close to talk privately with C.J. 'Just a little bit of friendly advice for you, Mr. Jones, if that is indeed your real name. This is a small community. Everyone knows everyone. If someone helps a little old lady cross the road, we find out about it. If someone throws rubbish in the street, we find out about it. We tolerate a lot of things, but we do not tolerate liars. If you are going to be a visitor here for some time, or even reside here, I suggest you start telling the truth.'

C.J. slinks back to the beach house, Emma's harsh words replaying in his mind.

While growing up, his mother told him to always be truthful. He always was.

Even C.J.'s friend Ellis Buckman once commented, 'Stroheim, you must be the only journalist on the planet not capable of telling a lie.' A witness to C.J.'s numerous relationships, Buckman regularly reprimanded his friend for not being able to 'lie to the ladies.'

His mother reiterated, 'Even when you are older and in a relationship, you should always be honest. A relationship based on lies is a relationship that shouldn't be.'

It was an ironic thing to say. Mary Stroheim was married to one of the most secretive men on the planet. Max never lied either, yet there was so much he obviously had not told his wife. She must have been a very understanding person to accept someone unwilling and unable to discuss so many things.

C.J. feels terrible he has lied. He has obviously offended Emma, but how can he make it up to her? He can't tell her the truth.

He reflects for a moment on his parents' relationship, knowing there was a time when his father needed to talk with Mary. The conversation C.J. had with his father on the golf course that day rings in his ear. 'I told your mother that my work was very important and top-secret. To talk about it would jeopardize what I and other people were working on. I vowed that, if she never asked me about my work, I would be open and honest about everything else in my life. Everything.'

CHAPTER NINE

The next morning C.J. sees Emma Burgess walking along the beach toward the beach house. He walks down the beach to join her; 'Good morning.'

She reservedly obliges.

C.J. asks 'Can I walk with you?'

'I guess so – it's a public beach.'

'Listen, I know you don't think much of me. To be called a liar is hurtful. I have never lied to anyone before, but you were right – I *am* a liar.'

She looks at him in bewilderment.

He somberly asks, 'Can I talk to you truthfully?'

She stops walking. 'I wish you would.'

There are rocks nearby. C.J. beckons her to take a seat. Emma sits down on a rock. C.J. faces her.

'My name is C.J. – that is not a lie. I've been called C.J. my whole life.'

'Your last name is not Jones though, is it?'

C.J. nods his head, before stating 'In the States, we have a thing called attorney–client privilege.'

'Yes, I'm aware of the confidential code between an attorney and their client. We have the same thing here.'

'And you're a lawyer, right?'

'Yes. In Australia a lawyer is a generic term that covers both solicitors and barristers. I'm a solicitor.'

'What is the difference?'

'Generally, solicitors deal directly with clients; working with things such as property searches and settlements, trust funds, wills, divorce settlements, private agreements – that sort of thing. Barristers are court specialists. I can do court work or representation but, if someone were facing a possible jail sentence, I would be using the specialist.' She looks C.J. directly in the eyes. 'Do you need a *barrister*?'

'What? No! Do you think I'm some sort of criminal, running from the law?'

'I don't know what to think.'

Talking with conviction, C.J. instructs, 'Now just sit and listen for a moment, please. I am not running from the law; jeez, I've never even had a parking fine. What I do need though is a solicitor; and maybe some legal advice down the track. Are you taking on new clients?'

'Well, yes, I guess.'

'Okay then. As of now, you are my solicitor. Okay?'

'So let me get this right; you want to engage my services?'

'Yes, I want you to be my Australian lawyer. Can you do that?'

'Well, yes, I suppose.'

'Good, then, as of this moment you are my lawyer, Emma Burgess. I can talk to you and whatever I say will be kept confidential?'

'That's right.'

'So it will go no further than us, so I can trust that I won't hear any of what I am about to tell you later in the café.'

'Of course.'

'Okay. My first name is Cole. My middle name is Joseph, thus the C.J. initials. I can't give you my last name.' Emma goes to say something; however, C.J. stops her. 'Please let me finish first, before you ask questions. I *am* a writer – a journalist, actually. I was born and raised in Pasadena, Los Angeles, then moved to Costa Mesa, also in LA. I have a university degree in journalism and I have written a book – albeit not a particularly good one. It was a self-indulgent piece of dribble published as an eBook not long after I graduated from university. It was only ever read by a few family members, a couple of friends, and friends-of-friends. I think I sold one copy to a man in Hong Kong, who mistook my title for another book.'

Emma laughs.

C.J. grins, before saying seriously, 'I know you lost your mother last year. I've lost both my parents. My father passed away just ten days before I arrived in Australia. Both my parents stayed here at Boat Harbour Beach – and it was their favorite place on Earth. Before my father died, he organized and paid for the beach house I am staying in. I have an uncle in Thailand, Uncle Joe – and I called in there on my way through to Australia. My Uncle Joe confirmed the reservation and gave me additional information and tickets to get here.

'I know very little about my father's career, but I do know he was an important man, not well known, but important. He wanted me to write a book – and he wanted me to research it here.'

'Why Boat Harbour?'

'My parents loved it here – and my dad thought it was a long way away from the States, I'd be less distracted to begin my Internet research.'

'So when you say *begin research*, that means you need to go somewhere else?'

Emma is insightful. C.J. knows he will need to choose his words carefully. 'Correct. It is too complicated to explain. I will find out soon where I need to go to next. I know it sounds a bit wishy-washy, but I'll be here a while longer. What I do know is the subject matter is highly classified and very sensitive. To be honest, I don't even know the full details myself. It's a work-in-progress, but I can't discuss it with anyone, even if I wanted to.'

'So you haven't signed some sort of confidentiality agreement with your publisher?'

'No, but I see you've been talking to someone?'

'So that was another lie?'

'Well, yes. I needed to get her off my back. You know how nosey she can be.'

'Okay, I'll allow you that one.'

'Please, believe me that what I'm now saying is the truth. To talk about it would jeopardize what I've been working on. What I can say though is: If you don't ask me about my research, I will be open and honest about everything else in my life.'

As she hesitates to answer, he reiterates, 'Everything.'

Recognizing his sincerity, Emma reaches across to touch his hand. 'I do believe you but, boy, are you dramatic!'

C.J. did not expect a statement like that. 'I don't know how else to tell you.' He pauses for a moment. He barely knows Emma Burgess. Yes, he likes her, but the last thing he wants is to give her information of any description that could endanger him or her. At the moment, C.J. doesn't even know what that information may be. But if his father has gone to all the trouble of sending C.J. to another country, under a different identity, then it must be taken seriously.

C.J. changes his tone, 'Look, I'm sorry – I've said too much already. It was a mistake to, well, um, I was just trying to be as honest as I can…'

She intervenes to say with a smile, 'You really are the serious one, aren't you?'

'I'm not normally. Forget what I said.'

He goes to walk away, echoing, 'I'm sorry; I've said too much.'

'Hang on; hang on. I'm sorry I mocked you but, you have to admit, it sounds all very melodramatic.'

'Again, I'm sorry. I shouldn't have said anything. Please disregard what I said. I'll see you tomorrow at the café.'

He walks away.

Emma sits in stunned silence, watching C.J. walk back to his beach house without looking over his shoulder.

Inside, C.J. sits on the lounge. Through the balcony railings he can see Emma still sitting on the rock. The conversation with her did not go as expected. He cannot recall a woman pressing his buttons like she has. As much as he would like to get to know this intelligent, feisty, and beautiful woman, now is not the right time. He sees her leave the rock, presuming she will walk to the café. Remaining on the lounge, justifying his decision to walk away from her, he does not notice Emma walking onto the deck. She knocks on the glass door.

Shocked, C.J. opens the door.

She apologizes for her sarcasm.

C.J. reiterates his decision to not tell her anymore, yet she is persistent. 'I *am* a lawyer. Research is what I do for a living. I could easily find out your real identity. How many men with the first names Cole Joseph, who are journalists, and have had a book published, could there be? In saying that, I'm not here to threaten you, nor do I really need to know about your life. I do, however, have two questions.'

'Two? Okay, what are they?'

'I presume this research and the subsequent book you are writing is relevant to the life of your late father.'

'That is highly observant, but that's not a question.'

'Touché.' Emma too is impressed by his insight. 'So, my first question is: Was your father involved in any criminal-related activity?'

'No, no, nothing like that. My father was a good man. I can't elaborate, but if you're thinking he was involved in illegal goings on, you'd be thinking wrong.'

'That's a relief.'

'So, what's your second question?'

'Am I still your solicitor?' she asks with a smile.

C.J.'s face lights up, 'Most certainly.'

'Well then, are you coming to have a coffee with your solicitor?'

'I think I could do that.'

As they walk along the beach toward the café, Emma affirms she will respect C.J.'s decision not to talk about his research and his book. She will, however, hold him to his comment about talking about everything else. 'So everything else then is open slather?'

'Absolutely.'

'You can trust me Cole Joseph whatever-your-last-name is,' she jibes, with an unquestioning grin.

'I do trust you, Emma Burgess. It is not about trust. One day it will all make sense.'

'So, who's paying for coffee?'

'As you are now my solicitor and I have used some of your time, then I guess it's my shout.'

'I AM your solicitor. You do know that I charge $250 an hour,' before looking at her watch. 'According to my calculations, you owe me coffee *and* a dinner.'

• • •

Over the coming days and weeks, C.J. and Emma spend more and more time together. C.J. paid for that dinner she jokingly charged him for. Their conversations have flowed effortlessly, meeting at the café at the same time each morning, as well as sometimes walking along the beach, continuing to chat. She has not asked any questions about his research – and the café staff have said nothing. C.J. is impressed she has respected his wishes.

It is ironic that C.J. has researched all the projects, departments, committees, divisions, and sub-divisions all clouded behind a veil of secrecy and he, too, has been forced to be secretive. It is not in his nature.

It has taken all of C.J.'s strength not to open up to Emma, as she is one of the few people he's felt a real connection with. C.J. thinks back to a moment with Ellis Buckman, where Ellis was ridiculing C.J. about the fact he cannot keep secrets. 'I wouldn't trust you with any secret, Stroheim. You don't know how to lie. I've seen you; one pretty woman comes along and you sing like a canary.'

At the time, Buckman was probably right. In recent times, C.J. has shown more maturity than any other time in his life. He thinks Ellis would be proud of his newfound maturity.

With thoughts of Ellis Buckman, it dawns on C.J. that he hasn't been in contact with him, not even in Bangkok. C.J. would love to send Ellis an email, yet can't risk it being traced back to Tasmania.

'One day, when this is all over, I'll be able to tell Ellis everything. He's an investigative journalist himself and often goes undercover for a story. He'll understand.'

The remaining codes and names on his father's list are:

CODE DREAMLAND
IPU, AEC, AFOSI

BOOKS YELLOW, RED & BLUE
YY-II, DNI/27
GREADA TREATY

Each time C.J. looks at the list, he is intrigued by the word RED. He has researched Project Redlight, but not yet Red Book – not knowing if they are related. He must be patient. *Code Dreamland* comes first.

Like some of the other projects, finding accurate information on this subject is rambling and varying. C.J. concludes that the term 'Dreamland' is a nickname for Area 51 and the 'off-limit' skies above; however, it also seems to refer to the area around Area 51's Groom Lake, which contains the underground facility S-4.

He learns of a UK documentary film, entitled *Dreamland: Area 51*.

C.J. watches the documentary on YouTube. It contains claims of UFOs sighted over Area 51, the housing of UFO crash debris, and reverse-engineering of the craft. From the documentary makers' viewpoint, there is no doubt that the US Government has kept Area 51 secret for a reason. C.J. concurs, continuing to research, digging deeper.

C.J. has previously read suggestions that a live alien was recovered from the UFO crash at Roswell. One article refers to the alien as an *EBE* (Extraterrestrial Biological Entity). It was reported that the EBE was ill, remaining in captivity for two years before passing away. Originally taken to Los Alamos, New Mexico, the EBE was then housed at new facilities within Area 51, Nevada. S-4. Medical personnel were unable to determine the cause of the entity's illness, as they had no background about its biological structure from which to draw. The EBE's internal systems were very different to our own. They were chlorophyll based, processing food into energy much the same as plants do. It was decided that an expert on botany was called for.

A botanist, *Dr. Guillermo Mendoza*, was brought in to help the EBE recover. Dr. Mendoza worked hard to save the alien's life, stabilizing the EBE for a period, before it died.

C.J. searches for more information on this EBE. What he finds next leaves him speechless.

Several Internet documents allude that this EBE actually had a name.

That name was *Krll.*

Krll is the name on his father's cryptic message for the code to the tin box, which C.J. buried: *The acronym for Krll in telephone numeric form.*

If the alien or, as it now termed, an *EBE*, was named *Krll*, then the acronym for KRLL has to be *E-B-E*; a three-letter acronym. His father's puzzle eluded that the three-digit acronym was to be converted to 'telephone numeric form.'

C.J. does not have a landline phone. He looks up the standard phone configuration on his computer. The telephone touch-pad keys for *E-B-E* are *3-2-3*.

'Three-two-three,' he mutters. 'This must be the code to open the tin box.'

C.J. reads as much information on EBEs as he can, yet in the back of his mind he ponder what the contents of the tin box are – and if the *323* code is correct. The C.J. of old would have raced straight down the beach, dug up the box, and tried the code. He has matured – but only somewhat – planning to dig up the box under the cover of darkness later tonight.

CHAPTER TEN

Even waiting for darkness proves a challenge for C.J.'s patience. He walks along the beach to meet Emma at the café for an 'afternoon coffee and chat.'

Sarah and Rob are behind the scenes prepping for dinner. Rob has just received a delivery of what he calls 'The biggest, fattest scallops I've ever seen.'

C.J. instantly commits to dining in a few hours' time. Emma needs little persuasion to join him. To date, she has kept their blossoming friendship discreet. In reality, the likes of Sarah and the rest of the café staff already know how C.J. and Emma feel about each other.

Sometimes nothing needs to be said; people just know.

C.J. and Emma savor the magnificent scallops. Despite not being able to talk about C.J.'s research and the book, their conversation flows effortlessly. Both have lost their mothers all too early, both are university educated, interested in travel and global affairs, and both are strong willed.

They also learn they share an interest for animal protection and conservation, with Emma revealing she is a member of Wildcare Tasmania, an environmental volunteer group that supports natural and cultural heritage conservation and reserve management. Emma is particularly passionate about saving whales, dolphins, and other marine animals, and learns that C.J. shares the same passion.

After dinner they walk along the water's edge. The full moon illuminates the unspoiled white sand and sparkling water. As if on queue, a pod of dolphins can be heard then seen, in the shallows. The resonances of spouting blowholes and playful splashing reverberate across the calm water. C.J. and Emma stop to appreciate the seemingly choreographed exhibition.

Once the dolphins have moved out to sea, C.J. offers, 'Come up to the beach house for a nice glass of Aussie wine.'

Emma declines. C.J. understands, walking her back to her car. She proposes to drop him off at his beach house. Before C.J. leaves the car, she leans across to kiss him tenderly on the cheek.

'This was nice,' she tells him, before driving away.

C.J. walks down to the beach alone to survey where the tin box is buried. As much as he would love to dig it up to see if the code *323* works, he hesitates. The full moon shines brightly on the spot C.J. would dig. His father's words 'Don't open the tin box until you feel the time is right' echo in his ears.

He'll research for a few more hours, before reevaluating the weather conditions. Justifying that he needs to update the buried USB memory stick, anyway, even though he bought another memory stick, which is updated regularly to be kept in his pocket or backpack at all times.

'If I'm opening the bag anyway, I might as well check that the code of three-two-three works. I won't open the box, but it would be nice to know that I'm on the right track. All I need to do is wait for a bit of cloud-cover.'

At just after two o'clock in the morning, clouds obscure the full moon.

Changing into a black T-shirt, C.J. walks down to the beach, grabbing the shovel on the way.

Taking a measured stride from the last step to the beach, then another to the west, C.J. digs.

Retrieving the sealed bags, everything is intact and dry. With the bags in hand, he races up the stairs to the beach house. Once inside, the first thing he removes is the tin box. He winds the wheels of the combination code to 3-2-3.

The locking mechanism *clicks*. The lock opens.

With a relieved smile, he quickly closes the lock, spinning the locking wheels around to hide the combination.

With the new information downloaded onto the memory stick, C.J. seals everything, including the tin box, back into the bags, before returning to the beach to bury them with the shovel.

Scattering the last scoop of sand, C.J. looks along the beach and out to sea to make sure the coast is clear, before walking over the disturbed sand. Just then the moon moves from behind clouds, illuminating the area. He quickly walks back up the steps, heading straight to bed.

C.J. sleeps exceptionally well. In a deep sleep, he dreams of hearing the beautiful Emma's voice calling his name. He stirs from his slumber to realize Emma is standing out on the balcony, actually calling his name. He can see her pretty face, with a puzzled expression, peering through the window.

There's a shovel in her hand.

Emma had walked past the beach house in the moonlight the night before. There was no shovel left on the beach then. It is something she would have seen and remembered. She is curious to know how the shovel was left out on the beach overnight or in the early morning – and why a shovel was there in the first place.

C.J. and Emma have become close, friendship close, not romantically close. Although there is definitely chemistry.

C.J. does not want to lie, but he can't tell her about the tin box. Even if he did lie, she would know.

'I could tell you some cock-and-bull story that I was digging for worms because I was thinking about doing some fishing, but you'd know I was lying anyhow.'

'You are damn right I'd know.'

'You know, I really like you.'

'You like me?'

'Yes, that's why I'm protective.'

'So somehow, because you like me, this has something to do with the shovel?'

'Bear with me. My father, when asked about his career, drummed a saying into me. "If no one talks, then no one dies."'

'So are you saying that if you tell me why there's a shovel on the beach, then I will die?'

C.J. doesn't appreciate being ridiculed, responding, 'Come on – you know what I mean.'

'I do not.'

'As you know, my father has me researching some very sensitive material. People in the past who have talked about some of these issues have mysteriously died. Also some of those people who have been told that information.'

'Aren't you being a bit theatrical?'

He shakes his head, then shrugs his shoulders, 'I don't know? All I know is that I made a promise to my father before he died – and I need to honor that commitment.'

She understands. It is the first real test faced in her promise to not ask questions. It is not an easy ask. It is not in her nature.

Emma waits a few moments. 'Well, if you want to tell me, I'm here for you. I can make the decision about whether it is information I want to know or not. Okay?'

'Okay. Will you have dinner with me tonight?'

'We had dinner last night.'

'That was because Sarah and Rob had fresh scallops.'

'What, so you want to ask me out on like a date?'

He shakes his head, 'Not *like* a date.'

'Oh?'

'I'm asking you out on an *actual* date.'

'What, at the café again?'

'No,' C.J. pauses a moment. 'Here.'

'Can you cook?'

'Maybe.'

Mary Stroheim was an excellent cook. She taught C.J. how to navigate his way around the kitchen competently.

'So, you'd like to cook a meal for me?' Emma asks.

'No. I'd like to cook a meal for both of us.'

'Touché.'

Excited by Emma's acceptance of 'the date,' C.J. drives into Wynyard to buy fresh seafood and champagne. Returning, he meticulously prepares dinner.

It is the first day since being in Tasmania that he hasn't turned on the computer.

When Emma Burgess arrives, looking absolutely stunning in an elegant dress, she carries a bottle of wine and a hot roast chicken in a foil bag. The chicken is a joke; a partial reference to her prior 'chicken skin' witticism of the sunburnt C.J. and also that C.J.'s food might be inedible.

As for C.J.'s possible lack of cooking skills, she will be proved very wrong.

When Emma hands the bottle of wine to C.J., he studies the label. 'I have a friend in the States, Ellis Buckman. He's quite the wine connoisseur. He once told me that Australian wines are some of the best in the world.'

Emma comments, 'This Ellis Buckman sounds like a smart man.'

C.J. refills their wine glasses after dinner, inviting Emma to step out onto the deck. It is another beautiful evening; the moon is virtually full, with the moonlight dancing across the water at high tide only a few paces from where they stand.

C.J. and Emma rest their drinks on the handrail to face the ocean. Looking down, they see the glistening whitewater – waves rolling in – waves rolling out; the soothing reverberations sounding like a splendidly choreographed symphony.

C.J. moves to stand behind Emma. She does not flinch when he wraps his arms around her waist. They spend some time draped as one, before Emma turns to face C.J. She was going to say something, but holds her words. She waits for C.J. to talk – he doesn't – instead they kiss.

• • •

Emma did not stay the night that evening.

Over the ensuing weeks she becomes a regular visitor to the beach house. They walk along the beach in the mornings to the café; not blatantly as a couple, but the staff could tell they were.

Boat Harbour Beach is a small community. Almost all the shacks and beach houses are either on the beach or located up the slopes and hills facing the beach. They all see what is going on – and if they don't, they hear about it. Emma wants her relationship with C.J. to remain private at this stage, yet concealing the sparkle in their eyes is impossible.

Sarah is thrilled that C.J. and Emma are so obviously smitten, commenting that C.J. should write a romance novel and call it *The Writer and the Lawyer*. C.J. and Emma failed to respond, their smirks confirming what Sarah already knew.

C.J. has remained tight lipped about his research into his father's life. He does talk to Emma about logistical issues; explaining how he is going to the write the book and how much information he has obtained on any given day. She would love to know why all the secrecy, but understands he will divulge all when the time is right. She knows he is writing a book with the intention of it being released to the public. At some stage he will tell her. She knows that.

C.J. now has a much better grasp of the elaborate and complex web of secret locations that were, and mostly still are, in existence in the United States. Most of these top-secret locations were set up in the late 1940s and early 1950s, while his father was an employee of the NSA. This was the period that launched most of the secretive bases and operations, including the formation of the NSA.

One creditable report stated that, between January 1947 and December 1952 there'd been at least sixteen crashed or downed alien craft, with sixty-five bodies, and one live alien recovered.

C.J. surmised that the live alien was Krll.

The report added that an additional alien craft had exploded yet nothing was recovered from that incident. Of these events, thirteen crashes occurred within the borders of the US—eleven in New Mexico, one in Arizona, and one in Nevada—areas reputed to be where the military were testing new frequency radar systems.

Two separate crashes were recounted in New Mexico in 1948. All previous crashes were of small disks, only 25–30 feet in diameter, yet one of the 1948 crashes was a UFO reputedly 100 feet in diameter, with seventeen dead alien bodies recovered.

The next snippet of information stopped C.J. in his tracks.

A report indicated that a large number of human body parts were stored within both of these vehicles, the large UFO and the small:

> A demon had reared its head and paranoia quickly took hold of everyone in the know. The secret lid immediately became a top-secret lid and was screwed down tight. This would be the beginning of a security blanket like no other. In the coming years, these events were to become one of the most closely guarded secrets in the history of the world. A special group of America's top scientists were organized, initially under the name Project Sign, but that was just the beginning.

This report, and subsequent commentary, were based on an anonymous whistleblower's account.

Finding further details proved elusive for C.J., yet the facts, timeframes, and terminology within the report were consistent with other well-researched articles C.J. had read. There was mention of 'America's top scientists.'

I wonder if my father was one of those scientists being talked about?

C.J. is ready to begin researching the next names on his father's list—IPU, AEC, AFOSI—but reflects on the earlier comment to Emma Burgess about the mysterious deaths of people associated with the subject matter he is researching. He will explore this notion further first.

What he discovers rocks his world.

Dozens, if not hundreds, of people speaking up about secret bases and hidden information relevant to UFOs and extraterrestrials appear to have died prematurely or in mysterious circumstances: researchers, former NSA employees, military personnel, scientists, industry insiders, whistleblowers, lecturers, journalists, and writers. Some were well-known identities.

C.J. spends all afternoon engrossed, stunned by the implications, realizing a pattern to the deaths. Apart from blatant murders, people were dying in three distinct ways: suicide, heart attacks, and cancer.

Most reported suicides were surrounded by suspicious circumstances, like the so-called suicide of James Forrestal. In almost every documented case there were questions asked—instances of suicide notes obviously written in someone else's handwriting, alleged suicides in locations it seemed impossible for the victim to be in, and victims who supposedly committed suicide after expressing fear for their lives. Several victims had, apparently, shot themselves in the head, yet no blood was found on the pistol barrel (as would be the case when a gun is shot at close range) and the handle of the weapon was free of fingerprints. There were also cases, like with James Forrestal, of people reportedly throwing themselves out of high-rise building windows or over cliffs.

Many of the heart attack victims were not old, did not have a history of heart issues, and died instantly. Of the cancer fatalities, an alarming trend became apparent; again, the victims were not old and in each case the cancer was aggressive, with the victim becoming debilitated quickly to pass away within days.

With so many of these deaths, C.J. reasons they all can't be coincidences.

He learns of the CIA running secretive programs from the early 1950s with the express intent of killing people and not getting caught. They experimented with cancer cells, poisons, and injection devices to administer lethal doses of the contaminants. The very concept that the CIA could entertain such programs, and the extent of how many people had died under mysterious circumstances, is staggering to C.J. He asks himself the questions: *Who runs the CIA? Why would they do it? How could they get away with such a thing?*

C.J. thinks long and hard, before concluding: 'The CIA Director was always a MJ-12 member, which means MJ-12 had access to the CIA's resources. The clandestine nature of the agency, along with massive government funding, allowed the CIA to run these sinister programs and not be scrutinized. There's no doubt the CIA developed high-tech ways of killing, but would they go out and murder anyone who talked about UFOs or secret underground bases? Probably not, well, not as a collective. Maybe the killings were authorized and carried out by a select few? The other option is that the technology developed by the CIA was given to someone else, say, like MJ-12? Oh God, this is scary stuff.'

CHAPTER ELEVEN

Emma is calling in to see C.J. after work. They planned to walk to the café for dinner. He is now perturbed about the information regarding the deaths and possible murders. When his father urged his son to search for the truth, C.J. only had himself to think about. Now he has Emma's welfare to consider.

C.J. has a new passport, ID, and credit card, a new identity in a remote part of the world, able to research in relative anonymity.

'Surely I am safe – and Emma, too,' he reassures himself.

Even so, he wants to talk with Emma.

When Emma arrives at the beach house, she recognizes something is troubling C.J. He explains that the more research he's done, the more he's come to realize how dangerous the knowledge could become. He hates talking in riddles, yet feels obligated to let Emma know the dangers he may face.

She does not allow him to finish. 'I only want to know one thing: Is it that important that it's worth the risks?'

'Yes, yes it is. I just want to let know how much you mean to me and the last thing in the world I would want to do is hurt you in any way.'

She smiles and leans forward to kiss him on the cheek. 'I'm a big girl. I can take care of myself. Come on, let me have a shower and get changed so we can walk to the café.'

'No, we need to discuss this.'

'We can talk about it over dinner,' she replies obstinately.

Over dinner, C.J. again hints at the threats he may face. 'If I am in danger, then you could be in danger.'

'Oh come on, C.J., stop being so theatrical. I'm sure you're being a tad melodramatic.'

'What if I'm not? I know we have only known each other a short while – and I've loved every second I'm with you, but maybe it's best …'

'Cole Joseph whoever-you-are, stop it right now. Listen and listen carefully. If you don't want to see me again, then fine. Tell me so and I'll deal with it. But if you do want to be with me, even if it's only until you leave here, then tell me that. I'll be the one who makes the decision on whether being with you is worth the risk.'

'Do you think being with me is worth the risk, even if my life was in danger and possibly yours?'

'I do. So what do you want to do?'

'I haven't felt about someone the way I feel about you. Believe me, the last thing I want to do is to not be with you. I don't want to sound overdramatic, but there is a chance, a distinct chance, that the information I am uncovering is damn important and someone, or some group, will do whatever they can to keep that information secretive. It's because I like you so much that I'm concerned.'

'Well, if you like me so much, then I'm not going anywhere. Maybe one day I'll find out your last name, as well as why all the secrecy. But, in the meantime, you're stuck with me, Cole Joseph.'

Emma stays overnight at C.J.'s. He holds her close – her arms wrapped tightly around him.

The next morning, Emma awakes first. 'We're here – we're still alive – no one tried to kill us overnight.'

'Very funny. It's not really a laughing matter.'

'You'd protect me, wouldn't you, C.J.?'

'Absolutely.'

Outside it's teeming with rain, so they forgo coffee at the café. C.J. makes breakfast.

Emma must leave for work so C.J. kisses her goodbye tenderly.

After he hears her drive away, he turns on the computer, eager to investigate who or whom might be responsible for the spate of deaths he has read about. He already knows the CIA ran secret operations to have people killed. He looks deeper into the CIA, as well as any other agency connected with his research.

The CIA's principal activities are:

> Gathering information about foreign governments, corporations, and individuals; analyzing that information, along with intelligence gathered by other US intelligence agencies.

C.J. thought that the CIA was a government agency, yet it is classified as 'independent.' Many of their intelligence-gathering divisions have been outsourced – to the private sector.

He researches the individual CIA Directors being MJ-12 members, particularly those during the years Max Stroheim worked for the NSA. The first four Directors were military men, until Allen Dulles, a lawyer and banker, became the first Director with a private enterprise background. Dulles was replaced by John McCone, a billionaire businessman from engineering, construction, shipping, and weapons manufacturing. The trend of powerful businessmen has continued to this day. C.J. notes that CIA Directors were 'given' the role. They were not elected nor appointed by the US Government. The CIA was run by MJ-12 – and it was MJ-12 appointing one of their own as Director.

The connections between the CIA and the NSA are obvious, but why the NSA, being the larger and possibly more powerful organization, has escaped public scrutiny is a question C.J. contemplates.

He continues to research, taking occasional breaks to prepare dinner as Emma is coming over after work. He relishes the opportunity to spend time with her, making every effort to cook interesting meals. She appreciates the effort, thoroughly enjoying his culinary skills.

They sit on the deck at sunset to look out across the ocean, twinkling with warm crimson tones. They see a pod of dolphins near the shoreline.

They walk down to the water's edge, with the dolphins seemingly playing in the shallows. C.J. wraps his arms around Emma, saying nothing, until the dolphins head out to sea.

Returning to the beach house, C.J. reveals his father took him to SeaWorld in San Diego many times to see the dolphins. His father knew a great deal about the animal; instilling in C.J. deep affection and respect for the mammals.

Emma participated in two separate incidences on Tasmania's west coast, trying to save and refloat stranded whales. Whale beachings are a common event in Tasmania. Emma zealously recounts her experiences, C.J. listening with interest.

They sit on the deck chatting until well after midnight.

• • •

Emma has stayed three nights in a row at the beach house. Although the skies are overcast with the threat of rain, they stick to their routine of having a morning coffee at the café. Emma tells C.J. she has promised to spend the evening with her father, as his shift finishes late in the afternoon. Emma and her father live just around the corner from the Police Station. Emma explains how her father has struggled since the passing of her mother. She and C.J. know what it is like to lose a loved one; Emma could only imagine the pain C.J. has felt in losing both parents. C.J. encourages her to spend as much quality time with her father as possible.

C.J. and Emma walk along the beach and into the café. Sarah doesn't bat an eyelid; she's now comfortable viewing C.J. and Emma together. Even a wry comment, 'What a great couple you make,' is met with a smile.

Emma leaves the café to go to work. C.J. returns to the beach house to further research the CIA, the NSA, and a host of other security divisions and agencies, including the DNI (Director of National Intelligence), the OFO (Office of Field Operations), the SRT (Special Response Teams), the SOG (Special Operations Group), and the FPS (Federal Protective Service). The more he reads, the more complex the web becomes.

He heeds his father's words. 'You will have a great deal to research. It will be like digging a hole in the sand – the more you dig, the more the walls will collapse, but you must keep digging. At some point an end will be in sight.'

C.J. researches most of the day, with intermittent rain-showers outside, until the sun breaks through mid-afternoon. Struggling to come to terms with all the information being presented, he decides to walk along the beach; 'I think another coffee will do me the world of good.'

After updating the USB memory stick from his pocket, he slides his computer under his bed to then step out the door.

'Just you on your own?' mocks Sarah.

'Just me; no legal advisor today,' replies C.J. with a grin.

Heading back along the beach C.J. can see movement on the beach house's deck – it looks to be a man – a tall, lean man – waving his arms in C.J.'s direction. C.J. quickens his stride.

Walking closer, C.J. can ascertain the man is … Ellis Buckman?

Ellis, realizing that it is indeed C.J., waves more frantically, before walking down the steps leading to the beach.

Ellis is dressed immaculately, as usual, wearing a designer suit. He greets a stunned C.J. on the beach.

C.J. should be excited to see his friend but, at the same time, C.J. asks himself, 'How the hell did he find me?'

Regardless, Ellis embraces C.J. 'Well, well, Stroheim – it's so good to see you – and before you ask how I found you, let me ask *you* a question: Why have you gone off the radar? No phone call, no text, no email, no Facebook, no Twitter, nothing – what's all that about?'

C.J. is still trying to process how and why Ellis Buckman is here. He starts to defend himself. 'My phone broke in Bangkok and …' but he needs to ask Ellis again, 'What on earth are *you* doing here?'

'I was worried about you, Stroheim. I phoned, I left messages, I sent emails, and you never replied. I told the network that my best friend had lost both parents, gone to Thailand, then disappeared off the radar. I told them there could be a story here. Cutting a long story short, they put me on a plane to Thailand and well, here I am – wearing four hundred dollar Italian leather shoes on a beach on the other side of the planet.' Looking up to the house, he asks, 'So, are you going to show me around?'

They walk up the stairs to the house. C.J. unlocks the door. They step inside.

'But how did you know I was in Tasmania?'

'I knew your Uncle Joe was in Bangkok and found him. It wasn't hard – I *am* an investigative journalist you know. He told me you were going to Tasmania and voilà – here I am!'

C.J. is dubious that his Uncle Joe would divulge information of his whereabouts to anyone, even C.J.'s best friend. Even so, Ellis is in Tasmania and appears genuinely pleased to see C.J.

'So you flew to Tasmania, but how did you find me in a little place like Boat Harbour Beach?'

'That was easy. A small community like this – how many good-looking Americans are there in this part of the world? There are *two* of us now! We should celebrate. I've got a bottle of red in the car, a very nice Barossa Valley Shiraz. The man in the bottle shop said it was 'bloody amazing, mate.' The car's parked up the road a bit, so I'll be five minutes or so.'

As he steps out the door, he yells, 'Let's celebrate, Stroheim. If there's one thing the Aussies do well, it's make a good wine. And I hear they love a drink. See you soon, buddy.'

C.J. is shell-shocked at the unexpected arrival. Being close friends for more than ten years now, C.J. has seen unusual behavior at times from Ellis. He knows he's a complex man. Ellis is a good journalist, but not a great journalist. For him to convince his employer for him to jump on a plane and chase C.J. halfway around the world sounds a little extreme, even by Ellis's standards. C.J. is also concerned that his Uncle Joe revealed information Max Stroheim briefed his brother not to say.

With Ellis momentarily gone, C.J. retrieves his computer from under the bed, then removes from his wallet the business card with his uncle's Facebook details.

'Why would Uncle Joe tell Ellis I was in Tasmania? There's something not right here. I wonder if there's something on his business Facebook page.'

What C.J. discovers shocks him to the core.

The page is flooded with tributes.

Joe Stroheim is dead.

Holding back tears, C.J. Googles: *Joe Stroheim Bangkok.*

Numerous newspaper articles appear.

Joe was murdered.

The reports say Joe Stroheim was tied up, tortured, and shot through the head. His Bangkok home, the same home C.J. had stayed in only two months earlier, was ransacked. Police had no suspects, assuming theft the motive for the vicious crime, yet it was noted that nothing appeared stolen. The crime occurred just the day before, in the morning, somewhere between 9:00 and 11:00 a.m. – 'most definitely before midday.'

C.J. is sick to the stomach. Grief is replaced by anger.

He slides the computer under the bed just moments before Ellis walks around the side of the beach house and onto the front deck.

Ellis waves the bottle of wine in the air to announce 'It's time to celebrate, Stroheim.'

He looks at C.J. 'What's up with you? You look like you've seen a ghost.'

C.J., deadly serious, looks Ellis in the eye. 'What are you really doing here, Ellis?'

'What do you mean?'

C.J. grits his teeth. 'Forget the lies, Ellis. How did you find out I was in Australia, and how did you know exactly where I was?'

Ellis takes his time in answering. There is now a slight nervous tone to his voice. 'I told you, I visited your Uncle Joe and he told me. Have you got two glasses?'

C.J. is unrelenting. 'You haven't answered the question! How did you know I was here?'

'And I told you – your Uncle Joe told me.'

'When were you in Bangkok?'

'I don't know. Yesterday, I guess.'

'What time yesterday?'

'Why all the questions?'

'You forget, I'm a journalist as well. Just answer the damn question. What time did you see my Uncle Joe?'

'Geez, Stroheim, chill out. I've never seen you like this.'

'Answer the damn question, Ellis, or get out.'

'Man, you'd think you'd be happy to see your best friend.'

'Answer the question or I will bloody-well throw you out!'

CHAPTER TWELVE

C.J. has always been more athletic and stronger than the leaner, awkward Buckman. Ellis has only seen C.J. lose his temper once. On that occasion, Ellis was not the cause of C.J.'s rage, but he knows full well C.J. is a capable fighter.

Ellis sweats profusely. C.J. can see how uncomfortable he is.

With C.J. probing aggressively, Ellis finally capitulates.

He admits, 'Alright, alright, steady on. Yes, I saw your Uncle Joe yesterday afternoon. He told me you were in Australia, so I flew straight here.'

C.J. shakes his head as his temper soars, closing in to Ellis to scruff him by the shirt. 'Yesterday afternoon, hey? So, yesterday afternoon?'

'That's what I said.'

'My uncle was murdered yesterday morning! You murdering bast—'

Before C.J. can finish his words or grab Ellis, Buckman backpedals. Sliding his hand inside his suit jacket, he produces a small pistol and aims at C.J.'s head.

With an evil grin, he tells C.J. to back off. Still full of rage, C.J. backs off.

Buckman waves the gun threateningly. 'Sit down and shut up, will you. Over there,' he beckons, looking at the lounge.

C.J. reluctantly takes a seat. Keeping the pistol trained on C.J., Buckman sits on a chair facing him.

C.J. asks, 'Why did you kill him?'

'I told you to shut up. I will do the talking.'

Buckman slowly and deliberately takes his time, keeping his right hand with the pistol pointed at C.J., using his left hand to reach inside his jacket to remove a pair of gloves. He expertly slides his long, bony fingers of his left hand into one glove. He then swaps the gun into his left hand to slip the other glove over his right hand, before returning the gun to his hand of preference. 'Yes, I killed your uncle – as I have others. Now, tell me, what do you know and who else have you told?'

'But why did you kill him?'

Buckman bellows, 'AND I SAID, SHUT UP.' He takes a few deep breaths. 'I'll ask you again: What do you know and who else have you told?'

'I don't know what the hell you are talking about.'

'I have known you long enough, Stroheim, to know that you don't lie. Your father told you some secrets before he died. They are secrets that could affect a lot of lives.'

'My father told me nothing.'

Ellis Buckman's face turns red with anger, the evil bubbling to the surface. 'Don't lie to me Stroheim! I am going to kill you anyway.'

'My father told me a fortnight or so before he died that he had some secrets from his career, but he didn't tell me what those secrets were. He told me nothing. He wanted me to research – to find the truth for myself. The only thing he gave me was a list of government departments and some project names. That's it.'

Ellis sneers, 'You expect me to believe that your father gave you basically no information and sent you to supposedly "research"' here at the bottom end of the world, knowing that we would be on your trail and would kill you, regardless of how much information you knew? You've got to be joking! I underestimated you, Stroheim.' Ellis licks his lips. 'I might have to try a different approach. Your uncle? You obviously know he's dead. Do you want to know how he died?'

C.J. protests. 'No.'

Buckman smirks. 'Tough luck, buddy. I'm going to tell you anyway. He was tied up and partially gagged. I pulled his fingernails off, one by one!'

Not taking his eyes off C.J., he reaches inside his suit jacket to remove a small plier-like tool, similar to a dentist's implement used for extracting teeth. 'He was a resilient old geezer, I must say. He didn't say much—not one mention of ol' Maxi's working life – but he did say that you had flown to Sydney. Finding out your new identity was even more painful for him than removing his fingernails. Everyone likes to think they won't talk, but they do. They always do.'

C.J. almost vomits. 'You sick, sadistic bastard.'

'I actually liked you, Stroheim. It would be a shame to see you suffer like your uncle did.'

He slides the tool back inside his jacket.

'I can tell you, my father told me nothing. I would have thought my uncle knew nothing as well. Yes, I've researched, but it's only stuff on the Internet that everyone has access to. Open your eyes man, why would I be here at 'the bottom of the world' as you call it? What's here that would have any relevance to my father's life?'

'That's what I'm here to find out.' Buckman thinks for a moment, never taking the gun from its position of threat. 'I have a better idea. You will tell me everything I need to know – the easy way. You see, I know about your little girlfriend – and don't act all surprised. Emma Burgess. She's a pretty thing – and smart apparently – a lawyer as I understand. Lives with her father, the cop. A real shame about her mother dying.'

There's a wicked tone in Buckman's voice, which scares C.J.

'She lives only a short drive away. It is probably considered miles away by hillbilly standards, but in LA it is closer than our next suburb. I have the address somewhere here in my pocket. It seems you two are quite the couple.'

'She knows nothing!'

'Oh no – on the contrary. You've spent a lot of time with pretty Emma Burgess – and I know you, Stroheim, you can't lie to the ladies. You never could and you never will.'

'You're wrong. She doesn't know anything. Leave her out of this.'

Ellis' expression turns malicious, 'You really don't know who you are dealing with here, do you? Listen and listen very carefully, Stroheim. You are dead. Emma Burgess is dead. It is beyond your control. How you both die is a whole different ball game though. If you tell the truth and tell me everything, I promise she'll die quickly and with dignity – and I won't kill her father. Lie to me again and she will die an excruciating death like your dear Uncle Joe. You got me?'

'I'm telling you the truth. I haven't found out any of my father's secrets yet. I've researched a great deal of information regarding the NSA and CIA's involvement in many of these projects on my father's list.'

C.J. divulges this real snippet of information to see if Ellis Buckman reacts in any way to the names NSA or CIA. He does not.

'Where's this so-called list of projects Maxi gave you then?'

'There wasn't that many names, so I committed them to memory. The day he gave me the list was the day I had coffee with you. Remember, it was the day I drove to Palm Springs and played golf with my father. It was on the golf course that he gave me the note.'

'So what were those names on the note?'

'Project Redlight, Project Sign, and Project Grudge. Those I have researched. He also mentioned Books Red and Blue, but I haven't starting researching those yet and I have no idea what they mean.'

'You expect me to believe you've been sitting down here for two months and spent all that time researching *three* projects?'

'My father wanted me to take my time and have a holiday as well. How do you think I got so tanned?'

'You naïve, dumb bastard. It's no wonder you ended up with a dead-end job,' mocks Ellis, keeping the pistol pointed at C.J.'s head. He brings his watch up to his eye level to glance at the time. 'Well, it looks like I'll be killing you soon.'

'Emma will be here shortly.'

Ellis licks his lips, 'Good, then I'll be killing two birds with one stone – so to speak.'

'She's bringing her father here, the cop. They're coming as soon as he finishes work. He'll be in uniform. I presume he'll be carrying a gun. You won't be able to kill all of us.'

For someone who'd never lied before coming to Tasmania, C.J. is excelling.

Ellis Buckman is unrelenting. 'I'll just have to kill you before they get here then. Actually, I have a much better idea. I want you to write her a note. Where's a pen and paper?'

'In the bedroom.'

Buckman instructs, 'Get them, but don't try anything stupid, Stroheim. You know I won't hesitate to shoot. I also have in my pocket a clever little device I can jab into you within the blink of an eye. It barely leaves a mark on the skin and the toxin brings on a heart attack within seconds. If I miss you with a bullet, and I won't, the jab won't miss its mark. I actually thought about killing you with the injection, but it *is* a horribly painful way to die – and you wouldn't be able to tell your dying secrets anyway. You see, the victim writhes around on the ground in agony. And they usually lose control of their bodily functions. It's not a pretty sight; there's no dignity dying in a pool of your own excrement. So no funny business, Stroheim. One false move and I'll put you in a world of pain you wouldn't believe existed.'

Buckman follows C.J. to the bedroom. There is a notepad and pen beside the bed. He cautiously maintains his distance from C.J.

'Now, sit back on the lounge.'

When seated, Buckman instructs:

'Now write this down: *Emma, feeling sorry for myself.*' Buckman pauses to allow C.J. time to write. '*It's the anniversary of my mother's death. Gone for a ride.*' He pauses again. '*Sorry about dinner plans. I'll phone you.*' He abruptly changes his mind. 'No, don't say "phone you" because I know you don't have a phone. Say: *I might see you tomorrow*, then sign it.'

The anniversary of C.J.'s mother's death is actually the following day. That Buckman knew this illustrates to C.J. just how meticulous Buckman has been with his planning. C.J. has many questions flying through his mind, but Buckman is waving the pistol at C.J.'s forehead, encouraging C.J. to write – and write quickly.

While C.J. writes, Ellis reflects, 'Yes, that's good. Go on, keep writing' until C.J. signs it *C.J. Stroheim.* Buckman's face contorts with rage. 'You must think I'm a complete and utter idiot! You signed it "C.J. Stroheim." I know your name down here is *Christopher Jones*. Don't try and play games with me. Do it again and sign it just C.J. I know she calls you C.J. Any more tricks and I'll kill you right here, right now – the agonizing way. Now damn well write it how I said.'

C.J. slides the rewritten note back onto the lounge. Buckman places it in his pocket.

'Grab your car keys. We're going for a little ride.'

'Where are we off to?'

Ellis boasts, 'You are lucky, you know. Now that you've left a suicide note of sorts, we're going to the cliff-top not far from here. Right now, as much as you think I enjoy killing, I don't. Some things in life are a chore. This is one of those chores.'

'So where are we going?'

'There's a farmhouse nearby, not far from the cliff. Isn't it convenient, the owners of the farmhouse live interstate? You poor depressed man; you drove up to the cliff, got out of the car and threw yourself over the edge.' Buckman is genuinely pleased with his self-assuredness. 'I can then walk back to where my car is parked. My new Italian leather shoes are not really made for hiking, but I guess one has to make the odd sacrifice here and there. Go get your car keys.'

'Before we go, can you just tell me why? Why are you doing this?'

Ellis grins. 'You really are naïve, aren't you, Stroheim? You had the right education, the right upbringing, you were a pretty good journalist, but you didn't make it, did you? I came from nothing. How do you think I made it to the top of my profession? Do you think it was luck? The world doesn't run on chance. It's run by those who make it run. I've done what I've done for a reason. Your father had access to the power and those with that power, but he didn't take advantage of it. He was, apparently, a brilliant scientist, but there are lots of brilliant scientists. He chose science over being one of the world's elite powerbrokers. Some people didn't like that. I am one of those people. Now get up.'

C.J. rises to his feet, 'Did you enroll at USC just to keep an eye on me?'

'You are kidding me, right? You had nothing to do with my university choice. I'd been involved with, well, let's just call them "powerful groups," and when I realized you were in my course, the opportunity came along and I took it. If you think you're the only person on the planet being watched, you're an even bigger fool than I took you for.'

'So who exactly sent you here?'

Buckman stands. 'Shut up, will you? Stop stalling me. Get your car keys!'

Buckman follows several paces behind, pistol pointed to the back of C.J.'s head. C.J. picks up the keys from the kitchen bench and walks out the door to the steps leading to the road above.

The earlier rain means the steps are still wet. Ellis can see this. He tells C.J. to walk very slowly, one step at a time. Buckman maintains his distance. Part way up the stairs C.J. deliberately slips, his left foot sliding from one tread to the step below. The moment his foot is anchored, he swings his body around, right foot lashing out, just like he was kicking for goal as a kid. The foot connects with Buckman's hand holding the gun. A single shot fires, missing C.J. The gun spills from Buckman's hand to lob over the railing.

C.J. jumps past Buckman; his clenched fist holding the car keys landing a weighted, passing blow. Buckman stumbles, blood dripping down his cheek where the punch landed and the keys scratched. He does not fall. He grabs the railing to slide his free hand inside his jacket, producing a device similar to an EpiPen. The pistol out of sight, C.J. plants his feet on the ground, turns to see the device in Buckman's hands, and continues running.

Knowing Buckman could retrieve the pistol at some point, C.J. can't risk looking for the gun himself or fighting, as he could be jabbed with the deadly device. He sprints along the side of the house – and then jumps athletically over the railings of the front deck. It is quite a drop. C.J. lands on the soft, fluffy white sand, rolling several times, before lifting himself to his feet unharmed. He turns right and runs. He darts behind one of the large boulders – angling his run to keep the rock between himself and the deck of the beach house. He knows Buckman will be hot on his heels.

CHAPTER THIRTEEN

Ellis Buckman appears on the deck, having re-gathered the gun. He wipes blood from his seeping cheek, raises the gun to shoot. He looks over the balcony to see an impression in the sand where C.J. jumped and landed. His eyes scan the beach, seeing nothing, then glimpsing C.J. scurrying behind a large rock.

Buckman fires repeatedly.

The pistol shots are muzzled, but the bullets *whizz* as they pierce the air. Bullets hit the boulder just behind C.J. – *pinging* – ricocheting away. C.J. drops to the ground, behind another rock. The shooting stops. C.J. pokes his head around the rock briefly. He can't see Buckman.

C.J. deduces Buckman must be stepping down onto the beach to change his angle of attack. C.J. knows he's a faster runner. Buckman knows this, too.

C.J. makes a dash for it, toward another larger boulder. Assuming Buckman will walk further down the beach to open up the angle of attack, C.J.'s course keeps the rocks behind him as shelter from the presumed new direction of gunfire. It is a big gamble. But it's the right choice. Buckman does move closer to the water's edge. Catching a glimpse of C.J., Buckman again opens fire. C.J. drops to the sand, bullets *zipping* over his head – crawling – rolling – scrambling behind another boulder.

Bullets ricochet from the rock – *pinging* – chunks of dislodged rock fly through the air.

Realizing Buckman will be changing the angles, edging closer, C.J. runs as fast as he can.

With enough distance, Buckman's shots are out of range. C.J. is now off sand and on rocks. He runs across the slippery and sometimes unstable surface until he sees a track leading up to farmland. This track will take him away from the beach – away from Buckman's view – as the track cuts a path through thick oceanfront foliage. Beyond is a large, grassy field.

He runs up the hill.

The farmhouse belongs to the Hope family. Thirty-five-year-old son, Craig, is inside. Hearing C.J. yelling, Craig opens the door as C.J. approaches.

'Are you okay, mate?'

Almost out of breath, C.J. replies, 'Hi. I'm C.J.—'

'Yeah, the American. I've heard about you. You're the bloke who found my wallet. Thanks for that, mate. I owe you a beer.'

'You're welcome. Listen, can I use your phone? It's an emergency. I need to call the police.'

'Everything alright, mate?'

Keeping an eye on the track below, C.J. promises to explain everything later. But now he needs to contact the local police. Craig happens to be good friends with the local Sargent, Gary 'Burgo' Burgess. His personal number is in his phone. Finding the contact, he hands the phone to C.J.

Sargent Gary Burgess knows exactly who C.J. is. He's in the police car on his way to Boat Harbour Beach.

'I've had a call to say some guy wearing a suit was on the beach. Looks to have a gun – and he's been shooting at something. Don't tell me, he was shooting at you?'

'The man's name is Ellis Buckman and he is very dangerous. He has an array of weapons.'

'Where are you now?'

'I'm at Craig Hope's house. I don't think Buckman saw me run up but, if he did, I'd see him coming. I've seen nothing yet, so he may be back at the beach house. If that's the case, I suggest you get backup.'

'Backup? You're in Boat Harbour, not Beverly bloody Hills.'

C.J. doubts Buckman would wait at the beach house for him to return. Too obvious and too risky. He'd probably return to his car, either to look for C.J. or to regroup and return later.

Sargent Burgess informs him, 'Well, I'm on my own and I'm still five minutes from the Boat Harbour turnoff. What sort of car is this Buckman fellow driving?'

'I don't know. He was parked up the road. I never saw the car.'

'When I do turn off, I'll keep an eye on any cars coming my way.'

C.J. interrupts in a panic. 'Before you go. Emma – where's Emma?'

'She'd be home from work already, I'd reckon.'

'What's the number? Craig, have you got a pen and paper?'

Craig's been listening intently. 'I have Emma's home and mobile numbers in my phone. Emma's our solicitor.'

C.J. tells Gary Burgess, 'The beach house is unlocked. I'll be going back to the house, so I'll see you there.'

Gary asks, 'Is Hopesy there?'

'I'm here, Burgo.'

'Don't you get involved, but can you give your rifle to C.J.? And show him how to use the bloody thing. Also show him the shortcut to his place. Tell him to keep off the main road and off the beach. I'll be there is ten minutes.'

C.J. walks along the road from the Hopes' farmhouse. He has a loaded rifle in one hand and Craig Hopes' cell phone in the other. He calls Emma.

Emma answers to hear C.J.'s voice: 'Get out. Get out of the house, now!'

She is a strong-willed, defiant woman. C.J. knows she won't leave the house without an explanation. 'Keep your phone on, but turn off the oven or anything you're using and jump in your car. I'll explain everything while you're driving.'

She does as C.J. says, replying, 'Okay, I'm on hands-free. I'm starting the car. Where do you want me to drive?'

'Anywhere, just not in the direction of Boat Harbour Beach.'

'What the hell is going on?'

She reluctantly drives in the opposite direction of Boat Harbour Beach.

C.J. begins to explain what has happened. He tells of being shot at, that the man's name is Ellis Buckman. He is armed, dangerous and could be after Emma. 'I know I've told you nothing, but they think you know things, so your life is in danger.'

'Who are "they"?'

'I thought it was a US government agency like the National Security Agency or the CIA, and it may well be, but I don't really know. What I do know is they think I know all my father's secrets, which I don't, and they want me dead. They think you know, too. You've got to trust me – you're in real danger.'

'I think you better tell me everything.'

'My full name is C.J. Stroheim. My father is Doctor Max Stroheim. He spent thirty-four years working for the National Security Agency. The NSA ran many of America's top-secret projects – things like Area 51, military research, secret underground bases. There's even talk of extraterrestrial activities – you know, UFOs, that sort of thing. Seriously Emma, that's about all I know.'

C.J. divulges someone from Boat Harbour Beach saw Ellis Buckman on the beach with a gun and had called the police, Emma's father Gary Burgess. Emma needs no more information. She stops the car and turns around. 'My father is going to the beach house? He could be face-to-face with an assassin. I'm on my way!'

No amount of protesting by C.J. will convince her otherwise. She keeps driving toward Boat Harbour Beach. Resigned, C.J. insists she stay on the line. He, too, is heading to the beach house.

Walking along a track, C.J. explains to Emma that he's nearing the street leading to his house. The sounds of Gary Burgess's police car's siren are in the distance, but getting closer. 'Okay, I'll put the phone in my pocket for a moment and I'll talk to you when I can. Stay on the line though.'

He places the phone in his pocket and raises the rifle to his shoulder.

Arriving at the house, C.J. sees no sign of Buckman's car. Hearing the police car siren increasingly louder, C.J. runs down the stairs. With the rifle cocked, he finds the house empty, but ransacked. Looking under the bed, he discovers his computer is gone.

He walks back outside and up the stairs to the road.

With the police car pulling up and the siren turning off, C.J. places the rifle on the ground. He greets Gary Burgess – extending his hand. Gary is a big, burly, ruggedly handsome man.

'C.J. Stroheim, pleased to meet you, sir.'

Shaking hands, Gary replies, 'I knew Emma had a boyfriend, but I didn't expect to be meeting him under these circumstances. Call me Gary.' Looking around, he asks, 'This Ellis Buckman character isn't here, obviously?'

'No sir, but he was. He's ransacked the place. There's no sign of his car, so he must have driven away.'

A neighbor, Barry Jakes, a single man in his seventies, steps from his house diagonally opposite C.J.'s. It was Barry who called Sargent Burgess.

He now informs them, 'I saw the guy, a tall, skinny man in a suit. He still had a gun in hand. I saw him leave with a computer and a bottle of wine tucked under his arm. He went to his car, which was parked up around the corner. I saw it leave. It was a medium-sized white sedan – it looked like a rental car.'

'Thanks, Barry. We've got it from here.'

As Barry Jakes leaves, C.J. removes the phone from his pocket. He explains Emma is on the line and on her way to Boat Harbour Beach.

'What?' bellows Sargent Burgess. 'Give me the phone.'

C.J. puts the phone on speaker and hands it over. Gary tells Emma, 'Sweetheart, it's Dad. I'm here with C.J. We're both fine. Where are you?'

'I'm only a few minutes from the Boat Harbour Beach turnoff.'

'We'll wait for you by the road outside the beach house. Keep on the line.'

'I'm turning off the highway now,' Emma says. 'I am only a few minutes away from … what the hell!'

'What is it?' asks C.J. with urgency.

'A car's just pulled out from behind the trees on the corner. It's spinning its wheels like a drag racer. Hell! It's not one of your unmarked cop cars is it, Dad?'

Before Gary can answer, C.J. yells, 'Drive faster – don't let him get close to you!'

Sargent Burgess and C.J. jump into the police car. They take off at speed.

Over the wailing siren, C.J. yells into the phone, 'We're on the way. Drive faster – drive faster!'

C.J. turns to Sargent Burgess, and asks for the siren to be turned off.

Gary obliges, then yells to Emma, 'Hang in there, sweetheart. Take the turnoff to the beach if you can; we'll shield you when you come down.'

'Christ, he's got a gun! He's shooting at me!' she screams.

'Drive faster!'

A loud *BANG* can be heard on the speaker phone:

'Oh God, the back wheel's blown out – I'm losing—'

Emma's car swerves violently, fishtailing from one side of the road to the other. Her foot is firmly planted on the accelerator. But the blown tire slows the car considerably, the wheel rim dragging along the bitumen – sparks flying from the road – the car shuddering from the grinding contact. Through the speaker phone, C.J. and Gary can hear the scraping of metal on tar, as well as a distressed Emma attempting to gain control of the car.

The police car takes the first sharp corner almost on two wheels, then the next bend even more dramatically. They turn the corner to see, in the distance, Emma's silver hatchback, sparks trailing, the car struggling to stay on the road. A mid-sized white sedan is closing in on her – and about to ram the rear of Emma's car.

It violently *slams* into the hatchback, sending Emma's car careening off the road, just as the police car enters the straight.

Gary and C.J. watch in horror as Emma's car veers from the road, careens over a small ditch, ploughs through a wire fence and into a grass paddock. It stops in the lush, rain-soaked pasture.

The police car drives down the middle of the road at full speed, hurtling toward the white sedan, which has now stopped on the side of the road, adjacent to Emma's stranded car.

Ellis Buckman, pistol in hand, steps from the car. He fires two shots at Emma's car just as Sargent Burgess turns the police siren back on. Distracted by the noise, Buckman looks over his shoulder to see the police car bearing down. He hastily jumps back in his car, back wheels spinning in the loose gravel on the apron of the road, before the wheels grip the bitumen. The car fishtails as Buckman U-turns to gain speed in an attempt to flee the fast-approaching police vehicle.

'Emma, Emma, are you there?' yells C.J. into the phone. 'Are you alright? We're here; we're after Buckman. Talk to me!'

Buckman has his foot to the floor, but before his car can reach full speed, the police car *thumps* into the back of the car – shunting it forward and sideways –off the road – two wheels forced onto the loose soil on the shoulder.

Over the sounds of crunching metal, Emma yells, 'I'm here – and I'm fine.'

Gary lines up Buckman's car, ready to strike again.

Foot still to the floor, Buckman brings the car back onto the main road surface. Just as the speed increases, the car is aggressively shunted again.

The highway turnoff is fast approaching. Buckman's car is clinging to the road, increasing speed.

Sargent Burgess places his foot to the floor; the police car rams into the back corner of Buckman's car once again. Buckman maintains control of his car, readying to take the highway turnoff at speed. Sargent Burgess brakes, backing off, while Buckman's car appears to be on collision-course with an oncoming semi-trailer truck. Its horn is blaring – it swerves – narrowly missing Buckman's car, using the full width of the highway, as well as the opposite shoulder to take the corner.

Buckman has turned in the opposite direction to Wynyard, his car fishtailing in the loose soil – two wheels sliding onto grass – mud and dirt spraying into the air. He maintains enough control to guide the vehicle back onto the road – and drive away at speed.

Sargent Burgess lets him go.

Turning the police car around to head back to Emma, Gary gives Buckman's car details and travel direction on the police radio.

Cars are being dispatched from several rural communities, including the direction Buckman is heading.

Emma saw the police car chasing Buckman. Now, seeing her father and C.J. driving back toward her, she jumps from the car to run toward the roadside. C.J. is the first to exit the car, Emma wrapping her arms tightly around him. Gary Burgess follows. Emma holds onto C.J. momentarily, before releasing her grasp to hug her father.

Gary Burgess gushes, 'Geez Em, I lost your mother way too soon; I don't want to lose you, too.'

CHAPTER FOURTEEN

Returning to beach house, Emma and Gary Burgess see the house is trashed. Buckman donned gloves after pulling the gun on C.J. – searching for fingerprints would be a fruitless exercise. The only item taken is C.J.'s computer. C.J. was diligent to back up all information to a USB memory stick, now in his pocket, as well as the other memory stick, still buried. He keeps the details of the buried items to himself for now.

When Ellis Buckman had arrived, C.J. was returning from the café. He had his wallet in his pocket, containing cash, credit card, ID, and the cards his Uncle Joe gave him.

'At least I have my wallet, but Ellis Buckman knows my identity and is able to trace me. My credit card and driver's license are probably also useless.'

Gary Burgess assigns a police constable to check every car taking the Boat Harbour Beach exit. At C.J.'s insistence, the police employed another plain-clothes constable to monitor every car turning off the highway, although they can only do this for a limited time.

Word is spread to the surrounding properties to monitor the beach entry from the rugged coastline-side of Boat Harbour Beach. A full description of Ellis Buckman and the events of the day have been circulated to Sarah at the café, as well as several local residents. The word is spreading through the little community like wildfire.

Gary Burgess comments, 'If Ellis Buckman is anywhere remotely near Boat Harbour Beach or Wynyard, for that matter, he'll be seen and reported. There are times when living in a small community has its drawbacks, but this is not one of them. The only way a fellow like Ellis Buckman can get into Boat Harbour Beach is to parachute in.'

The sun is going down. Emma and Gary decide to stay at the beach house for the night. It doesn't seem like an appropriate time to be drinking alcohol, but C.J. has learnt from the locals that there is never an inappropriate time to have a drink. Gary is not much of a wine drinker so he rings Craig Hope. Craig arrives at the beach house with beer. C.J. thought it might be a bottle or two, or even a six-pack. Craig brings a full carton of twenty-four bottles.

Over red wine and beers, C.J. is prepared to tell Emma and Gary Burgess, as well as Craig Hope, everything. Any hope of secrecy in the small community went out the window the second Ellis Buckman pulled a gun on him – and threatened Emma's life. If one person in Boat Harbour Beach knows the truth, everyone will know.

Whoever Ellis Buckman was working for, they can't kill a whole community. From C.J.'s perspective, the more people who now know, the better.

Before explaining the whole situation, C.J. apologizes profusely for dragging both Emma and Gary into the circumstances they are now in. He is particularly remorseful toward Emma, although she defends him vigorously.

'Even if you'd told me the truth from the beginning, I don't think anything would have been different.'

Gary is more introspective. Emma is well aware of her father's reluctance to accept the situation. She tells her father C.J. told her nothing and it was he who warned her to stay away.

'Dad, it was me who made the decision to be involved.' She turns to C.J. with affection. 'And I have no regrets.'

Craig Burgess accepts Emma's explanation grudgingly. He focuses his attention on C.J. 'Well then, Mr. Stroheim, I guess you'd better tell us why a man would travel halfway around the world to try and kill you – and my daughter.'

C.J. chooses his words carefully. 'My father, Max Stroheim, was a scientist; an astrobiologist – the best in the country. An astrobiologist is someone who looks at biological life in the universe and how it might relate to us here on Earth. Anyhow, after World War II, the US Government set up a secretive agency with a number of projects relative to UFO and extraterrestrial activity …'

'Sorry, did you just say *UFOs and aliens*?' says Gary.

'Well, yes. You must understand that, before I came to Tasmania, I knew nothing. While my father was alive, I was aware he'd worked for thirty-four years with the NSA, which is the US National Security Agency, but apart from knowing he was a scientist, I was never told anything. Before my father passed away, he asked me if I wanted to know the truth and if I was willing to write a book about it. He also pointed out the danger I might face if I accepted. Of course, I said I would do it. He gave me instructions to visit Bangkok. That's where my uncle lived, my father's brother. I was given a new passport, ID, money, and airline tickets with instructions to come to Boat Harbour Beach.'

'Why Boat Harbour?' queries Gary.

'My parents had stayed here on holidays. My father thought it would be the ideal place to research some of the projects and secretive divisions he'd placed on a list – and it was a long way from the US. In Bangkok I was given a code to access a bank's security box – and I retrieved a list of names my father wanted me to research.'

Emma asks 'What was on this list?'

'At first glance, it looks like a whole lot of codes and numbers, but they're all relevant. Look, it's very hard to explain.'

'Try,' urges Gary Burgess.

'I was only about three-quarters through the list, but I'll try and explain what I have learnt so far. Have you heard of the Roswell incident?'

Emma has. Craig and Gary haven't.

'Apparently, in 1947 a UFO crashed in the New Mexico desert. Supposedly, dead aliens, as well as a live alien, were found. The then-

President, Harry S. Truman, commissioned his Secretary of Defense, James Forrestal, to set up a whole lot of secretive divisions and projects. Eleven men were chosen to join Forrestal to head up and control all these agencies and tasks. These twelve men were given the name The Majestic 12, or MJ-12 for short. From there, it looks like many secret locations were created or existing military bases were expanded, mainly underground – and very few people knew about them or knew the complete story. I can surmise that my father was one of those who knew.

'Look, I know this appears to be an American thing, and at first glance it looks like being exclusively the US Government, but it's much broader than that. Private enterprise appears to be involved and the ramifications of what's been going on in secret will have global consequences.'

Emma is stunned. She'd speculated what C.J.'s father's work may have been. She would not have guessed in a million years it'd be ET or UFO related. That in itself is enough to understand why the government, or whoever else knew, wanted everything kept under wraps. But why private enterprise involvement? From C.J.'s tone, she knows he's yet to find the answers. There is obviously much more to learn. She knows she will help C.J. find those answers. She may not have a choice, anyway.

Gary Burgess accepts C.J. is telling the truth, but is far from impressed with the situation. 'For whatever reason, this has happened, it has happened. What do we do about it? We have a well-armed lunatic still on the loose. Maybe the road blocks will snare him?'

Gary loosens his police uniform to ask C.J. questions about Ellis Buckman and who he might work for.

C.J. tells him, 'I've known Ellis Buckman for over ten years, but I obviously never knew him at all. For him to find me, then pull a gun on me, is baffling. My first thought is he must work for the NSA or even the CIA, but I mentioned both names and he didn't flinch. My father worked for the NSA, so it would make sense Ellis Buckman worked for the NSA, too, but now I'm not so sure. In my research I found so many different secretive networks and subdivisions. There are security agencies within security agencies. This is the sort of stuff that they do. In saying that, I asked him directly, 'Who do you work for?' His answer was strange.'

Emma asks, 'What did he say?'

'He told me he came from humble beginnings. That I already knew. But he became one of the most successful journalists in the country.'

'Buckman is a journalist?' queries Gary Burgess.

'Highly respected. He was on TV in the States with one of the major news networks.'

'So, what did Buckman say?' asks Emma.

'He teased me with riddles. He said, "The world does not run on chance," then he said something like "It's run by those who make it run" and that he did what he did for a reason.'

'What do you think he meant?'

C.J. takes a deep breath, 'Okay, this is what I know and what I think. Ellis Buckman did come from modest beginnings. He rarely talked about his past, but I know he didn't have a happy childhood. As soon as he could, he left Los Angeles. He actually worked for a year at Yale University, on the other side of the country. He wasn't a student, but a janitor. He didn't have the academic ability to become a Yale student, and yet he traveled from LA to be a cleaner at Yale, just on the off chance he could become enrolled. He was not, but after a year he was accepted into the University of Southern California and that's where I met him. We studied journalism together.'

'Was he a good student?' asks Emma.

'He was terrible. He only just scraped through the course. But he still made it to the top of his profession – and quickly. This is the thing I'm struggling to understand: Ellis Buckman is one of the best-known reporters in Los Angeles. This guy is on the news every day. He's not a fulltime hit-man, he couldn't be, yet he appears to have the arsenal and the training to be one. He talked of a powerful group. I am guessing it's not a government group but an influential group who control many things. Maybe he became involved when he was at Yale University somehow? Either way, he has information and weapons very few people have access to.'

Addressing Gary, he says, 'I know Australia has stringent gun control laws. I've seen your gun and it's nothing like Ellis's pistol. He also had an injection device. He claimed that, when jabbed, it contained a poison that would bring on a fatal heart attack. When I came into this country, I saw how strict the customs and immigration system was. How can someone like Ellis Buckman waltz into Australia with the weapons he has and not be detected?'

Gary Burgess shrugs his shoulders.

'The other thing is, and you don't know about this, but before Buckman came to Tasmania he went to Thailand. My Uncle Joe lives there, I mean, lived there …'

C.J. has a lump in his throat and tears in his eyes. 'Ellis Buckman obviously had the gun in Thailand because he killed my uncle.'

Learning of C.J.'s uncle's death jolts Emma. They all are shocked, particularly realizing C.J. only found out about his uncle's death after Ellis Buckman had arrived only a few hours earlier. Emma knows the day's events have overshadowed C.J.'s chance to absorb the tragic news. She wraps her arms around him, holding on tightly.

When Emma finally unlocks her arms, she stops for a moment to think.

She then discusses her thoughts on a subject so insightful and so thought provoking, it will make C.J.'s mind spin more than it already is.

Emma Burgess worked with a large Melbourne law firm. As a junior lawyer, she was assigned mainly research work for the senior partners and associates. One of those research assignments involved what at first looked like a somewhat innocuous case. A wealthy middle-aged businessman had imported a car, a 1967 Corvette convertible, from the United States, to be hit with a rather large tax bill for the importation of the car. The money wasn't necessarily the concern; the reasoning for the bill became the real issue.

The client thought to himself, 'Why should the Australian Government profit from the fact he had traveled to the States, purchased a car for which the local authorities had taken the appropriate taxes, and had paid for the shipping all the way to Australia? He would then be paying local tradespeople to convert the car to right-hand drive, registering the car in Australia, then paying local insurance premiums and taxes.'

Upon researching, he was astounded to discover that the excise he was required to pay was not to the Australian Government, but the Customs division – and they operated under a separate identity to the Federal Government. He dug deeper. By the time he had taken the information to Emma's company, he'd ascertained that the excise money, or tax, never went to the Australian Government at all. It went to Customs. And, in turn, it was transferred, to his utter astonishment, to Washington DC. Where that money ended up, he could never find out. The fact the money went offshore and not to his own government made his blood boil.

Emma explains that her law office decided not to take the case as legal restrictions meant the Customs Office were technically operating within a different domain to that of the Australian Government.

'To put it bluntly, Customs have their own set of rules. They operate outside the standard law. Or you could even go further and say that they are above the law.'

C.J. is fascinated. Much of what he read about the NSA and even the CIA had concluded the very same thing. One document had stated:

> MJ-12 and similar agencies operate at Above Top-secret levels and beyond. The charter for the NSA, for instance, states that the NSA is exempt from all US laws, which do not specifically mention the NSA within the text.

This means that the NSA is indeed 'above the law,' unless they actually created a special law for themselves.

The ramifications of this information are immense.

Could Ellis Buckman carry weapons from country to country and be operating 'above the law'?

It would seem so.

C.J. would later find, in the US alone, there are more than ninety different federal law enforcement agencies able to travel on commercial airlines, which are armed onboard at one point or another.

It is perplexing how so many people are able to carry armed guns on planes. Additionally, countless more agencies and departments transport weapons in luggage, carried within the hold of aircrafts.

Someone like Ellis Buckman, with the right clearance, could easily bring into Australia whatever he wanted – or any other place in the world for that matter.

It is a scary thought.

CHAPTER FIFTEEN

With midnight approaching, Craig Hope finishes his last beer and uses the shortcut to stagger home.

Gary is exhausted, almost falling asleep on the lounge. He struggles to his feet, eventually sliding into a bed in the second bedroom.

C.J. and Emma step out onto the deck to keep talking.

C.J. cannot be any more sincere in his apologies for dragging Emma into this mess. She pulls him in close to kiss him with feeling. Breaking the kiss, she looks him in the eyes.

'I know you're now a fugitive. I know I am as well. This Ellis Buckman is not working alone. He's part of something much, much bigger. I know that; you know that. If it is not Buckman after us, it'll be someone else.

'I haven't known you all that long, C.J. Stroheim, but I know a good man when I see one. I trust you. And I'm beginning to fall in love with you.'

C.J. cups her pretty face in his hands. 'I fell in love with you the first time I saw you. And I've fallen further every day since.'

'So the big question is: Where do we go from here?' she says. 'We can't stay here. Where do we go? And how do we get there?'

C.J. takes her by the hand to lead her down the steps to the beach. He takes a seat on the last step, beckoning Emma to join him.

'When I was talking earlier, there was one thing I didn't mention. My father gave me a tin box with a code. Inside that box is information to help me on the next leg of this journey. I haven't opened the box yet.'

'Where's this box?'

'Just there,' replies C.J., pointing to the spot on the beach where the bags are buried.

'So that's why the shovel was left here,' she deduces. 'Well, don't just sit there; get the shovel and start digging!'

C.J. and Emma take the sealed bags up to the house. With Gary sound asleep and snoring loudly, they enter the bathroom, closing the door behind them. Opening the bags, C.J. places his passport, money, and USB memory stick in his pocket. Then he removes the tin box. He pauses momentarily, having waited so patiently for this moment.

He aligns the code: 3-2-3.

It opens.

His heart races. He looks inside. There is very little to see – another passport, ID, and credit card, plus a single piece of paper.

The paper is the first item he removes. It is in Max Stroheim's handwriting:

> FOUR-DIGIT POSTCODE: DOUGLAS ADAM'S ANSWER + YOUR AGE WHEN WE GAVE YOU THE TAG.
> THERE IS A MAILBOX UNDER YOUR NEW NAME. THE PASSWORD IS: THIS TINBOX CODE + THE NUMBER OF PET FISH YOU HAD AS A CHILD.

'It's another riddle?'

C.J. opens the seemingly well-worn passport. All the documents carry the name *Calvin Jacob Reiner*. Calvin was C.J.'s maternal grandfather's name and Jacob his paternal grandfather's. Max Stroheim has retained the initials *C.J.* Where the last name *Reiner* comes from is, at this stage, a mystery to C.J.

He tells Emma, 'Ellis Buckman mentioned James Forrestal and a Frank Reiner supposedly fell to their deaths but, the way he said it, he was inferring they were pushed. Whether this Frank Reiner is relevant to my new identity, we'll need to investigate when we get time.'

'At least this time your name isn't *Welsh*,' jokes Emma. 'What does the riddle mean?'

C.J. reads the riddle out loud. 'Four-digit postcode: Douglas Adam's answer plus your age when we gave you the tag. There is a mailbox under your new name. The password is: this tin box code plus the number of pet fish you had as a child.'

C.J. takes a deep breath. 'Let's look at the first clue: *four-digit postcode.* Postcodes in the US are normally five digits.'

'The postcodes in Australia are all four digits. Maybe he's referring to somewhere here?'

'You might be right.' Looking at the next clue: *Douglas Adam's answer plus your age when we gave you the tag*, C.J. reveals 'I know these numbers. This is easy. My father's favorite author was Douglas Adams and his favorite book was *The Hitchhiker's Guide to the Galaxy*. For a habitually serious man, my father had a sense for the absurd.'

Emma has heard of the book. She hasn't read it, but she had seen the movie.

C.J. enlightens her. 'Okay, the central theme to *The Hitchhiker's Guide to the Galaxy* is to answer the question: *What is the answer to life, the universe, and everything?* A super computer is specifically built to answer the question. It then takes seven-and-a-half million years for it to calculate that answer.'

Emma vaguely remembers the scene from the movie.

'So, generation after generation maintained the computer and, finally, after seven-and-a-half million years it gave the answer.'

'So what is the answer to "life, the universe, and everything"?'

'Forty-two' C.J. tells with a smirk. 'That's what made it so absurd – and so funny.'

'The first two digits are *four* and *two*. What does *your age when we gave you the tag* mean?'

C.J. holds his watch up to show her, 'A *tag* is a Tag Heuer watch. My parents gave it to me when I graduated high school. I was 17 at the time.'

'So the code is four-two-one-seven. *Four*? Tasmania's postcodes start with *seven*, Victoria's start with *three*, and New South Wales with *two*. I'm pretty sure that *four* is the postcode for Queensland.'

Max Stroheim went to Queensland twice; once with Mary and again earlier this year. He'd visited an old buddy now living on the Gold Coast. C.J. wonders if there may be a connection. It makes sense it is related.

Emma searches for the postcode on her phone. 'Got it – it's Surfers Paradise – and Surfers Paradise is on the Gold Coast.'

The next part of the puzzle reads: *There is mailbox under your new name. The password is: this tin box code plus the number of pet fish you had as a child.*

C.J. already knows the code for the tin box is 323. 'My father asks *how many pet fish I had as a child?* I never had pet fish.'

Emma concludes 'There's your answer then – *zero*. The code is: *3230*.'

C.J. recognizes the new credit card will have the same password as the mailbox code, with the mailbox presumably in Surfers Paradise, Queensland. 'We must get to Queensland.'

The next morning C.J. and Emma wake with the sun to formulate a plan to get to the Gold Coast. C.J. has a new identity, credit card, and cash; he should be able to book a flight, accommodation, and hire a car without being traced. Unfortunately, Emma has no false documents.

C.J. is confident Ellis Buckman had help with locating him in Tasmania. Whether that help came via the US or actually came from inside Australia, C.J. is unsure. Leaving from commercial airports will be risky though. They'll be monitored.

Gary Burgess is awoken by his phone ringing. It is not his police radio, but his personal phone. News of Ellis Buckman and his car traveled fast; a friend-of-a-friend has discovered the burnt-out remains of a white sedan. The car has a number of dents and scrapes and was abandoned on a country road about thirty minutes' drive west of Wynyard. Buckman's body was not in the car nor was he seen near the area.

How could Ellis Buckman drive to a remote location, deliberately dump his car, torch it, then disappear?

Someone must have picked him up.

C.J. concludes that someone, or more than one person, helped Buckman. If that is indeed the case, then the tentacles of the organization or group affiliated with Ellis Buckman have spread much further than C.J. imagined.

Another phone call to Gary comes from a friend who works at the local airport's rental car desk. They are positive it was their rental car involved in the saga. It was booked the previous afternoon, not under the name Ellis Buckman, but *Nathaniel Goldberg*. He is described as being a tall, lean, well-dressed American. The rental was paid for on a credit card under the same name.

C.J. does not recognize the name, but the description sounds like Buckman.

Gary receives another call on his police radio. He steps out onto the deck to take the call. They can hear Gary yelling expressively into the radio's mouthpiece. 'What do you mean, my guys are being taken off? When?' He swears loudly. 'I have my daughter's car sitting in a paddock riddled with bullet holes and a lunatic on the loose with weaponry out of a Terminator movie and you expect me to wear this? Get me Bob Crawford on the line, will you?'

While an enraged Gary is on hold, his daughter steps outside to ask if everything is okay.

It is not.

The officer checking vehicles into Boat Harbour Beach is finishing his shift in less than an hour and will not be replaced. The investigation is being handed directly to the Wynyard police station; effectively meaning there will be no support to Gary and total team of three policemen, inclusive of Gary. He is waiting to talk to the State Superintendent.

When Gary does talk to Bob Crawford, the news is grim.

The Superintendent is apologetic, repeatedly saying 'But Burgo, my hands are tied. This is coming from higher up.'

'Higher up? You're the bloody State Super, who the hell is higher up than you?'

But Bob Crawford elaborates no more.

C.J. starts packing.

Fuming, Gary hangs up. He comes inside, head bowed. 'I am so sorry.'

Within half an hour, they have a plan.

C.J. is reluctant to use commercial airlines to get to Queensland, so Gary made a quick phone call. Being the likeable local cop, Gary has friends and contacts all through the region. One of those helpful contacts lives an hour's drive away, near the picturesque fishing village of Stanley.

Gary Burgess's first police basing was in Stanley. Gary was a country lad, but had fallen in love with a beautiful Hobart girl, Nicole Wiley. Nicole had just finished her private-school education and she decided to follow Gary where-ever he would be stationed. She did not think it would be the furthest distance from Hobart possible.

Gary spent three years in Stanley, during which time he and Nicole were married. She fell pregnant shortly after. Gary was an outstanding footballer. In the Stanley region, the main winter sport was Australian Rules football. Gary played with the local footy team when he was not on duty. One of his fellow players, Mick Heath, lived on a farm just outside Stanley.

One of Mick's passions was flying planes. These days Mick owns his own four-seat plane.

Gary phones Mick Heath, partially explaining the situation. Mick is only too happy to help.

Emma and C.J. hide in the backseat of the police car. Gary has told his regional headquarters that, although his car is slightly damaged, he will drive to where the burnt-out rental car was reportedly found and investigate. He is told they have already investigated and there is no need to go.

Gary states, 'You guys have passed the buck and handed all responsibility to my station. If I want to see the burnt-out car, I'll bloody-well see the burnt-out car. I'm on my way there now.'

In reality, Gary will drive past the turnoff to take Emma and C.J. straight to the airstrip in Stanley.

The weather around Stanley is closing in. The aging, single engine aircraft is fueled and ready to fly. Gary Burgess hugs his daughter in an emotional farewell. He shakes Mick Heath's hand, before Mick jumps up into the plane.

Gary then turns to C.J. with a tear in his eye. 'Promise me, look after Em and bring her back to us safe and well.'

'I give you my word, sir.'

Mick Heath is a tall, barrel-chested larrikin with a wicked sense of humor and a broad Aussie accent.

He looks to the sky, shakes his head, and comments 'It's startin' to look nasty. We better choof-off, before all hell breaks loose.'

The plane takes off into the dark, foreboding skies.

They plan to fly to King Island; a large, remote island off the north-west tip of Tasmania, almost halfway to mainland Victoria. C.J. and Emma's strategy is to reach King Island, catch a commercial flight to Melbourne, then another to the Gold Coast.

The weather is getting worse – and quickly. The turbulent winds rock the plane severely. Mick Heath flies the plane under the black, menacing clouds, with little choice but to fly close to the water. Through the torrential rain they can see the whitecaps of the churning waters below.

Bass Strait is infamous for its wild weather and treacherous seas. Sometimes referred to as 'the Bermuda Triangle of the South,' a number of boats and aircraft have gone missing.

Mick Heath is as tough as any man, but even he is concerned at the buffeting his small plane is receiving. Emma's hand holds C.J.'s so tight his fingers are starting to turn blue.

'Geez, you'd pay a fortune at Disneyland to go on a ride like this!' says Mick. His sense of humor hides the fear. 'It's normally only a thirty-minute flight, but it's pretty blowy out there. It often gets blowy around King Island. The last time I was there, I walked down the main street and the wind was so strong it blew me right into the pub!'

Although scared witless, C.J. and Emma manage a smile.

Breaking waves become visible. Land is not far ahead.

Mick grins in relief, 'Land ahoy.'

They cross the coastline, Mick maneuvering the plane to line up the small runway through the pelting rain and howling winds. The more they descend, the more extreme and inconsistent the wind gusts.

To make landing matters worse, they're now in a crosswind.

Mick knows he's in for a struggle to land the plane. He's landed in some fairly difficult conditions in the past. This is extreme, even for him.

The wind and the turbulence seem to be increasing. Mick jokes, 'The tourist slogan for King Island is "You'll be blown away." They aren't bloody-well lying.'

He takes a deep breath, struggling to keep the plane on line.

'Tighten your buckles – we're goin' in!'

The little plane is rocking violently from side to side. C.J. and Emma look out the window to see the ground, then sky, then ground again. As the plane nears the tarmac, the aircraft lurches again. This time Mick pulls up the joystick. The plane rises sharply into the air – the landing aborted.

Mick fails to be fazed. 'Crikey, we were a bit all over the shop there; 'best we have another crack at it. They say practice makes perfect.'

C.J.'s fingers are no longer blue; they are white.

Mick does a 360-degree circuit to line up the runway one more time.

Again the plane rocks. Mick manages to straighten the aircraft before a gust of wind hits moments before the wheels touch down.

'Whoa there! Hang on folks, I think we're in for a bit of roo hopping,' he hollers.

The plane lands on one wheel, bounces, lands on the other wheel, and bounces again before landing on both wheels. It hops two more times before coming to a stop at the very end of the runway.

Mick takes several deep breaths then sighs. He turns to the ghostly white faces of C.J. and Emma.

'Well, that was fun – anyone like to do that again?'

CHAPTER SIXTEEN

Mick had planned to drop off C.J. and Emma then fly straight back to Stanley. Now he'll stay until the weather improves.

He jokes, 'In a place like King Island that could be in ten minutes time, but ten minutes after that, all hell could break loose.'

The weather system battering the island is expected to last an hour or two longer.

The commercial flight scheduled for two hours' time may indeed go but, in Emma's words, 'I doubt C.J. and I will be on it.'

They decide to stay, C.J. says, 'Until the blood has returned to our faces.'

Mick refuses to take any money from C.J., even when he removes $100 from his wallet to insist, 'At least put this towards the fuel – and a carton of beer.'

The more C.J. insists on paying, the more Mick shakes his head. Eventually, he agrees on C.J. paying for lunch instead.

'I'll take you to a pub I've been to once or twice,' he says.

It's becomes clear that Mick has downplayed the number of times he's been inside the hotel.

He greets the lady behind the bar. 'Gidday Shirl, how you been, luv?'

She smiles instantly. 'Well, well, if it isn't Mick Heath.'

Mick and Shirl chat like long-lost friends. He asks her recommendations for lunch.

'Just got some fresh crays.'

'They're not those scrawny little things you tried to pass off as your "special" last time? Struth, Shirl, my thumb was bigger than that bloody cray.'

'Today you're in luck, Mick, we've just had a couple of thumpers bought in; fresh off the boats.'

'You better give us one of them, then.'

'Got to charge you though, Mick.'

'Not a problem, Shirl. Lunch is on my friends here.'

Mick introduces C.J. and Emma to Shirl. C.J. jokingly mentions he might need some more cash, asking Shirl if there is a cash machine. There is. C.J. goes to walk away, but breaks stride to ask Emma if she is having crayfish too? She nods emphatically.

'Better make that three crays, thanks Shirl,' confirms Mick. 'You said you had a couple of thumpers – can you find a third?'

'Anything for you Mick, you big lug.'

C.J. doesn't really need any cash, but is anxious to find out if the *3230 code* will work on the new credit card. It does. He removes a few hundred dollars and checks the balance. This account has around AU$60,000. C.J. now has access to approximately AU$120,000 between the two accounts his father set up. However, Ellis Buckman now knows Christopher Jones, so the account could be traced. Even so, AU$60,000 in *Calvin Jacob Reiner's* account is a huge sum of money and is safe from prying eyes for now. C.J. decides to withdraw only small amounts at a time. A large withdrawal, especially in a small place like King Island, may set off alarm bells.

Eating the biggest crayfishes C.J. has ever seen, Mick tells Emma he met her when she was a baby.

Nicole Burgess had a complicated delivery. She'd spent a further three weeks hospitalized, requiring a hysterectomy.

Then he conveys his condolences at the recent loss of her mother. 'I adored your mum. We all did. She was a very special person, was Nic. I remember when she first came to Stanley. I don't think little ol' Stanley had seen such a glamorous and sophisticated woman like your mum.

She was a good sort, that's for sure. I used to tell Burgo he was punching well above his weight with that one.

'She was still down-to-earth though. Everybody loved her. I can see where your goods looks come from.' He turns to C.J. 'Burgo used to joke, when Emma was born she got all *his* good looks – because Nicole kept hers!'

They all laugh.

A phone rings. It is coming from inside Emma's handbag.

'Oh hell – I forgot to turn my phone off,' she says, concerned. The call could be traced.

'Quick, turn it off.'

'I'm so sorry; with all the drama and everything that has gone on, I forgot. I know the phone has got to go.' She turns to Mick. 'Hey Mick, how'd you like a brand-new phone?'

Emma removes her SIM-card and f hands the phone to Mick.

They now have little choice but to take the commercial flight they were reluctant to board.

The flight has seats available. It's still small, but compared to Mick Heath's, it's a comparative jumbo. It's to land at Moorabbin Airport. Emma explains it's close to Melbourne's CBD, yet some distance from Melbourne's main domestic airport, where they'll find a flight to the Gold Coast.

C.J. is aware Emma has no spare clothes, almost no make-up, and no toiletries. She left Tasmania with the clothes on her back and her handbag, yet has not complained once.

C.J. suggests, 'When we land in Melbourne, why don't we catch a cab to the city? We can get a nice hotel and you can have the world's longest bath. Then we'll go out and buy you some new clothes and whatever else you need. We'll go to the Gold Coast tomorrow.'

She kisses him.

Emma says goodbye and gives a big hug to Mick Heath, while C.J. organizes the tickets.

The short flight to Moorabbin is nowhere near as dramatic as the flight from Stanley but, by the time the plane lands, they feel like they've spent a full day in a tumble dryer.

Emma knows Melbourne CBD well. She knows a boutique-style hotel on the city's fringe.

'Sounds perfect,' says C.J.

Emma immerses herself in the filled bath and closes her eyes. The warm water and soapy bubbles soak all the way to her soul.

C.J. has many things on his mind, until he stands in the bathroom doorway, looking at Emma lying in the bubble bath with her eyes closed.

Without opening her eyes, she asks, 'Are you staring at me?'

'Yes, I've been here for a while now.'

'You know, there's enough room in here for two.'

Emma loves Melbourne and she loves shopping. As traumatic as the last day-or-so have been, she relishes the opportunity to buy a new wardrobe – or as C.J. put it – 'to fill a suitcase.' That's the first thing they buy.

Emma reluctantly allows C.J. to pay. Even so, she is surprised at how much fun she is having. She buys some beautiful yet practical clothes. Queensland will be warm, but who knows where they will be after that. Emma is conservative with her retail spending but, according to C.J., new lingerie and a sexy bikini are classified as 'essential.'

C.J. also buys some clothes for himself, with Emma's guidance. The one thing C.J. is most anxious to buy is a new computer. He leaves Emma in the cosmetics and beauty section of a large department store, and returns with a laptop computer for himself and a tablet for Emma.

She has already declared her willingness to help C.J., so an extra computer will be invaluable.

The next morning, C.J. and Emma sleep in. After a room-service breakfast, they set up their new computers, loading all the data from C.J.'s memory stick to both computers. C.J. can now show Emma the research and information he's uncovered thus far about his father's career. Emma is eager to learn as much as she can.

C.J. made notes about the various secretive projects on his father's list and now elaborates on MJ-12 and their role in many of these ventures. Ellis Buckman has access to those same notes; now knowing C.J. knows more than what he admitted.

C.J. books a ticket online for a flight from Melbourne to the Gold Coast. In a taxi to the domestic airport, C.J. further discusses the projects researched.

'When we get on the plane, I'll show you some of the files I downloaded onto your computer.'

On the flight to the Gold Coast, Emma is so absorbed by the material on the computer she can neither eat nor drink. An extremely intelligent woman, finding solutions to intriguing questions is what motivates Emma. She had little choice in becoming tangled in C.J.'s father's web of secrets, but she is savoring the thought of helping C.J.

C.J. shows Emma the full list of names his father wished him to research:

OPC MJ-12, S-4
PROJECTS: SIGN, GRUDGE,
GRUDGE 13, REDLIGHT, SIGMA, POUNCE, BLUE TEAM,
PLUTO, MOONDUST & BLUE FLY
CODE DREAMLAND
IPU, AEC, AFOSI
BOOKS YELLOW, <u>RED</u> & BLUE
YY-II, DNI/27
GREADA TREATY

'I've researched all the projects and Code Dreamland. These are the ones I've yet to do.' C.J. points to *IPU, AEC, AFOSI; BOOKS YELLOW, RED & BLUE; YY-II, DNI/27* and *GREADA TREATY*.

Arriving on the Gold Coast, C.J. hires a rental car, a small hatchback. They are both anxious to get to Surfers Paradise to view the contents of the mailbox.

Could it be his father's notes of his secretive career?

Could it be the information and truth C.J. has been searching for?

Will whatever's in the mailbox reveal the six secrets?

The post office is in the heart of Surfers Paradise, bustling with tourists. C.J. and Emma anxiously wait in line. Producing his new *Calvin Jacob Reiner* ID, C.J. punches in the code: *3230*. He waits. It is the right code. He is given a key to a mailbox.

C.J. turns the key. Both he and Emma are trembling with anticipation. They are not sure what to expect. A single, small envelope comes as a mild disappointment. C.J. immediately opens the envelope. It contains a single piece of paper:

> PACIFIC BLEAU APARTMENT TOWERS. ASK FOR STEVE POMEREL. SAY YOU ARE MAX'S SON.
>
> TWO WEEKS OF RESEARCH: PROJECTS: JOSHUA, GABRIEL & EXCALIBUR.
> GROUPS: BILDERBERGS, THE COUNCIL ON FOREIGN RELATIONS, CHATHAM HOUSE, THE TRILATERAL COMMISSION, THE CLUB OF ROME & THE BOHEMIAN CLUB.
> THE JASON SOCIETY.
> THE DEFENSE INTELLIGENCE AGENCY & MAJIC.
>
> CHECK MAILBOX IN TWO WEEKS.

This message seems clear; Pacific Bleau Apartment Towers is obviously accommodation. Max must have paid for two weeks' accommodation to allow C.J. time to research this new material. The only problem is C.J. hasn't finished researching all the letters, numerals, and codes on his father's original list.

Will two weeks be enough time to finish that list, as well as the names on the new list?

C.J. now has a secret weapon: Emma Burgess.

Firstly, though, they need to find out where the Pacific Bleau Apartment Towers are. The Post Office staff explain it is on the beachfront only a short distance away.

Steve Pomerel is in his mid-fifties. Born in the USA, he moved to Australia in his thirties after falling in love with a local girl, Janelle.

Steve's father is retired Air Force General Vince Pomerel. When Vince retired from nearly forty years with the US military, Surfers Paradise was his desired location. Although Vince Pomerel is several years younger than Max Stroheim, they came from the same town in Missouri.

Janelle Pomerel stands behind the reception counter of the Pacific Bleau Apartment Towers.

'I am Max's son; I've been told to ask for Steve Pomerel,' says C.J.

'I'm Steve's wife, Janelle. You must be C.J. We've been expecting you. I'll just get Steve for you.'

Janelle steps behind the scenes, returning moments later with her husband. He walks around the reception desk, with a beaming smile and hand outstretched.

'Hi C.J., I'm Steve Pomerel. It's nice to meet you. A great man, your father. I met him several times. I'm sorry for your loss.'

C.J. acknowledges the kind words, before formally introducing Emma.

Steve explains that he wasn't sure when C.J. would be arriving, but all the accommodation had been pre-paid for.

He asks Janelle to check the bookings in the registrar for the next two weeks. 'Honey, is the penthouse available?'

'I know it's free this week. I'll just check. Yes, no worries.'

Steve suggests they use the car space next to theirs, #102:

'Nobody is using that space and its right near the lifts. Your unit is number twenty-six oh-one.'

'Thanks, Steve,' says C.J.

Steve says, 'I know you guys will be here for a while, so I'm sure I'll get the chance to chat. But, in the meantime, why don't you get comfortable and settle in? I'm sure you'll enjoy the views.

The penthouse occupies the entire twenty-sixth floor. Featuring a full kitchen, separate lounge, a huge bathroom with a spa bath, and a wrap-around balcony, it looks directly over the beach and rolling surf of Surfers Paradise.

Both are eager to get started, so C.J. suggests a compromise. 'We can't waste a view like this. I mean, what a day – what a view.'

'So we'll set up the computers out here? Great idea.'

C.J. shows Emma the remaining codes and names from his father's original list again:

IPU, AEC, AFOSI
BOOKS YELLOW, RED & BLUE
YY-II, DNI/27
GREADA TREATY

'What would you like: IPU or AEC?' asks Emma with a smile.

'Your choice,' replies C.J.

'I'll take IPU then.'

Before C.J. begins on *AEC*, he searches for any information on the man Ellis Buckman mentioned: *Frank Reiner*. He finds nothing of any relevance. C.J. is not surprised. He'd once Googled his father's name, but there was also nothing.

About to type *AEC* into his computer, C.J. pauses momentarily. He looks across to see Emma engrossed at her computer screen. *She looks so beautiful*, C.J. smiles to himself.

CHAPTER SEVENTEEN

Emma's had little time to absorb all the incredible information presented to her. If she were sitting at a dinner table and C.J. started talking about secret organizations, aliens, and UFOs, she would have been skeptical indeed. Being shot at and rammed off the road by an assassin who traveled halfway around the world is a sobering way for Emma to sit up and take notice.

When Emma was a child, staying at her grandmother's house, she saw bright lights in the sky. In the early hours of the morning, the lights brilliantly shone through the blinds of her bedroom window, waking Emma, who in turn woke her grandmother. They watched the lights travel in formation then take off at incredible speed – out of sight. The next morning, the local radio station was inundated with calls. Local astronomers, the Army, the Air Force, and meteorologists could not explain the phenomenon.

Emma had read a few books and seen several documentaries on UFOs; however, it was not a subject impacting her day-to-day life. When she'd been asked if she believed in UFOs, she'd diplomatically say 'I don't know? I definitely think there's other life in the universe, but whether they're capable of traveling the immense distances to get to Earth is debatable.'

Deep down, she is not surprised to learn, if these secretive projects are to be believed, that UFOs and extraterrestrials *do* exist – and they have visited and continue to visit Earth.

Emma sits beside C.J., eyes glued to her computer screen. She is researching *IPU*, which stands for Interplanetary Phenomenon Unit. The first thing that strikes Emma about the name is the implications of the words: Interplanetary Phenomenon Unit. They're so blatant. Every other department or project C.J. researched and mentioned used smoke and mirrors, but not this IPU. This is not the only oddity; the IPU didn't seem to be formally organized, it was not accountable, and official records were either not kept or, if they were, they were so secretive that little evidence of the unit could be found.

The unit was set up by the Army in 1947 to investigate UFOs. It was disestablished during the late 1950s and never reactivated. All records were surrendered to the AFOSI (Air Force Office of Special Investigations) in conjunction with operation Blue Book.

AFOSI and *Blue Book* are two names on Max Stroheim's list yet to be researched. Mentioning the fact to C.J., he encourages her to research AFOSI first, then Blue Book.

AFOSI is the Air Force Office of Special Investigations. It 'identifies, investigates and neutralizes criminal, terrorist, and espionage threats to personnel and resources of the Air Force and Department of Defense.' They are a specialized military department.

C.J. notes that specialist departments within the NSA, as well as the CIA, performed similar functions. 'How many of these secretive investigative departments could there be?'

'Ellis Buckman could work for any number of these organizations,' Emma says.

C.J. has remained silent about his research into AEC.

Over cups of coffee, he explains to Emma what he has found to date. 'You know how I talked about the Manhattan Project? Well, that was organized and run by Dr. Vannevar Bush. He later became the head of MJ-12. He brought in leading physicist Robert Oppenheimer, who was attributed with making the first atomic bomb. After the war, the

American public were concerned about nuclear weapons so, from what I read, the Manhattan Project morphed into the AEC. It's short for the Atomic Energy Commission. I found basic details of the AEC on Wikipedia, so I'll read what it says:

> AEC was an agency of the United States Government established after World War II by Congress to foster and control the peacetime development of atomic science and technology. President Harry S. Truman signed the McMahon/Atomic Energy Act on August 1, 1946, transferring the control of atomic energy from military to civilian hands, effective from January 1, 1947.

'Did you just say that it was a Government agency, but was transferred into civilian hands in 1947?'

'That's what it says here.'

'So, as of 1947, the United States nuclear program was given to civilian hands? That means it was given to private enterprise.'

'Or MJ-12, which effectively was becoming private enterprise anyway.'

'Has this "civilian hands" thing changed?'

'No. The AEC remained named that way for almost thirty years. It then split into two separate divisions, but effectively remained the same. From what I could gather, the whole American nuclear program is funded by the US Government, but is fully in the hands of private enterprise.'

'Oh God, that's scary.'

The Atomic Energy Commission was set up at Sandia Air Base, New Mexico. This was close to Los Alamos, recognized as the birthplace of the first atomic bomb.

Sandia Air Base was the principal nuclear weapons installation of the US from 1946. James Forrestal and Vannevar Bush were instrumental in the setting up and administration of the base.

Max Stroheim was not a military man nor was he a nuclear scientist.

Why would Max want his son to research nuclear development and testing?

Was his father involved in some way?

Why would the Government, at the time, literally give away the nuclear program, for which it had invested so much time and money?

The next day C.J. and Emma rise early to stand on the balcony overlooking perfect, small, glassy waves rolling in to the sandy shore.

'Do you feel like a swim?' asks Emma. 'I have that new bikini to try out.'

The thought of sitting on the beach with a scantily clad, stunning woman like Emma is a no-brainer for C.J.

'What a great way to start the day,' says C.J., on their return from the beach to the penthouse. On today's agenda are: *BOOKS YELLOW, RED & BLUE*, with Emma taking *Yellow* and C.J. *Red*. They decide to research independently, to share their findings at the end of the day over a glass of wine.

With the sun setting and the high-rise shadows lengthening over the beach, C.J. and Emma sit on the balcony, wine in hand and computers on.

'You go first,' offers C.J. 'So, Emma Burgess, what did you find out about *Yellow Book*?'

'Firstly, let me say that the information on the Net is disjointed and contradictory. But, if any of it is true, then wow – it reads like something out of a science-fiction movie. Yellow Book is portrayed as a history of extraterrestrials, written by the extraterrestrials themselves.

'Now, from what I read, Yellow Book is not really a book as such, but, and I'll quote (looking at her computer screen): "a sort of holographic compact disk containing astonishing material about the aliens themselves, including information about the universe and the history of the aliens."

'One report submitted that the aliens met with certain members of the Government and were able to project images visually to explain some of this incredible material. These aliens were called *Tall Greys*.'

After Emma has finished, C.J. asks, 'So what do you think? You're a lawyer; you're used to making judgments on what's real and what isn't.'

'I found what was reported as devoid of real facts. Excuse my lawyer-speak, but the reports were based on conjecture and hearsay. It could be a real document; however, there's not enough evidence for me to make a definitive judgment. The jury is still out.

'How did you go with Red Book?'

'Well, Red Book doesn't seem to be as fantastical as Yellow Book, but equally fascinating all the same. Again, Internet information is fragmented, but I gather that Red Book, or Project Red Book as it was also known, is a database of underground sites and subsurface facilities. It's predominately a chronology of alien activities, their craft, technology, and the physiology of the extraterrestrials. Many of the projects on my father's list would fit into Red Book. That might be why my father highlighted this project. Either it was very important, or maybe my father was involved?'

'It's an intriguing thought. What else did you find out?'

'Red Book was not really an actual book, but a compilation of documents and information, amassed over several decades. From my understanding, some of Blue Book, which we'll both look into, was incorporated into Red Book, yet Red Book was apparently far more detailed and accurate. It would seem few knew of the compilations and even fewer had the opportunity to read any of it. The few reliable reports about Red Book on the Internet relay that the project was well researched and written convincingly. There are suggestions that Red Book was the real catalogue of all things ET and Blue Book was a diversionary exercise.'

'Well, I guess we'll find out more about Blue Book in the morning. Or do you want to start researching it now?'

'Tomorrow sounds good,' replies C.J. 'I was thinking that a nice relaxing spa bath would be nice.'

'Is there enough room for two?'

'Absolutely.'

The next day, C.J. and Emma learn Project Blue Book was one of a series of systematic studies by the United States Air Force of unidentified flying objects (UFOs) – or, as they called them: 'Alien Aerial Phenomena.' This terminology was linked to the IPU (Interplanetary Phenomenon Unit), as well as AFOSI (the Air Force Office of Special Investigations).

C.J. and Emma determine that Blue Book appeared to start with all the right intentions, being an evolved division of Projects Sign and Grudge, but it quickly changed. It would seem Blue Book was selective on what UFO information it would investigate. Its primary objective was to disprove UFOs existed, explaining some of the reports as misidentified comets or other natural phenomena.

'I find this quite amusing and contradictory,' says Emma. 'For all the Air Force's so-called "secret investigations," they basically determined there was little-to-no evidence UFOs exist and, if by chance they did, the UFOs were deemed non-threatening to national security. Could you imagine if I was representing someone in court for plotting to kill someone and said, 'Your Honor, my client is innocent of all charges but, even if he is not, he was never going to hurt anyone?'

Even though Blue Book was supposedly 'top secret,' a string of congressional hearings and committees regarding UFOs used Blue Book findings to basically refute the existence of UFOs. As of today, much of the Blue Book's documents are declassified (most, not all).

Emma tells, 'I find the American system of classifying then declassifying confusing. Would you like me to look into it further and give my thoughts on it later this afternoon?'

'Absolutely.'

'What's the next name on your father's list?'

'YY-II,' replies C.J. 'I'll start researching that, while you're looking at all these classified systems.'

With the sun setting, C.J. pours two glasses of wine to join Emma on the balcony, eager to hear her 'thoughts' on the many previously classified US documents released to the public in recent years.

She starts, 'I must say, I'm still a bit confused. There are so many layers and exceptions to the rules. Before the official formation of MJ-12 and agencies such as the CIA and NSA, any secret files or documents considered sensitive or secretive, or not in the interest of national security to be publically divulged, were placed in secured rooms or vaults. The Government didn't want files destroyed, yet they did not want them released either. Realistically, they didn't know what to do with these growing piles of top-secret material.

'It wasn't until the early 1950s that a more structured scheme of classifying things was implemented, putting time constraints on each file. Some were marked as being classified for twenty-five years, some for thirty years, fifty years, and so on.'

'So in the early nineteen-fifties, when this time limit was placed on classified items, it also coincided with MJ-12 controlling many of the underground bases, as well as the start of the Atomic Energy Commission and the formation of the CIA and the NSA?' asks C.J.

'Correct. Obviously, many files were destroyed and some were marked not to be released for as many as one hundred years; however, the documents classified prior to the nineteen-fifties, as well as selected files that passed their declassification dates, were taken from these overflowing vaults to make room for newer files. Additionally, under the US *Freedom of Information Act*, some of those files needed to be declassified. There'd been legal challenges and court requisitions or orders requiring some of the classified files to be released – and in doing so, they were declassified.

'In some instances, these documents were copied or photographed – and some of that information has been released to the public. So some of these files are now public domain, but certainly not all. Even so, we seem to know more today than what even the Government would have known fifty or sixty years ago. That said, I'm amazed at how little press coverage some of this information has received. Maybe there's a reason – and maybe we'll find out more down the track?

'How'd you go with YY-II?'

'Not that well. Internet information is disorganized and limited. YY-II appears to have been, or still is, an additional secret facility either within or nearby the underground base at Los Alamos. This is one of the major nuclear development sites in America and the home of the Atomic Energy Commission, yet the few references I found relevant to YY-II are not about nuclear involvement, but extraterrestrials. The suggestions are that YY-II is much like S-4, where ET artifacts and UFO debris is stored, although there was no reference of research happening there. That seemed to be done at S-4 in Area 51. Unfortunately, that's all I found.

'The last two names on my dad's original list are DNI/27 and GREADA TREATY. This treaty has me really intrigued.'

'Why don't you research that tomorrow and I'll look into this DN/27?'

'Sounds good.'

At the end of the day, C.J. and Emma sit on the balcony to discuss their findings.

Emma talks first. 'The only creditable reference to *DNI/27*, is a YouTube clip. I've downloaded it, but before I play it, I'll give you some background information. There are varying reports about when the clip was made, but, from what I can gather, the footage was shot in 1948, then digitally enhanced in the 1990s. The film is of a supposed telepathic interview recorded with a Grey alien, which they call *an EBE.*

'Extraterrestrial Biological Entity' confirms C.J.

'Yes. The EBE was kept in a dark room because it was sensitive to light – and it was filmed behind a glass screen, so at times there's a reflective glare. I'll play the clip – and you can make up your own mind about the authenticity. There's no sound though. I'll talk you through it.

'You can see that the EBE appears distressed. There's some sort of recording equipment in front of it, apparently recording brain waves and vibrations. You see that the more the tape rolls, the more distressed the EBE appears to become … see it struggling to keep its head up? Then two men walk behind it, here they come, and they have a torch of some sort. See how they're wearing surgical gloves. Now they help hold the head up and clear some sort of liquid or discharge from the EBE's mouth. I'll pause it, here.'

'You can see some of the body … see the shoulders and the chest; it's only small – very skinny – you can tell by the size of the men's hands.'

'Wow,' gasps C.J.

'And the neck is also thin. If it is a puppet or something, then the neck is too small for a hand to fit inside. Also, in most of the clip, because of the lighting, we only see the head, yet when the torch or torches shine we can see glimpses of the upper torso. Would someone go to this extreme, back in the nineteen-forties, to make a whole fake alien when they could have just made the head?'

'There's also reflection from the eyeballs, which change every time it moves. That would be hard to fake – and I've seen its mouth move. Wow Emma.'

When the clip finishes, C.J. asks to watch it again. They watch it multiple times, before pausing it to watch the video frame-by-frame.

Emma reveals she saw other videos and images she determined to be faked, but this video has her perplexed.

'The equipment is consistent with the type they used in the nineteen-forties and it is filmed in front of glass; that's obvious. Why would someone film from behind a glass screen if they didn't have to?'

'So, what do you think?'

'I don't know. It could be faked, but experts are divided. From the frame-by-frame analysis, it seems to be authentic, although it's possible the alien is a puppet. That said, the mouth and the head have quite a range of motion – and so does the body.'

'And the way the men in the shot move around the body, it seems highly unlikely there are strings. If this is from the nineteen-forties or even the fifties, sophisticated puppetry just wasn't around then. As a kid I loved watching reruns of the TV show *The Thunderbirds*, but you could tell they were puppets – and the Thunderbirds was made in the sixties, not the forties.'

Emma explains the video's origins. 'A former employee, who wished to remain anonymous, for obvious reasons, claimed to have been in the room at the time. He said he was one of four men, with the "interview" conducted at S-4. He described things about the facility the general public would not have known, so there might be some merit to his claims.'

'Did you find out what the DNI/27 meant?'

'Possibly. One theory is that it's the twenty-seventh interview in a series of interviews. I also read that the *DNI* was probably the security code for the "interviews." From what I could gather, the various top-secret clearances ranked from one, being the lowest, to thirty-six, being the most secretive. If that is the case, if filming a telepathic interview with an alien only ranks a twenty-seven, then what kind of colossal secret would constitute a ranking of thirty-six?'

CHAPTER EIGHTEEN

'I might just know of one such colossal secret,' tells C.J. with a grin.

'You found out what the Greada Treaty is?'

'I think so. Emma Burgess, you might want to fill your glass and strap yourself in!

'Okay, in nineteen-fifty-four Dwight Eisenhower was President, inheriting the NSA and its many secretive subdivisions from Harry S. Truman. Not only had Eisenhower taken an active interest in everything UFO or alien, he also expanded many of the operations. In doing so, he shared much of that information with some of the top players in the private sector, allowing them to run most of the secretive projects and subdivisions. The Government helped fund many of the operations, yet we've learned that the private sector also contributed – and greatly benefited.

'With greater corporate involvement, the Government deliberately distanced itself from any information deemed "not in the public's interest to know."

'The Greada Treaty appeared to be one such event; the secrecy surrounding the treaty was arguably tighter than anything else in US history. Whether or not my father was there, I can only speculate at this stage, but this event would be perfect for my father's expertise. In late February, President Eisenhower and a select few had an extraordinary meeting at the now-named Edwards Air Force Base, but some reports suggest it was at Holloman Air Base in New Mexico. There is some confusion – there may have been more than the one meeting – regardless, it would seem the Eisenhower Administration signed one of the most monumental agreements imaginable: an official agreement with *an extraterrestrial species.*'

'Oh my God. What, the Greys, like the EBE?'

'Yes. I'll tell you soon what the treaty was all about. First, let me explain. It appears Eisenhower and these men also had a meeting with a different alien species.

'Another alien species? Oh wow. So they weren't Greys?'

'No; they apparently looked a bit like us, although they were at least a foot taller and they had fair skin, blonde or lighter-colored hair, and blue eyes. Because of their Scandinavian appearance, they were referred to as the Nordics.

'I read that these Nordics have visited our planet for thousands, if not millions, of years. Like the Greys, the Nordics have the ability to communicate telepathically. Unlike the Greys, they appear to be very spiritual.

'These entities seemingly approached several governments around the world, including the US, to discuss "the Grey problem." Their agenda was simple: Stop the global development of nuclear weapons and, in turn, the Nordics would help keep the Greys from interfering in world events.

'This was unacceptable to the Eisenhower Administration. The Nordics offered no technological information and the nuclear agenda was very much part of the Eisenhower Government's strategy.

'No Nordic craft had ever been recovered and there had been no previous capture or subsequent study of any of the Nordic individuals. Consequently the US secret agencies and organizations knew very little about them. From the Government's perspective, all the alien craft recoveries, technological information, and study of alien life forms had been with the Greys. Most of these secretive projects were based around the Government, the military, or the private sector obtaining information and using that data to improve the military might of the

United States. Much of this material came from the Greys, thus the Eisenhower Administration rejected the Nordic alien's offer. They chose to align themselves with the Greys.

'Let me read what the Greada Treaty allegedly stated: "The Grey aliens would not interfere in our affairs and we would not interfere in theirs. We would keep their presence on Earth a secret. They would furnish us with advanced technology and help us in our technological development. They would not make any other treaty with any other Earth nation."

'Many of these projects and information-gathering agencies, such as the NSA, had become aware of the Grey aliens' program of human and animal abductions. Communications with the Greys, including Krll, talked of a need for their species to learn from our genetic make-up. It was the main reason for their visitations and bases on our planet.

'The Greys and the Eisenhower Government agreed that the Greys could abduct humans on a limited and periodic basis for the purpose of medical examination and monitoring of our development, with the stipulation that the humans would not be harmed, they would be returned to their point of abduction, and they would have no memory of the event.'

'What? So the US Government would allow their citizens to be abducted?'

'As long as they weren't harmed – and with a few stipulations.'

'This is incredible, C.J. How authentic do you think this Greada Treaty is?'

'I don't know. There are conflicting accounts of the location of the meeting, but everything else appears to be consistent. At that time, being nineteen-fifty-four, MJ-12 appeared to be heavily influencing the Government's viewpoint on ETs and UFOs. With issues of national security at stake, everything was classified top-secret. MJ-12 apparently advised the Government that, under no circumstances, was the general public or the press to learn of the existence of these entities.

'The official Government policy was: "Such creatures do not exist and no agency of the Federal Government was at the time or ever engaged in any study of ETs or their artifacts."

'Any deviation from this stated policy was absolutely forbidden and was actually against the law.'

'Let me get this right: Somehow the Government passed a law forbidding anyone within a Government department or affiliated agency to talk about aliens? This I have to look up when I get the opportunity. It sounds utterly ridiculous.' Emma thinks momentarily, before continuing. 'I know the American system is different to Australia, so I guess it could be covered by any one of their secrecy acts. I remember reading about a couple in the fifties who were alleged to be Russian spies. It was a major media event. The evidence was circumstantial to say the least, but under these special laws they were prosecuted – and both sent to the electric chair. So I guess talking about top-secret information, including aliens, would be covered under the same umbrella. I'll research it further a bit later.'

C.J. remarks, 'It's obvious that the Government, or whoever is in control of this information, would not like the press to cover such a media event about aliens and secret treaties. Rather than prosecuting someone for revealing such sensitive secrets, what would they do instead?'

'Use someone like an Ellis Buckman to nip the potential problem in the bud before it ever got that far?'

'Bingo!'

'As far as Ellis Buckman goes, at some stage, I'd like to look into his life.'

'Me too.'

'Best to finish your father's lists first.'

'You are right as usual, Emma Burgess.'

It's almost midnight. C.J. and Emma sit on the balcony, discussing the ramifications of this new material.

C.J. is positive his father was either present during the signing of the Greada Treaty or somehow had a hand in setting up the meeting. 'No wonder these secrets have been so zealously guarded.' His thoughts race:

If this meeting between an alien species and a group of men actually occurred, then is the Government right in concealing it from the public?

Should an obviously superior species be involved in what is basically a 'peace treaty' where the trade-off is allowing experimentation on a percentage of the human population – even if it is only a small percentage?

He ventures an opinion. 'My father was the most deliberate and ethical man I knew. He said and did nothing without a reason. If he wants me to write a book and tell the truth to others, then there is a reason. He also made two separate lists of subjects and projects. Again, there's a reason.'

C.J. looks at the names on the new list:

PROJECTS: JOSHUA, GABRIEL & EXCALIBUR.
GROUPS: BILDERBERGS, THE COUNCIL ON FOREIGN RELATIONS, CHATHAM HOUSE, THE TRILATERAL COMMISSION, THE CLUB OF ROME & THE BOHEMIAN CLUB.
THE JASON SOCIETY.
THE DEFENSE INTELLIGENCE AGENCY & MAJIC.

'We'll start on it first thing in the morning,' Emma says.

• • •

Over the ensuing days, C.J. and Emma research projects *Joshua, Gabriel,* and *Excalibur*. All these projects are about UFOs and extraterrestrials, but with a marked difference; each are examining different aspects of how UFO craft might operate and how to destroy them.

C.J. and Emma are confused.

Numerous projects and agencies were specifically set up to study and learn from Grey alien communication and technology – and even a treaty was agreed upon.

Why would the same people and departments who made these agreements turn their attention to possibly destroying the very species they made a peace agreement with?

It reeks of deceit.

Projects Pluto, Aquarius, and Pounce were established to evaluate data pertaining to alien technology. Projects Joshua and Gabriel, as well as further projects Galileo, Project Sidekick, and Project Looking Glass were apparently trying to develop different ways to 'neutralize alien weapons.'

One project attempted to develop a low-frequency pulsed generator, specifically as a weapon to bring down UFOs. Another looked at the role of gravity as a possible UFO propulsion mechanism, attempting to produce an artificial gravity wave with the intent of using gravity to harness power as a type of beam weapon.

Excalibur was the most disturbing of these projects. The project's objective was to build a missile capable of destroying existing alien underground bases. The idea was to build a nuclear device able to penetrate deep underground, exploding at the target without operational damage on the surface. This project was located at Los Alamos, New Mexico, close to where one of the alleged alien bases was.

Prior to researching this latest list of projects, C.J. had not read anything suggesting the UFOs, or the EBEs, had weaponry of any description. Both he and Emma research further.

Finding reliable and accurate material regarding aliens with alleged weapons proves fruitless.

C.J. asks, 'If we can't find any reference of aliens having weapons, why would all these projects be set up to destroy, or as they say, "neutralize" these so-called weapons? Is it paranoia or is it an excuse to develop their own weapons?'

Emma thinks it could be a little of each, 'Call it insurance, if you will, but maybe they just wanted to make sure the aliens wouldn't be a threat.'

'It would appear the Government, or whoever has dealings with the Greys, did not trust them – and the Greys have every reason not to trust them either.'

C.J. and Emma walk to the beach most mornings, generally chatting with either Steve or Janelle on the way through. Steve reveals he loves the surf 'across the road.' Today, he joins them 'for a quick dip.'

Steve is aware C.J. is doing research here.

Max Stroheim told Steve and Vince Pomerel, 'my son will be coming to Australia to research a few things.'

What those 'few things' might be, the Pomerels could only speculate.

They knew Dr. Stroheim spent time with the NSA, but little else. Steve is aware of the NSA, having taken a keen interest in the Edward Snowden revelations. He'd love to ask C.J. what his 'research' has uncovered, yet realizes it's not the appropriate time. He does, however, mention that his father would like to meet C.J. and Emma. He organizes for Vince Pomerel to visit the following week.

'My dad talked very fondly of your father,' says C.J., 'we'd love to see him while we're here.'

C.J. and Emma are ready to investigate the groups on Max Stroheim's list: *BILDERBERGS, THE COUNCIL ON FOREIGN RELATIONS, CHATHAM HOUSE, THE TRILATERAL COMMISSION, THE CLUB OF ROME & THE BOHEMIAN CLUB.*

C.J. has heard of The Trilateral Commission and vaguely remembers hearing of the Council on Foreign Relations, yet cannot recall specifics. The other groups are unfamiliar.

First on the list, the Bilderbergs, also referred to as The Bilderberg Group, are allegedly a clandestine society group evolving into a secret world Government that now controls almost everything, including the world banking system.

'Did I just read that they control *almost everything*?' says Emma. 'I've never heard of them.'

They continue to read, learning that the Bilderbergs are named after the hotel in Holland where the first meetings took place in 1954. C.J. notes that the first meeting was only weeks after the Greada Treaty.

The Bilderberg headquarters are located in Geneva, Switzerland. Although their early meetings were in Holland, each year they now meet in a different hotel and country. They have their own security team and details of the meetings are kept guarded. The exact number of members is debatable, with about eighty being the commonly accepted figure. Members include European royalty, former and current presidents and prime ministers, and the most elite, wealthy, and powerful people on the planet, particularly from global banking.

Until now, Max Stroheim's list of codes, projects, and organizations has been exclusive to the United States. The Bilderbergs are a global organization, dealing with international issues.

C.J. and Emma look at some of the family names associated with the Bilderbergs. The term 'old money' appears apt. C.J. comments, if the most influential business people on the planet were meeting annually, it should be reported extensively in the press. C.J. is a journalist and, like Emma, had not heard of the Bilderbergs or their meetings until now.

Why would such important and powerful people, who apparently make decisions affecting the global economy, be ignored by the media?

Maybe the Bilderbergs are deliberately ignored?

This seems to be the case. The most powerful media moguls are invited to meetings, on the understanding that 'what is said in-house, stays in-house.'

The Council on Foreign Relations (CFR) is considered to be: 'the USA's most influential foreign-policy think tank.' Formed just after WWI, the CFR believe that 'national boundaries should be obliterated, and a one-world rule established.'

Even though the CFR is meant to be non-governmental, a thirty-year-study found the majority of all US Federal Government officials were members of the council. Today, the CFR has reportedly around 3,000 members, yet they control over three-quarters of the nation's wealth. Their members have included 'senior serving politicians, more than a dozen secretaries of state, former national security officers, bankers, lawyers, professors, former CIA members and senior media figures' – and of course; 'presidents.'

C.J. and Emma learn the CFR is a sister organization to England's Royal Institute of International Affairs, which is also called Chatham House. Formed just a year or so before the Council on Foreign Relations, the goal of the UK's Chatham House is to influence global affairs. They later worked closely with, and guided, NATO.

Introducing a rule known as the Chatham House Rule, the guests attending a meeting may discuss the content of the meeting in the outside world, but may not discuss who attended or identify what a specific individual said – keeping the participants and what they said confidential. The Chatham House Rule has been adopted by all these 'think tanks,' including the CFR and the Bilderbergs.

'No wonder they are able to keep everything hush-hush,' comments Emma.

CHAPTER NINETEEN

The Trilateral Commission was formed in 1973 by members of the Bilderberg Group. Close links and shared members with not just the Bilderbergs, but also the Council on Foreign Relations, meant The Trilateral Commission became the unofficial political arm of NATO. Both organizations encompassed the same three regions: (Western) Europe, North America, and Asia.

The idea was for Western Europe and Asia to forge greater ties with America, with the US becoming increasingly influential in the organization's focus. According to the Trilaterals, the most powerful men from 'the major foundations, all of the major media, publishing interests, the largest banks, all the major corporations, the upper echelons of the Government, and many other vital interests' became members.

The Trilateral Commission is a non-governmental, and supposedly non-political group, with around 400 members only, with individuals not elected, but selected. It is estimated that the collective members of The Trilateral Commission manage more than 60 percent of international wealth.

Emma gasps, 'Four hundred people control over sixty percent of the world's wealth? That is staggering, especially for an organization based mainly in America.'

It is noted that one *cannot* become a major player in US politics these days without being a member of the Council on Foreign Relations or The Trilateral Commission; preferably both.

'It says here that Trump, the Clintons, the Bushes, every Secretary of State … geez, just about everyone at the top end of American politics in the last thirty or forty years is or was a member,' says C.J. 'And they contain the powerbrokers of the media; no wonder the media never talks about these groups. I spent over a decade in journalism and even I knew next to nothing. I'm now starting to know why.'

The Club of Rome is described as a 'global think tank that deals with a variety of international political issues.' Like the Bilderbergs and The Trilateral Commission, they are supposedly non-political. Founded in 1968 in Rome, Italy, they define themselves as a 'group of world citizens, sharing a common concern for the future of humanity.'

They have a very select group of members, consisting of current and former Heads of State, United Nations bureaucrats, high-level politicians and government officials, diplomats, scientists, economists, and business leaders from around the globe.

C.J. notes the word *scientists*, wondering whether his father had something to do with this group, although the fact they weren't formed until 1968 would rule out Max Stroheim's involvement during the earlier years of his career.

Emma finds a graphical depiction of these groups, as well as the United Nations:

'According to this flow chart, all these organizations feed to a central group – *The Round Table*.'

'Maybe we should research this Round Table,' offers C.J.

'I think we should finish your father's list first. Then we can look into it. What do you think?'

'I think you are a very smart woman, Emma Burgess.'

The last of the groups on Max Stroheim's list, which Emma notes is not on the flow chart, is The Bohemian Club.

Founded in San Francisco in 1872 by journalists, along with artists and musicians, the club began to accept businessmen, entrepreneurs, and high-level academics and government officials as members.

Known as a 'private men's social club,' The Bohemian Club is closely aligned with the Freemasons, being steeped in Illuminati traditions and rituals.

Just outside San Francisco, in Sonoma County, is the club's 2,700 acre campground, called Bohemian Grove.

When C.J. reads 'Bohemian Grove,' he stops. 'I've heard of this; Ellis Buckman mentioned it, just the once, but I'm sure he went there – at least a few times that I know of.'

'Tell me more,' encourages Emma.

'Until Buckman pulled a gun on me, I hadn't noticed anything remarkable or overly suspicious about his life or career. He had few friends and few hobbies, apart from drinking fine wines and buying expensive clothing. I knew Buckman was a Freemason, but lots of people in the media are Masons. Buckman attended meetings but rarely talked about it. I didn't think he was obsessed or high up in the organization.

'The only person outside of his work colleagues he ever mentioned was a man named Ben Hamermesh. Ellis and Hamermesh went to Mason meetings together.

'Did you ever meet this Hamermesh?'

'Just the once – and that was by coincidence. They just happened to be having coffee at a café in LA, when I was walking past – so I joined them. Ellis introduced Hamermesh as "a close friend." He mentioned Ben worked for a construction company. Ellis then boasted "He doesn't just work there – he's a VP," which means Vice President. The way Ellis bragged about the position, I didn't know if he was being sarcastic or serious. I just presumed Ben Hamermesh had come from humble beginnings, like Ellis, and that Hamermesh had risen up the ladder in a small construction firm.

'Ben Hamermesh was about five or six years older than Ellis –I knew they went to Freemason meetings together, as well as two-week-long summer camps or meetings in San Francisco. Ellis once said 'the Grove,' which I think slipped out by mistake. At the time, I didn't give it a second thought. I assumed the San Fran trips were Freemason forums and 'the Grove' was where they were held. After what we've just read, I'm sure he was talking about Bohemian Grove.'

'Wow; then that would mean that Ellis Buckman was rubbing shoulders with some of the powerbrokers of the world.'

They discover the powerful past and present members of the Bohemian Club, including famous meetings housed within the club. The initial assemblies, held at Bohemian Grove, led to the formation of the Manhattan Project. Doctors Robert Oppenheimer and Vannevar Bush were both members of the club.

C.J. comments, 'Amazing, this Dr. Bush seemed to be involved in everything.'

More digging into the Bohemian Club and the Grove reveals the clandestine nature of the exclusive club facilities. There are stories of members dressing in medieval robes, performing pagan acts, and worshipping a giant owl.

'This sounds like pagan rituals from the Middle Ages,' says Emma. 'They had academics and scientists as members. Do you think is it possible your father was involved?'

C.J. shakes his head, 'We went as a family to San Fran when I was about twelve – and I know for a fact that was my father's first time in northern California. With that said, he put the Bohemian Club on his list, so he must have known about it.'

As the sun sets over Surfers Paradise, C.J. and Emma get ready to go to a seafood restaurant Steve and Janelle Pomerel recommended.

'No talk of New World Order organizations, secret projects, hidden bases, or UFOs tonight,' says C.J. 'Tonight is going to be just about us.'

'Like a date?'

'Not *like* a date, an *actual* date!'

Eating succulent seafood and sipping divine wine, Emma is the one eager to talk about their research. C.J. reluctantly allows the conversation to drift back to their latest findings.

Emma says, 'I can see why your father had you research two separate lists and examine them in two different locations. The first list was relevant to his work and the infrastructures around what he did. The secret projects, the underground bases, like S-4, and the information about UFOs and ETs, as well as the Greada Treaty were to give you a sense of what was really happening behind the scenes, particularly in desert areas of America after WWII.

'This new list, so far, is about global politics and economics. We haven't looked at the JASON Society, the Defense Intelligence Agency, and MAJIC, whatever they are, but it seems clear what your father was implying.'

'That the majority of global influences are in the hands of a powerful few?'

'It looks that way.'

'William Cooper talked about the same thing. He also insinuated that these powerful individuals and families had much control over MJ-12. Maybe my father knew this? In a few days, we can pick up whatever is being left in the security box at the Post Office,' says C.J. 'I wonder if that'll be the end of it? And if whatever is in the mailbox will give us some answers?'

'I'd be surprised. From what I'm learning about his character, I'd expect there are more "holes to dig in the sand".'

'I suspect you're right. Also, someone needs to place whatever it is in the mailbox.'

'That someone could be Vince Pomerel?'

'Yeah. I'm really looking forward to meeting him,' says C.J.

The next morning, C.J. and Emma enjoy a sunrise swim, before returning to the penthouse to work. Over breakfast they investigate the *JASON Society*. Also known as the JASON Scholars, they are described as 'an independent group of scientists advising the US Government on matters of science and technology.'

'Scientists,' notes C.J., excited by the discovery. *Maybe this society includes my father?*

They quickly discover JASON aren't officially linked to the NSA or the government, being controlled and run by a private corporation. It is highly unlikely Max Stroheim was a member.

Details about JASON are kept highly confidential. C.J. and Emma do learn that JASON was established in 1960 with somewhere between thirty and sixty members. JASON members all had, and continue to have, high-level security clearances. They include physicists, biologists, chemists, oceanographers, mathematicians, and computer scientists. They are apparently selected for their scientific brilliance, as well as their ability to keep secrets. Over the years they have included eleven Nobel Prize winners.

There are suggestions that the JASON Society was set up and consequently controlled by MJ-12. Dr. Vannevar Bush was instrumental in the formation, funding, and the running of JASON.

'It's Dr. Bush again,' remarks C.J. with a grin.

C.J. and Emma then learn that JASON's activities are run through *MITRE Corporation*, which has contracts with the Defense Department and manages Federally Funded Research and Development Centers (FFRDCs). These support the Department of Defense (DOD), the Federal Aviation Administration (FAA), the Internal Revenue Service (IRS), the Department of Veterans Affairs (VA), the Administrative Office of the US Courts on behalf of the Federal Judiciary, the Centers for Medicare and Medicaid Services (CMS), and the Department of Homeland Security (DHS).

'This isn't a government department, but a corporation. How can that be? They're running government departments?' mutters C.J.

Emma is also miffed. 'If I understand correctly, this MITRE Corporation is a private company, with a board of directors. Yet it appears to be either partially or fully funded by the US Federal Government and they seem to have direct ties to the MJ-12, as well as manage the IRS, the Department of Homeland Security, the Department of Defense, and a host of other government departments. They also have access, through the JASON Society, to the most brilliant scientific minds in the country. Um, how can that be? We have to look into this in more detail down the track.'

'Absolutely.'

Later in the day C.J. and Emma recharge their batteries with another refreshing dip in the ocean, before tackling the last two names on Max Stroheim's list: *THE DEFENSE INTELLIGENCE AGENCY & MAJIC.*

'Would you like research MAJIC and I'll do the Defense Intelligence Agency?' suggests Emma.

'Sure.'

Emma learns that the Defense Intelligence Agency (DIA) is 'the central producer and manager of foreign military intelligence for the United States, both in the US and overseas.'

They operate under the US Department of Defense and liaise with other intelligence agencies. Established in 1961 by President Kennedy's Defense Secretary, Robert McNamara, the DIA was involved in US intelligence efforts throughout the Cold War and Vietnam War to rapidly expand in both size and scope. Due to the sensitive nature of its work, the spy organization has been embroiled in numerous controversies, including those related to its intelligence-gathering activities, its role in using torture to extract information from prisoners of war, as well as attempts to expand the DIA's activities on US soil.

At first glance, the DIA looks like a typical governmental military department.

How wrong could that assumption be?

The DIA employs nearly 20,000 people worldwide; many of them based overseas. What really stuns Emma is when she learns that the vast majority of those employees are not military personnel. They are civilian – and not government employees. Even though the DIA is designated 'a combat support agency,' most of its funding, operation, and employees come from the private sector.

On the balcony at sunset, Emma tells C.J., 'This is the body monitoring other countries' military strategies, weaponry, and threats. If a foreign country poses a menace in any way, shape, or form to the US, it is primarily the DIA who collect and analyze the data, then recommend the appropriate action the military are to take. To give you an example: If North Korea is about to test nuclear weapons, it would be the DIA who report the intelligence information to the US Government, then in turn to the press. Yet they are controlled by private enterprise, or at the very least they are aligned with the private sector.

'Go figure?

'And the other thing that made no sense to me is that the DIA directives are almost identical to those of the NSA.'

Reading from her notes on her computer: '"The NSA is described as 'responsible for the collection and analysis of foreign communications and foreign signals intelligence, as well as protecting US government communications and information systems." I'll read the DIA's description again: "The DIA are the central producer and manager of foreign military intelligence for the United States, both in the US and overseas."

'As a lawyer. I can tell you that these are almost identical mission statements. There is one major difference I found; most of the DIA's work is done overseas, whereas much, but not all, of the NSA's work is done within America. Why they are not under the same umbrella is baffling, although many things uncovered by us to date, initially at least, defy logic.'

'I know what you're saying, Emma. I had a similar experience researching MAJIC.'

'What did you find out? I'm all ears.'

'Well, I initially found nothing, then I "dug a little deeper." Although there is little information available, it would seem there are two linked organizations: MAJIC and MAJI. I'll start with MAJI, which is the Majority Agency for Joint Intelligence. According to what I read, MAJI is, and I'll quote: "responsible for information, disinformation, and intelligence."'

'Disinformation?'

'Yes, disinformation. MAJI apparently operates in conjunction with the NSA, CIA, the Office of Naval Intelligence, and the DIA. I read that MAJI has control of all alien projects, as far as intelligence operations go.

'It appears MAJI was set up at the same time as MJ-12; most likely by MJ-12, thus MAJI is short for "*Majestic*." The name *MAJIC* apparently means "MAJI Controlled".'

'So this would imply that MJ-12 had their own intelligence agency?'

'That's what I concluded. Even though MAJI operate alongside the NSA, CIA, the DIA, and Naval Intelligence, they have no responsibility to any of these groups. MAJI were initially run by MJ-12, yet were answerable to the US President only. However, it appears that, over time, even the President was excluded from MAJI's operations.

'If this is the case, then MJ-12 effectively had their own intelligence agency, as well as the additional resources of the NSA, the CIA, and the DIA.'

'Oh my God, that's massive.'

'And it seems that, over time, MJ-12 drifted away from Government accountability, yet they maintained access to information from just about everywhere, including the military and the Government. The irony is that the Government and the military appear to have lost access to MJ-12.'

CHAPTER TWENTY

C.J. and Emma anxiously await the arrival of Steve and Vince Pomerel. While waiting for the Pomerels, they begin researching The Round Table.

An initial search provides information about a *Round Table Club* for young men, formed in England more than ninety years ago, as well as articles on the King Arthur's Round Table, being the famed table in the Arthurian legend.

'I'm not sure this is it,' comments C.J.

They dig deeper.

'I'm keying in '*Round Table Bilderbergs*' just to see what comes up,' says Emma. 'A-ah, here we go! There's not many articles, but there are some.'

Emma and C.J. learn The Round Table was officially formed in the late 1800s by two of the most powerful individuals and families in the British Empire. Cecil Rhodes heads up the secret society. Further research is put on hold when the interphone rings. Steve Pomerel informs he and his father are on their way up.

Vince Pomerel is a frail old man, a shadow of his former physical self. He still speaks with authority and strength. He carries an envelope. C.J. can see his name on it in his father's handwriting.

When C.J. calls Vince 'General,' Vince instantly reprimands him. 'Call me Vince; it's been a helluva lot of years since I left the military.'

'Can I make you a tea or coffee?' asks Emma.

'You better make it a tea, dear,' tells Vince, placing the envelope on the table.

He tells C.J., 'Your father told me to put this in the mailbox at the Post Office two weeks after you arrived. I wanted to deliver it personally, if I was alive. He said that was fine. I haven't opened it. You can do the honors after Steve and I leave. I know it's only a single sheet of paper – my solicitor has a copy of this note, too, in case anything happened to me.

'He was a good man, your father. He told me you'd be researching into his career at the NSA but, before you ask me what I know, you must understand. Max never talked about it to me. I understood. I had my own secrets. Max knew that also.

'I don't know about the specifics of what you've researched so far, but I'll tell you what I know. Even though I was with the Air Force, we often did joint ventures or sub-projects with the NSA. Have you heard of Project Snowbird?'

'No sir.'

'Well, I was involved in Snowbird. Apparently a number of projects were called Snowbird – all unrelated. I guess it was part of the secrecy game. I used to call it "controlled confusion".'

Emma places tea, milk, and sugar in front of Vince.

'Thanks dear,' he says, taking a satisfied sip. 'Okay, where was I? That's right, Project Snowbird. Snowbird was an offshoot of Project Redlight …'

'I've researched Redlight,' reveals C.J.

'Good. You'd probably know more about Redlight than me. Son, can you tell me what you know?'

'From my understanding, Project Redlight was to test and reverse-engineer recovered craft.'

Vince's eyes light up. 'When you say "craft," what exactly do you mean?'

'Unidentified flying craft – UFOs.'

'Tell me more, son.'

'Project Redlight was specifically set up to test recovered alien craft, UFOs. From what I read, the basic idea of Redlight was to reverse-engineer alien technology.'

'Do you know where they did the testing?'

'Yes sir. The facility was somewhere inside Area 51, deep underground in "Dreamland." Some of Project Redlight was actually a diversionary exercise. They'd build a craft using conventional technology to cover up and explain the accidental sightings or the real reason for much of the research at Area 51.'

'You've been doing your homework there. When I was involved with Snowbird, I was led to believe I was part of the inner workings. The reality is, I was nowhere near it. I suspect your father was close to the truth, but I can only speculate. He knew about Project Redlight, but I don't think he was actually involved in it. I certainly never saw his name attached to any of the documentation.

'Redlight was an NSA operation, kept top-secret within Area 51. We were given some of the work started in Project Redlight and told to build a flying saucer, like you said, using conventional technology. The Air Force doesn't build planes; that's private enterprise's domain so they gave us a couple of engineers and the specifications they wanted. When I say "they," it wasn't a government initiative. We never knew who was pulling the strings. We were told not to ask questions.

'Generals like me were brought in to give the project some legitimacy. We were told very little – and quickly moved on before we found out too much. I was told that Snowbird was top-secret, yet before I was "moved on," I became aware that the UFO-type craft we were creating was to be paraded in front of the media. The whole exercise was a crock; a PR exercise to show that UFOs were actually military experiments. Of course, I didn't know what the motives were at the time.'

'So I gather that Project Snowbird wasn't based at Area 51?'

'We were at the Tonopah Test Range, which was also known as Area 52. It wasn't that far from Area 51, but far enough away that the Air Force knew nothing of the operations within Area 51. It was off the radar for us. Tonopah, on the other hand, was purely an Air Force base.

'I know Max spent time at Area 51, but that's all I know. Have you pieced together anything about Max's career yet, C.J.?'

'Not yet, sir.'

'I spent nearly forty years in the Air Force. As a three-star General, I had access to incredibly sensitive material, but I knew very little indeed. Some of the Air Force's schemes were joint ventures with the CIA, the NSA, or even private corporations. Where the money came from, and who were pulling the strings, I have no idea. There must be some very, very wealthy individuals and corporations spending the money and doing the research. The amount of money being thrown around was staggering. Someone had to be making a buck out of it.

'If and when you discover what your father really did, I'd love to know. Your father said you might be writing a book. That's one book I'd like to read.' Vince coughs. He looks tired.

Before Vince leaves, he tells C.J., 'Max Stroheim was a great man. He was one of the most intelligent men I knew. If it's his wish for you to find the truth, find the truth. It won't be easy. I'm sure it will be dangerous. Don't be discouraged. General George Patton once told me: "If a man does his best, what else is there?"

'Just do your best, son.'

'Thank you, sir. We'll come down in the lift with you,' offers C.J., helping Vince stand.

'No need to come down, son. You must be dying to find out what your father has left for you in the envelope. I'm sure I'll see you both again soon. Don't forget – I want a copy of that book.'

'I won't, sir.'

The Pomerels walk out the door.

As soon as the door shuts, C.J. and Emma go straight to the envelope on the table. C.J. opens it, revealing the single piece of paper:

> SON, I AM SURE BY NOW YOU HAVE EDGED CLOSER TO THE TRUTH. EVERYTHING WILL BE REVEALED. RETURN TO THE LOCATION OF YOUR MOTHER'S FAVORITE MUSICAL. THE BANK IS: THE NATIONAL BANK AT THE MUSICAL'S LOCATION + A REGULAR QUADRILATERAL.

THE PASSWORD IS: THE NUMBER OF DOUGLAS'S TRILOGIES + THE NUMBER OF TIMES YOU'VE BEEN TO SEA WORLD + YOUR FAVORITE GERMAN WORD FROM HOGAN'S HEROES, PHONETICALLY + THREE DOG NIGHT'S ONLY NUMBER
GOOD LUCK. I LOVE YOU

The code and puzzles, for the moment, fade into the background. The words of *I love you* override everything else. This is the first time Max Stroheim has said anything personal in his messages.

Seeing the tears in C.J.'s eyes, Emma wraps her arms around C.J.

After hugging for some time, Emma asks, 'Your father wants you to go somewhere, but where?'

'*Return to the location of your mother's favorite musical.* What was my mother's favorite musical? She loved musicals. There were so many. She loved *The Sound of Music* – that was set in Switzerland, but was that her favorite?'

C.J. thinks for a moment, then it dawns on him. '*The King and I*, that's it! She absolutely adored *The King and I*. She read the book, watched the movie, and saw the play a number of times. The book was called *Anna and the King of Siam*. SIAM? My father is talking about Siam – the old name for Thailand. It's also the name of the central district of Bangkok.'

'So it's Bangkok again. That would make sense, but what does *plus a regular quadrilateral* mean?'

'A regular quadrilateral is a square. The inner center of Siam district is called *Siam Square*.'

'Excellent; so you know the location and that you need to go the National Bank.'

'That would mean the Bank of Thailand, in Siam Square. That's close to the area I stayed last time. Remember, I told you I was meant to stay with my uncle again?'

'I'm so sorry about your uncle,' Emma empathizes.

She turns her attention back to the puzzle of the password. There are four individual clues to unlock the code.

C.J. reads out loud, '*The password is: The number of Douglas's trilogies, plus the number of times you've been to SeaWorld, plus your favorite German word from* Hogan's Heroes *phonetically, plus Three Dog Night's only number.*' He licks his lips. 'Okay, the first part of the clue is easy – *the number of Douglas's trilogies* refers to *A Hitchhiker's Guide To The Galaxy*. The books came out as a trilogy.'

'So the answer is *three*.'

'I told you my father loved Douglas Adams's sense of the ridiculous. Adams deliberately wrote the trilogy in *five* parts. So the first number in the code is actually *five*.'

Emma smiles and reads the next clue, '*How many times have you been to SeaWorld?*'

'Seven,' is C.J.'s instant reply.

'Wow, seven times?'

Emma is not just impressed at how many times C.J. had been to SeaWorld, but at the instantaneous answer he gave. These must have been important moments in C.J.'s youth, and it must have been significant for Max also.

Emma deduces, 'So the first two numbers are *five* and *seven*.' She reads the note once more. 'Okay, the next clue is: *What is your favorite German word from* Hogan's Heroes*, phonetically. Hogan's Heroes* was an old TV show, wasn't it?'

'It certainly was – and my favorite word was *nein*, which is German for "no." Phonetically, the answer would be the number *nine*.'

'Five, seven, nine. Now for the last clue: *Three Dog Night's only number*. So, is the answer three – and what's a Three Dog Night?'

'Three Dog Night were a band in the late sixties and early seventies. It was before my time, but my father loved them. He had an old vinyl album he used to play on a turntable. It would crackle and crunch, but I must say the music was pretty good. There were two songs my father played all the time. One started with the lyrics "Jeremiah was a bullfrog, was a good friend of mine". I think the song was called "Joy to the World." The other song was called "One".'

The penny drops. 'That's it, that's the number – ONE!' He sings, 'One is the loneliest number. One is the loneliest number that you'll ever hear.'

'So the full code must be: *5791*. When do we go to Bangkok?'

'I'm not sure it is wise we both go to Thailand. I have a new passport and ID. Your passport is in Tasmania – even if you could get it, Ellis Buckman or whoever he works for could probably trace it. I think it's best if I go to Bangkok alone. I'll only be gone a couple of days.'

Emma nods in agreement. Her best friend from university now lives in Brisbane, only an hour away from Surfers Paradise. 'I'd love to catch up with Anna. And it'll give me time to research Ellis Buckman or whoever he really is.'

'And I'll download what I can about The Round Table, as well as MITRE Corporations, for the flight. And do a backup.'

'I'm sure they'd be flights from Brisbane to Bangkok. When do you want to go?'

'No rush. It's such a beautiful day, after we've downloaded what we need, what say we hit the beach for a while? We can pack in the morning and head to Brisbane after that.'

'Sounds like a plan.'

CHAPTER TWENTY-ONE

The next morning C.J. and Emma head to the beach for one last swim, before returning to their room to pack for Brisbane. With swimwear under casual clothing, C.J. and Emma stop to chat with Steve in the reception area.

Steve says he's interested to hear more about Max and the NSA, saying, 'Thirty-four years is a long time to spend with such a secretive agency. I've read all about Edward Snowden's revelations – the spying, the hacking, the big brother stuff, but I didn't know the NSA had scientists.'

C.J. tells him, 'My father told me little, but he did say that by the end of the fifties there were around ninety thousand working for the NSA.'

'This was before the Internet and mobile phones. What did ninety thousand people do for the NSA back then?'

'That's what we are trying to find out' replies C.J. with a smile.

Five minutes after C.J. and Emma leave for the beach, two men enter the reception area. They ask Steve for 'a man known as either C.J. Stroheim or Christopher Jones.'

Steve hesitates.

One of the men is an Australian Customs and Quarantine official, in uniform. The other is a tall, lean man wearing a suit: Ellis Buckman.

The customs official does all the talking. He explains he has the authority to search any part of the premises without a search warrant.

He asks again, 'Do you have the man I mentioned staying here? He is American, thirty years of age, known as either *C.J. Stroheim* or *Christopher Jones*. He's possibly traveling with an attractive twenty-eight-year-old woman named *Emma Burgess*?'

Steve Pomerel shakes his head.

The official asks to see the booking registrar. 'We will search every apartment one by one if we have to.'

Steve hands the registrar to the official who, in turn, passes it to Ellis Buckman. Buckman studies the recent entries until seeing the name *Max*; 'Here it is – apartment two-six-zero-one.'

Steve Pomerel is reluctant to allow someone else into a guest's apartment.

'You have no choice in the matter. Get the key and accompany us to the apartment,' the customs official instructs.

'I am here on my own; I can't leave the desk unattended. My wife will be back in a few minutes and then I can …'

Before he can finish, Steve is unsympathetically instructed to get the key and take the men to the apartment, 'Now!'

In the elevator, Ellis Buckman asks, 'Do each of the apartments have their own car space?'

As the door opens, Steve answers, 'Yes.'

Ellis Buckman steps from the elevator, holding the door open. He reaches in to press the 'G' before instructing Steve to return to the ground floor.

'When we're finished, we'll return the key to reception,' says Buckman, as the lift door closes.

Ellis Buckman draws his gun to position himself along the wall beside the door to #2601. The customs official, electronic key in his hand, knocks loudly on the door.

Steve Pomerel exits the lift just as his wife steps into reception. He quickly tells Janelle that two men, one a customs official, are searching unit 2601. C.J. and Emma are down at the beach.

'Something's not right. I'm going down the beach to tell C.J. and Emma. If the men return to reception before I'm back, tell them nothing. Nothing, you hear. I won't be long.'

He grabs a beach towel on his way out.

On short beach track leading to the beach, he glances over his shoulder to look up. Ellis Buckman is on the balcony of the penthouse apartment, scanning for C.J. Before Buckman looks in his direction, Steve ducks low and hard up against the track. He sneaks along the track then peeks upward again. Ellis Buckman's back is turned.

Steve peels off his shirt and runs. Just in shorts, from behind he looks like a regular beach-goer. There are many people on the beach and nearly as many in the water. Steve looks up and down the beach, but can't see C.J. and Emma. Walking closer toward the water's edge, he spots them directly ahead in the water. Steve throws his towel down on the sand and wades in. They see him coming.

'Steve?'

'Stay where you are,' yells Steve

He points toward the penthouse balcony at Pacific Bleau. Ellis Buckman steps out onto the balcony. C.J. can't be sure, but there's someone on their balcony and that someone looks to be wearing a suit. It has to be Buckman.

Buckman looks toward the water. Both C.J. and Emma dive under an approaching wave. Steve looks over his shoulder briefly to monitor Ellis Buckman's movements. As C.J. and Emma surface, Steve voices instructions.

'He's looking this way. Dive under another wave!

'He's looking over the balcony toward the road and the entry to the apartments.

'He's now looking down the other end of the beach. I'm pretty sure he hasn't seen you.

'He's going back inside.'

C.J. and Emma come closer to Steve, positioning so they too can look back at their apartment balcony. Steve tells of the customs official and the tall, lean man wearing a suit.

C.J. asks 'Did the man in the suit have an American accent?'

'Yes, it was the American who asked to see the guest's registrar. He saw the name *Max* – and knew it was your booking. I tried to stop them, but I couldn't.'

Emma understands. 'If the man was a Customs and Quarantine Official, they don't require a search warrant.'

Steve mentions the tall American had asked about the car space. C.J.'s rental is not parked in the penthouse car space, so the two men would see the space empty and presume C.J. and Emma have driven somewhere.

C.J. and Emma decide to stay in the water until Buckman and the Customs Official have left the building.

C.J. asks a favor of Steve, 'When you go back to Pacific Bleau, could you take the keys to my car, which are in my backpack on the beach? Then in an hour, can you drive two blocks north and two blocks inland and drop the car off there? Leave the keys on top of the driver's side wheel.'

'No problems,' replies Steve. 'I can pack your clothes and things and put them in the car.'

'Thanks, but don't take any extra risks,' says C.J. 'They'll be watching the penthouse. One last question Steve: Did they ask for me by name?'

'Yes. They said your name was either C.J. Stroheim or a Jones name. Chris or Christopher, I think.'

C.J. says 'We'll be back some time down the track, and we'll explain everything. When we've finished the book, I promise I'll send you and your father copies.'

Steve Pomerel walks back to the apartment block, already dried by the sun.

Janelle informs him the two men have yet to return to reception. Moments later, they step from the elevator. The Customs Official, handing over the key card, explains they'll return later. They leave.

Steve watches them carefully, noting that the men are not carrying anything. When they leave the reception area, Steve races behind the counter to watch a CTV monitor. He sees Buckman pointing to the car park entry. Buckman slowly and deliberately walks away from the camera view. Steve can sense the tall American will take a position of surveillance nearby.

With the key card for 2601 in hand, Steve takes the lift to the penthouse floor, surprised to find the apartment tidy. C.J.'s computer is on the kitchen bench beside his computer bag, charging. Steve packs everything he can find into suitcases, including the computer, taking all to the basement car park – and C.J.'s car. He checks his watch.

Opening the car, C.J. is amazed to learn his computer was still in the room and Steve was able to pack it. He is skeptical as to why Buckman did not take the computer, but, for now, they're in a hurry to leave.

C.J. and Emma drive toward the Brisbane turnoff and the hinterland area called Mount Tamborine.

Looking in his rear-vision mirror, C.J. sees a car traveling extremely fast – closing in quickly. He's about to say something to Emma when he sees an arm extend from the driver's side window.

In his hand is a gun.

'Oh hell – it's Buckman. Hang on!' says C.J.

C.J. puts his foot to the floor as bullets *whizz* through the air.

Still accelerating, C.J. drives past the Brisbane turnoff. Buckman's car is hot on their heels. C.J. has managed to keep some distance between the two cars, but several bullets hit the back of the car – *bam* – the rear window shatters. Buckman now aims at the rear tires of C.J.'s car.

The cars chase up the mountain range toward Mount Tamborine. With bushland either side of the road, the vegetation becomes denser. The further the cars chase, the more the road narrows, the tighter the bends. C.J. is a good driver, but Buckman's car is larger, with more power. The steeper the road becomes, the more Buckman gains.

Now Buckman is close enough to fire with greater accuracy. On a hairpin bend, the car's rear tire is pierced by bullets. The tire blows; the car veers out of control off the road – careening over an embankment and into the bush. C.J.'s foot presses firmly on the brake pedal but the car knocks over small tree after tree, slithering down the slope toward thicker bushland. Small trees are knocked down – bushes run over. The out-of-control car glances a eucalypt tree and rebounds into another, before coming to rest against a larger tree.

C.J. and Emma are shaken, but unharmed.

Emma's door is jammed against the tree, so C.J. helps her out from the driver's side. They know Ellis Buckman would have pulled over. He pursues them on foot, his pistol raised and ready to fire.

Ping; bullets hit the car, most ricocheting and failing to penetrate the car's body. C.J. and Emma hide behind the eucalypt tree; bullet shells imbed in the timber.

C.J.'s car gouged a clear track for Ellis Buckman to follow. C.J. and Emma keep the tree between themselves and the advancing Buckman, running as fast as they can into the thicker vegetation. A hail of bullets *whizz* past them, glancing off trees, sounds reverberating through the bush.

They continue to run; bullets continue to fire.

Ahead is a clearing under a small, rocky rise. At the foot of the rise is a cluster of native plants called grasstrees; a unique plant with a black stump, tufts of grass-like foliage, and a flowering spike that looks like a spear.

In the trees, C.J. and Emma are shielded from Buckman's vision. The shooting stops.

C.J. instructs Emma, 'Climb the rocks, then keep running and don't stop until you find a safe hiding spot. I have a plan. Don't argue. I'll yell out when it's safe to come back – now go-go-go!'

C.J. attempts to yank the spike from the top of the nearest grasstree, thinking of using it as weapon. It won't budge; the spike is firmly fixed.

C.J. begins climbing the rocks to a small plateau, with the idea of waiting at the top, out of sight, until Buckman comes by. That strategy, too, is abandoned as Buckman catches a glimpse of C.J. scampering over the last rock to the plateau. Shots are fired – narrowly missing C.J. – *pinging* from the rocks. Still firing, Buckman sees C.J. rise to his feet, crouch, then run away at speed – out of sight.

He can't see that C.J. doubles back, crawling deliberately and quietly toward a boulder just behind the plateau clearing. He is crouched and ready to pounce.

Buckman climbs the rocks toward the plateau. C.J. can hearing him coming, his grunts of exasperation and curses about his new Italian shoes not being made for rock-climbing.

Buckman stretches to lift his head over the ledge. He sees no sign of C.J. He places one hand on the shelf, followed by the hand with the gun, readying to hoist himself up and over.

Just then C.J. springs from behind the rock, lunging at Buckman. Seeing the hand with the gun on the ground, C.J. changes his angle of attack. His foot lashes out to connect flush with Buckman's hand – the gun spills free – and drops over the ledge.

C.J. pulls up just at the edge, teeters on the brink of falling, rolls away to regain his feet. Buckman curses at losing his gun. Regaining his footing at the same time as Buckman, C.J. pounces again. Buckman backpedals to the edge of the ledge, sliding his hand inside his jacket, searching for the injection device. He doesn't have time to remove it fully before C.J. clenches his fist to unleash a ferocious right hook.

Whack.

The blow hits Buckman flush on the jaw, spinning him a full 180 degrees – knees buckling – falling face-forward over the edge.

C.J. races to the plateau edge to see Buckman leaning against the closest grasstree. The injection device is on the ground beside his leather shoes. Buckman's arms are limp, his fingers dangling. The gun is on the ground nearby.

As C.J. scampers down the rocks, he can see the grasstree's spike has impaled into Buckman's neck; the spike driven deep into the base of his skull.

Blood trickles from Buckman's neck – *drip, drip* – onto his shoes – slithering down the Italian leather to form a deep crimson puddle on the ground.

Ellis Buckman is dead.

CHAPTER TWENTY-TWO

As C.J. views Buckman's skewered body, Emma appears on the plateau above to look over the edge. Now is not the time for C.J. to remonstrate with her for not heeding his instructions. Seeing the puddle of blood and Buckman motionless, she climbs down the rocks to run into C.J.'s arms.

Alongside the lifeless body, Emma grasps C.J. resolutely – tears streaming down her face – his strong arms holding her tightly.

C.J. searches Ellis Buckman's suit jacket and pockets, finding his phone.

'There are no car keys, so they must still be in his car.' He then picks up the injection device and places it and the phone in his pocket.

Emma suggests leaving the gun where it is. 'It will have Buckman's fingerprints all over it. Whoever finds him, and the gun, will realize he fired it.'

C.J. and Emma walk up the hill, along the path cleared by their car. Approaching Buckman's car, they find the keys in the ignition, as well as a tracking device mounted on the dash. The device is on, a red blinking light highlighting their location.

'We were bugged somehow,' says C.J. 'And they'll know we're here. Let's get what we can from our car and then get the hell out of here.'

He pulls the tracking device off the dash to hand to Emma. She throws it deep into the bush.

C.J. and Emma return to their damaged car. The bullet-ridden trunk opens easily. They remove the suitcases Steve Pomerel had packed. Searching every item carefully, they find four small bugging devices, including one in C.J.'s computer cover. C.J. leaves the bugging devices in the trunk.

As C.J. and Emma were on the beach in swimming outfits when Steve Pomerel raised the alarm, Emma is still wearing her bikini with a little wrap-around dress, and C.J. just his board shorts and T-shirt. They change into new clothes, C.J. retrieving his backpack from the back seat and Emma her handbag from the passenger seat floor of the car. The bag has a small rip, which must have occurred when the car slammed into the tree. Unperturbed, Emma slings the torn bag over her shoulder, before helping C.J. carry their luggage back up to the road and into Buckman's car.

A map in Buckman's car confirms a nearby train station in a town called Helensvale, which should have trains going to Brisbane. They will leave Buckman's car at the station and catch a train to Brisbane.

As they drive toward Helensvale, Emma inspects Buckman's phone, surprised she is able to access his recent calls, as well as his phone contacts.

'He has all his contacts in acronym form,' she tells C.J. 'The last fifteen phone calls have been to just two people; most to *B.H.* and several to *M.R.* Do those initials ring any bells?'

C.J. originally draws a blank, then realizes *B.H.* are the initials for *Ben Hamermesh*.

Emma says, 'If that's the case, then Ellis Buckman has called Ben Hamermesh three times today, including only an hour ago.'

On the train to Brisbane, Emma uses the camera on her tablet to photograph all the files and contacts on Ellis Buckman's phone.

When they exit the train at Brisbane's central station, she throws the phone in the first rubbish bin she finds.

Inside a hotel room near the station, C.J. removes Buckman's injection device to inspect it closely. It is a small, high-tech piece of equipment, featuring a flick-lid and a syringe system similar to an EpiPen. There is liquid inside, which C.J. presumes is poison. C.J. took the device out of curiosity, but now it's in his possession it's a potential weapon or possibly evidence against Ellis Buckman. C.J. will keep the device.

Emma freshens up to visit her lawyer friend, Anna. C.J. and Emma have already discussed what to tell Anna. Emma trusts Anna implicitly.

C.J. asks Emma to get passport photos while she's out. C.J. will organize tickets for his flight to Bangkok.

'You should stay in Bangkok for a few days,' suggests Emma. 'You said the massages are amazing – and I hear the shopping's pretty good, too.'

After seeing Anna, Emma returns to the hotel. She'll be staying with Anna while C.J. is away. Anna will also get a message to Emma's father. 'I gave her Mick Heath's number. Mick will go and see Dad to give him the message personally. How'd you go with a flight to Bangkok?'

'All booked. I leave just after lunch tomorrow and don't arrive in Bangkok until midnight, so I won't be able to go to the bank until the following morning.'

'We need to find a way of communicating, just in case things don't go to plan.'

'I've thought about that. I was thinking that we have a list each, say with twenty or thirty phrases or instructions. We can email each other and just use numbers.'

''Sounds like a good idea. We'll work on the list tonight or in the morning. By the way, I have the passport photos you were after.'

'What name would you like on the passport?'

'My Mum's maiden name was Wiley and I've heard Emma as being short for Emmeline – so Emmeline Wiley. How's that sound?'

'Very nice.'

C.J. grabs a pen and paper, asking Emma to sign it *Emmeline Wiley* and to write down her date of birth.

C.J. looks twice at the birthdate. 'Is this your real birthdate?'

'It is.'

The date in question is in five days' time.

Despite Emma saying, 'It's no big deal,' C.J. promises to be back from Bangkok in time to celebrate her birthday.

C.J. and Emma dine at a riverfront seafood restaurant Anna had recommended to Emma. They speculate on what Max Stroheim will have waiting for C.J. in Bangkok.

'My father said he was going to write a book, but with all the surveillance and bugging it became difficult. That, to me, indicates that he at least tried to write something. Maybe he has written notes or memoirs for me? I saw him write; he was very quick.'

'I guess you'll find out soon.'

'We'll both find out.'

Earlier today they were chased in a car, shot at, and crashed their car into bushland, only to be shot at again. They saw a man die; an assassin, who only a short time ago pretended to be one of C.J.'s best friends. Emma will research Ellis Buckman while C.J. is away. She wants to learn as much as possible about him.

C.J. tells her that Ellis Buckman won several media awards for his work, forging a reputation for taking difficult stories to expose the truth.

'Buckman's disclosures ruined the careers of a string of high-profile politicians, as well as several successful businessmen. On reflection, I never saw Ellis spend much time researching his stories, so now I'm thinking, "Where was Buckman getting his information?" Ellis was based in LA, not Washington DC like most political reporters, yet many of his stories were from Washington. He didn't appear to have contacts within Government, but he was able to ruin the promising careers of a number of political aspirants who weren't living in the Los Angeles area.

'I'm sure there are plenty of politicians who've done far worse things than those Buckman alleged and proved they did – and these other men survived politically. So why were these particular people burned at the political stake?'

'How did Buckman get to the top of his profession with limited talent and limited experience?'

'Ellis said to me, "I came from nothing. How do you think I made it to the top of my profession? Do you think it was luck? The world does not run on chance. It is run by those who make it run. I have done what I have done and I do what I do for a reason." He obviously had help.'

'I'd be very surprised if he didn't,' says Emma. 'Maybe I can find out who helped him.'

• • •

Waiting to board his flight to Bangkok at Brisbane International Airport, C.J. reads information on The Round Table.

The Round Table was shaped to its current format toward the end of the 1800s in London. At the helm was Europe's (and England's) most powerful family, who happened to control the vast majority of the banking industry, not only in the UK, but internationally. The Round Table's first official leader was Cecil Rhodes, himself a very wealthy and influential man from his mining interests in Africa.

Rhodes and others left money in wills and foundations to fund the now-celebrated Rhodes Scholarships – where exceptional overseas students have their expenses paid to study at Oxford University in England. The aim of the scholarships is for persons of the right character and leadership to study at Oxford, then return to their countries to enter positions of political, economic, and media power. Consequently, some of the world's leading figures have been Rhodes Scholars, including prime ministers, premiers, governors, and presidents. In the 100-or-so years of Rhodes Scholarships, there have been just over 7,000 Scholars, with many prominent on the world stage.

Several articles suggest that The Round Table spawned the Royal Institute of International Affairs, as well as the Council on Foreign Relations, plus the other key organizations, including the Bilderbergs, the Club of Rome, the UN, and The Trilateral Commission. C.J. finds credibility in the idea that these organizations are close aligned. There are far more similarities in these groups than differences.

He further reads of The Round Table's Illuminati ties, until a PA announces his flight to Bangkok is ready for boarding.

Sitting in business class and reopening his computer, C.J. is ready to investigate the next organization he's downloaded information on: MITRE Corporation.

MITRE Corporation is 'an American not-for-profit organization, managing Federally Funded Research and Development Centers (FFRDCs), supporting several US government agencies.'

C.J. already knows it is more than 'several,' with the term 'sponsored' being used to describe MITRE's relationship with the Department of Homeland Security, the FAA (Federal Aviation Authority), the IRS (Internal Revenue Service), the Administrative Office of the United States Courts, the Department of Defense, and several other government departments and agencies.

C.J. learns that MITRE also works closely with the NSA (National Security Agency), and is responsible for the majority of the NSA's computer and monitoring systems. For such a large and powerful company, MITRE is virtually unheard of.

Maybe they're ignored for a reason?

MITRE was formed in 1958 to provide overall direction to the companies and workers involved in the US Air Force's SAGE project; a multi-billion dollar project funded annually. SAGE (Semi-Automatic Ground Environment) was a system of large computers and associated electronic networking equipment that coordinated data from a number of radar sites to create a single unified image of the airspace over a wide area. From the late 1950s into the 1980s, it was the backbone of NORAD's air-defense system.

NORAD is the North American Air Defense Command, a US and Canadian aerospace warning and protection body for Northern America.

Much of SAGE's research and development was based out of MIT (the Massachusetts Institute of Technology), one the world's most prestigious universities – and also privately owned and run.

C.J. notes that the Manhattan Project also used MIT's facilities. He discovers that Dr. Vannevar Bush was born and raised in Massachusetts, he studied and graduated from the electrical engineering program at Massachusetts Institute of Technology (MIT) – and would continue his affiliation with MIT throughout his working career. Bush even became the Vice Dean of the university, as well as the head of the Engineering department.

Surely it is not a coincidence that the Manhattan Project and SAGE were affiliated with MIT – as well as Dr. Bush?

Reading further, C.J. nearly falls out his business-class seat when learning that MITRE's name is short for MIT-REsearch.

C.J.'s plane touches down late in the evening, Bangkok time. He catches a taxi to Siam Square to stay in a hotel just a block from the Bank of Thailand. As enthralled as he was learning about MITRE Corporation and the links to Dr. Bush, the Manhattan Project, SAGE, and MIT, his thoughts are now with what awaits him in the morning at the bank. He is certain he'll be the first customer to walk through the bank's doors when they open.

He is.

The code *5791* is correct. The bank's security box opens. C.J. trembles with anticipation.

Inside is a single envelope. Again, he expected more.

He opens it to find yet another passport and credit card, this time under the name *Chad Jacobson*. Also inside area wads of cash in USD and Thai Baht. There is a single sheet of paper, in Max Stroheim's handwriting:

> Son, I have always had the greatest love and admiration for you. The fact that you have come so far in this journey is a credit to you. I know it could not have been easy. You will no doubt be overloaded with information from your research. You have probably found out about many things that I knew little of. I spent the majority of my working career cocooned, but there are some things that I, and very few others, know.
>
> You are close to learning the truth, these six secrets I mentioned. However you still have some work ahead of you. Don't be disgruntled – you are in the home stretch. Your next set of research topics don't need to be thoroughly investigated, although your research is for a reason; to know the structures and processes implemented – why they were applied – and how. Look into the following, then I have one last puzzle for you to solve:
>
> FAMOUS SCIENTISTS, IN RELATION TO MJ-12:
>
> ROBERT OPPENHEIMER, ALBERT EINSTEIN, EDWARD

TELLER, VANNEVAR BUSH, JOHN VON NEUMANN, and WERNHER VON BRAUN. (Realize these men were administrators, as well as scientists. Also look at the era when most of the secret organizations and projects were set up.)
DR. WILLIAM REICH, DR. FRANK REINER, and CAPTAIN EDWARD RUPPELT.
COMPANIES/CORPORATIONS: RAND, MITRE, RAYTHEON, and BECHTEL.
DWIGHT EISENHOWER (NATO and THE COUNCIL ON FOREIGN RELATIONS).
After you have researched these, you will easily solve my puzzle. Go to Uncle Joe's apartment at Jomtien Beach to research. He'll let you stay as long as you need.
THE FINAL PUZZLE: FROM UNCLE JOE'S APARTMENT BLOCK, TAKE THIS MANY MEASURED PACES ALONG THE STREET TO THE RIGHT: THE YEAR I LAST TOOK YOU TO SEAWORLD MINUS THE YEAR ALBERT EINSTEIN AND ROBERT OPPENHEIMER WROTE THE DOCUMENT 'RELATIONSHIPS WITH INHABITANTS OF CELESTIAL BODIES.' INSIDE THAT BUILDING IS A LOCKER. THE LOCKER NUMBER, IN TELPHONE NUMERIC FORM, IS FOR A THREE-LETTER ACRONYM: A HIGHER-LEARNING PLACE LINKED TO VANNEVAR BUSH, MITRE, RAYTHEON, AND THE MANHATTAN PROJECT.
When you find the location, ask for Ploy. Say you are Max's son and give the locker number. Take a medium-sized magnet with you. Remember that there is no such thing as empty space, you'll be drawn to the answers.
Good luck, son.

C.J. clearly remembers the last time he and his father went to SeaWorld; it was 2008. C.J. has never heard of Einstein's and Oppenheimer's document.

'I didn't even know they worked together,' mutters C.J. as he closes the security box.

As far as the locker number is concerned, C.J. has just read about Vannevar Bush and MITRE. He knows of the Manhattan Project and has heard of Raytheon, having seen their buildings near LA Airport and knowing they are a major defense contractor.

C.J. mumbles 'A higher-learning place with a three-letter acronym linked to these names must be *MIT*.' He thinks again, then justifies it, 'It has to be MIT.'

He places the envelope in his backpack, before returning to the bank's front counter. He then authorizes the credit card to be jointly used by *Emmeline Wiley*, having Emma's signature and details with him, before leaving the bank to return to the hotel.

CHAPTER TWENTY-THREE

C.J. contemplates the puzzle and other quandaries. He needs to go to Jomtien Beach at some point, even though his Uncle Joe is now dead. He also needs to do more work before being able to fully solve his father's final puzzle. He only anticipated coming to Thailand for a few days; Emma is waiting for him – it's her birthday soon. He made a promise. He also made a commitment to his father, and is so close to finding out what these six secrets are.

'Surely I can condense my research to solve the puzzle? Emma and I can then further research. I've already examined MITRE and a little on the other names. The locker number has to be *MIT*.'

He looks at the phone in the room, to deduce that if MIT is the correct answer, then the locker number must be 18, as M=6, I=4, and T=8.

'I know I need to subtract a number from the last time I went with Dad to SeaWorld, which was 2008 to work out how many steps from my Uncle's apartment this place with the locker will be. Dad said that Einstein and Oppenheimer wrote the document called 'Relationships with Inhabitants of Celestial bodies.' Oppenheimer was busy with the Manhattan Project in the early-to-mid 1940's, so I doubt he became involved with Einstein until 1946 or later. I'll find this document on the Net, as well as quickly research to confirm *MIT* is indeed the answer for the locker number.'

He turns on his computer to type in: *Einstein and Oppenheimer Document Relationships with Inhabitants of Celestial bodies.*

What he initially reads blows him away, hastily learning the document was written in 1947:

'The steps from Uncle Joe's is 2008–1947; that equals 61. That was easy. Now to see if MIT is the correct answer for the locker number.'

C.J. soon recognizes he was on the right track. Vannevar Bush was heavily involved with MITRE, Raytheon, and the Manhattan Project – and they were all associated with MIT.

'It must be MIT,' he says out loud. 'I need to buy a magnet and get to Jomtien Beach.'

C.J. buys a magnet and then catches a taxi to Jomtien Beach, a two-hour drive.

With his backpack slung over his shoulder, he stands in front of his Uncle's Apartment regal building. Without hesitation he begins walking the sixty-one measured paces along the street, walking past small shop-fronts. He can soon see where the steps will finish, a massage and spa business. He enters the humble entry door to find the interior luxuriously appointed.

A young Thai woman behind a counter smiles to say, 'Good afternoon, sir.'

'Good afternoon. Is Ploy here?'

'Yes sir; she's upstairs.'

'Can you tell her that Max's son is here for locker number eighteen. Make sure you tell her eighteen.'

'Yes sir, I'll get her for you. Eighteen, yes sir, I won't be long.'

Ploy is a stunningly beautiful Thai woman in her early forties. She approaches C.J. 'You must be C.J.; I hear all about you. I'm Ploy,' she tells him in poor English. 'Your father very nice man. I so sorry about Joe. I miss Joe. I loved Joe very much.'

C.J. will learn that Joe Stroheim actually owned the massage premises, having bought the business for Ploy. She was once a masseuse and now runs the business.

'I have key for locker,' Ploy reveals, handing the key to C.J. 'Come with me. The locker just here.'

She leads C.J. to a bank of metal lockers, with eighteen being at the top. She tells C.J. she will leave him on his own.

As Ploy leaves, C.J. nervously opens the locker.

It is empty.

'Remember that there is no such thing as empty space; you'll be drawn to the answers,' were his father's words.

C.J. carefully inspects the 'empty space.' The empty locker looks normal. He removes the magnet from his backpack to point at the back of the locker, it latches to the metal panel. Pulling the magnet toward him, the whole panel removes to reveal a small cavity; the width of two fingers. In the space is a bulging A4 envelope.

C.J.'s face lights up.

He opens the envelope to remove a bound, thick wad of papers, all in Max Stroheim's handwriting. There is a single note:

> C.J., this will give you the answers you've been looking for; my memoirs. Everything is in here: the six secrets, my thirty-four years with the NSA … the truth. I am so proud you have made it to this point. I never doubted your ability, your dedication, and your courage.
>
> You now have the tools to write the book that the world needs to read. At the end of the book, I've reiterated the publisher's details, as well as those of my lawyer here in Thailand, but first, write the book. Now, more than ever, cover your tracks and be diligent. I'm sure the book will take time to write. Take all the time you need. Money should not be an issue, so enjoy your surroundings – and don't forget to 'stop and smell the roses.'
>
> I love you son. If there's a way for me to look over and protect you, I will.
>
> Again, I am so proud of you.
>
> I love you always.

Still smiling, tears stream down C.J.'s face. His father must have been confident that his son would pursue, and find, the truth. That show of faith has touched C.J. more than anything else he has read to date.

The memoirs in hand, he stands in silence, contemplating the gravity of the situation.

In the taxi, with a two-hour ride ahead back to Bangkok, C.J. begins reading his father's memoirs.

The first pages of the memoirs are his father's instructions, directing C.J. how to interpret the information. Max did not keep a journal or diary, so some dates are omitted, as well as summarizing some of the 'countless number of secret projects and divisions.'

After months of researching, C.J. knows exactly what his father is alluding to.

Max Stroheim also makes reference to 'very influential families and individuals.'

He writes:

> Throughout my notes, I will avoid naming these powerful individuals or families. I urge you to remain secretive even if you think you know who they are or if you actually discover their identities, which I'm sure you will.
>
> IT IS NOT FOR THEIR BENEFIT, BUT YOURS.

C.J. understands what this warning means. Very influential people are at the core of all these societies, with clear links to most of the secret projects C.J. has read about.

> These are obviously people you don't mess with. With that said, here are my thoughts and recollections …

As eager as C.J. is to learn the truth, he pauses in momentary reflection. He wishes Emma was with him to share in the revelations about to unfold. He will email Emma as soon as he gets to the hotel, using their devised coded system.

In the taxi, C.J. reads the opening pages after the introduction, with Max Stroheim writing about his initial interviews and meetings with the NSA:

> You must understand that the NSA is not easy to define. The official name came in 1952, but when I joined in 1948 the structures and processes were already in place; the name change was merely

an evolutionary process. When I had my first interviews, I don't think I was actually told who I was being interviewed to join. I assumed it was a government top-secret department; something to do with scientific research. The name was irrelevant.

I wasn't even told the names of the men conducting the interview. It was only later that I discovered they were members of what I term 'The Group,' but some of the paperwork referred to them, or their immediate department, as 'MJ-12' or 'Majestic 12.' I'm sure you've read much about them already. In all my years of dealing with these men, usually individually or several at a time, I have never heard them refer to themselves as these names. I will call them 'MJ-12' because, in later years, that is what I was told was their code name. They simply referred to themselves as 'The Group,' so whenever I was told several members of The Group were visiting our facility, I knew what they meant.

My interviews were not with all twelve MJ-12 members. The numbers and members throughout the numerous interviews and psych tests varied; however, the key assessors were Vannevar Bush, Navy Admiral Roscoe Hillenkoetter, Detlev Bronk, and Donald Menzel.

Dr. Bush was the main panelist through the interview stages; however, government official and future Secretary of Defense, James Forrestal, was the instigator for setting up MJ-12 and the NSA after consultations with President Truman. MJ-12 were to oversee secretive scientific research and data collection and it was Dr. Vannevar Bush who ran much of the day-to-day administrative duties of the group. Dr. Bush was also the chief administrator with the Manhattan Project, continuing to head the whole nuclear program – among other things. He was a very powerful man. I'm sure you will realize this.

I accepted that I was not necessarily employed for my scientific skills and achievements, but more for my character and ability to keep secrets. Secrecy was everything.

Two other men were employed at the same time as me; Frank Reiner and Bill Nedersham.

Frank REINER? C.J. thinks to himself, *So that's where Reiner fits in. This should be interesting.*

Dr. Reiner was a physicist, not as prominent as Robert Oppenheimer, Edward Teller, Werner Von Braun, and Albert Einstein. But Frank worked briefly on the Manhattan Project during WWII with Vannevar Bush. He proved himself to be a man of integrity, a well-organized documenter, and a competent scientist. This I can concur. Frank was a good man. He'd sometimes stir the pot, but by-and-large he was professional and highly efficient.

Bill Nedersham was a naval intelligence officer during WWII, one of their top code-breakers. He was one of the men responsible for breaking the Japanese Diplomatic Code (dubbed Code Purple), which led to the US gaining a decided advantage in the Pacific War. Bill had worked with naval Captain Roscoe Hillenkoetter, who would later become an Admiral, an inaugural MJ-12 member, and then Director of the CIA. I assumed Hillenkoetter was responsible for Bill's recruitment, because Bill did not sit through the rigorous interviews and psych-analysis tests that I and, to a smaller degree, Frank, were subjected to.

Bill and I weren't close, not like Frank and I were. I never fought with Bill and, although we had a reasonable working relationship, we were very different people.

I met Frank and Bill for the first time in a military convoy taking us through to Nevada's Area 51, alongside S-4's chief coordinator, Colonel Ian Berkmeyer. Berkmeyer's no-nonsense style and intricate knowledge of the secretive underground facilities would be vital.

S-4 was already built when I arrived. It was well below ground, under (and to the side of) Groom Lake (within Area 51), which incorporated what was formerly called the Nellis Air Force Range (NAFR). Our facility was often referred to as 'The Dark Side of the Moon.' The security of the installation was incredible. There were over a dozen checkpoints before entering the inner core. This is where we learned the first of many astonishing discoveries. I didn't really know what to expect that first day. I knew I was taken deep below ground and passing checkpoint after checkpoint for a reason, but when I found out the reason – I was totally stunned. In a dimly lit room, lying on a medical-grade bed, was a live alien. By now you should realize that the alien, or EBE (Extraterrestrial Biological Entity), was Krll. You may have read descriptions of Krll; however, I am unsure what the Internet articles will report or how accurate those accounts may be. I will tell you what I know, given that I spent around a year with Krll, along with Dr. Guillermo Mendoza. I'll talk later about Guillermo.'

C.J. is so excited. Sitting in the backseat of the taxi, for some reason he looks around to see if anyone is watching him. Of course nobody's watching. He continues reading.

Krll was only about four feet tall, with a small frame and long, thin arms and shorter legs. His weight was only 56 pounds, either myself or Guillermo were easily able to pick him up. I'll call Krll a 'he,' but Krll was an asexual being. Autopsy reports on other EBEs confirmed that all were asexual, with no internal or external reproductive organs.

Krll's head was domed and proportionately very large, larger than a human head. His cranium appeared firm, yet pliable. There was no discernable jaw or cheekbones, with the face, as well as the whole body, being hairless, including no eyebrows or eyelashes. Even under a microscope, we saw no hairs or hair-like structures. There were no distinct ears, only small bumps on either side of the head, although his hearing was exceptionally good, probably better than our hearing.

He had a small nose with two cavity openings and a tiny slit-like mouth without lips. I'd estimate the mouth to be less than half the size of a human mouth. The mouth cavity had no teeth, although inside the mouth was hard cartilage-like gum. Even so,

> the mouth was not designed to chew things.
>
> He could not talk or make noises. Autopsy reports of other EBEs revealed no throat or vocal chords. Krll was the same.
>
> His eyes were his most distinctive feature – large, almond-shaped, slightly slanted, and very dark. They had a clear lens covering and were sensitive to light, thus the reason for the dim lighting. Any bright light would make him very uncomfortable.
>
> Krll was badly injured in the Roswell crash and never seemed to recover. He would often seep a clear fluid from his eyes, and sometimes his mouth. We'd frequently wipe the residue away. This was the only way for him to clear toxins or waste from his body, as he had no bowels or discharge systems.
>
> Krll's hands consisted of four very long fingers that were slightly webbed, with no discernable thumb. They were not as functional as human hands. Krll's hand movements were slower and more deliberate than our own. Even so, he had the ability to grasp and hold most items.
>
> His skin was grey in color, like a dolphin, yet sometimes this changed tones, becoming lighter or darker depending on his wellness. Like us, when he was not feeling well, his skin would become pale. Although his skin looked smooth from a distance, it was actually a little rough, also like that of a dolphin.

When C.J. was nine, Max and Mary drove to San Diego to spend the whole day at SeaWorld. This was the first of C.J.'s seven visits. C.J. remembers that first time as if it were yesterday; both he and his father were privileged to enter the water and pat a dolphin. Max Stroheim knew some of the staff so he'd organized to take a thrilled C.J. into the water with the dolphins.

Thinking back to that day, C.J. wonders if his father, touching the dolphin's skin, was thinking about the EBE. It must have been difficult for C.J.'s father to keep secrets to himself. Max Stroheim was one of the few people in the world who had spent time, and touched a live species from somewhere else in the universe, and yet he could not talk about it.

Imagine being one of the twelve astronauts who walked on the Moon, but you were not allowed to talk about the experience?

That day at SeaWorld must have been just one of hundreds of moments Max Stroheim yearned to share with someone else, but could not. It is something that lingers in C.J.'s mind. He knows his father's memoirs are extensive and the paperwork incredibly thick; there is clearly a lot more information to come. Even though C.J. has read only a small portion of his father's notes, the monumental significance of circumstances from events over sixty years ago are clear.

CHAPTER TWENTY-FOUR

With C.J. sitting in the back of the taxi driving back to Bangkok, C.J. continues to read his father's descriptions of the alien.

> The skin was devoid of scales, bumps, or any imperfections, although under a microscope we could see tiny lines, similar to grooves on a vinyl record, running horizontally from head to foot. We presumed these grooves were to increase skin surface area to assist absorption. The autopsy reports revealed the surface under the skin resembled a thin layer of fatty tissue unlike anything we'd seen before. This layer was spongy and completely permeable. The porous nature of this layer was consistent with how the EBEs nourished themselves, through the skin.

So it didn't eat using its mouth? thinks C.J.

> As a result of his injuries, Krll was unable to walk; he could sit up in bed, but I never saw him walk. Although it was obvious he was unwell, I could tell from his physiology that he and his kind were not physically strong. The body was not designed to carry heavy loads; in fact the body was very simplistic, yet functional. I'll talk about the internal organs, as well as body and brain composition

> later, as we had many cadavers to work on, from before, as well as after Krll's arrival.
> You would have read about the Roswell UFO crash in 1947. Although there were many crashes prior to this, and subsequent recovery of craft wreckage and cadavers, this was the first crash where a live EBE was recovered, Krll. I heard stories that another EBE survived that crash, that it was accidentally shot and died in the desert, but I can't confirm that allegation. I do know that I inspected many frozen EBE corpses, so my descriptions of the internal workings of the EBEs are defined and accurate, although pathology was not my field of expertise. Dr. Detlev Bronk oversaw the majority of the autopsies, although, from my understanding, there were other pathologists, mainly military men, who assisted Bronk at various times.

Dr. Bronk was named as one of the original MJ-12 members, a prominent scientist, educator, and administrator, working alongside Vannevar Bush as an advisory member of the Atomic Energy Commission (AEC), as well as becoming president of the National Academy of Sciences and affiliated with numerous science-based privately owned institutions.

> Dr. Bronk was exceptionally thorough. He, along with Dr. Bush, and sometimes Dr. Don Menzel, were the main scientists and administrators controlling S-4 and the EBE information, the funding, and the secrecy.
> I mentioned Dr. Guillermo Mendoza earlier. Guillermo was a botanist. Krll was badly injured when he was taken, initially, to Los Alamos, where medical doctors attempted to treat Krll – without success. Previous alien autopsies had revealed some of the physical make-up of the EBEs, so they already knew it was nothing like our human anatomy. Some of the functions appeared more plant-like than human-like, therefore Guillermo was brought in to treat Krll. Guillermo attained better results.
> At this point, S-4 was being built and specifically fitted for Krll's arrival. I was brought in shortly after Krll was moved from Los

Alamos to Area 51 – and the S-4 facility.
Guillermo explained to me that Krll exhibited some humanoid-like functions, but was closer to plants in how he operated. He already knew EBEs systems were chlorophyll-based; processing food into energy much the same as plants do, with waste material also excreted similarly to plant life.
From autopsy reports, the EBEs had a single organ, which appears to work like our bladder and kidneys, where it converted any solid waste to liquid. The waste material either seeped through the skin, by way of osmosis, or it was secreted through the mouth or, in extreme cases, through the eyes. As Krll was not well, his eyes were often the source of secretion.
Krll did not feel pain, yet the eye secretion was a cause of irritation to him and one of the reasons we regularly wiped them.
Krll would take in nutrition from a liquid genetic mixture (a biological slurry mix), either smeared into the skin or taken orally. We gather that the skin smearing was the principal method, yet most mixtures we gave to Krll were ingested orally.
I said that the skin was similar in appearance and texture to dolphin skin, but on a molecular level it was far more permeable, being able to absorb liquids into its system with ease. From the autopsy reports we knew that Krll had no discernible digestive tracts, meaning there was no throat or tubes below the mouth, or stomach or intestines for that matter. The nutrition from his food intake was via a system of internal seepage, being like osmosis. This is closer to a plant's function than a human's.
The EBEs did have a two-piece organ, which appeared to be a combined heart and lungs; functioning a little like ours, helping to push blood and nutrients throughout the body. With that said, the EBEs don't have blood like us. It has a colorless, viscous fluid, which smells like ozone and ammonia. The heart/lung organ was not as dynamic as a human heart. Both Dr. Vannevar Bush and me used a stethoscope on Krll, yet could find no heartbeat or pulse, although we did hear some kind of faint resonance; a subtle murmuring.

The specimens studied during autopsies had no sign of disease or inflammation; their bodies were devoid of toxins, germs, or bacteria. Dr. Mendoza found this fascinating. The more we studied the EBE, the more unlike humans we found them to be. I'll elaborate later on the cellular and chemical structure of the EBEs and the challenges we faced trying to categorize EBEs.

You would be aware that there are obvious differences between plants and animals, but at the chemical level the cells of all plants and all animals contain DNA in the same shape – and all plants and animals have RNA and DNA, with RNA often referred to as 'the building blocks of life' and DNA as 'the blueprint of life.' Every living thing on Earth is DNA-based – or so we thought. We found no DNA in any of the EBEs.'

C.J. can sense the excitement and the curiosity his father must have felt in recalling these momentous events from over sixty years prior. Totally absorbed, C.J. doesn't even realize the taxi is now entering Bangkok's outer suburbs.

We were initially dumbfounded about finding no EBE DNA. We thought that DNA was essential for a living entity to replicate. The EBEs were asexual, yet there are some animals that are asexual, albeit they are simple organisms, yet they can reproduce. Again, even these simple organisms are DNA-based. Our years of training, with preconceived ideas, went out the window.

The EBEs body and internal organs were all simplistic, yet functional. The skeletal system of the autopsied EBEs was very different to that of a human. The bones were less dense, more slender, and had an elastic quality, being more of a cartilage material, similar to sharks. Many human bones are designed to protect internal body parts, as well as to support our frame, whereas the EBE's skeletal system was more for support than protection.

The brain, on the other hand, was extremely complex. The EBEs' heads were large because their brain capacity is around double that of humans, with the brain taking up most of the head's size and weight. Krll, at times, struggled to keep his head upright. We had his head propped up on the bed. Even then he would still struggle to keep his head in one position.

I spent much time going over the other EBEs' brain dissections and autopsy reports, as there were some similarities to a human brain; however, overall, they were very different. Not only were the EBEs' brain dissimilar in size to ours, but also the look and texture appeared darker and more jelly-like. The brains of all species on Earth are composed primarily of two broad classes of cells: neurons and glial cells. The EBEs had neither. Guillermo and I found this intriguing.

We humans have two lobes. The EBE's brain has three. The additional lobe was made of some sort of crystalline substance we were unfamiliar. It almost looked artificial. It may well have been synthetic. From the autopsy reports and extensive testing, the crystalline substance appeared manufactured, although it was made of material unfamiliar to us. I know this sounds contradictory, but the material of this lobe exhibited both organic and inorganic traits. With no other earthly material to compare, we were baffled.

We thought this additional lobe was responsible for EBE's higher learning and telepathic communication abilities.

Everything Max has written about the entity to this point are physical descriptions. When C.J. reads that the EBE is able to communicate, he is blown away.

We were able to communicate with Krll via telepathy. It is hard to explain, but Krll was able to project images to our brains. We could not understand everything, but mostly we could interpret those images and put them into words. We would talk to Krll. He could hear, although we presumed he was actually reading our minds to retrieve information.

Krll's telepathic abilities were exceptional. He did not need to face us or even see us to be able to read our minds or project images to us. And he could do it over quite large distances. I even received images while in a nearby room, with metal doors and other structures between us.

Guillermo and I discussed Krll's telepathic abilities at length and how, at times, Krll would attempt to manipulate our thoughts. How successful he was we couldn't be sure, but we did know that there was never any emotional connection with the EBE; everything was data based, information was given on a need-to-know basis only. What was evident from the beginning was that Krll was not an emotive entity. Not once did he display any emotion, no anger, no anxiety, no excitement, no joy – nothing.

He never tried to escape. We humans have innate survival instincts. Krll had no such instincts. Self-preservation was not on his agenda. I don't know of one species where self-preservation was not one of the highest priorities, yet Krll showed no survival dispositions whatsoever.

Colonel Berkmeyer did not like nor trust Krll. I must say that, after the euphoria of looking at, then communicating with a unique species, after a while I tended to agree with Berkmeyer. Krll was inexpressive, yet he had an agenda. The information he relayed was measured and contrived. When humans lie, we do so for selfish reasons, for self-preservation, to save face, or for personal gain. Krll did lie; not blatant, easily distinguishable lies, yet lies all the same. Berkmeyer would ask 'Why?' It was the topic of debate behind the scenes. Why would this entity, which had no regard for his own well-being, try to deceive us?

I will talk about this later.

Inner-city car horns blast, C.J. looks up for the first time since being in the cab. He is in the heart of Bangkok's CBD, almost at his hotel.

As the taxi pulls into the hotel's entry, C.J. tucks his father's memoirs back into the envelope to place in his backpack.

He pays the taxi-driver, then dashes toward his hotel room, eager to contact Emma and to continue reading.

After sending an email to Emma, C.J. sits down with his father's memoirs. C.J. noted that his father, when describing Krll, used words like *entity* and *unique species*, not *a being from another planet* or *extraterrestrial.* He is anxious to learn why his father chose these words.

> I'd been at S-4 for almost a year when Krll passed away. Although he'd been ill the whole time, it still came as a shock. There were no defining telltale signs he was going to pass away; no dramatic last breath. Krll was taken away to have an autopsy performed but, at that time, we'd already had many frozen EBE corpses and numerous autopsies. We would find nothing new about Krll than we already knew.
>
> As I had access to the previous autopsy reports, I was by then well aware of the EBE's physiology. I spent the last months of Krll's life trying to ascertain the psychology of the EBE – his mindset, strengths, weaknesses, knowledge, and possibly spirituality. For all the hours Guillermo and I spent trying to evoke some sort of emotive response from Krll, we came up empty handed.
>
> Colonel Berkmeyer once commented, 'That thing is smarter than what we think. Everything it relays to us has been carefully planned – even the lies. And we all know that it does lie.'
>
> I spent much time dissecting Berkmeyer's comments. Berkmeyer was far more direct with Krll than Guillermo or me. He'd question Krll repeatedly: Where do you come from? Why are you here? Will others of your type try to rescue you? That sort of thing. Krll never gave a response – and never a reaction.
>
> Intelligent animals can formulate a feeling or sense about another animal or human. A dog can like one person and not another. I found the same thing with dolphins, yet Krll treated everyone the same. He should have realized myself and Dr. Mendoza had his best interests at heart – and, conversely, been afraid of Berkmeyer, but Krll's responses were identical to all of us. Berkmeyer became agitated, but no matter how much he ranted and raved, Krll was never flustered, never showed a hint of emotion. This only made Berkmeyer madder.
>
> When Berkmeyer was not around, Dr. Mendoza and I would

discuss Krll's psychology. There's no doubt the EBE was an intelligent specie, yet it lacked the ability to question and wonder; in other words, it did not seem to be able to learn. It made us think that Krll was preprogrammed or partially preprogrammed. The crystalline substance in the third lobe may have been implanted, the same as every other EBE. The more we explored this hypothesis, the more convinced we were that this was the case. We formed the opinion that Krll was part of a telepathic community or think-tank. He lacked individualism; his answers and motives may have been part of a collective process. Dolphins appear to have a similar ability, with a number of studies suggesting dolphins can communicate as a group; having a collective consciousness. This may be connected with the dolphin's echolocation (biosonar) skills, where they send out frequency sound waves to bounce off objects, then interpret the returning waves to form images in their brain. This would mean other dolphins could interpret that information also.

Using echolocation, dolphins can identify prey, as well as communicate with each other. Regardless of any similarity with dolphins or that train-of-thought, I feel that the EBEs had the ability to telepathically be part of a larger group-thought process. The more time I spent with the EBE, the more convinced I became.

Krll was able to project vivid images into our brains. This was done by using frequency and waves. We were able to record those brain waves. Although we knew this as fact, we were unable to interpret those thoughts; not with mechanical instruments anyhow.

I became quite adept at receiving the images from Krll. Once, as an exercise, I tried to block Krll from telepathically transmitting to me. I was somewhat successful. Much like deliberately not paying attention to someone when they are talking, it was possible to ignore the information he was sending – and for him not to read my mind. Even so, Krll's telepathic abilities were exceptional. He could have used them to manipulate our brains for information; to maybe try and escape or even direct other EBEs to our location

> to attempt rescue him, but this never happened. As I said, he had no agenda to save himself.'

C.J. orders hotel room service, the memoirs barely touching the desk next to the phone, as he calls before picking up the memoirs again.

He reads his father's reiteration that the EBEs had no DNA, revealing their genetic make-up was a form of RNA. Max writes a number of pages on the scientific differences between DNA (Deoxyribonucleic Acid) and RNA (Ribonucleic Acid), as well as the role they play together.

C.J. comes to the understanding that all living matter on Earth is made up of both DNA and RNA. DNA is double helix strands of genetic information, whereas RNA is a single strand with a slightly different molecular structure. The RNA assists the DNA to replicate.

According to Max, RNA is capable of carrying both genetic information and getting metabolic work done, making it the 'origin of life' molecule; however, DNA carries the genetic blueprint to replicate. Max Stroheim has made it clear that the EBEs were asexual and had no DNA.

> We had access to all EBE autopsy records, as well as frozen bodies of the retrieved dead aliens. All the corpses appeared identical to each other. Although some were badly damaged, they were all the same height and appeared to be similar or the same weight. From my earliest examinations of the bodies, I felt the species may have been cloned or produced in a similar type of process.

'Clones? Wow,' mutters C.J.

CHAPTER TWENTY-FIVE

> Back in the late forties and early fifties, the word 'clone' was almost unheard of. Even the understanding of genetics was in its scientific infancy. Few knew about DNA and RNA, however this was a topic both Guillermo and myself learned about as much as possible. We were of the opinion that a RNA-based entity would be simpler to clone than a DNA-based one. The more we hypothesized that the EBEs were 'manufactured,' the more convinced we became that Krll and the other EBEs were duplicates. This meant that someone or something was producing them. The questions were frequently asked: Who? How? And Why? I'll speculate later; however, I will say at this point that we doubted the EBEs themselves were of extraterrestrial origin.

This statement comes as a shock to C.J. Here's this species so unlike anything on Earth and yet his father doubts they are from another planet. This implies that the EBEs were from here or, at the very least, manufactured here. C.J. reads on.

> We had retrieved a number of crashed disks. These were not designed for traveling long distances. I'll describe the disks later, as they, like the EBEs, were unique. Dr. Bronk was the one who

used the term EBE: Extraterrestrial Biological Entity. It was initially assumed the disks and the EBEs were from another planet. It was a fair assumption given the technology of their craft and the biology of the occupants. Note that I use the term 'EBE' because that's how everyone at S-4 referred to Krll. We did not call it an 'alien,' a 'Martian,' or any other outer-space-type term, especially when we came to realize the EBEs were probably not from outer space anyhow.

Frank Reiner and Bill Nedersham worked in different facilities within Area 51. We would meet regularly to discuss our individual projects – to find correlations, work on hypotheses, and to document our findings for The Group. We generally worked in our specific areas within S-4, but we had security access to visit each other's facilities. Only a handful of people had this access, but there were still protocols and procedures to follow. The security was incredible.

I was never given a map or layout of the underground facilities at Area 51. The facility was expanding rapidly. I'm sure there were people in charge of construction and expansion, but I never met them. MJ-12 did a very good job of keeping S-4 segregated and compartmentalized. I will say that I saw the results of the technology used in underground digging and I did hear rumors of the incredible tunnel-boring machines used, particularly from the mid-to-late 1950s onwards.

I won't elaborate here, but will reinforce that the underground facilities in not only Area 51, but dozens of other, often linked, secret bases was extensive and well-hidden – and hidden for a reason.

Back in the late forties and early fifties, we had just finished WWII and then we came across this spectacular discovery of crashed UFOs, dead alien bodies, and a live EBE. As secretive as the Government wanted to keep it, everybody wanted a piece of the action: the Air Force, the Navy, the Army, and the Intelligence Agencies. There were projects and power struggles happening everywhere. I am sure the Government was unsure what to do at first. That was why MJ-12 was created and, ultimately, the NSA. MJ-12's first task was to delegate different assignments to different departments and agencies. A lot of this was 'smoke and mirrors.' They set up secret divisions for each of the various factions and often fed them only snippets of information. Sometimes that information was deliberately incorrect or set up to be confusing. You'll read of the term 'disinformation.' Deception was rampant. An example of this disinformation was the use of the name 'Dreamland,' given to a variety of different installations, assignments, and areas over the years. I am sure it was a deliberate ploy to obscure the truth. MJ-12 did this very well.

Harry S. Truman himself said, 'If you can't convince them, confuse them.'

Remember that it was Truman and James Forrestal who set up MJ-12 – and ultimately the NSA, the CIA, and so many of these secretive projects.

I later learned that MJ-12 would deliberately keep each organization or agency from knowing all of the information. Some had scraps of the truth, but often they were given manufactured lies. MJ-12 were the only ones holding all the information – and they wanted to keep it that way.

Frank, Bill, and I were only given information relevant to our projects, nothing else. We would furnish MJ-12 with huge amounts of data, but received little in return. This we accepted from an early stage.

We did not technically work for the NSA; in fact, we did not formally work for anyone. We were paid well, but it was always in cash. We were never officially recognized. We knew that if any of our research went public, or came under government or media scrutiny, then all ties with The Group's individual members or the agency would be denied. Even so, we were given whatever resources and funds we needed. The Group's favorite saying was an old military term: 'Do whatever it takes.'

Although our role was not officially recognized or defined, we were once introduced to a member of The Group as: 'The three men in charge of all scientific data relevant to extraterrestrial activities,' but that was a one-off reference. During our training we were told we'd be given 'all the power and resources we needed to get the desired results' (do whatever it takes), but we were never to question the processes behind the scenes. Frank Reiner began questioning these processes. Frank was a good man, thoughtful, intelligent, and thorough. I know, at times, he struggled with the enormity of the implications of what we were involved in. We all did.

Frank was a great administrator, excelling with all the documentation, including the thoughts and conjecture based on what we saw. The Group wanted to know everything, with Frank's skills contributing to the majority of the paperwork MJ-12 saw. Frank, Bill, and I would meet weekly to discuss and document our findings, with Frank the designated scribe.

Bill was a hard-nosed military man, who dealt with facts. His expertise was cryptology, spending much time discussing the markings or symbols found on many of the recovered disks (UFOs), found mainly on internal beams or columns inside the disks. Even though Bill was reputedly the best cryptologist in the world, he struggled to decode these symbols. His contribution to our meetings was limited.

Bill had taken copies of all the symbols to Krll in the hope some light would be shed on them, but Krll never responded. I know this frustrated Bill; however, he was always one to keep his emotions in-check. After Krll passed away, Bill became increasingly involved with other projects relevant to alien communications and collaborations. He rarely talked of the project names or specifics, yet always listened carefully to both my and Frank's revelations.

I was always a little wary of Bill's involvement. Bill was close with MJ-12 member Admiral Roscoe Hillenkoetter; the first Director of the CIA. I knew more than our documents would be going to MJ-12. In private, I warned Frank to be careful revealing his personal thoughts and opinions in Bill's company. Frank heeded my cautions for a while; however, Frank was becoming more and

> more disillusioned with some of these processes we were told not to question.

There is a knock on the door; C.J.'s room service has arrived. As soon as the attendant has left with a handsome tip, C.J. resumes reading, nibbling on Pad Thai noodles.

> Frank was a physicist. He'd spent thousands of hours investigating retrieved UFO wreckage. The alien craft were unlike anything he'd seen before; devoid of instrumentation as we know it. The outside covering was a thin, metallic-colored substance, which appeared to be like a biological skin. We tested the material. It did not resemble anything on Earth, nor did it contain DNA or RNA. The internal columns and beams were metallic looking, yet made of different materials from the outer skin – also unknown to our science.
>
> The craft themselves were not very large – about 20–30 feet in circumference – by comparison, a Boeing 747 (Jumbo jet) is more than 230 feet long with a wingspan of around 200 feet. The crafts at Dreamland were symmetrical with a smooth, featureless surface. There were no seams, no rivets, and no weld marks – and the whole craft was incredibly lightweight. Two men could easily pick the craft up.
>
> No one at Area 51 had much idea about how the crafts were powered or how they were controlled. This became Frank Reiner's field of expertise. He consulted with other physicists; many famous scientists – some you would have researched. Apart from MJ-12 members and their support team, as well as a handful of prominent physicists, Bill and I were some of the few privy to this information. When I say 'information,' I am talking about 'real information.' There was a lot of disinformation spread about the supposed existence of these craft. At the time I was shielded from this disinformation. In later years, I discovered just how extensive and elaborate the cover-ups were.
>
> For the record, Frank never called them UFOs, preferring to call them 'disks.'

The Government and the Military documented numerous public and military sightings of the disks. We read findings from several secret UFO projects, consistently reporting that, in flight, the disks were luminous and moved in ways defying logic. Of the wreckage recovered, there was no indication that the craft had a separate or external lighting system, yet they emitted a bright light during flight. Frank surmised that the disks were surrounded by some sort of energy field, or corona, which created the illumination many witnesses reported. This energy field may have also contributed to the energy source of the crafts.

I must admit that, in the early stages of research into the disks, little was known – and little found out. MJ-12 became more interested in the technology of these disks than anything else. Dr. Mendoza and I were encouraged to communicate with the EBE to learn as much technical information as possible. Krll was not forthcoming. MJ-12 became increasingly frustrated and we faced additional pressure to get results – without success.

Frank told me there were all sorts of projects involved in trying to reverse-engineer the retrieved crafts. MJ-12 had the best scientists, access to the best facilities, no bureaucratic red tape, little accountability, and massive funding. And yet, they could not discover the full secrets to the alien craft's amazing flying abilities and power source. With that said, some of the greatest scientific breakthroughs of the fifty years came from the processes set in place during the 1940s and 50s. This was more of a bi-product from the research, given the huge leaps in technology achievable using the best people, few restrictions, and bucket-loads of money.

Dr. Mendoza and I obtained no worthwhile information from Krll in respect to the disks/UFOs. Before Krll passed away, Frank (Reiner) was badgered by The Group to pursue 'interrogating' Krll. Of course, this proved pointless.

We knew Krll's health was deteriorating. The telltale sign was his color, becoming progressively paler, with increasing secretions of a clear mucus-type substance through his eyes and mouth.

We were so concerned about the EBE's condition, we suggested to The Group that maybe, as a show of good faith, we should release Krll. A resounding 'no' was the reply. Dr. Vannevar Bush did, however, talk with Bill Nedersham, with Bill relaying that, through his work with Project Sign and a new project, Plato, radio communications using a computer binary language had been somewhat successful in communicating with the EBEs on a collective level. Dr. Bush had agreed to send a message as a show of goodwill.

Guillermo, Frank, and I were not included in the specifics of this 'alien communication attempt,' although we saw or heard nothing to suggest it worked. Krll passed away with no response or direct contact from other EBEs.

I must point out that, at this point, the EBEs were now sometimes referred to as 'Grey aliens' or 'Roswell Greys,' in reference to the Roswell crash incident. Obviously, I wasn't at Roswell, nor were Guillermo, Frank, or Bill. However, this seemed to be the event that sparked much of the secretive divisions and projects. I believe that MJ-12 formed around this time. The exact details of The Group were kept from everyone. I doubt even the President knew all the information. Harry S. Truman the President at the time. You remember, I used to play golf with Harry. I'll elaborate on some of our conversations a little later.

C.J. finishes his last mouthful of Pad Thai, eager to keep reading.

I was cocooned from many of The Group's activities, but I knew of the AEC, as well as the formalization of the NSA and the CIA. Apart from President Truman, two key players are behind the formation of these three agencies: Secretary of Defense Jim Forrestal and Dr. Van Bush. I only met Jim on three occasions, although Harry talked highly of him, once referring to him as his 'right-hand man.' I found Forrestal to be a decent, stable, thorough, and intelligent man.

Jim was interested in S-4 and all things extraterrestrial. I am sure he was in regular contact with the President over these matters. I am also sure there was some dissent over the direction The Group were taking and what to do with all of this incredible information.

Jim wanted President Truman to inform a few of his fellow government colleagues about some of this evidence. From my understanding, The Group, led by Dr. Bush, were opposed to any UFO or extraterrestrial information being circulated, either to the Government or the media. It was a divided but majority decision. Apparently, in defiance, Forrestal did inform some of his government colleagues. This resulted in pressure for Harry Truman to stand Forrestal.

Forrestal was relieved of his cabinet position and told to 'take a holiday.' He was placed in a low-security military rehabilitation facility, which happened to be a high-rise building. He was put in a room on the sixteenth floor and allegedly jumped over the balcony to his death. You probably read about this.

We all knew the truth. 'If no one talks, then no one dies.' Jim wanted to talk. Obviously the other MJ-12 members didn't want the truth to come out.

From my understanding, Vannevar Bush became the new head of The Group. I had a huge amount of respect for Dr. Bush's scientific and administrative skills, but I harbored some uncertainties about his agenda – and the lengths he would go to achieve what he wanted. He could be ruthless. We always got along well, but he was a driven man. You'd know that Dr. Bush ran the Manhattan Project during World War II, and was a key instigator behind the Atomic Energy Commission, RAND Corporation, MITRE Corporation, the JASON Scholars, and he just happened to have his own military supply company – Raytheon.

'Raytheon?' gasps C.J. 'I know it's on Dad's latest list – oh my God, Raytheon was Vannevar Bush's company?' C.J. composes himself to keep reading.

> Van Bush was incredibly powerful. From the best of my knowledge, he never actually worked for the Government; however, he was responsible for ensuring government funding for a host of private enterprise or 'independent' ventures. He advised Harry Truman and, in some instances, decided what information would be revealed to the Government and what was to be kept inside The Group. You must also understand that the Government was paying for the vast majority, if not all, of The Group's activities. We are talking billions of dollars annually, even back in the late 1940s and early 1950s.
>
> I did not always agree with how Bush did things, but he was a scientist at heart. He advanced science technology in The US more than anyone else I knew. But at what cost?

'But at what cost?' repeats C.J. He's starting to think his father began to question the 'processes' he'd been asked to trust and accept.

CHAPTER TWENTY-SIX

Dr. Bush brought the best scientists on the planet into MJ-12's operations. Some I met, others I heard mentioned by Frank, and still more had their names associated with reports I read. Most of my scientific dealings were with Vannevar Bush, Detlev Bronk, and Don Menzel.

I also met Edward Teller, albeit briefly, and Robert Oppenheimer, on two occasions. On the second meeting, Oppenheimer was accompanied by none other than Albert Einstein. I so wanted to talk with the great man, yet passing him in the corridors of S-4 was the closest I came. I was surprised how short in statue he was; yet Einstein had a gleam in his eye and a spring in his step. He was obviously excited to be at our facility. Frank spent time with Einstein, recalling with fondness Einstein's quick wit, willingness to learn, and his fascination with our research.

You would have seen Einstein and Oppenheimer's 1947 paper 'Relationships with Inhabitants of Celestial Bodies.' Read it again. I was only given access to the paper some years after it was written. You would no doubt realize the ramifications, if the recommendations of two of the world's most prominent scientists were made public? Those recommendations were never given the chance to be implemented.

Bush, Bronk, and Menzel were all in The Group. I had the feeling Robert Oppenheimer may have been as well, but I can't be certain. I can confirm he was close to The Group. All documents to The Group were listed generically as 'MJ-12,' with no itemized list of who received the memos. There may have been more than 12 members by the time I joined S-4. There may have also been associate members. I can't be sure. I can relay that I was not fond of Dr. Don Menzel. He would not have known my distaste. Diplomacy takes strength of character. Menzel was a powerful administrator and influential scientist – a theoretical astronomer and astrophysicist. In principle, we should have had much in common, but we didn't. Don Menzel was two faced. He'd come to S-4 and spend hours with the EBE. I know from Frank that Menzel also spent a great deal of time looking at disk crash wreckage. then he'd write all these memoranda and papers to different military departments, announcing that he'd researched into all these 'so-called UFO sightings and found them to be bogus.'

At the time, I didn't know why he'd do such a thing. Van Bush and Detlev Bronk were both administrative geniuses but at their core, they were scientists. Menzel was different. He seemed more intent on spreading propaganda than actually learning from the rare and privileged scientific position we were in. Don Menzel may have been The Group's designated 'disinformation' expert; however, I did not trust Menzel. An opinion I formulated from our earliest meetings.

C.J. writes down *Dr. Don Menzel* to research later, before continuing.

I remember a conversation with Menzel, shortly after Krll passed away. He wanted to know just how much more intelligent the EBE was compared to us humans. He would have seen Dr. Mendoza and my reports, with our discussions

> of the EBE's third lobe and speculation whether the crystalline substance was implanted – it was possibly non-biological. Never once did we say the EBE was smarter than humans.
>
> Menzel said flippantly, 'Come on Stroheim, you must think that the alien was much more intelligent than us?'
>
> Menzel's manner made my blood boil, but I composed myself to tell him that defining intelligence was subjective. There is no doubt the EBEs had extraordinary telepathic abilities; however, some suggest so too do dolphins. We know that the dolphin brain is some 65 million years ahead of the human brain in cortical development, yet the dolphins maintain a social structure totally without tools and devices. In the case of the EBEs, for all their programmed intelligence, they lacked the emotional and individual development of mankind. Just because the EBEs had a big brain didn't automatically mean they were smarter.
>
> Menzel did not like my answer.

C.J. would later learn Dr. Donald Menzel was considered 'a prominent skeptic concerning the reality of UFOs.' He authored or co-authored three popular books debunking UFOs, including *Flying Saucers: Myth – Truth – History*, published in 1953.

This was less than two years after the experiences Max Stroheim described.

All of Menzel's UFO books argued that UFOs are nothing more than misidentification of prosaic phenomena such as stars, clouds, and airplanes, or the result of people seeing unusual and unfamiliar atmospheric phenomena. He often suggested atmospheric hazes or temperature inversions could distort stars or planets, making them appear to be larger than in reality, or unusual in their shape and in motion.

In 1968 Menzel testified before the US House Committee on Science and Astronautics, a symposium on UFOs. Menzel stated that he considered all UFO sightings to have natural explanations. He even told a story of his own 'supposed' UFO experience when in 1955 he observed what he first thought might be a 'flying saucer,' but later identified it as 'a mirage of Sirius.'

Further investigation revealed Menzel was a consultant to both the CIA and NSA, also with close ties to the Council on Foreign Relations and The Trilateral Commission. This was a very well connected man, with powerful allies.

> For all of Menzel's badgering, he actually helped me consider the EBE's real intelligence. I discussed this with Dr. Mendoza. Guillermo used this analogy: a man with an IQ of 160 stands obliviously on a train track in front of an oncoming train, and a man with an IQ of 80 steps to the side. The man with the high IQ gets hit and dies. Who is the most intelligent?
>
> Krll had no inclinations for self-preservation. Surely self-preservation is the most basic innate intelligence a species can have? Krll could have simply communicated what he required from us to maintain his health or be comfortable, but he didn't. We knew he had the ability to lie, to manipulate situations. If he wanted to end his life, he could have.
>
> He appeared not to feel pain, emotionally or physically. I think that, even if Krll had survived longer, we would not have found out any new information. The capture and study of another EBE would be pointless, although I did not relay this to The Group. The one thing to accept when you work in a top-secret environment is to realize you are dispensable.
>
> The secrecy surrounding Area 51, and particularly S-4, was unprecedented. Before we joined the project, what was expected of us was spelled out clearly– and reiterated on a daily basis. The security systems were impenetrable. Every conversation in the complex was monitored. It was something we needed to accept. Frank became frustrated at the lack of privacy. I remember, one day we were in the restroom and he said, 'You know, Max, they even watch us while we're in the crapper.'
>
> I laughed at the time, but he was right. We were kept men.
>
> Initially, I lived within Area 51. A windowless, sterile room was

not my idea of fun so I soon followed Frank's lead and moved to a house in Las Vegas. I'd fly from Vegas to Groom Lake. These weren't commercial flights though – they were windowless charters that ferries us to and from Area 51. All buses within the area had blacked-out windows and we were forbidden from talking with other workers, apart from saying, 'Good morning,' or 'How's it going?'

When I first started working at S-4, I didn't care less where and how I lived. I was so excited to be involved in a project that surpassed any of my career expectations. After Krll's passing I spent more time in Las Vegas, flying in and out most days. My house was supplied (I'm guessing by the NSA), including all my electricity and phone bills. I had an inkling the phone would be bugged, but I didn't contemplate listening devices being planted throughout the house or constant surveillance from cars. It was something I came to accept. While I knew Frank Reiner began to question the intrusiveness of being constantly monitored, I was good at keeping my emotions in check.

After Krll passed away, Dr. Mendoza and I had little to do. We'd been reprocessing all the information we had – notes, autopsy reports, that sort of thing – to pass on documentation and hypotheses to The Group, but we were at a crossroads. Then things changed.

More disks and EBE bodies were retrieved after the Roswell crash; however, the disks and corpses were identical to what we already had. In 1952 a substantially larger disk crashed in the desert, badly damaged. Over a dozen dead EBEs were recovered – and, for the first time, it appeared there were vats of some description within the craft.'

'Vats?'

I was not given access to the wreckage or the bodies, as I was told the corpses were severely damaged. They appeared to be all the same size and weight as previously recovered EBEs.

'There is nothing new to learn here,' I was told.

Then they gave me a container of what appeared to be some type of liquid, with blood and chunks of flesh in it. They told me that they'd already tested the contents. What they then told me came as a huge shock: The contents included blood and body parts – some bovine and some human.

Apparently, this disk had numerous vats inside; it appeared that the vats were full of human and cow body parts. Guillermo and I were very concerned. I'd read reports of Grey aliens abducting people, as well as cases of cows being mutilated, with some of their body parts surgically removed, especially the eyes, the tongue, and around the anus. Back in 1940s and early '50s, information about abductions and cow mutilations was limited. From the few credible abductee accounts we had, the Grey aliens described were the same as Krll.

These abductees all reported the same thing: being beamed up somehow into a UFO, with Grey aliens performing intrusive medical procedures on them. The abductees were returned, mostly unharmed, with little-to-no memory of the incident. In some cases, people were abducted multiple times. The abductees often recalled only snippets of information, with a clearer description generally recounted during hypnotherapy. What this information meant to us at the time was ambiguous. Colonel Berkmeyer had interrogated Krll on why his species were abducting people and of what interest bovine body parts were to them but, again, Krll refused to answer. I too broached the subject with Krll, but also came up empty-handed.

Then, after Krll's death, we discover this larger crashed craft full of human and cow body parts.

Initially, it was a scenario almost too gruesome to contemplate. We were perplexed. The EBEs are plant-like entities. They do not eat food as we humans do and they certainly aren't meat-eaters, so why the body parts?

This question I wrestled for months, if not years.

This is what I now think: The EBEs had no personal use for

the contents of the vats. I believe the EBEs were all cloned or manufactured through a similar process. This means someone else made them. The EBEs are being used like worker bees; collecting things for someone or something else. I think they are collecting genetic material: human and bovine DNA and RNA. Why cows, I was never able to answer, but human DNA might be key. Maybe the species manufacturing the EBEs is DNA based – and somehow they need, use, or experiment with our DNA?

It is unlike me to speculate. These are my opinions based on thirty-four years of research. After that amount of time dealing with reams of paperwork on the Greys, spending a year with a live EBE, and seeing their disks, I'm entitled to some suppositions.

C.J. smiles to himself, as his father's rare moment of sarcasm is noted.

Now I want to detail my relationship with Harry Truman. It was at this time that I first met Harry. In 1952 he was nearing the end of his presidency. To be honest, I didn't know much about the President. I knew he took over from Roosevelt, after he died in office toward the end of the war, but I knew little else. When I was recruited to the NSA, initially, I was unaware that Truman, Forrestal, and Dr. Bush had set up MJ-12 and the secretive processes I found myself a part of. I'm sure Truman took an active interest in the evolving UFO and EBE information. My name, as the resident astrobiologist, would have been on some of the reports. I hadn't really thought that the President would read some of my findings until I received a phone call. I was at the Las Vegas house, and had just returned from playing a round of golf. I thought it must have been a prank call. But the President was direct and authoritarian.

He said, 'I am President Harry Truman. Please listen, Max. I know you are an astrobiologist working at S-4. I have not been there, but I know the facility. I've heard that you've been doing some excellent work for us. I also understand you're a golfer. Is that right?'

'Yes sir,' I replied nervously.

Truman said, 'Well, we'll just have to play a game. I'll be in Vegas in a few days. I'll check my schedule and my people will be in touch.'

The President does not go out and play golf with someone just for the hell of it. I knew there had to be a reason. Three days later, I'm on the golf course with the leader of the free world.

As mesmerized as C.J. is by his father's revelations, he places the memoirs down momentarily. C.J. would have loved Emma to share in the disclosures. He turns on his computer to see if Emma has responded to his email.

She has reported, in code: 14 = All is good here; 19 = Have researched; 22 = I love you.

She has; reporting in code. She's made inroads into Ellis Buckman's life and career.

C.J. replies:1, 5, 6, 14, and 22. 1 = I have what I came for, 5 = I'll catch a flight to Brisbane tomorrow, 6 = We'll meet at the designated spot, 14 = All is good here, 22 = I love you.

He then turns off his computer to continue reading the memoirs.

CHAPTER TWENTY-SEVEN

C.J. reads of his father playing golf with the then president Harry S. Truman for the first time.

I instantly liked the President. When he shook my hand, I said, 'I'm pleased to meet you, Mr. President.'

He said 'My name's Harry. We are here to enjoy a casual round of golf, so please call me Harry.'

I asked him to call me Max. He may have been the President, but to me he seemed direct and sincere.

It was just he and I playing. A team of security was following. We did not have caddies; Harry preferred to carry his own clubs. He informed his security team to not get too close. At the time, I thought this was so they didn't distract his golf game but, later, I thought it was so he could talk to me privately.

On the first fairway, he told me the reason for the golf game. He'd heard I was not only a good scientist, but a good man. He knew where I worked and what I did. The President told me he was fascinated with what he termed the 'Alien Situation.' He said that, because of the ramifications of what was unfolding, he needed to keep everything from the public until we were in a better position to accurately assess and relay that information, not only to the American people, but to the world. For that reason, he and the

Government had to distance themselves from the many projects that had begun.

Between golf shots, Truman mentioned he played golf regularly with James Forrestal. It was on the golf course that he'd asked Forrestal to head up the team that would 'get the best people and the best outcomes.' He was talking about The Group, MJ 12.

Truman told of his interest in the secret projects being carried out in Area 51. He knew about S-4, having read a number of reports, mostly from Frank Reiner, in relation to the 'Alien Situation.'

What the President wanted from me was a one-on-one update. He said, 'You seem like a no-nonsense type of fellow, Max. I don't need all the facts. I just want to know what you think.'

He already knew that human body parts had been found and he knew of the EBE living in captivity for two years; one year at Los Alamos and one at S-4.

When the President asks you for your opinion, you give it. He assured me our conversation was confidential. I think he said, 'We're just two Missouri farm boys having a hit of golf, so this is just between us.' I didn't know Harry was originally from Missouri. He must have done his homework on me. We discussed our home state and even talked about baseball. We hit it off right from the start.

He said, 'This EBE. Did you think it was ever a threat?'

I told him I never saw any aggression, no emotion whatsoever.

'So, you don't think it was capable of violence?' he asked.

'Not that I could tell,' I replied.

Harry didn't really ask too many hard or intrusive questions. It was, as he said, just an informal chat while playing golf.

I was so nervous about meeting the President, I barely paid attention to the actual golf game. At the end of the round, I discovered that I'd actually scored pretty well. Harry genuinely loved hitting a golf ball so the round was enjoyable on all fronts – and even though there was an agenda for the game, he seemed to like my company.

We played one more round of golf together before Harry came to

> the end of his term, but afterward we played regularly.
>
> Even years later, he was still surrounded by personal bodyguards. He was the first former President to have this ongoing protection. He said, 'I didn't ask for it. You may think that it's for my benefit and wellbeing. Like hell it is; it's for *their* benefit. They don't trust anyone. My phone is bugged, my house is bugged, and probably the golf buggy, too. I'm sure you'll get the same treatment, if you haven't already. It's a world we need to learn to live with.'
>
> I'm sure The Group knew about each and every golf game Harry and I played. I was actually questioned on several occasions by MJ-12 members Don Menzel and Roscoe Hillenkoetter about my relationship with Truman. I told them, Harry and I were just a couple of Missouri farm boys playing golf.
>
> Menzel didn't like that answer. I explained we were both from Missouri and both loved baseball. I began telling Menzel that Truman even wore a St. Louis Cardinals baseball cap on the course one day, but Menzel turned his back on me and walked away.
>
> The new President was Eisenhower. Harry didn't like Ike, irrespective of Eisenhower being a Republican and Truman being a Democrat. Ike had some powerful allies and was backed by some of the wealthiest individuals and corporations in the country. Harry knew Ike from when he helped form NATO.

'What, Eisenhower helped form NATO?' mutters C.J., not having researched that information on his father's newest list.

> Ike looked after those who looked after him – and those who looked after him were from the private sector. Harry knew he'd no doubt bring them into many of the top-secret projects and agencies. The 'Alien Situation,' as Harry called, it was not just about America's and the world's security, it was about power. Those with the power would have the control. Truman feared that the Government would lose all control; a fear well based.
>
> Around then, I spent more time sifting through previous documents and reports of UFO sightings and extraterrestrial

encounters. Under the name 'Project Red Book,' there were chronicles of legitimate UFO sightings, as well as our own recent research. According to Frank, The Group were becoming increasingly frustrated at the lack of scientific results from the testing and attempted reverse-engineering from the disk wreckage. We had numerous disks, but they were all badly damaged. Some were only fragments and crumpled pieces. We thought there would be more disks retrieved in the future and that we would learn more. But by 1953, the incidences of crashes and retrieval of wreckage appear to stop.

Frank Reiner surmised that the disks were crashing due to a new military radar frequency being tested in the desert. From my understanding, radar emits a strong electromagnetic wave. At the right frequency, the wave caused the disks to oscillate, lose control, and crash. Whoever was making the craft must have fixed the 'frequency' problem; electromagnetic energy may have been the source of power for the disks. We discussed these scenarios but never shared them with The Group.

The Group wanted Frank Reiner to wrap up all the UFO information into a simple package. He suggested to them that I might be of some help, so I assisted documenting what facts we knew. But Dr. Van Bush wanted us to speculate. This made me nervous. Frank was a little more flippant. Just to confuse matters, we had reports, through Red Book, of all sorts of UFO types and shapes. We had assess wreckage from two different-sized craft, being essentially identical in material and design. We read numerous credible reports of UFOs that were 'flying saucers' like the EBE's craft, but that were also triangular-shaped, cigar-shaped, some like spheres, some huge, some small – the variances were extreme but they all appeared to exhibit similar technology, with the ability to change direction quickly and fly at incredible speeds.

We decided to completely review what we already knew about the EBE's craft. If Dr. Bush wanted us to 'speculate,' then it would be from information we knew firsthand.

Krll and other retrieved EBEs were found wearing a suit, like a spacesuit, covering their bodies from head to toe. The material was soft and easy to remove. It resembled nothing like we'd seen before. It was incredibly durable, almost armor-like, and it appeared to be conductive, like it was part of an electronic circuitry system. Under a microscope, the material revealed an intricate spider-web-type molecular structure, but the atoms all aligned in one direction. Frank believed the suit was indeed a conductor or conduit of some kind. When the craft was powered, he felt that the suit became part of the craft's system, with power running through the suit to protect the EBEs. With the power turned off or the circuit broken, then the suit behaved like regular material.

In most of the crashed crafts, we retrieved a type of headband device, embedded by some advanced vulcanizing process into a form of flexible plastic. We presume these electrical conductors or sensors worked similarly to the conductors on an electroencephalograph or polygraph machine, interacting with brain waves when worn. This is speculative, as the craft retrieved, as well as the bands, were badly damaged. No amount of testing could simulate the technology being used.

The internal structures of the craft – beams, columns, and flooring – were made of similar materials to the suits. Structurally, however, they were more like a metal. Frank believed they, too, were conductive. Everything pointed to the craft and its occupants being like a super-conduit, like some sort of electrical or magnetic wave.

I've been in many conventional aircraft. They have an array of electrical circuitry, controls, and panels. The EBE's craft had none of that; it was devoid of anything remotely resembling our planes or rockets. There were no obvious signs of any way to control the craft, or even of a fuel source to power them. When they crashed, there were no explosions. Crash witnesses recalled the craft skimming off the ground a number of times before coming to rest; albeit crumpled and badly damaged. At no time was there smoke, fire, or smoldering of any description.

I read a number of eyewitness reports where they claimed to be close to a UFO, either in-flight or hovering just above the ground. They all commented how silent they were. Some recalled hearing a buzzing sound, quiet, yet distinctive. Many recounted seeing these disks making incredible maneuvers, turning 180 degrees almost instantaneously, then taking off at speeds defying logic.

We asked each other: How were the craft controlled? What was its fuel source? and Where do they come from?

Frank believed the crystalline section of the EBE's enabled the craft to be controlled by the EBE's mind. The headband device became a link from the EBE to the craft. The spacecraft was navigated by direct interaction between the electronic waves generated within the minds of the pilots and the craft's directional controls. These were interpreted and transmitted by the headband devices, which served as interfaces. This was a difficult concept to grasp back in 1953, but now technology has advanced to where mechanical devices can be controlled by circuitry interacting with brain waves.

I remember seeing a computer in the mid-to-late 1950s. It was the size of a small house. Now the smartphones you have are smaller than your hand – and it has thousands of times more functions and storage capabilities than the archaic computer. We have come so far technologically in the last fifty or sixty years, much of it achieved from the scientists and systems under The Group's guidance and control. The EBE's technology is not beyond the realms of probability, however, at the time, it was beyond our full comprehension.

What was the fuel source?

Everything points toward an electrical or magnetic charge, probably creating some type of wave around the vehicle. Frank believed the EBE's disks used a technology to 'cut through' our atmosphere, as well as water. Being electrically or magnetically charged, he felt it created a current or barrier surrounding the craft during flight. Similar to a hovercraft, which creates an air cushion between the vehicle and its surrounds, the craft would glide through the air or water without actually touching the atmosphere or water. A hovercraft still has resistance from air and gravity, but Frank believed the disks had little to no resistance. Without friction, the craft could achieve incredible speeds and maneuverability, and be under virtually no stress. I concurred with Frank's theories.

Where did they come from?

We found no evidence to suggest the crafts we investigated at S-4 had traveled long distances; well, not from another planet anyhow. We concluded that the disks either came from a larger mothership or they were from here. When we say 'here,' we are presuming they came from a base or bases, either underground, underwater, or both. I'd read accounts that UFOs had been reported entering the ocean or large lakes. We tested the outer skin of the EBE's crafts and it was indeed waterproof. From reports read, Frank and I concluded that the disks could cut through water, without actually touching it; much like a hovercraft does.

Most sightings of UFOs entering the water claimed that the UFOs emitted a bright light that was visible underwater. Both Frank and I were of the opinion that the UFOs did not produce light, not purposely anyway. They would not want to draw attention to themselves. We believed the light seen by so many eyewitnesses was a byproduct, generated by the electrical or magnetic shield around the craft.

You should have found out about the 'Greada Treaty.' I am sure that snippets about what happened early in February 1954 would have found their way to the Internet. Bill Nedersham and his team were somewhat successful with communicating with what he termed 'The Greys.' I thought little of it at the time, but noted the subtle change in Bill's terminology. I wasn't privy to all of Bill's department's findings; however, Frank and I were aware of the communication breakthrough and that a meeting between MJ-12, and possibly President Eisenhower, with 'The Greys' was imminent.

> I'll elaborate on the Greada Treaty and subsequent meetings later, but first I want to talk about my dealings with another species.'

'Another species? What the—?' C.J. mutters out loud. He knows he needs to sleep, but can't – not just yet anyway.

> There was some historical documentation on the existence of this species, but for them to contact us came completely out of the blue. I remember the day Bill told me. He rarely showed emotion but, on this day, he couldn't stop smiling. We were unsure of what was to come. All we knew was the excitement of it all.
>
> The species in question never formally identified themselves by name, although they've been referred to as The Whites, Ancient Elders, Pleiadians (named after their star-system origin), the Watchers, and Nordics.
>
> We chose to call them 'Nordics' as their appearance looked Scandinavian; very human-like, but much taller – at least a foot taller than the average man. They had fair hair, a light complexion, and looked to have blue eyes.

C.J. reads the description of these Nordics again. His father isn't describing these Nordic aliens from some report or document. He's seen them firsthand. C.J. licks his lips in anticipation. There's no way he can go to sleep now.

CHAPTER TWENTY-EIGHT

These Nordics wanted to meet with President Eisenhower. The meeting was hastily arranged. Frank, Bill, Colonel Berkmeyer, and I were taken by helicopter to Muroc Test Center in southern California (I believe it's now called Edwards Air Force Base). Eisenhower arrived, with several other men with him. They were businessmen; dressed in suits. I thought it odd that the President would bring civilians into such a secure and secret location. Several MJ-12 members arrived separately; I noted that Vannevar Bush and Don Menzel were not present.

The meeting was hastily arranged and somewhat chaotic. I thought the meeting may not happen, but realized that, if the President and a team of important business men were able to come, at short notice, then they must have been confident that it was really going to happen.

Some time after midnight, a bi-convex 'saucer-style' craft flew in, extended tripod landing gear, and alighted on the landing strip. A ramp extended and two very tall and athletic men appeared. I say 'men', because they looked human. Both had blonde hair, pale complexions, and pale blue eyes. They both appeared to be between thirty and forty years-of-age. One walked down the ramp and approached President Eisenhower. He obviously knew who

Eisenhower was. He stopped short of the President and indicated for no one to come any closer, while the other man stayed on the aircraft's ramp.

The Nordic on the ground addressed the President; not telepathically, but with actual words. He was confident, direct, and spoke perfect English. There was an accent of sorts, but at the time I could not compare.

I could tell both Nordics also had telepathic capabilities. I didn't think about it at the time because the Nordic was speaking, but I realized he was communicating telepathically, as well as verbally. My prior dealings with the EBE had sharpened my ability to understand telepathic communication. Even so, I, like everyone else, listened to the words intently.

The Nordic explained they had been visiting Earth for thousands of years and were aware of what he termed 'The Grey Problem.' He also stated, in no uncertain terms, that the Greys, as well as themselves, knew about the Government's nuclear experimentation and testing. He suggested they could help us get rid of the Greys, but only if the United States Government were prepared to abandon their nuclear testing program.

Eisenhower asked if the Nordics could help the US with technological information. The Nordic ignored the question and repeated his original offer: they could help with controlling the Greys if the US Government abandoned the nuclear program.

Eisenhower turned down their offer.

I personally think Eisenhower expected more dialogue with the Nordic, but the Nordic turned around and walked up the ramp to join his colleague. The ramp raised and hatch closed. Within a matter of seconds, the craft took off, leaving at speed.

It all happened so fast; it was like a dream. We looked up to the sky in bewilderment. Eisenhower looked shocked. I knew Eisenhower didn't want to give up the nuclear program, but I was surprised that he answered 'no' so quickly. We did not hear from the Nordics again.

Eisenhower's handling of the meeting with the Nordic aliens

> created a lot of conflict behind the scenes. Frank and I spent hours discussing the interaction, as well as Eisenhower's poor management of the event. We knew little about the Nordics, but felt assured they had our best interests at heart.
>
> Why would they wish to help us with what they termed 'The Grey Problem'? They were also concerned at America's nuclear program. Why? They seemed genuine – and I was so surprised how similar in appearance these Nordics appeared to us humans. They may be DNA-based entities. I'd be highly surprised if they weren't.

C.J. recognizes the enormity of his father's statements. Reading between the lines, his father is hinting that these 'Nordics' may share some type of lineage with humans.

> Bill Nedersham sustained his communication with 'the Greys,' arranging a meeting to include Eisenhower and select officials in February 1954. This time, the Government and officials had time to prepare. Only a few of The Group attended the hastily arranged meeting with the Nordics but, this time, every MJ-12 member was in attendance. We were fully briefed about the upcoming meeting. Bill, Frank, and I were asked to prepare a dossier of information The Group would find beneficial, regarding any agreement or negotiation with the Greys.
>
> We had a heated debate over the subject. I really wanted to know the answers to a lot of the questions Krll was unwilling to answer – the real reason for the human and bovine genetic material discovered, why they were abducting humans, and where they came from. Bill wanted the Greys to supply communications technology, and Frank wanted to find out the power source of their disks. In a perfect world, we would find out everything. In reality, we found out nothing.
>
> The meeting between 'the Greys,' Eisenhower, and MJ-12; and Bill, Frank, and I took place at Holloman Air Force Base, near Roswell, New Mexico. This time Eisenhower was well prepared. There were more than thirty people present. Some of the same

businessmen who attended the meeting with the Nordics were in attendance, plus several more. It was an overcast night and a little windy. We assembled in a hanger, before being asked to step outside. We could see no craft, but two EBEs stood out in the open. I use the term 'EBEs' loosely because, although the beings looked like Krll, they appeared taller. It was difficult to judge, as there was no point of reference nearby to compare and the EBEs were some distance away. Where they stood was poorly lit and the weather conditions weren't ideal.

Like Krll, they used telepathy to communicate; the images were vivid. Even so, communicating with Grey aliens using telepathy in front of a large group of people was an arduous task. Eisenhower and his business associates had an agenda and the Greys had their own agenda. I was probably the most experienced in the assembly with translating telepathic images, but even I was confused.

Eisenhower had a prepared speech, talking about peace and prosperity; the usual diplomatic hogwash, before talking about alien abductions. He didn't use the term 'abduction,' it was more diplomatically worded; something about 'experimentation,' but we all knew what he was alluding to. I was surprised that Eisenhower would mention such a thing; however, the planning of this speech and the meeting was meticulous and choreographed, so I doubt Ike was adlibbing.

Eisenhower communicated that his government would, in essence, turn a blind-eye to the abductions, given a few guidelines and, in turn, the Greys would assist and furnish the US Government with technology and research.

After this awkward and confusing exchange, Eisenhower produced a document. This was the Greada Treaty (with Greada pronounced Gree-arda). I don't even know if the Greys could read English, yet Eisenhower stepped forward to hand it to the two Greys. They looked at it, transmitted some telepathic images of them looking at it, and then returned it to Eisenhower. He and several of advisors signed it. I don't know why, but they did.

On face value this was a groundbreaking treaty like no other

> in the history of the USA: A pact between human inhabitants and (possibly) extraterrestrial beings. The reality was that it was a farce. The basic terms of this so-called treaty were: the Greys would assist the US Government with technology and research, while the Government ignored the alien's abduction of humans, as well as genetic experimentation on humans and animals. Within the wording of the prearranged document, Eisenhower and his advisers only stipulated that the Greys would only be allowed to abduct a small number of persons, with the Government periodically given a list of those abducted. The abductees were to be returned unharmed.
>
> Excuse my skepticism, but did the President expect the Greys to drop into the Whitehouse once a month with a typed list, saying, 'We only abducted ten people this month: They were John Smith from Pasadena, California; Sue Citizen from Fort Worth, Texas …' you can see where I'm going with this.

C.J. chuckles over his father's outburst of sarcasm, agreeing with his father's summation.

> On the Greys' instructions, we returned to the hanger. We did not hear a craft land but, minutes later, the two Greys were gone, with no trace of any craft landing and no trace of a UFO in the sky. Eisenhower, his businessmen, and his advisers seemed pleased. Frank and I were unimpressed. We suspected the EBEs, or 'Greys' as they were now known, would not supply any data on abductees and would continue seizing and experimenting on US citizens unabated.
>
> And we were proved correct. As for the Government receiving technological assistance from the Greys, well, there was little evidence to suggest that happened either.
>
> We returned to S-4 with no questions answered and more questions asked. Frank was agitated, having not seen the EBE's craft in flight. He'd spent thousands of hours meticulously studying disk wreckage, yet never saw a UFO in the air. The

Nordics' craft, albeit larger, looked a little similar to what he'd imagined a complete Grey's craft would look like. Not seeing the EBE's disk, as well as the farcical nature of the Greada Treaty, contributed to Frank's frustration.

The Greada Treaty became a defining moment in the direction of the S-4 operations. I was unaware of what discussions occurred between Eisenhower, his government, and The Group; however, things changed – and changed rapidly. With no warning, I discovered Dr. Guillermo Mendoza was no longer working at S-4. Colonel Berkmeyer told me Dr. Mendoza had been moved to another facility, after six years of working together. Before I could ask, Berkmeyer shut me down. I could see the angst in his eyes when he told me, 'You know the rules Max. You need to trust the processes.'

And that's all he said.

C.J. would later search the Internet, attempting to discover where Dr. Guillermo Mendoza moved after the Greada Treaty. There are articles about Dr. Mendoza's work up to that point, but nothing after. It is as though he fell off the face of the planet.

Maybe he did?

Only a few weeks later, Frank Reiner and MJ-12 member Roscoe Hillenkoetter exchanged heated words. Frank was unsatisfied with the situation, believing the scientific component of his research was being compromised. In a moment of anger, Frank threatened to tell others about what he termed 'a loss of integrity.' I presumed Frank was talking about telling other scientists, not the press, but even so, Hillenkoetter was not impressed. The next day, Frank, said to me, he was told to 'take a holiday.'

I knew it was a mistake for Frank to threaten The Group, even in anger or jest. When I was told, some days later, that Frank had committed suicide by jumping over the balcony of a high-rise hotel, I kept my true feelings to myself. I knew Frank was murdered. I didn't need to see the police report or the official cause of death. I knew. So did others. It was a message, and those at the base received it loud and clear.

Frank was not just a colleague, he was a friend. Deep down, I was fuming. I knew the work we were doing was important, but to kill a man because they thought, on the off chance, he *might* talk was sobering. 'If no one talks, then no one dies' ran through my mind for days.

I've always told you that, sometimes, you need to step away from a problem to look at it from a different viewpoint. I went back to Vegas, played golf for three days, and thought.

With Krll gone and the likelihood of another live EBE being captured unlikely, I knew my career was at a crossroads. But I could not leave. They would never allow it. I was still in a privileged situation; I had access to information other astrobiologists would give their eyeteeth to have. With Dr. Mendoza gone and Frank dead, I was one of the few with firsthand knowledge and dealings with an EBE.

When Dr. Vannevar Bush called me in for what he termed 'a little chat,' I was understandably anxious. He put me at ease, explaining that The Group were extremely pleased with my work.

'You know about Red Book?' he asked.

I nodded.

'Well, Max, we want you to take over Red Book. You'll be in charge of gathering and documenting all information relevant to the work you've already started. This is a very important project. We want to know everything. You will still work here at S-4 from time to time, but we will give you the clearances and the access to enter other facilities, as well as whatever resources you need. What do you think?'

I did not hesitate to say 'yes.' Red Book would be a dossier for MJ-12's eyes only, but I would learn more. I'd been wondering what they would do with me. It was an affable outcome for all of us.

I spent the rest of my career working on Red Book.

C.J. was in Surfers Paradise when he researched Red Book. It was a database of underground sites and subsurface facilities, a chronology of alien activities, their craft, technology, and the physiology of the extraterrestrials. Little more information was available on the Internet. C.J. asked at the time, *I wonder who was in charge of researching and writing Red Book?*

He now knows.

C.J. finally succumbs to tiredness, placing the memoirs on the bedside table and falling asleep within seconds.

CHAPTER TWENTY-NINE

After only a few hours, C.J. barely rubs the sleep from his eyes before picking up his father's memoirs. Anxious to learn of his father's revelations within Project Red Book, he reads:

> One of the first tasks assigned to me was to dissect the Air Force's Project Blue Book, which began in 1952. Blue Book was an initiative from projects Sign and Grudge. MJ-12 member Nathan Twining, who was the Air Force's Chief of Staff at the time, told me Blue Book had started with the best of intentions, gathering interesting and useful information about UFO phenomena, but then the project changed direction. He suggested I read what he called 'the useful information,' as it was about to be 'sanitized.'
>
> Blue Book was to become a propaganda device, saying that the Air Force had looked extensively into UFO sightings and activity and debunked them. Even though it was classified as a top-secret exercise, it reeked of deception. If any leaks from the factual top-secret operations, such as Red Book, ever became available to the public, then Blue Book would be released – or leaked.
>
> Identifying what was real, contrived, masked, or disinformation became a skill I honed. I learned that the UFO and extraterrestrial reports were locked away, often put in the 'too hard basket,'

and rarely shared. The Air Force had files, the Navy had files, the Army had files, the CIA had files, the Government had files, and NASA had files, but one department or agency seldom communicated with any of the others – not on UFO- and ET-related matters anyhow.

From my experiences with Krll and autopsies on many other EBEs, I found no evidence the species could reproduce or replicate, and no evidence of growth or aging. I believe the EBEs, now referred to as 'Greys,' were cloned or manufactured here on Earth, as well as being based here. I found no suggestion that they were aggressive or violent, yet they appeared to be responsible for a spate of sustained abductions of humans, as well bovine mutilations.

The Greys at the Greada Treaty may not have been identical to Krll. They appeared taller. This prompted me to start referring to Krll and his kind as 'Roswell Greys,' in reference to Krll being rescued from the crash at Roswell in 1947. Even though I spent a year with a live EBE and had access to frozen corpses and autopsy results from many others, over the years, the science of autopsy examinations improved dramatically. I revisited and reviewed the results periodically, particularly after the formation of MITRE Corporation's JASON Society in 1960. They had the best scientists in America, and I was fortunate to have access to some of their results. The more autopsy reports I read, the more I justified my belief that the Roswell Greys were cloned and the crystalline substance in their brain was implanted.

Prior to Red Book, I knew little of the Nordic species. The meeting with them came out of the blue. There was next to nothing available about them in any of the documentation I had access to, or it was inconclusive. I'd read more about another species, termed 'Reptilians,' who supposedly lived underground. They were described as being slightly taller than an average man, yet human-like in body shape. Their name comes from the reptilian-type skin covering their body, which includes scales of varying sizes and color. Their eyes are defined as human shaped, yet catlike and large. They allegedly have twin nostrils at the end of a short stubby muzzle; the mouth is more like a slit, with some teeth-like structures inside. They have three fingers, with an opposing thumb. I noted that the reports of this species sounded very different to the EBEs I studied. I was eager to learn more.

Prior to Frank Reiner's death, we spent many hours discussing the EBE's and the Nordic's craft, as well as speculating about the thousands of other UFO sightings from around the world. All shapes and sizes have been reported; certainly dozens of different craft types, maybe more. Even if only a quarter of these UFO accounts are real, it's still a lot of variances. Frank was not surprised to see such variety. He speculated that the EBE's craft generated an electric or magnetic field, which encased the craft in flight. This meant that the craft never touched any surfaces, such as air or water. Given this type of technology, it would matter little what the shape of the craft was – friction and drag would not be a factor.

Some of the craft described by witnesses were exceptionally large; much larger than any commercial aircraft. Some were small, like we discovered with the majority of the EBE's craft. I speculated that Roswell Greys were not from outer space; their craft were unlikely to be used for long-distance travel. Frank concurred. Where all these other different shaped and sized craft came from, we were unsure.

Back in the mid-1950s, NASA and the space program were in their infancy. You may recall, I was recruited to the NSA from what is now known as NASA. During Project Red Book, I was reacquainted with NASA personnel; specifically those close to the Gemini, Mercury, and Apollo missions, and including several well-known astronauts. These men were willing to talk to me about their experiences, yet reluctant to officially put their name to documents.

According to those I talked with, the NASA missions were monitored by UFOs – between Earth and the Moon and on the Moon itself. Sometimes these craft were at a distance; other times they were close-by, particularly with the earlier missions. Dozens of astronauts reported sightings and many of the alien craft and lights were photographed or recorded. All evidence was kept in-house, with astronauts briefed to remain silent. Just like NSA employees, they were made to sign privacy agreements before joining NASA, so everything was kept from the media – and the Government as well.

There were numerous accounts of UFOs on the Moon, both in the air and on the ground. The first man to walk on the Moon, Neil Armstrong, reported enormous spacecraft lined up on the far side of a nearby crater. He relayed this to mission control. While information was filtered from the public, a number of radio hams listening to the communication heard the exchange.

One of the astronauts I talked with had also walked in the Moon. He restated Armstrong's comments. Knowing I was working with the NSA and investigating UFO reports, he had as many questions to ask me as I had to ask him. He chose a location he felt was 'safe,' meaning not bugged, and we talked for several hours. This was in 1972; only three years after the first manned moon landing.

I was surprised at how much he knew about the formation of the NSA and our subsequent operations, as well as the CIA, the Roswell crash, and the The Group (who he called 'the Majic 12'). He told me that the Roswell incident happened at a time when the intelligence-gathering agencies created by Truman and Forrestal (becoming the CIA and the NSA) were taking over roles previously undertaken by the military and the Government. After World War II, we were also at odds with the Soviets – we'd entered the Cold War. It was paramount that information about the crashed UFO at Roswell, as well as other sightings and reports throughout America were kept secret. The military and the Government knew little of the UFOs and aliens, not knowing if they were hostile or not. He told that President Truman and Secretary of Defense Jim Forrestal formed a committee, comprising very high-level military, academic, and politically powerful people. He was talking of MJ-12.

This new committee, he told me, took control of the Atomic Energy Commission, which had morphed from the Manhattan Project, as well as the Armed Forces Security Agency, which transformed into the NSA, plus the Office of Strategic Services, which became the CIA. The Government passed a National Security Act, allowing, under highly classified auspices, this newly formed committee to have virtually unlimited power to deal with any issues relevant to national security. That's exactly what 'Majic 12' did; they took control, then slowly excluded everybody, including Presidents.

I was surprised at just how much this NASA astronaut knew. In many ways, at that time, he knew more about the NSA and the power of MJ-12 than I did. It made me stop and think. At that point, I'd been with the NSA for more than 20 years and yet, I was not only learning more about UFOs, I was now learning about the organization I worked for and the corporations surrounding them.

From the moment at Muroc Test Center, when I saw those high-powered businessmen alongside President Eisenhower, I realized the role private enterprise was playing in secretive projects and agencies. In my golf games with Harry Truman, he also warned that Eisenhower was letting big business control areas that should have remained under government control, even though the Government was funding the operations. Harry and I knew that, over the years, MJ-12 increased their numbers, with more businessmen involved. Additionally, CIA Directors were always MJ-12 members and, as time went by, the Directors were recruited from the private sector. Allan Dulles, an influential lawyer, joined MJ-12 to become the CIA Deputy Director in 1951, then became Director in 1953. Dulles fine-tuned and transforming the CIA into a powerful clandestine operation. I didn't have much to do with the CIA. As far as I understood, any information the CIA had that was relevant to ETs or UFO was forwarded to the NSA and me anyhow. As the CIA was an extension of MJ-12, it made sense to do it that way.

What the CIA did do well was to instigate cover-ups and disinformation regarding UFO sightings and abduction accounts. Investigate Operation Mockingbird thoroughly – in essence, the operation was for the CIA to influence the media, to push MJ-12's agenda. Officially, Mockingbird ran for around twenty years from the early 1950s. Unofficially, it continued.

Anyone who claimed to have seen a UFO, or implied they were abducted, were ridiculed in the media. In my research, I came across many thousands of reported UFO sightings, as well as human abductions, cow mutilations, and physical evidence of UFOs that had either scorched the earth when landing or created interference to electrical and mechanical equipment while nearby. How the media could ignore or mock all accounts had me perplexed at the time. Yes, some stories were inaccurate, fake, or were allegations made by crackpots, but to dismiss all reports was brash – and, as I would later discover, orchestrated.

I had some access to CIA files and personnel, so I knew snippets about Operation Mockingbird and the concerted efforts to keep all information on UFOs and extraterrestrial activities from not only the public, but also the Government. I also became aware of other procedures, most likely instigated by The Group, of muzzling scientists, researchers, and journalists who dared make this information public. It was 'If no one talks, then no one dies' all over again.

C.J. realizes his father is insinuating that those who talked were killed. C.J. read of dozens of writers and journalists, investigating or writing about UFO themes, who died under mysterious circumstances. His father is suggesting that scientists died as well.

The media manipulation was on a grand scale. I heard that, by 1953, Operation Mockingbird had around 3,000 CIA agents working fulltime, and was a major influence on more than twenty-five newspapers and wire agencies. These networks were run by people with well-known liberal pro-American big business views. Journalists were paid extraordinary amounts of money to publish certain stories or embellish others. Journalists stepping outside the boundaries faced ridicule – or worse. Mockingbird was a political tool, but also served to keep information about ETs and UFOs concealed. Not only were the CIA directly influencing the media, MJ-12 were also becoming closely aligned with the major media owners in the US, particularly while Dulles was CIA Director and Eisenhower the President.

One day on the golf course, Harry told me that Ike had lost control. He said, 'These business people already control NATO and the UN, and they now control most of the military's infrastructure, intelligence, and weapons supplies. And now Eisenhower is going to let them control alien technology as well. God help us.'

I know you've researched the Council on Foreign Relations, The Trilateral Commission, and a host of other collective private enterprise groups. So you understand their agendas to influence governments and global decision-making decisions. Additionally, in America, we now had corporations created specifically to receive government funds to help run MJ-12 projects, particularly the secretive desert projects of the AEC, the CIA, and the NSA. I had you research corporations such as RAND, MITRE, Raytheon, and Bechtel for a reason. They grew very large very quickly – again, for a reason.

They weren't the only companies to benefit from the billions of dollars being spent annually on secret projects and bases; however, each had a close affiliation with MJ-12 and these 'think tank' groups I asked you to research.

'So that's the connection,' says C.J., realizing why his father had him research the groups that seem to be connected with The Round Table. He'd thought this was the reason, but for his father to spell it out justifies C.J.'s (and Emma's) viewpoint.

C.J. has already forgone breakfast, but now must ready to go to Khao San Road. He will need several hours to copy the memoirs, buy Emma a birthday present, have passports and I.D made, and then return to the hotel to catch a cab to the airport.

Even though it's only a short taxi ride to Khao San Road, C.J. continues to read his father's memoirs in the cab.

> Harry Truman and I discussed private enterprise's involvement in the underground bases, and the formation of MITRE Corporation in 1958 to control the scientific development of much of the alien technology. It is no coincidence that Eisenhower, with Vannevar Bush's influence, granted federal funding to MITRE and, in turn, JASON.
>
> The idea behind JASON was to have the best scientists in the country working together, with the highest security clearances – and little-to-no bureaucratic or monetary impediments. Although it was a private enterprise venture, the theory was for these scientists to advise the Government on matters of science and technology. Of course, most of that information stayed in the hands of the corporate world and MJ-12, even though our own government bankrolled it.
>
> Throughout my notes, I will avoid naming the powerful individuals and families behind these organizations. I'm sure you know that Dr. Bush and others worked closely with these people. I urge you to remain secretive, even if you think you know who they are or if you actually discover their identities, which I'm sure you will. IT IS NOT FOR THEIR BENEFIT, BUT YOURS. These are people you don't mess with.

The taxi enters Khao San Road. C.J. closes the memoirs to place in his backpack.

CHAPTER THIRTY

Vendors are all throughout Khao San Rd, selling everything from fake IDs and driver's licenses to bogus university diplomas. It doesn't take much enquiry to find someone who makes up passports, as well as licenses. C.J. is led down a narrow arcade to be whisked behind the scenes of a shop selling fake handbags. He has Emma's photos and details with him. He organizes Australian and US passports, plus a driver's license, under the name of *Emmeline Wiley*.

Ninety minutes later, the passports and license are ready, and his shopping and photocopying is done. In a cab returning to the hotel, C.J. opens up the memoirs.

> Over the years playing golf with Harry, we could see what was unfolding. MITRE and JASON only sought scientists they thought were able to help MJ-12 and private corporations in a military sense or with technology relevant to intelligence gathering. That meant JASON's sponsors included the Department of Defense, DARPA (Defense Advanced Research Projects Agency), the Navy, the Department of Energy, and the US intelligence community. The scientists chosen for JASON were physicists, chemists, mathematicians, and computer scientists. I knew it was unlikely I would be asked to join. On

Harry's advice, I would not have joined anyway.

Around the time of setting up JASON, the corporate powerbrokers who helped get Eisenhower into office, as well as who initiated and controlled the Council on Foreign Relations, The Trilateral Commission, NATO, and the UN, to name a few, donated a large parcel of land to MJ-12. They then built a magnificent and private resort named 'The Country Club,' specifically for MJ-12 members, selected guests, and JASON members.

Getting these busy men together at the one time was becoming increasingly difficult, so The Country Club became the perfect meeting place, usually for two- or three-day sessions. I know this information because I was invited; I attended on five different occasions.

The only access was by air. I was taken by helicopter – always on my own. I was never told specifically where The Country Club was, but I was not blindfolded and the windows of the chopper weren't blacked out. I knew the facility was either in Virginia or Maryland – most likely Maryland.

The Country Club was a magnificent state-of-the-art complex, with its own eighteen-hole golf course. I must point out that each stay was by invitation only. There was an agenda. I would meet with MJ-12 members to discuss the progress of Red Book. They also knew I played golf with Truman, asking informally what we talked about on the golf course. I reiterated we were both 'Missouri boys' and we both loved golf. I did tell them that I phoned Harry every year to wish him 'Merry Christmas' and that, as he was getting older, we played golf together less frequently. They already knew this. They knew everything.

I suspected the CIA were behind the phone tapping, the listening devices, and the monitoring of not only myself, but countless others, including former-President Truman. MJ-12 ran the CIA, as well as the NSA; however, they also created their own internal security group, referred to as 'MAJI.' MAJI staffs were given the highest possible clearances, accountable only to MJ-12. I gathered that Allan Dulles was instrumental in the formation of MAJI, as

> well as transforming the CIA into the culture of surveillance we still see today.
>
> I can't tell you a lot about MAJI, and I doubt there would be much reported on the Internet, but I do know that they worked with the CIA and some of the CIA's projects. As the NSA evolved, MAJI also had access to the NSA's surveillance and intelligence-gathering networks. But it was a one-way-street; no one had access to MAJI's files or systems.
>
> When I was recruited in 1948, I was not told who I worked for. I was told that names and labels meant little, as departments and projects changed frequently. Technically, I joined the AFSA, the forerunner of the NSA, which was initially a science-based cryptology agency. The retrieval of the crashed disks and the live EBE triggered massive growth, with the recruitment of thousands of scientists, like myself, to work in secret desert locations, mostly underground in areas like Area 51.
>
> During the late 1950s, the MJ-12-linked private enterprise manufactured massive nuclear-powered underground boring machines; often expanding deep underground natural cavities already there. I never saw these devices in action, I only saw the results of their work – and it was impressive. The facilities were far more extensive than any citizen could fathom – and they were expanding swiftly, both down and sideways.

The taxi arrives at C.J.'s hotel. He changes clothes, packs, then catches another cab to the airport, memoirs in hand.

> I was not allowed to keep any documentation retaining to Red Book at my home. Every document I worked on was not to leave the bases where I worked. The security risks were deemed too great.
>
> Even though the NSA headquarters was set up in Fort Meade, Maryland, I did not work there. I had the distinct impression that Fort Meade was not only the administrative headquarters, but the home of the rapidly growing intelligence-gathering arm

of the NSA. I'll discuss this branch of the NSA later. What I was working on – UFO and extraterrestrial information – was a separate agenda.

I was based in desert areas – New Mexico, Nevada, Colorado, California, and Arizona – moving regularly from base to base. Sometimes I'd live at the base and other times I'd live nearby and commute. This was my directive, not my choice. I must say it wasn't a great way to live, but I had few options. On the positive side, I was in a privileged position to accumulate and document some incredible information.

There were only a handful of people in government who knew about the alien and UFO projects – most of those, if not all, were MJ-12 members anyway. MJ-12 wanted to know from me if any of the ET species were a threat, whereas private enterprise wanted the technology from these perceived technologically advanced species. With no more crashed craft recovered, however, learning the science of UFOs stagnated. Through the systems MJ-12 had put in place (funded by the Government), they had the best scientists, the best resources, and almost no bureaucratic red tape. Scientific research within America boomed. As private enterprise was running most of the secret bases and their infrastructures, it was only a matter of time before the technological discoveries filtered through to society. Most of America's computer, mechanical, medicinal, and military advances came via the systems set up and controlled by MJ-12.

Companies such as Raytheon, MITRE and RAND Corporations, Bechtel, Halliburton, pharmaceuticals like G. D. Searle & Company, many of the Silicon Valley high-tech companies, and a host of military supply businesses grew dramatically as a result of MJ-12's support and influence.

At the time I was aware of the private enterprise technical advances, as many improvements filtered through to the work and the facilities I would visit.

While my work with Red Book continued, I came to realize that few eyes would read my reports, yet I was still in a privileged position. Every now and then my research would take me in unexpected directions. One such occurrence was a report that Grey aliens might have the ability to use their mind as a weapon – to transmit a powerful frequency capable of injuring or killing humans. I saw no evidence of this power in my dealings with Krll, but other species of Greys have been reported.

I did read an article suggesting Cetacea (whales, porpoises, and dolphins) had a similar ability to the mind-power of the aliens.

During the sixties and seventies, research into Cetacea was in its infancy. Even so, some interesting information, particularly from dolphin research, came to light. I learned that terran dolphins use a form of sonar to navigate, as well as to stun prey and enemies. Dolphins were found to emit powerful and focused ultrasonic bursts from the anterior section of their skulls. These sonar-type bursts stunned larger animals, such as sharks and barracuda, and even killed smaller fish instantly. The military were willing to explore this apparent skill, as well as to train Bottlenose dolphins to perform tasks such as ship and harbor protection, mine detection and clearance, and equipment recovery.

The Navy had set up a dolphin research and training program in 1960 at Point Mugu just north of LA. Called the NMMP (Navy Marine Mammal Program), it was moved to Point Loma in San Diego toward the end of the 1960s to be under the control of the Space and Naval Warfare Systems Center. The program was purely military, it had nothing to do with SeaWorld. I based myself in San Diego during the late 1970s. I kept up with dolphin research until my retirement. And I met your mother in San Diego, do you remember?

I had full access to NMMP's facilities and reports, although, at the time, the Cetacea program did not officially exist. Like so many other projects, the funding came from Government Black Budget allocations. Simply put; the financing was considered 'not in the interest of national security to be disclosed.' This, too, I will discuss later. I think the NMMP's work was declassified in the 1990s but, when I was there, everything was top-secret.

Working with dolphins was fascinating. Trying to compare their brain functions with a Roswell Grey alien proved difficult. As much as I wanted to find similarities, I couldn't. The dolphin's higher learning functions appear to have been honed over a long period of evolution, whereas I believe the EBEs brain, or at least part of it, was artificially implanted or grafted.

Frank Reiner and I felt this artificial crystalline component of the brain was conducive to receiving and sending electrical currents. We felt this was responsible for the EBE's telepathic abilities, as well as for controlling the disks/UFOs. In essence, we thought the crystalline matrices, along with the headbands the EBEs wore, became a part of the crafts' electronic circuitry. Possibly the crafts' sole circuitry system, as nothing was ever found within any of the retrieved disk wreckage to suggest otherwise.

Whether other species used similar technology in their craft, I could only wonder. We had many EBE disks to scrutinize; however, to the best of my knowledge, no other crashed or identifiable UFO types were ever retrieved. All the reports of other UFO types were based on eyewitness or radar accounts only. The different craft had many similarities in flying behavior so I assume they used similar technology, yet noting anything beyond that would be pure speculation.'

The taxi arrives at Bangkok's International Terminal. After C.J. has checked in, he finds a café near his boarding gate to sip coffee and read.

Throughout my twenty-eight years with Red Book, I came to realize that UFO and extraterrestrial descriptions varied considerably so it was difficult to be generic. I could be accurate and detailed with EBEs because I knew them firsthand. I wish I could be as exact with other species, yet I can't. The best I can do is form speculative opinions based on what I have read and correlated from others' eyewitness accounts. Firstly, from the varied UFO craft identified, it's fair to assume that not all of them came from Earth. Frank Reiner suggested that many of these craft came from

> other planets, even other galaxies, and they may not have traveled in conventional terms to get here. Frank had studied the theories of brilliant physicians, such as Nikola Tesla and Albert Einstein, theorizing that other dimensions, outside the three we see, existed.

Although Max Stroheim acknowledges not being a theoretical physicist, he spends several pages discussing 'string theory' and 'superstring theory,' with the notion that many physicists believe that as many as eleven dimensions exist throughout the universe.

> I readily accepted that at least one other dimension exists, understanding that the fourth dimension is time. I acknowledge that other dimensions could also exist. Frank Reiner talked about the idea of the multiverse was talked in the early 1950s. He tried to explain it to me then; however, it was a difficult concept to grasp. Frank suggested that if other species had access to one or more of these extra dimensions, then traveling vast distances through time and space would be possible and probable. Your book *Grains of Sand in the Universe* explored the notion that there are more than five times the number of stars and planets in the universe than grains of sand on Earth. If only a miniscule percentage of these planets had intelligent life, with the capabilities of accessing the technology I've talked about, then the numbers would be enormous. The Earth may have been visited by many species over a great period of time.
>
> It is not unreasonable to assume that some of those species built bases here. Around the world are structures and evidence of advanced civilizations having been on Earth for thousands, if not millions of years. The Nordics said they'd been visiting Earth for thousands of years. I have no reason to doubt that.
>
> Some species may have been and gone; others stayed, which I surmised was the case with whoever manufactured the Roswell Greys. I'd heard rumors there were numerous underground ET bases throughout the world, including in the US, with places like Mt. Shastra and Dulce mentioned frequently. My security

> clearance did not allow admission to these sites, nor did I have the opportunity to talk directly to those with access. The fact that these sites do exist, but I was not given access to them, made me somewhat suspicious.

C.J.'s flight is boarding. He places his father's memoirs in his backpack to walk to the gate. Onboard, C.J. indulges in a business class pre-takeoff glass of champagne, while he reads.

> Many reports talked of Greys, which at first sounded like Krll's kind, but there were differences. Some accounts recounted male and females of the species. If you researched Yellow Book, you would have learned that it is supposedly the alien's history of our universe written by the aliens themselves, as well as their interactions and involvement with Earth's development and evolution. It was purportedly brought to Earth and presented to the US government at Holloman Airforce base, presented by a female Grey in 1964. I was not there, nor do I know anyone who was. I also did not find out about this apparent event until almost ten years after it occurred, which makes me wary of its authenticity.
>
> Whether this really occurred is speculative; however, I found it interesting that the Grey was referred to as a female EBE. Although not many people knew of Krll or the other EBE autopsy results, those in the know would have known that the EBEs researched firsthand were asexual.
>
> The vast majority of witness reports of Grey aliens define individuals matching Krll's description, but some reports describe Greys being similar in height to humans. In some instances, these taller Greys were referred to as 'male' and 'female.' Roswell Greys were only about four feet tall. I remembered that the Greys present at the Greada Treaty appeared taller than Krll. I came to the conclusion that there must be two (or possibly more) kinds of Grey extraterrestrials.
>
> To simplify my cataloging, I began referring to the lankier Greys

as 'Tall Greys.' I had no corpses to inspect or personal close contact with theses Tall Greys. I had to rely on others' accounts. What did seem clear was that the Tall Greys and the Roswell Greys, apart from physical similarities, were very different. If the Tall Greys had genitals, then it may be they were DNA-based. I explored the possibility that the Roswell Greys might be cloned hybrid versions of the Tall Greys, yet this did not fit the science of biology as I knew it. It's like trying to crossbreed an animal with a plant. One day it might be done but, for now, it's a concept I can't comprehend. All I can is guess that the Tall Greys may have produced the smaller RNA-based Roswell Greys, speculating that the EBEs were partial hybrids and partly artificially produced.

I mentioned earlier another species, the 'Reptilians.' I've read and heard suggestions that this species also live underground. Some reports claimed the Tall Greys and the Reptilians are aligned, with the Reptilians responsible for producing the Roswell Greys. Again, these are others' suppositions. They may be right; however I don't have enough accurate data to be sure. What I can be certain is the species we referred to as 'Nordics' were not aligned with the Greys or Reptilians. The two Nordic individuals at Muroc Test Center warned us about the Greys, offering to help us with 'The Grey Problem.' After that meeting, I wished to find out as much as I could about the Nordic species.

C.J. is so engrossed in his father's writings that he barely notices the plane taking off.

CHAPTER THIRTY-ONE

Red Book gave me unprecedented access to witness's testimonies and accounts. I came to the conclusion that the Nordics did not live in bases here on Earth; they actually lived, as well as traveled, in another dimension. Again, this is a difficult concept to fathom, but it is what I determined. Many witness reports described religious or angelic interactions. You know I am not a religious man, although I'm respectful of those who are. I could see where the likenesses arose. The Nordic men I saw – I will call them 'men' as they looked human – were almost like biblical replications of Jesus Christ, without the beards. Witnesses claimed to have seen the Nordics appear like angels, they were often described as having an aura or glowing light around their body and head. The word 'halo' was sometimes used.

Although I dismissed some of the Nordic encounter reports as being contrived or embellished, the believable accounts I read conveyed similar experiences. None recalled the Nordics as being aggressive or threatening; in fact, it was the opposite – the experiences were enlightening. At Muroc, I'd felt the same. I thought about this afterward. The Nordics did not appear to have a selfish agenda; they simply wanted us to quit nuclear weapons research and production and they, in-turn, would help us with

'The Grey Problem.' This appeared to be for our benefit, not theirs. Maybe they were looking out for our best interests?

Until the end of WWII, the world had not seen nuclear weapons. Other intelligent life forms had been visiting our planet for thousands, if not millions of years with the developing human species. With the explosion of atomic bombs, their interaction with humans became more pressing.

President Eisenhower's rejection of the Nordics offer to forge a treaty with the Greys was a big mistake. The Greada Treaty was a mockery. The Tall Greys, using the Roswell Greys, continued abducting and experimenting on humans unabated, as well as mutilating cows and other animals. I think the two events are unrelated. I'll discuss the animal excisions first. Reports worldwide suggested that mostly cows were mutilated, but also targeted were horses, sheep, goats, pigs, rabbits, cats, dogs, bison, elk, and deer. In several instances sea animals, including whales, had been found dumped inland, nowhere near water.

Most evidence, however, is of cows being beamed up to a craft, mutilated, and returned dead. In the 1970s, I read reports indicating that thousands, possibly tens of thousands, of cows were mutilated within the United States alone. This phenomenon appeared to be occurring globally and systematically.

Eyewitnesses attested to seeing a live animal being lifted high in the air to a bright light in the sky, presumably a UFO. The dead animal is then returned to roughly the same area they were taken from, with the bodies having bloodless excisions of ears, eyeballs, jaw flesh, tongue, lymph nodes, genitals, and rectums. I know that the Roswell Greys used a genetic slurry-like mix to rub into their skin as nutrition. There might be genetic material in these removed body parts that was ideal for the EBEs' (or other Greys') nutritional needs but, again, this is speculative.

From my research, I found no evidence to suggest that humans abducted and returned by the Greys had body parts removed. The standard abduction accounts by Greys had the person or persons beamed up to a disk, with the victims explaining feelings of weightlessness and helplessness. Arriving inside the craft, abductees told of being in a paralyzed state, while one or more Grey aliens performed medical-style procedures on them. They were then beamed back to where they were taken, seemingly unharmed, with memories of the experience either masked or obscured. Most abductees had dreams of the experience, often recalling the full details of the event during hypnosis. Many abductees reported being abducted on more than one occasion.

Some abductees had a small, metallic-like device surgically inserted. The position of these varied between victims. Some of the devices, when discovered, usually by x-ray, were removed by doctors; however, some were inserted in areas, such as near the spinal column or the brain, which were deemed too dangerous to be surgically removed. The reasoning for the insertion of these devices is unknown. My belief is that it is a tracking and monitoring strategy. Although metallic in structure, the devices did not react with the victim's body. Normally, in these instances, the body's immune system attempts to eject foreign objects, but this was not the case with these devices. The devices tended to be integrated into the victim's body, with no signs of rejection and little-to-no side effects.

I was of the opinion that the Greys purpose for abducting humans was to retrieve genetic information. Not all abductees were inserted with the metallic-like devices, so I would assume the Greys earmarked some individuals for further investigation and monitoring, while leaving others alone. What the Greys did with this genetic information is uncertain, but as the Roswell Greys were not DNA-based entities, I would assume it was not for them. As I suspected, the EBEs acted as gatherers or collectors. Further speculation is fruitless, as I don't have enough concrete evidence to substantiate any theories I may have entertained. I want you to write a book; however, I don't want you to stray from the truth. I had you research the projects, corporations, and various private think-tank organizations for a reason: to understand the complexities and the events that have contributed to the agencies and processes in place today.

My role during my time with the NSA, or what I thought was the NSA, was specialized. I saw the growth and directional changes but it wasn't until the last years of my career that I came to understand just how diverse and large the organization had become. I'm certain the scientific processes put in place by MJ-12 contributed to the birth of the computer and Internet era – and who better to manipulate and monitor the new technology, but MJ-12 and their affiliated corporate powerbrokers. MITRE Corporation ran computer systems, with the NSA expanding operations rapidly – and globally. I read with interest the revelations of Edward Snowden. I was unsurprised to learn of the NSA's global surveillance capabilities. The clandestine operations of the previous fifty or sixty years were perfectly suited for the NSA to adopt and expand.

The NSA was often referred to as 'No Such Agency.' I'm still surprised at just how little media and government attention the NSA has received over the years. This is not a coincidence; it is by design. It has become increasingly evident that the efforts of the NSA and CIA, with the additional help of projects like Blue Book and Operation Mockingbird, helped to keep information about UFOs and aliens from the general public. Not only was the media manipulated to ridicule all things 'extraterrestrial,' but the Government was also kept in the dark, particularly after the Eisenhower Administration left office. Also understand that the individuals and families controlling most of the world's press were either affiliated directly with MJ-12 members or were involved in societies such as the Bilderbergs, The Trilateral Commission, and the Council on Foreign Relations. It is no wonder why the media reacted the way they did.

As the NSA expanded to become more surveillance oriented, the methods they used to cover up UFO and extraterrestrial information were employed to conceal their foreign intelligence and counterintelligence operations.

Edward Snowden was not the first to blow the whistle on some of the NSA's operations. But by using WikiLeaks, and with Snowden fleeing the United States, they were able to bypass some of the systems MJ-12 and others had carefully orchestrated to keep their secrets covered up. I remember Barack Obama holding a press conference, justifying the NSA's hacking into global phone and Internet systems, using the words 'in the interest of national security' regularly. Even when it was revealed that the NSA had been caught hacking into German Chancellor Angela Merkel's phone, as well as other European and world dignitaries, Obama used this justification as an excuse.

Let me blunt, son. The NSA is classified as 'independent.' Yes, it is funded predominately by government funds; however, I would imagine the President, whether it is Obama, Clinton, Bush, or Trump, knows very little about the true function and processes of the NSA. There is one exception to this statement. That is, if the President is not a member or affiliate of MJ-12 or its subsidiaries. In most, if not all, instances the Presidents have been.

This is not the forum for political commentary, but for your benefit only, son. Know that even someone like Donald Trump, who, as a presidential candidate campaigned as being an 'outsider,' was far from what he claimed. Donald Trump is deeply entrenched in most of these organizations I refer. When Trump became President he, just like those before him, surrounded himself with fellow members of the organizations I've been writing about.

Budget allocations for the NSA, CIA, DIA, and the like would be increased. I doubt future Administrations will deviate from this course, with the threat of national security issues their justification.

I saw a TV interview where Trump said that Edward Snowden was a spy, saying words to the effect that Snowden should be executed immediately. Snowden is not a spy. This is the type of bigotry and bullying you may encounter. Be prepared.

From my understanding, Edward Snowden, at the time of the disclosures, was not an NSA employee. He was employed by NSA contractor Booz Allen Hamilton, a private company. It begs the question: What is a private corporation doing with confidential

information and data on world leaders, other private corporations, and individuals from around the world, as well as the US?
Of course, this question has never been addressed. The media's attention turned on Edward Snowden and where this 'alleged spy' had fled to. It is an old political ploy when trying to avoid answering a question. The politician turns the blowtorch onto a similar or related subject, a subject they are prepared to discuss or make political mileage from. I had never heard of Edward Snowden before his whistleblowing allegations; however, I would be amazed if dozens, hundreds, or possibly thousands of people who have had access to the information he had would have the courage to come forward like Snowden did.'

The lights in the cabin dim. C.J. turns on his reading light; he is nearing the end of his father's writings.

By now, you must have some sense of how the world really works. With that said, I don't want you to write about the current political landscape. Just know that most of the wars and global conflicts are not what they seem. Usually, they are a ruse or an excuse for an ulterior motive – the 'justification' to which I refer. Governments employ the soldiers and troops who fight the wars and, ultimately, it's the Government making the decision to go to war. However, they have outsourced most of the technical and infrastructure analyses that contribute so much to the decision-making. Private enterprise supplies the vast majority of intelligence information from around the world, handling weapons technology and manufacturing, and private enterprise advises the Government whether or not to go to war. So it isn't just countries making the decisions to go to war; it is conglomerations: NATO, the United Nations, agencies such as the DIA, NSA, CIA, and AEC; corporations like RAND, MITRE; Bechtel and Raytheon; military supply, infrastructure, and support businesses; and world banking and oil companies. They are as much a part of the war-machine as any individual country or government.

Without conflict, most of these organizations would not exist – and without these organizations, most global conflict would not exist.

This is relevant to past and recent events as well as so-called conflicts – and will continue to be so. The systems and processes put in place in the 1940s, '50s, '60s, and beyond have not abated. If anything, they have become stronger and even more clandestine. The scale of deception is intricate and saturating.

What you read in the media and what is the truth are often poles apart. You will no doubt realize this.

I know your research has uncovered much. I'd expect you to find out more than what I know, but I have a hint: the same people who belong to the Council on Foreign Affairs, the Bilderbergs, NATO, and The Trilateral Commission, to name a few, also sit on the boards of the MITRE and RAND Corporations, and a host of private companies associated with weapons manufacturing and supply, as well as so-called government contracts with agencies such as the NSA, CIA, DIA, and others. Some of these same people have also been given the highest positions within the Government. Note that most were appointed to government roles, not elected. I knew men who were top-level government officials while also sitting on the boards of these corporations and private companies. They were also members of one or more secret global organizations. Many of the names you will recognize; however, as I keep stating, do not, under any circumstances, name these people.

I want your book to educate the general public about the truth of events, not to expose individuals or families. It is a can of worms well left alone. Also recognize that not all the people involved in secret organizations, agencies, and societies are necessarily evil. Much good frequently comes from these collective 'think tanks' and the world often benefits. Life is far too complicated to place some things in a 'good box' and others in a 'bad.' To expose these people would have repercussions too great to consider. Know who

> they are and why they do what they do, but keep that information to yourself.
>
> You'll need to go into hiding. Only be after the book is published will you be safe. At that point, do not talk with the press. You'll need to fly under the radar until the book is distributed. Money for you will not be an issue. I have anticipated you will not be able to return to the US in the short-term. Contact Joe and his lawyers in Bangkok, but only after you have written the book. They have been instructed on what to do.

C.J. turns the page to see he is about to read the last page of his father's memoirs. He has a lump in his throat.

> I have talked about six secrets. Of course, there are many more, but these key secrets are:
>
> 1. UFOs and extraterrestrials do exist. Although the Government has known about their presence since the late 1940s, that information, and the subsequent technology, was kept hidden – only to be known by a select few.
>
> 2. There is a network of deep underground bases throughout the USA. They are mostly run by private enterprise, yet are funded by the Government.
>
> 3. The USA's nuclear program is fully privatized. After the formation of the AEC in 1946, Government funds were given to private companies who, in turn, control all nuclear development, technology, and supplies.
>
> 4. The media has helped to manipulate the general public. Many media owners and infrastructures are part of the systems and processes that run these secretive projects.
>
> 5. Most wars and conflicts are contrived. They are planned and instigated not by governments, but the people and companies behind governments (understanding that many of the Government's highest-ranking officials now come from this system anyway).
>
> 6. The people and companies I have mentioned are part of a well-

orchestrated network of think tanks and organizations, not just within the USA, but globally.

A small minority controls the majority; their influences saturate world affairs.

If my years with the NSA have taught me anything, it is that nothing is simple and rarely are things as they first appear. To deceive the general public like they have requires a complex web of integral components – and the public has been deceived. As a nation, we need structure and we need guidance, but we also deserve to know the truth. That is the least of what we should demand.

I know how big this story is and how deep it goes. I have used the analogy that it is like digging a hole in the sand; the more you dig, the more the sides of the hole will collapse. Reading this should have given you some clarity and structure but, in many respects, you have only just scratched the surface. Now it's time to start writing the book. Don't become engulfed, research further where you feel you need to; however, take time to reflect.

If I have one regret in my working life, it is that I didn't, as your mother would say, 'stop to smell the roses.'

I can only imagine how you are dealing with all this information and the consequent effect it is having on your life. I have entrusted you with a huge responsibility. I was not prepared to gamble on my family's wellbeing while I was alive. It is with a heavy heart that I involve you, but I am sure you have come to realize the importance of sharing the truth with the world.

I am at total peace knowing you are in charge of such a responsibility.

I love you, I trust you, and I am so very proud of you.

I will always be with you. Always.

C.J. turns off his reading light. He sits in the dark, tears streaming down his face.

CHAPTER THIRTY-TWO

In C.J.'s absence, Emma spent her time researching Ellis Buckman and who he was working for. She eagerly awaits C.J. arrival, sitting in a coffee shop they'd prearranged to meet. C.J. sent a coded message to say he has landed back in Brisbane.

C.J.'s taxi pulls up at the curb. Emma races outside to hug him, gripping him tightly. 'I've missed you so much.'

They have so much to discuss, the words can't come quickly enough.

They venture inside to sit in a quiet corner.

'How are you?'

'I've missed you—'

'I have so much to tell you—'

'You go first.'

'No, after you—'

'You're not going to believe—'

Emma is first to insist. 'So, what did you find? What did your father leave you?'

'Firstly, at the bank I found another list. You said my father might want me to do some research. You were right. I have the list here:'

> FAMOUS SCIENTISTS, IN RELATION TO MJ-12:
> ROBERT OPPENHEIMER, ALBERT EINSTEIN, EDWARD

TELLER, VANNEVAR BUSH, JOHN VON NEUMANN, and WERNHER VON BRAUN. (Realize these men were administrators, as well as scientists. Also look at the era when most of the secret organizations and projects were set up.)
DR. WILLIAM REICH, DR. FRANK REINER, and CAPTAIN EDWARD RUPPELT.
COMPANIES/CORPORATIONS: RAND, MITRE, RAYTHEON, and BECHTEL.
DWIGHT EISENHOWER (NATO and THE COUNCIL ON FOREIGN RELATIONS).
After you have researched these, you will easily solve my puzzle. Go to Uncle Joe's apartment at Jomtien Beach to research. He'll let you stay as long as you need.
THE FINAL PUZZLE: FROM UNCLE JOE'S APARTMENT BLOCK, TAKE THIS MANY MEASURED PACES ALONG THE STREET TO THE RIGHT: THE YEAR I LAST TOOK YOU TO SEAWORLD MINUS THE YEAR ALBERT EINSTEIN AND ROBERT OPPENHEIMER WROTE THE DOCUMENT 'RELATIONSHIPS WITH INHABITANTS OF CELESTIAL BODIES.' INSIDE THAT BUILDING IS A LOCKER. THE LOCKER NUMBER, IN TELPHONE NUMERIC FORM, IS FOR A THREE-LETTER ACRONYM: A HIGHER-LEARNING PLACE LINKED TO VANNEVAR BUSH, MITRE, RAYTHEON, AND THE MANHATTAN PROJECT.
When you find the location, ask for Ploy. Say you are Max's son and give the locker number. Take a medium-sized magnet with you. Remember that there is no such thing as empty space, you'll be drawn to the answers.
Good luck, son.

'So you need to solve this riddle to take you to this locker near your Uncle Joe's apartment at Jomtien Beach?' says Emma.

'I solved the riddle – I cut corners and went to Jomtien Beach.'

'So you found the locker?'

'I did.'

'Oh my God. What did you find?'

'At first the locker appeared empty, but the reason for the magnet was to pull out a false metal panel at the back,' says C.J., before removing Emma's bound copy of Max Stroheim's memoirs. 'And this is what I found.' With a broad smile, he hands the papers to Emma. 'This is what we've been waiting for: my father's complete memoirs.'

Emma is gob-smacked, staring at the opening page.

'This is your copy. I read them in Bangkok and on the flight over. They reveal everything, but I don't want to talk about specifics, not just yet anyway. I want you to read them first. This is your journey, too.'

Emma wraps her arms around C.J., knowing the significance of what he just said. She can't wait to begin reading.

'I've booked us a hotel just around the corner for tonight. Then, in the morning, we can catch a bus to Noosa Heads.'

Before leaving to Bangkok, they'd discussed where they would go after Brisbane. Emma holidayed in Noosa with her parents, and loved it – and it's only two hours by bus from Brisbane.

C.J. says, 'I have all the things on my father's newest list to research. Noosa Heads sounds like the perfect place to buckle down – and a great place for you to read my father's memoirs.'

'Hey, I'm not waiting till we get to Noosa! You look beat anyway. Why don't you shower and take a nap and I'll start reading?'

'Sounds good, but first I'm dying to hear what you found out about Ellis Buckman.'

'Firstly, Ellis Buckman *is* his real name. he was born in LA in 1986. He had a few misdemeanors as a teenager – petty stuff really. At the age of fifteen, he left home to live with his mother's brother. His uncle became his legal guardian – and here's the kicker – his uncle's name is Nathaniel Goldberg – the name on Buckman's credit card, as well as the rental car booking.'

'No way.'

'You see, Goldberg was a wealthy and very powerful man. He was a former Yale University graduate and reputed to be active in an old secret society within Yale called Skull and Bones. Skull and Bones has links with the Illuminati and has all sorts of pagan and secret society rituals. They are highly selective in who they choose as members; it's a breeding ground for some of the most influential people in America. Their members are a who's who of America's rich and famous. I'm an Aussie, yet even I've heard of most of these names. Anyhow, Nathaniel Goldberg was also a Freemason and, reportedly, a member of The Trilateral Commission, as well as the Council on Foreign Relations.

We know Buckman worked at Yale for a year. I presume Goldberg used his contacts to get his nephew the job, with the hope of him being accepted as a student. I guess the rest you know, but this you wouldn't. Buckman's uncle was in a business partnership with another man, as well as sitting on the board of two corporations with the same man. Those corporations were RAND and MITRE – and the business partner and fellow board member was Ely Hamermesh – the father of none other than Ben Hamermesh.'

'Wow, you have been busy. This is valuable stuff, Emma.'

'However, there's more,' she reveals, opening her computer tablet to check her notes. 'I stumbled across a 2010 newspaper article from a small, independent newspaper in Willington, Delaware. The article asserts Hamermesh and Buckman were questioned by police in relation to the death of a man, Jack Wheeler. Both men were reported as, and I quote: "persons of interest in the death of prominent lawyer Jack Wheeler." Wheeler was an important man, a West Point and Harvard graduate, an official on the Securities and Exchange Commission, a Presidential Aide in not one, but *three* Republican Administrations – Ronald Reagan, George Bush senior, and then George W. He happened to be a member of the Council on Foreign Relations and, at the time of his death, he was a consultant for none other than MITRE Corporation.

'Jack Wheeler was murdered near his law practice and home in Delaware and placed in a dumpster. He was consequently dumped at a nearby landfill. His body was always going to be found. If this was a professional hit, then someone wanted the body to be found. A message was being sent.

'Apparently, Wheeler was becoming concerned at some of this MITRE's projects and direction. It sounds like he was about to blow the whistle. Obviously, he did not get the opportunity.

'"But why would the police want to talk with Buckman and Hamermesh?" you might ask. Even if the two men were involved in some way, and they weren't formally charged, the perplexing issue is that although Hamermesh worked in Virginia at the time, near Delaware, while Ellis Buckman was based in Los Angeles.'

'When was he killed?'

'Just after Christmas in 2010.'

'2010? I knew Ellis then. After Christmas, you say? I'm sure Ellis spent that Christmas over east with his Uncle and Aunt in Maryland.'

'Guess where Nathaniel Goldberg and Ely Hamermesh live?'

'Maryland?'

'Bingo. I also have some information on Ben Hamermesh. You know how you said he was a Vice President, probably of a small construction company? Well he's a VP alright, but for one of the largest construction and engineering companies on the planet – it's on your father's list.

'Hamermesh's resume is pretty impressive. He went to Yale, then scored a plum job straight out of uni with another company on your father's list, RAND Corporation. He left RAND to become a junior executive with BAE Systems, who produce combat vehicles, artillery, naval guns, missile launchers, and precision munitions. They employ more than a hundred thousand people. Their annual revenue is larger than many countries' GDP. BAE is one of the largest military suppliers in the world – and it'll come as no surprise that they're linked with both RAND and MITRE Corporations. These corporations had a close working relationship with another defense contractor, United Defense Industries. You won't be shocked to learn that United Defense Industries were taken over by BAE Systems in 2005. And you'll be less surprised to learn that Ben Hamermesh joined BAE Systems at the same time.

'Apart from the newspaper article from Delaware, I couldn't find any other immediate connection between Hamermesh and Buckman. They appeared to move in similar circles, particularly with these think tank and Illuminati-type organizations.'

At the hotel C.J. slides under the bedcovers, falling asleep the moment his head hits the pillow.

While C.J. sleeps, Emma begins reading Dr. Max Stroheim's memoirs.

Seven hours later, C.J. opens his eyes to see Emma sitting beside him, reading.

Seeing C.J. stir, she places the memoirs on the bedside table to teasingly whisper, 'Hello there, sleepy.'

'What time is it?'

'Nearly midnight.'

Conversation is the last thing on Emma's mind. She slips under the covers, removes her clothes, and cuddles up to an obliging C.J.

They fall asleep locked as one.

C.J. wakes first. The bedside clock reads: 5:30 a.m. He snuggles back up against Emma's warm body.

Before breakfast, C.J. hands Emma her new passport and ID. They pack and head to the bus depot.

On the bus to Noosa, Emma reveals she is about halfway through reading C.J.'s father's memoirs.

'I know you don't want to discuss it until I've finished, but C.J. – wow! You must be so excited to have learned all this about your dad?'

'I am.'

'I'll try to finish the memoirs in the next day or so, then we can research the names and corporations on his newest list together.'

'Sounds like a plan. I can start looking into the famous scientists on Dad's list – and they ARE all very famous. Robert Oppenheimer is known as *the father of the atomic bomb*; Edward Teller is *the father of the hydrogen bomb*; and we've read about Vannevar Bush already. I know John von Neumann was a nuclear physicist involved in thermonuclear reactions and the hydrogen bomb; Werner Von Braun is known as *the father of rocket science*; and everyone on the planet has heard of Albert Einstein. Obviously, they are connected.'

'You can start researching now if you like; I'm keen to keep reading your dad's memoirs anyhow.' Emma opens her ripped handbag, now with tape covering the rip, to remove the memoirs.

The bus arrives at Noosa Heads. Emma has booked an exquisite apartment on the hill overlooking the trendy shopping strip. The views are breathtaking. They stand out on the balcony to absorb the scenery; panoramic views of sparkling ocean, coastline, hinterland, and rainforest.

'A very good choice, Emma Burgess,' says C.J., before wrapping his arms around Emma. 'I know you're keen to keep reading, but let's explore first – and maybe pick up a few supplies?'

'Sure.'

C.J. and Emma walk hand in hand along the beach. Emma points out a beachfront restaurant. 'Mum loved this restaurant. We had breakfast there three mornings in a row.'

'I might duck in and see if we can make a booking for tomorrow morning,' says C.J.

'I don't think you need to book.'

'I'll check anyway. You keep walking; I won't be long – I'll catch you up.'

C.J. and Emma buy groceries and bottles of wine to return to the apartment. With a glass of wine each, they sit on the balcony. The sun begins to set behind the hinterland hills, C.J. assembles a platter of cheese and dips, topping up their glasses. He joins Emma to watch the remarkable sunset.

'You know, I only have a dozen or so more pages to go' says Emma. 'I should be finished tomorrow, then I can help with your research.'

C.J. knows its Emma's birthday tomorrow. He has plans, but says nothing.

The next morning, C.J. and Emma rise early. C.J. suggests walking on the beach, followed by breakfast, but doesn't mention her birthday.

C.J. leads her to the restaurant her family loved. A table right next to the beach features a vase brimming with flowers and two filled glasses of champagne. C.J. walks her straight to that table.

'Happy birthday, Emma Burgess,' he says, before kissing her tenderly.

C.J. opens his backpack to remove two gift-wrapped presents. The first is a bottle of perfume he purchased at the duty free shop at Brisbane's International Airport.

'The girl at the counter said this was their best perfume.'

Emma sprays perfume on her wrist to smell. 'She has good taste; it's beautiful. Thank you.'

Emma then unwraps a handbag. It's almost identical to her ripped bag. She is stunned at C.J.'s thoughtfulness.

'Wow, this is perfect. I love it.' She leans across to kiss him.

C.J. confesses that the handbag is a copy. He vows to buy Emma the 'real McCoy' when he can. He then hands Emma a credit card in the name of *Chad Jacobson*.

What's this?'

'My new credit card. While I was at the bank in Bangkok, I took your Emmeline Wiley details and signature and opened a joint account. I know you can't use your own credit card, so I thought you'd appreciate…'

'So I'm a kept woman?' interrupts Emma jokingly.

'You might like to buy some new clothes for your birthday. There seem to be some nice boutiques nearby. Please use it; don't be shy – and don't ask permission. The password is five-seven-nine-one.'

C.J. returns to the apartment. Emma buys herself a beautiful 'birthday outfit'. She will wear it tonight – C.J. has booked another oceanfront restaurant for dinner.

Although C.J. implored Emma to be self-indulgent on her birthday, she is anxious to finish the memoirs. She returns to the apartment to read, while C.J. researches.

CHAPTER THIRTY-THREE

Mid-afternoon, Emma turns to C.J. with tears flowing down her flushed cheeks. She places the papers down to wrap her arms around C.J.

When she finally breaks the embrace, she says, 'My God, C.J., it's no wonder your father kept this information secret, but wow, it must have been so hard to keep it to himself. To live with all of this knowledge – and not be able to share it. He was an amazing man.'

'I know.'

C.J. opens a bottle of French champagne. 'It looks like we have a double celebration. We've both discovered the truth behind my father's career – and it's your birthday. I think it's time to party!'

Readying for dinner, Emma steps from the bedroom wearing her new dress and shoes.

C.J.'s jaw drops. 'You look absolutely stunning.'

At sunset, they walk down to the restaurant. Their table overlooks the beach. The view outside is spectacular but C.J. only has eyes for Emma.

I know the past few weeks and months have been a roller coaster. At times, it's been downright dangerous but, Emma, in finding you I found a beautiful intelligent woman, and someone I trust implicitly. Every day you amaze me. Happy birthday.'

The next morning C.J. and Emma sleep in. They head to the beach for an invigorating swim.

Returning to the apartment, Emma says, 'Okay C.J., we had a late night last night. It's time to get to work. What do you want me to do?'

'I've researched Robert Oppenheimer and Albert Einstein – and I must say I was surprised to learn they were involved in some of MJ-12's most secret projects, particularly Oppenheimer. He may have even been an MJ-12 member at one time. Either way, Oppenheimer and Vannevar Bush were close, working side-by-side on a number of projects, including the Manhattan Project.

'It would seem that both Oppenheimer and Einstein were privy to crashed UFO disks debris, even before the Roswell crash in 1947. Remember how my father mentioned that Albert Einstein and Robert Oppenheimer wrote a document called "Relationships with Inhabitants of Celestial Bodies"? I've downloaded it for you to read. There's lots of legal jargon, so your expertise as a lawyer would be greatly appreciated.'

'I can't wait.'

'If you read it out loud, I'll also point out something really interesting at the end of the paper.'

C.J. plugs his USB memory stick into Emma's computer.

She opens the file in question.

The first things she's sees is the title *Relationships with Inhabitants of Celestial Bodies* and the date of the paper's draft: June 1947.

'So this was written in June 1947?'

'Yes, just a month *before* the Roswell incident. They intended to give the document to the Government, with the President being Harry S. Truman, and then it was to be forwarded to the United Nations. I'll let you read it, then I'll explain the note at the end of the document.'

'Okay.'

> Relationships with extraterrestrial men, presents no basically new problem from the standpoint of international law; but the possibility of confronting intelligent beings that do not belong to the human race would bring up problems whose solution it is difficult to conceive.

'Oh wow, this is talking about extraterrestrials. I'll continue.'

> In principle, there is no difficulty in accepting the possibility of coming to an understanding with them, and of establishing all kinds of relationships. The difficulty lies in trying to establish the principles on which these relationships should be based. In the first place, it would be necessary to establish communication with them through some language or other and, afterward, as a first condition for all intelligence, that they should have a psychology similar to that of men.
>
> At any rate, international law should make place for a new law on a different basis, and it might be called 'Law Among Planetary Peoples.' Obviously, the idea of revolutionizing international law to the point where it would be capable of coping with new situations would compel us to make a change in its structure, a change so basic that it would no longer be international law, that is to say, as it is conceived today, but something altogether different, so that it could no longer bear the same name.

'So Einstein and Oppenheimer are talking of not just having international law, but an intergalactic law. Oh boy, I'd love some of my legal colleagues to see this. Sorry, I'll try not to make too many comments.'

'Please do. I've read the papers several times. I'm fascinated to get your take on it.'

'Okay.'

> If these intelligent beings were in possession of a more or less culture, and a more or less perfect political organization, they would have an absolute right to be recognized as independent and sovereign peoples, we would have to come to an agreement with them to establish the legal regulations upon which future relationships should be based, and it would be necessary to accept many of their principles.
>
> Finally, if they should reject all peaceful cooperation and become an imminent threat to the Earth, we would have the right to legitimate defense, but only insofar as would be necessary to annul this danger. Another possibility may exist, that a species of *Homo sapiens* might have established themselves as an independent

> nation on another celestial body in our solar system and evolved culturally independently from ours. Obviously, this possibility depends on many circumstances, whose conditions cannot yet be foreseen. However, we can make a study of the basis on which such a thing might have occurred.

'So, they are talking about laws covering aliens coming to Earth and settling here, as well as covering us doing the same on another planet or planets sometime in the future. Wow, this is incredible stuff. I'll keep going.'

> In the first place, living conditions on these bodies; let's say the Moon, or the planet Mars, would have to be such as to permit a stable, and to a certain extent, independent life, from an economic standpoint.
>
> Much has been speculated about the possibilities for life existing outside of our atmosphere and beyond, always hypothetically, and there are those who go so far as to give formulas for the creation of an artificial atmosphere on the Moon, which undoubtedly have a certain scientific foundation, and which may one day come to light. Let's assume that magnesium silicates on the Moon may exist and contain up to 13 per cent water. Using energy and machines brought to the Moon, perhaps from a space station, the rocks could be broken up, pulverized, and then backed to drive off the water of crystallization. This could be collected and then decomposed into hydrogen and oxygen, using an electric current or the short wave radiation of the Sun. The oxygen could be used for breathing purposes; the hydrogen might be used as a fuel. In any case, if no existence is possible on celestial bodies, except for enterprises for the exploration of their natural riches, with a continuous interchange of the men who work on them, unable to establish themselves there indefinitely and be able to live isolated life, independence will never take place.
>
> Now we come to the problem of determining what to do if the inhabitants of celestial bodies, or Extraterrestrial Biological Entities (EBEs) desire to settle here.

'Oh C.J., they use the term "EBE." This is amazing.'

'And this is before Krll,' reiterates C.J. 'I know my father used the term "EBE" to describe Krll. He started at S-4 over a year after the Einstein-Oppenheimer paper was written, so Einstein and Oppenheimer must have known about the small Greys, as well as the term "EBE", before the Roswell crash. Very few people would have been privy to this information.'

> If they are politically organized and possess a certain culture similar to our own, they may be recognized as independent people. They could consider what degree of development would be required on Earth for colonizing. If they consider our culture to be devoid of political unity, they would have the right to colonize. Of course, this colonization cannot be conducted on classic lines. A superior form of colonizing will have to be conceived, that could be a kind of tutelage, possibly through the tacit approval of the United Nations.

'When was the UN formed?'

'Late 1945, I think, so this document was less than a year later.'

> But, would the United Nations legally have the right of allowing such tutelage over us in such a fashion?

'I think "tutelage" means "control".'

> Although the United Nations is an international organization, there is no doubt that it would have no right of tutelage, since its domain does not extend beyond relationships between its members. It would have the right to intervene only if the relationships or a member nation with a celestial body affected. Another member nation with an extraterrestrial people is beyond the domain of the United Nations. But if these relationships entailed a conflict with another member nation, the United Nations would have the right to intervene.
>
> If the United Nations were a supra-national organization, it would have competency to deal with all problems related to extraterrestrial peoples.

'What they are recommending is for the United Nations to be given powers to arbitrate in conflicts outside of Earth, so they would be the chosen body to represent Earth. I'll continue.'

Of course, even though it is merely an international organization, it could have this competence if its member states would be willing to recognize it.

It is difficult to predict what the attitude of international law will be with regard to the occupation by celestial peoples of certain locations on our planet, but the only thing that can be foreseen is that there will be a profound change in traditional concepts. We cannot exclude the possibility that a species of extraterrestrial people more advanced technologically and economically may take upon itself the right to occupy another celestial body.

How, then, would this occupation come about?

The idea of exploitation by one celestial state would be rejected; they may think it would be advisable to grant it to all others capable of reaching another celestial body. But this would be to maintain a situation of privilege for these states. The division of a celestial body into zones and the distribution of them among other celestial states. This would present the problem of distribution. Moreover, other celestial states would be deprived of the possibility of owning an area, or if they were granted one it would involve complicated operations. Indivisible co-sovereignty, giving each celestial state the right to make whatever use is most convenient to its interests, independently of the others. This would create a situation of anarchy, as the strongest one would win out in the end.

A moral entity?

The most feasible solution it seems would be this one: submit an agreement providing for the peaceful absorption of a celestial race or species in such a manner that our culture would remain intact with guarantees that their presence not be revealed. Actually, we do not believe it necessary to go that far. It would merely be a matter of internationalizing celestial peoples and creating an international treaty instrument preventing exploitation of all nations belonging to the United Nations. Occupation by states here on Earth, which has lost all interest for international law, since there were no more *res nullius* territories, is beginning to

> regain all its importance in cosmic international law. Occupation consist in the appropriation by a state of *res nullius*.

'*Res nullius* is a legal term meaning a thing that does not have an owner, like a yacht abandoned at sea or birds in the sky.'

> Until the last century occupation was the normal means of acquiring sovereignty over territories, when explorations made possible the discovery of new regions, either inhabited or in an elementary state of civilization. The imperialist expansion of the states came to an end with the end of regions capable of being occupied, which have now been drained from the Earth and exist only in interplanetary space where the celestial states, present new problems. *Res nullius* is something that belongs to nobody, such as the Moon.

'There you go, the two most famous scientists in the world at that time are giving us a legal lesson.'

> In international law, a celestial body is not subject to the sovereignty of any state is considered *res nullius*. If it could be established that a celestial body within our solar system, such as our Moon was, or is occupied by another celestial species, there could be no claim of *res nullius* by any state on Earth (if that state should decide in the future to send explorers to lay claim to it).
>
> It would exist as *res communis* that is that all celestial states have the same rights over it.'

'You rarely hear of *res communis* these days. It usually refers to international law, with relevance to things being of common law, so it's the opposite of *res nullius*. I'm amazed that Oppenheimer and Einstein used such official legal terminology. This reads like a formal legal document. I would be very surprised if they did not seek legal advice before writing this. They obviously thought it important. Okay, where was I?'

> And now to the final question of whether the presence of celestial astroplanes in our atmosphere is a direct result of our testing atomic weapons?

'I'm guessing "celestial astroplanes" are UFOs. I presume we'll find out soon, so I'll keep reading.

> The presence of unidentified space craft flying—

'Ah, there we go, they are talking UFOs.'

The presence of unidentified space craft flying in our atmosphere (and possibly maintaining orbits about our planet) is now, however, accepted as de facto by our military. On every question of whether the United States will continue testing of fission bombs and develop fusion devices (hydrogen bombs), or reach an agreement to disarm and the exclusion of weapons that are too destructive, with the exception of chemical warfare, on which, by some miracle we cannot explain, an agreement has been reached, the lamentations of philosophers, the efforts of politicians, and the conferences of diplomats have been doomed to failure and have accomplished nothing.

The use of the atomic bomb, combined with space vehicles, poses a threat on a scale which makes it absolutely necessary to come to an agreement in this area. With the appearance of unidentified space vehicles (opinions are sharply divided as to their origin) over the skies of Europe and the United States has sustained an ineradicably fear, an anxiety about security, that is driving the great powers to make an effort to find a solution to the threat.

Military strategists foresee the use of space craft with nuclear warheads as the ultimate weapon of war. Even the deployment of artificial satellites for intelligence gathering and target selection is not far off. The military importance of space vehicles, satellites as well as rockets is indisputable, since they project war from the horizontal plane to the vertical plane in its fullest sense. Attack no longer comes from an exclusive direction, nor from a determined country, but from the sky, with the practical impossibility of determining who the aggressor is, how to intercept the attack, or how to effect immediate reprisals. These problems are compounded further by identification.

How does the air defense radar operator identify, or more precisely, classify his target?

At present, we can breathe a little easier knowing that slow-moving bombers are the mode of delivery of atomic bombs, which can be detected by long-range early warning radar. But what do we do in, let's say ten years from now? When artificial satellites and missiles find their place in space, we must consider the potential threat that unidentified spacecraft pose. One must consider the fact that misidentification of these space craft for an intercontinental missile in a re-entry phase of flight could lead to accidental nuclear war with horrible consequences.

Lastly, we should consider the possibility that our atmospheric tests of late could have influenced the arrival of celestial scrutiny. They could have been, curious or even alarmed by such activity (and rightly so, for the Russians would make every effort to observe and record such tests).

In conclusion, it is our professional opinion, based on submitted data, that this situation is extremely perilous, and measures must be taken to rectify a very serious problem are very apparent.

Respectfully, Dr. J. Robert Oppenheimer, Director of Advanced Studies Princeton, New Jersey and Professor Albert Einstein, Princeton, New Jersey.

'Wow!'

CHAPTER THIRTY-FOUR

Emma is gob-smacked. While she shakes her head in disbelief, C.J. explains the note at the bottom of the document:

> Myself and Marshall have read this and I must admit there is some logic. But, I hardly think the President will consider it for the obvious reasons. I understand Oppenheimer approached Marshall while they attended a ceremony at (location deleted). As I understand it Marshall rebuffed the idea of Oppenheimer discussing this with the President. I talked to Gordon, and he agreed.

The note is followed by handwritten initials.

'I dissected this memo, line by line, as I initially did not know who wrote and signed the memo. I did realize the note was written by someone other than Einstein or Oppenheimer, because it is in a different style of writing and the first paragraph was not indented. The paper was written for President Truman and the UN, so it obviously went to someone very important before it could be forwarded to its intended audience. Researching the sentence '*Myself and Marshall have read this and must admit there is some logic*', I concluded that the *Marshall* mentioned is General George C. Marshall, one of the leading Generals and organizers responsible for the Allied victory in World War Two. He was the Army's Chief of Staff under Presidents Roosevelt and Truman, then served as Secretary of State at the same time James Forrestal was Secretary of Defense.

'The next part of the memo conveys that Oppenheimer talked with George C. Marshall; however, the writer of the memo relays that Marshall felt President Truman would not entertain implementing the recommendations, '*for obvious reasons*.' The writer then said he talked with Gordon, and this Gordon agreed the President should not be involved.

'I assume that *Gordon* is Gordon Gray, who was a government official in Truman's Administration, heavily involved in the formation and running of the Atomic Energy Commission, as well as one of the Government's leading defense and national security advisors. Gordon Gray was reputedly close to Truman, Forrestal, and Vannevar Bush, and, allegedly, one of the original MJ-12 members.

'I racked my brain, thinking, *Who would be important enough to be discussing all of this with Marshall and Gray – and advising them on what to do?* I came up with only one person. See the initials V.B. on the document'

'V.B.?'

'VANNEVAR BUSH! I researched Dr. Bush's signature – and the initials match his writing.'

'Let me get this straight,' says Emma. 'Vannevar Bush was a non-government employee, yet he consulted with two of the leading members of Truman's Administration – to recommend the document, a document written by the two most prominent scientists on the planet at that time, was *not* to be shown to President Truman? It just goes to show how powerful Dr. Bush really was – and what direction MJ-12 were heading. Your father mentioned the document in his memoirs.'

'I have it stored in another file,' says C.J., leaning across to open it on Emma's computer:

> You would have read Einstein's and Oppenheimer's 1947 paper 'Relationships with Inhabitants of Celestial Bodies.' I'd suggest you read it again. I was only given access to the paper some years after it was written. You would no doubt realize the ramifications if the recommendations of two of the world's most prominent scientists were made public? Sadly, it never was.

'Einstein and Oppenheimer also warned that testing of nuclear weapons and technology in the atmosphere may attract unwanted attention.'

'Here it is, here.' Emma finds the relevant words in the scientists' document, reading out loud, 'We should consider the possibility that our atmospheric tests of late could have influenced the arrival of celestial scrutiny. They clearly knew the ramifications of the nuclear program—'

'Ironically, it was Oppenheimer who developed the first nuclear bomb and – along with Vannevar Bush — he was one of the administrators in charge of the AEC and the US's nuclear program direction.'

'This was years before the Greada Treaty and the meeting between Eisenhower and the Nordics. Einstein and Oppenheimer were smart men; they even predicted future space travel and satellite technologies. Wow C.J., this is an incredible document. Your father was right when he said that it was sad that the document was never made public.'

The next scientists on Dr. Stroheim's list are *Edward Teller* and *Vannevar Bush*. C.J. will further research Dr. Bush and Emma will investigate Edward Teller.

C.J. encourages Emma to reveal her findings first.

Computer in front of her to refer to her notes, she begins, 'As you know, Edward Teller is referred to as the father of the hydrogen bomb. He was also instrumental in the development of the atom bomb in the Manhattan Project, working alongside Oppenheimer and Dr. Bush. Teller was then influential in the early years of the AEC then, in 1952, cofounded the Lawrence Livermore National Laboratory (LLNL), which was another private enterprise nuclear weapons venture. Several high-profile companies were involved, including Bechtel. Bechtel is on your father's list, so we'll research that further down the track.

'Although Teller's venture was fully privatized, it was funded by the Government using Federally Funded Research and Development Center money.'

'We've read a little about this form of funding. MITRE Corporation was set up using the same Government funding,' notes C.J.

'And I'm sure they'll be more companies set up specifically to take advantage of this kind of funding. But for now I can tell you that Teller was at the peak of his administrative powers when Ronald Reagan became President in 1981. He worked closely with Reagan – and lobbied the President to implement what was later called the Strategic Defense Initiative, which the press dubbed "Star Wars".'

'I know about Star Wars; it was a plan to use ground- and satellite-based lasers, particle beams, and all sorts of high-tech missiles to destroy rockets, presumably from the Soviets. This was still during the Cold War.'

'The key word is *presumably*. Teller was less concerned with the Russians – and more concerned by UFOs.'

'No way!'

'Yes. Teller knew a lot about UFOs. He'd visited Area 51 many times. He was part of a secret 1948 meeting, *the Conference on Aerial Phenomena*, which was held at Los Alamos specifically to discuss UFOs. He'd also seen bright lights in desert areas, as well as crashed disk debris, so he knew more than most about the disks. He wasn't just fascinated. He deemed them a threat to not only the United States, but the world.

'I'll read some snippets of a detailed memo written by Teller to President Ronald Reagan:

> I wish to bring to your attention a very real and dangerous situation that threatens not only us, the world, but our very existence as a race.

'He also said:

> Today all on Earth are close neighbors. The first world which is liberal, the second world which is dictatorial, the third world where changes are rapid and often violent. The fate of all hinges on the development and use of UFO technology. If we want to understand and influence the future, we should review and understand humankind's new tools.'

'Wow, they were profound words,' says C.J.

'Profound indeed. So, what extra information did you find out about Vannevar Bush?'

'We already know how powerful Dr. Bush was, but he was also an innovative scientist and engineer in his own right. He invented what is called a *memex*, a forerunner to modern computers. It was designed to compress and store information and data, such as books, records, and communications. He then became instrumental in the development of analog computers, as well as inventing and patenting a mapping device to assist surveyors.

'As inventive as he was, he is best known for his administration skills. As we know, he managed to convince the Government to fund private enterprise to experiment, develop, and ultimately produce nuclear bombs. There were more than 120,000 people working on the Manhattan Project – and he managed to keep the whole project secret. He mastered the art of deconstructing a venture and breaking it up into smaller pieces. I liken it to building a car, piece by piece. One company makes the spark plugs, another makes tires, another the seats, and so on. Individually, they mean very little, but put it all together and we have a fully functioning car. The same thing happened with making a nuclear bomb.

'The key was to only have a handful of people at the top who knew the full picture. The Manhattan Project was deconstructed and controlled expertly by Bush. Even when the bombs were dropped on Japan, the individual companies, private institutes, and universities had no idea their individual components were involved.

'Bush took the business model and success of the Manhattan Project to MJ-12 and their various projects. He was able to secure Government funding, while all still run by private enterprise.

'He then helped set up several corporations, also privately run, but backed by Government funds. The two main organizations were RAND Corporation and MITRE Corporation. And, of course, he was responsible for the JASON Scholars, who were housed and furnished under the MITRE Corporation umbrella and their funding. But Bush didn't stop there. While all this was going on, he was the Vice-Dean then Dean of a massive private institute, MIT – the Massachusetts Institute of Technology. You'll note that the first three letters of MITRE Corporation are M-I-T. This is not a coincidence. MITRE is short for *MIT Research*. MIT was also heavily involved in the Manhattan Project, as well as the AEC.

'I know I'm sounding like an infomercial, but wait, there's more. Vannevar Bush also had his own little company. That "little company" is now the biggest weapons manufacturer in The United States – Raytheon.'

'I know a little of Raytheon,' says Emma. 'In Australia, our Navy has submarines, called Collins Class. I'm sure Raytheon do most of the fit-outs, as well as the weaponry.'

'Raytheon are the world's biggest manufacturer of guided missiles. They are huge. If you ever hear of a missile being fired, like a Patriot, Stinger, or Tomahawk, you can bet it was made by Raytheon. Dr. Bush started Raytheon and worked closely with MIT and many of the secret projects and subdivisions under the AEC's and NSA's umbrella.'

'It's no wonder then, Raytheon became so big so quick.'

'Funny that,' says C.J., heavy with sarcasm. 'There's no doubt Dr. Bush was a busy man – and incredibly powerful. It seemed like everything he asked for, he got. President Truman gave him power –then Eisenhower gave him even more power – and, in turn, Bush steered his projects further away from the Government – and further away from scrutiny. The more I read about this man, the more impressed I am with his administrative skills.

'My father wrote: "I had a huge amount of respect for Dr. Bush's scientific and administrative skills, yet I harbored some uncertainties about his agenda – and the lengths he would go to achieve the desired results. He could be ruthless. We always got along well, but I knew he was a driven man."

'I think my father was a good judge of character.'

The last two famous scientists on Max Stroheim's list are *John von Neumann* and *Wernher von Braun.*

'Which "von" do you vant?' asks Emma cheekily.

Vant! Very good. 'I'll research von Neumann.'

'I'll take von Braun then.'

Over the next hours and next day C.J. researches von Neumann and Emma von Braun.

Emma talks first. 'Wernher von Braun was described by NASA as

"The greatest rocket scientist in history." He was the lead scientist in the development of the Saturn V booster rocket, which helped land men on the Moon. But, before von Braun headed the US space program, he was in Nazi Germany – the central figure in Germany's rocket development program. He was responsible for the design and realization of the V-2 combat rocket during World War II. The V-2 was the world's first long-range guided ballistic missile. It flew more than sixty miles in the air. Toward the end of the way, it was fired from occupied France to kill thousands of people in London.

'When the war finished, the Americans raced to capture key German V-2 manufacturing sites and technology. Von Braun and more than one hundred key V-2 personnel surrendered to the Americans. Von Braun should have been executed for war crimes; however, he and his team were relocated to the US. They were brought to secret bases in the US desert to help Americans in their own rocket and scientific research. From what I could gather, some of those men ended up at Area 51. It seems highly likely that some would have been at S-4, where your father worked.

'Later in his life, von Braun told in private of being at Roswell in 1947 just after the UFO disk had crashed. He and some of his associates were taken to the crash site after the bulk of the military personnel left the scene. Von Braun told of doing a "quick once-over of the site" and acknowledged that alien bodies were found. He told of seeing the bodies in a medical tent near the UFO debris.

'This was his description of the bodies: "The beings were small, very frail, and almost reptilian in nature."

'He was also puzzled by the nature of the UFO debris, saying: "The material was very thin, aluminum colored and similar to chewing gum wrapping."

'He related how the exterior of the space craft was not metal as we know it, but appeared to be made of something biological, like skin. Von Braun was convinced the craft was made of something organic living.

'His description of the craft's interior was equally bizarre: "It was very bare of instrumentation, as if the creatures and the craft were of a single unit."

'Von Braun rarely talked about the incredible secrets he obviously knew, yet on his deathbed he revealed a few of these mysteries. He was very wary of the extraterrestrials' presence on Earth, believing they possessed an enormous threat to mankind. He admitted the Government knew it and the rationale for the space-based weapons programs was a lie to the public, so it was clearly evident that he knew the real reasons for Edward Teller and Ronald Reagan's Star Wars program.

'I'll read what von Braun said:

> I have debated Generals and Congressional Representatives. I have testified before the Congress and the Senate. I have met with people in over 100 countries, but I have not been able to identify who the people are who are making this space-based weapons system happen. I see the news. I see the administrative decisions being made. I know that they are all based on lies and greed.

'He then said:

> But I have yet to be able to identify who the people are. That is after tracking this issue for 26 years. I know that there are big secrets being kept and I know that it is time the public and decision-makers pay attention to the people who are now going to be disclosing the truth. I have concluded that it is based on a few people making a lot of money and gaining power. It is about ego. It is not about our essence and who we really are on this planet and loving each other and being at peace and cooperating. It isn't about using technology to solve problems and heal people in the planet. It isn't about that. It is about a few people who really are playing an old, dangerous, costly game for their own pocketbooks and power struggle. That is all it is.

'Wow,' says C.J., 'He's talking about the same groups and people my father mentioned.'

'And on his deathbed, he didn't talk about his regrets of being a Nazi and contributing to thousands being killed. Instead, he talked of ETs, their threat to Earth, and the people with the power. He admitted it was not the Government, yet the Government knew. This was in the 1970s, when Reagan was President. Von Braun and Edward Teller were warning of the same thing at the same time. Wow.'

CHAPTER THIRTY-FIVE

When revealing his research into John von Neumann, C.J. says, 'He was a mathematical genius. He could take complex mathematical calculations and solve them in his head instantly. He also had a photographic memory – he'd read a book then, years later, recite it word-for-word from memory. Apart from arguably being the greatest mathematician of all time, he was involved in physics, quantum mechanics, and computing. Von Neumann is often attributed with being the founder of computers. This guy was an out-and-out genius. It's no wonder he was brought in to be a major player in the Manhattan Project.

'He worked closely with Oppenheimer, Teller, and Bush – and continued this association after the Manhattan Project morphed into the AEC. He was based out of Los Alamos with Edward Teller when the Lawrence Livermore National Laboratory was set up. He sat on several government bodies and committees dealing with national security and military advancement, as well as being a consultant to the CIA.'

'The CIA?'

'I know. It sounds unusual. What he actually did with the CIA I couldn't find out, but he certainly was in demand in the late 1940s and early 1950s. He was also a consultant with RAND Corporation before he died in 1957, at just 53, reputedly from cancer caused by radiation exposure while with the Manhattan Project. As far as von Neumann knowing about UFOs and ETs, or his association with MJ-12 is concerned, I couldn't find any reliable information, but it was clear that he worked closely with Dr. Bush. He was colleagues and close friends with Edward Teller and Robert Oppenheimer – and worked alongside Albert Einstein on many projects. Von Neumann was well connected and brilliant; he must have known what was going on around him.'

C.J. checks the next line of his father's list: *Dr. William Reich*, *Dr. Frank Reiner*, and *Captain Edward Ruppelt*.

'These men are listed separately for a reason. My father talked in-depth about Frank Reiner. There's nothing about him on the Internet, but we already know that he was a physicist at S-4, working alongside my dad. Dad's story is that he became disillusioned and spoke out – and was quickly dealt with. My father kept saying, 'If no one talks, then no one dies.' MJ-12 must have been afraid Reiner would talk.

'I'm surprised Ellis Buckman mentioned Frank Reiner to me. He must have known about Reiner and how he died. Buckman must have had inside information. Maybe he mentioned Reiner's name to provoke a reaction from me? Of course, I didn't know anything about Reiner at the time.'

'I wonder if Reich and Ruppelt were involved in any of the projects your father mentioned? He didn't name them in his memoirs, yet he obviously knew about them.'

'Maybe they were like Frank Reiner – they threatened to speak out?'

'Hopefully, we'll get to find out. I know you want to start writing the book. Would you like me to start researching Dr. William Reich and Captain Ruppelt?'

'Sure.'

'I'll start tonight and share what I find out in the morning.'

The next morning C.J. and Emma wake at dawn.

Walking hand in hand along the beach, Emma says, 'I found some interesting articles on both Dr. Reich and Captain Ruppelt. Firstly, let me say that they worked in a similar era, but they didn't seem to work together or know each other, so I'll talk about each separately. I did find a conspiracy book that talks about both men. I downloaded the book, so I'll read it when I have time. I did note that the book has some similar themes to what your father wants you write – and here's the good news: the book was published, sold quite a few copies, AND the two authors are still alive! When your father said you should be safe after the book is published, he knew what he was talking about.'

'Well, that's good news.'

'I've still some more to research to do on Captain Ruppelt so I'll start with Dr. William Reich. He was a prominent psychoanalyst, fleeing Austria to live in America before the outbreak of World War II. He was not only brilliant within the field of psychology, but also in physics and energy fields. He interacted on several projects with Albert Einstein. He believed he had discovered how to affect the propulsion systems of some of the alien disks.

'How Reich knew about UFOs is a little puzzling. He didn't seem to work for any of the projects, organizations, or agencies associated with UFO research. This man should have been perfect candidate to join one of these secret projects, yet he didn't. Instead, he was harassed by government agencies. All his books, notes, and written texts were seized by the FBI and burned.'

'Burned?'

'Like a bonfire. Reputedly, three tons of literature were scorched. This is not in the dark ages, but the early 1950s – in a democracy supposedly encouraging "freedom of speech." Before Reich's paperwork was impounded, he was arrested on some ridiculous, obscure charge and jailed for two years. Just a few days before his release, he was found in his cell bed – dead.

'The official report stated Reich had a heart attack in the middle of the night, dying in his sleep; somehow fully clothed and wearing shoes. Forgive my sarcasm but, if I was suffering a heart attack in a jail cell, ,the last thing I'd be doing is getting dressed and putting on shoes.

'Now for Captain Edward Ruppelt. I haven't read that conspiracy book yet, so I haven't got the authors' take on it. From what I saw on the Net, Captain Ruppelt was the Director of Project Grudge, then Project Blue book.'

They walk back from the beach. Emma's plans are to keep researching Ruppelt after breakfast, and check her emails to see if her friend, Anna, has forwarded information to her father in Tasmania.

'You need to concentrate on writing,' she adds.

'The quicker it is written and published, the safer we should be,' says C.J. 'We'll need to go to the UK at some point, as that's where the publisher is.'

'I've always wanted to go to England,' says Emma. 'Anna and I talked of traveling to England, possibly via Africa and go on safari.'

Back at the apartment, Emma checks her emails. Anna has sent an email: 'Read today's Brisbane Courier Mail – urgent!'

Emma looks at the newspaper's homepage. Photos of C.J. and herself appear under the headline: 'WANTED: US SPY HIDING DOWN UNDER.'

The article continues: 'Wanted man C.J. Stroheim, also known as Christopher Jones, has reportedly fled the United States and is in hiding somewhere in Australia with his girlfriend, Tasmanian woman Emma Burgess (pictured below).'

Emma yells to C.J. 'Quick, come here.'

C.J. is as stunned as Emma to see their photos in the newspaper.

The newspaper article does not mention what C.J. is actually being accused of, apart from being a suspected 'spy.' There is a contact phone number for 'anyone who may have seen this man.'

Emma researches the phone number.

It is not the police; it is Australian Customs and Quarantine.

C.J. begins packing immediately, while Emma checks which other newspapers are carrying the story. The first three papers she sees – Melbourne's *Herald Sun*, Sydney's *The Daily Telegraph*, and Tasmania's *The Advocate* – all feature the story. Emma's seen enough; she joins C.J. packing.

C.J. and Emma wear sunglasses to catch a taxi heading south toward Brisbane, formulating travel plans on the way. Knowing their photos are being circulated around the country, traveling by plane today from a major airport, such as Brisbane, is not wise. They'll pre-book Brisbane-to-Sydney train tickets and go direct to the train. The newspaper article is unlikely to be the only unwanted publicity they'll receive in Australia.

'Maybe we can lie low for a day or two, then catch a flight overseas somewhere?' speculates C.J. 'We have new passports.'

'So where do you want to go?'

'Are there direct flights to Africa?'

Arriving in Brisbane, they head straight to the train station. On the fourteen-hour trip to Sydney, there'll be plenty of time for Emma to read the book she downloaded and for C.J. to write.

In their private sleeper compartment, Emma and C.J. turn on their computers.

Emma had downloaded *The Secret Treaty – The United States Government and Extra-terrestrial Entities*, written in the late 1980*s* by Richard K. Wilson and Sylvan Burns. The authors had published several other controversial books and sent open letters to a number of government officials with alien-related themes. *The Secret Treaty* was the culmination of much of the authors' research.

Emma soon discovers the book connects secret organizations, such as The Trilateral Commission and the Bilderbergs, with the US Government, citing Illuminati-driven agendas for covering up knowledge of extraterrestrials and their technology. The authors seem thorough in their investigations, listing some of the secret projects Max Stroheim had C.J. research, including Project Sign, which morphed into Project Grudge. The authors confirm that the Director of Project Grudge was Captain Edward Ruppelt.

An Air Force officer, Ruppelt headed up Grudge, which had extraterrestrial and UFO information for MJ-12's eyes only. All the reports were later ordered to be destroyed. Project Blue Book was created shortly after Grudge, with Captain Ruppelt placed in charge. According to *The Secret Treaty* authors (and Max Stroheim), Blue Book was the 'public version' of ET data – should it need to be released.

Ruppelt became frustrated with the Air Force's treatment of UFO information, particularly as his budget and staffing were slashed. He resigned from the military in 1953. Working in the private sector as a qualified aeronautical engineer, he wrote and published a book called *The Report on Unidentified Flying Objects.*

Emma thinks to herself, *This man knew secrets that would have made MJ-12 nervous. Although Ruppelt's book was thoughtfully written, it still divulged top-secret information.*

When Emma reads that Edward Ruppelt died of a sudden heart attack at just thirty-seven, she gasps out loud.

Hearing Emma's gasp, C.J. looks up.

She explains, 'I still have more to read, but already there are a number of people with knowledge of UFOs who mysteriously died, including William Reich. I also read that, around the time of Ruppelt's death, RAND Corporation, held several conferences on deep underground construction. Apparently these conferences were attended by various military services, as well as large corporate construction firms like Bechtel.'

'Yes. Massive underground construction works began shortly after these meetings. I think your father, by having you research these corporations, was hinting at the same thing. That's all I have to relay for now. I'll let you get back to your writing. You seem to be tapping away quite frantically there.'

'Oh yes, the first chapter is taking shape. Only another thirty or forty to go,' quips C.J.

In *The Secret Treaty – The United States Government and Extra-terrestrial Entities*, Emma reads that FEMA (Federal Emergency Management Agency) is referred in the book as 'the secret government of the United States.' Hardly anyone knows about this organization (including Emma), yet it is, according to *The Secret Treaty*, the most powerful entity in the US:

> It has more power than the President of the USA or the Congress; it has the power to turn the United States into a police state in time of a real crisis or a manufactured crisis.

Although emergency management and contingency plans had

existed for some time in the US, FEMA was officially formed in 1979 as an 'independent agency.' In 2003, under George W. Bush's Presidency, FEMA become 'a major agency of the Department of Homeland Security.'

FEMA is not an elected body; it does not make public disclosures; and it has an annual budget of more than US$14 billion. It has the power to suspend laws, arrest and detain citizens without a warrant and hold them without trial, to seize property, food supplies, transportation systems, to move entire populations, and FEMA can even suspend the Constitution.

'In times of emergency, FEMA is in indeed in control,' she says under her breath.

The Secret Treaty implies that elected government officials not only lacked influence, but that the vast majority of them were unaware of many of these secretive agencies and organizations. The more Emma reads, the more she realizes where the real power in the USA seems to be.

C.J. and Emma discussed ways of staying in Sydney with minimum chances of being recognized. Emma suggested 'We could stay in a hotel near the airport, however I think we might be safer in a place with backpackers and tourists who are not likely to be reading papers. I think Bondi Beach might be good. We should be able to get a cheap hotel; some place that has room service and Internet facilities, so we don't need to leave the hotel until we're ready to catch a flight to Johannesburg.'

'Sounds like a good idea.'

'I can wear glasses and my hat, so why don't we catch separate taxis when the train arrives in Sydney. I'd suggest you change into your board shorts and a T-shirt and meet me at the northern end of Bondi Beach after I have booked a hotel.'

When C.J. arrives at iconic Bondi Beach, his eyes search the crowded foreshore for Emma. She sits on a towel on the sand at the northern end of the beach, raising her hand subtly when seeing C.J., then picks up her towel to walk from the beach. C.J. follows at a distance.

Crossing the road, Emma enters a large hotel. When C.J. steps inside the foyer, she hands him a key card and whispers 'Room three-o-five', then walks away.

'Wow, what a view' says C.J. when stepping inside the room to see a balcony overlooking the beach. 'I thought you said you were getting a cheap hotel?'

'It is cheap. When I was a poor uni student I learnt a few tricks to get good value for money – and they upgraded us as well.'

C.J. cuddles Emma, to say 'You never cease to amaze me Emma Burgess.'

Their room's balcony is high enough from the street to be private, yet they can still see the ocean waves breaking on the shore. On the balcony, Emma researches RAND Corporation, while C.J writes.

With the sun setting, Emma divulges 'Some things you already know and some information will be new. I'll just tell it as I see it: After World War II, the Government began outsourcing much of their military technology, including intelligence gathering, weapons advancement, military analyses, and military engineering and construction. Under the umbrella of Federally Funded Research and Development Centers, dozens and dozens of privately run companies started receiving huge amounts of money from the US Government.

'Many of these corporations were specifically set up to take advantage of this system – and some of the companies created further divisions under different names, yet blatantly under the control of the main corporation. These new divisions received separate, additional federal funding. We are not talking a few dollars here, we are talking billions of dollars – each. RAND Corporation was the first beneficiary, creating the blueprint that would kick start this whole federally funded concept.

'RAND was conceived and run by the Douglas Aircraft Company. They were the US's largest military supplier during WWII. In 1945 they convinced the Government to hand over massive amounts of money to assist their research and development arm, thus the name RAND – *Research ANd Development*. The Government gave them the money on the proviso that RAND was a non-profit organization. RAND were the Douglas Aircraft Company, but under a different name.

'In 1967 Douglas merged with McDonnell Aircraft to become McDonnell Douglas, then thirty years later, they came under the control of Boeing. Yep, Boeing Aircraft Company. Regardless of the name and ownership changes, RAND continued to be a separate entity, maintaining their federally funded status; actually receiving more money and setting up further subdivisions.

'RAND refer to themselves as a "think tank," advising the US Government on military strategies, nuclear policies, and communication and global spying. It was RAND who developed the first spy-satellites to spy on the Russians back in the 1950s, expanding that program in the 1960s and beyond.

'RAND also studied and categorized terrorism and terrorist acts back in the 1970s. At that time, the United Nations didn't even have a working definition for the word *terrorism*. The US Government, as well as the UN, now use what's called the *RAND Terrorism Chronology Database*, which catalogues all acts of terrorism.'

'So this is a private corporation advising the US Government and the United Nations on global military strategies?'

'Yes. It's a scary thought.'

CHAPTER THIRTY-SIX

RAND Corporation's influence extends into technological advancements in the communications industry. Working with the Government to create the Advanced Research Projects Agency Network (ARPANET), this packet switching communications network became the technical foundation of the Internet.

'As you can see,' Emma says, 'RAND have been a major player in influencing the US Government, especially in telecommunications and the military.

'Now, I just want to go back to the late 1940s again. RAND was officially named and set up in 1948. At the time, there was something called the Institute for Defense Analyses. It's not an institute by educational definition; it is yet another organization involved in military assessment. I know it sounds like this 'institute' should have no the connection with RAND Corporation. But I'll explain: The Institute for Defense Analyses morphed from what was the Weapons Systems Evaluation Group. You won't believe who set up this up – James Forrestal. After Forrestal's death, and with Eisenhower the President, it was outsourced to the private sector to work hand in hand with the NSA. It then changed names to the Institute for Defense Analyses and, according to their own website, they are considered, and I quote: 'Major clients and grantors of RAND Corporation.' And this is the kicker –

they also get separate funding from the Federal Government.'

'So RAND, as well as the Institute for Defense Analyses, both received funding through the Federally Funded Research and Development grants?'

'Absolutely. You'll also be interested to learn that, besides James Forrestal's involvement, Dr. Vannevar Bush was also instrumental in the early formation of the Institute for Defense Analyses, with some of the operations and research based at … guess where?'

'I'll take a stab in the dark: MIT?'

'Bingo. It's Dr. Bush and MIT again. I also have another institute to talk about.' She glances at the computer. 'I bet you haven't heard of The International Institute for Homeland Security, Defense and Restoration – or usually it is simply called The International Institute?'

C.J. hasn't.

'Well, this is yet another intelligence-gathering organization. As their name implies, they work internationally. It ties in and works closely with NATO, the World Customs Organization, the European Union, the European Defense Agency, and the US Congress and Interagency, which includes the Department of State, the Department of Justice, the Department of Defense, and the Department of Homeland Security. Here's the bit you'll like: *It is not a government agency*. It is privately run – and any guesses who runs it?'

'Surely not RAND?'

'Sure is!'

C.J. is shell-shocked. 'So RAND have their own intelligence-gathering agency?'

'It's crazy, right? And they're not just US-based, but internationally. RAND works closely with the CIA, and obviously the NSA as well, but they have their own intelligence division – and they work hand in hand with many other intelligence organizations around the world, including the US's Department of Homeland Security and the Department of Defense. I'm dumbfounded.'

'That makes two of us. Before I started on this journey. I'd never heard of RAND, or MITRE for that matter. I'm starting to think that the American general public hasn't heard of them for a reason.'

'I'll research MITRE in the morning; however, I can already tell you that MITRE and RAND are intertwined. I read that board members often swap from one of the corporations to the other. I downloaded some of the board members over the years. Look at these names.'

Showing the list on her computer to C.J., he recognizes many of the names. 'Wow, these are some seriously powerful individuals.'

At the end of the following day, Emma reveals her findings on MITRE.

'MITRE Corporation was set up in 1958 from a project termed *SAGE,* which is short for Semi-Automatic Ground Environment. It was a Cold War operator for what was known as the Automated Air Defense. This air defense system was basically a network of computer systems providing support for radars and the whole military operations.

'Of course, you know Vannevar Bush was heavily involved in MITRE's creation. Dr. Bush helped the corporation receive immediate government funding through the Federally Funded Research and Development Centre grants. MITRE grew rapidly, becoming involved with many of the secret projects controlled by MJ-12, as well as gaining additional funding and support for the JASON Scholars. And it didn't stop there. As far as I can tell, MITRE now has at least seven other subsidiaries all receiving federally funded money. We are talking billions of dollars annually. Figures were hard to come by, but I did find some from just a few years ago. The Government was spending nearly one hundred and fifty billion dollars US on these federally funded schemes. Annually.'

'One hundred fifty billion in one year? That's incredible.'

'I know; it's a hell of a lot of money – year in, year out. MITRE has the best scientific minds, pursuing technological advancement, particularly military with defense systems. They also supply expertise not only to the US military, through the Department of Defense, but to a host of government departments. From what I read, MITRE have contracts with what they call 'their sponsors,' which include the Department of Defense, Homeland Security, Customs and Border Control, and the IRS. Didn't William Cooper have 'issues' with the IRS?'

'He did. I was wondering how and why they could avoid the normal protocols to declare Cooper a "fugitive of the law".'

'You might have found your answer,' says Emma.

It is a poignant statement. Both pause to reflect on the implications of MITR, a private company, influencing, advising, guiding, and even managing prominent government departments.

C.J. says, 'I was labeled a *spy*, with no proof, no explanations, and no recourse. I'm starting to realize, this may not have been initiated by the Government.'

'It's looking that way.'

Breaking the sudden somber mood, Emma suggests she look into flights and accommodation in South Africa.

'Could you handle another day here, then fly out the day after?'

'Absolutely.'

Emma makes separate bookings for the flight to Johannesburg, being wary of not being seen together Although it is now a number of days since their photos were featured in national newspapers, they're still fearful of being recognized. They'll catch the same flight, but will check in separately and sit in different sections of business class, with C.J seated downstairs and Emma in the upper-deck of a Boeing 747. Emma also books several nights' accommodation in a trendy area of Jo-burg, called Sandton. This will give them time to recover from jetlag and make plans for their next leg of the journey: safaris in the north of South Africa, before planning to fly to Cape Town in the south.

'I heard Cape Town is amazing,' gushes Emma. 'The coastline is apparently incredible.'

'Sounds like a great place to write a book' replies C.J. with a grin.

• • •

Onboard the aircraft, C.J. continues to write, intermittently reviewing his father's notes. His father was right in insisting C.J. research extensively before uncovering the memoirs.

Max had cautioned, 'You won't be able to grasp the truth, well, not initially. This is the hardest thing you will ever do in your life. Not only will you discover things that'll be very hard to comprehend, but you'll have to do it while traveling and moving frequently.'

Emma researched and downloaded information on Raytheon and Bechtel, as well as the final line on Max Stroheim's list:

DWIGHT EISENHOWER (specifically his relationship with NATO and THE COUNCIL ON FOREIGN RELATIONS).

She told C.J. of both Raytheon and Bechtel's rise to prominence. Both had close ties with MJ-12 and their projects, as well as links to and joint ventures with RAND and MITRE Corporations.

'I don't normally like to talk generically, but I could see a pattern evolving with both Raytheon and Bechtel.

'Raytheon benefitted immensely from the technology from MITRE, the JASON Scholars, and of course MIT's research. Vannevar Bush founded Raytheon – it would be damn easy to take some of the technological advances and give them to your own company to expand – and commercialize. And Raytheon grew rapidly. Over ninety percent of their revenue comes from military sales: weapons, radar, satellite, and sonar systems, and technical military support.

'Bechtel, on the other hand, were heavily involved in building secret bases and working on many of the Atomic Energy Commission's nuclear projects and infrastructures. During WWII, Bechtel was known as Bechtel-McCone. You won't be surprised to learn that the *McCone* in Bechtel-McCone was John McCone, who dropped his name from the company when he became the first Chairman of guess which organization?'

C.J. shook his head.

'McCone was one of the richest men in America at the time – and was made the inaugural Chairman of none other than the Atomic Energy Commission.'

C.J. laughed aloud, comprehending the significance of such an appointment.

Emma told 'McCone was influential in the Council on Foreign Relations, as well as being close to President Eisenhower. McCone left being Chairman of the AEC to become the Director of the CIA.'

'So he was an MJ-12 member?'

'It seems so. During this period, Bechtel received numerous lucrative federally funded grants, as well as the Government's black budget allocations. There seemed little-to-no tender processes, so Bechtel quickly became the largest construction and civil engineering company in the USA.'

Emma now reads information on Dwight Eisenhower, regarding his relationship with NATO and the CFR.

Although she thought she knew who NATO was, she soon realizes she knew very little indeed.

NATO is The North Atlantic Treaty Organization – a military alliance formed from the bones of Japan's WWII surrender to the US and its allies. It covers North America and some of Europe, mostly Western Europe, and Asia. This Emma knew.

These days, there are fewer than thirty member states (countries), which she notes is very few in global terms. But the combined military spending of all NATO members apparently constitutes more than 70 percent of the world's defense spending.

Much to Emma's surprise, NATO is not a government-controlled alliance, but formed and funded by private enterprise, with 'private sponsors.' The same names who created The Trilateral Commission and who control the Council on Foreign Relations appear in the founding of NATO, with the organization seemingly controlled by The Trilateral Commission, the CFR, and the Bilderberg Group. It appears that the leaders of NATO are not only members of these groups, but are also appointed to NATO by these groups.

Emma doesn't bat an eyelid when she discovers the first Supreme Allied Commander appointed to NATO was Dwight D. Eisenhower.

Prior to becoming NATO's 'first Supreme Allied Commander,' General Eisenhower chaired the Council on Foreign Relations Study Group on Aid to Europe from 1948–51.

Emma also learns that, through the CFR, Eisenhower requested the Council on Foreign Relations advise the Secretary of Defense James Forrestal on unification of the armed services. It was reported that, through his involvement in the CFR, Eisenhower also gained exposure to economic analysis, which would become the bedrock of his understanding in economic policy during his Presidency.

So Eisenhower was influential with the CFR at the same time he was in charge of NATO, Emma thinks to herself. *Oh boy, what a conflict of interest.*

Emma reflects on the information she has learned.

'NATO is referred to as "the World Army," yet they are not global at all – and they are not a governmental organization. They are privately funded, backed by some of the richest and most powerful people in the world. They take an American five-star General as their first Commander (Eisenhower), then that same man becomes the President of the United States shortly after. This sounds almost too incredible to believe.'

Several articles Emma downloaded link NATO with the UN. She learns President Truman was influential in the UN's formation, with Eisenhower the driving force behind the creation of NATO. The two organizations were set up separately and were theoretically unrelated; however, over time they have become very much entwined. Given the same powerful names and backers behind both organizations, this is not surprising.

In recent times, UN Security Council resolutions have provided the mandate for NATO's operations in a number of countries, including Afghanistan and Iraq. The level of cooperation has increased year in, year out, yet Emma notes the United Nations has around 200 member states, whereas NATO has less than 30. She also realizes that in official documentation both the UN and NATO refer to the countries involved as being *states*, not *countries*.

Former secretary-general of the United Nations, Kofi Annan, once said, 'arguing against globalization is like arguing against the laws of gravity.'

Emma thinks '*This is talking about a New World Order.*'

Max Stroheim's memoirs made it clear that Truman and Eisenhower were political foes but, behind the scenes, they would have circulated with the same people. Both men and the organizations they supported had 'New World Order' agendas.

The European Union was born from this agenda, with 'global think tanks,' such as the Bilderbergs, the Royal Institute of International Affairs (Chatham House), the Council on Foreign Relations, and The Trilateral Commission instrumental in the EU's creation. Emma sees many similarities in the European Union and NATO, with both having a similar number of 'member states.' Many of those same 'states' are in both alliances.

Emma leaves her seat to stretch their legs. The cabin lights were turned off hours ago and most of the business class passengers sleeping. She sneaks downstairs No one has appeared to recognize either C.J. or Emma, so she's confident they're now safe. Emma sees C.J. writing and winks at him as she passes by. Closing his computer, C.J. rises from his seat. He finds Emma standing on the other side of the curtain, illuminated by sunlight; she stares out of the aircraft door window. Sensing C.J.'s arrival and with no passengers or crew in-sight, she turns around to kiss him tenderly on the lips.

'We've so much to discuss, but first look at this,' she instructs, beckoning him to look out the window.

'Wow,' gasps C.J.

Beyond the tiny window, expansive sheets of ice stretch to the horizon, the sharp gaze of sunlight making the ice gleam. In this sea of white, interspersed cracks of cobalt appear to be flicked across the icy canvas.

'We must be right down near the Antarctic Circle,' concludes Emma. 'I knew we flew south, but not this far south. Isn't it magnificent?'

'Just this morning we were watching surfers at Bondi Beach, now we're looking at Antarctica on our way to South Africa. I bet you could never have imagined this, Emma Burgess?'

'There's lots I couldn't have envisaged, but I wouldn't have it any other way,' she says, wrapping her arms quickly around him.

CHAPTER THIRTY-SEVEN

C.J. and Emma manage a few hours' sleep, before landing in Johannesburg. They pass customs control separately and only meet up outside the terminal.

Catching a taxi to Sandton, Emma summarizes what she researched on the plane, before explaining, 'I had time to reflect on why your father asked you to research all these groups and organizations. He clearly knew what the big picture was. He worked with MJ-12, but he was aware they were involved and influenced by these organizations, such as the CFR, Trilateral Commission, and the Bilderbergs.

'Your father's career was in an era with no Internet and very little literature available about these groups – and these groups were never talked about in the press, so he must have had firsthand information or experiences.

'You said that Ellis Buckman acknowledged your father was a brilliant scientist. But what did he say – he had access to the power, but didn't take advantage of it?'

'Buckman said to me, "The world does not run on chance. It is run by those who make it run." He said my father chose science over becoming one of the elite powerbrokers of the world. Then said that he and the other "powerbrokers" didn't like that.'

'Your father clearly made his own choices. He was obviously a man of principle, working in a secretive environment where few had such ethics. You should be so very proud of your father, C.J.'

'I am.'

Showered, refreshed, and changed, they ask the concierge at the Sandton Hotel if there is a nearby restaurant he can recommend. There is.

C.J. and Emma dine at the Butcher's Shop, with a butcher's counter inside the large restaurant.

'I'll have the most tender steak you've got,' declares Emma, 'I'm not overly concerned about size.'

'Then I recommend the eye fillet,' replies the man, smiling cheerily from behind the counter.

'Make that two,' chimes in C.J.

Over succulent steaks, potato mash, creamed spinach, steamed vegetables, and green peppercorn sauce, washed down with local Pinotage wine, C.J. and Emma discuss their travel itinerary. They plan to stay at Sandton for another night, before driving north to spend several weeks in various game lodges in and around Kruger National Park. Emma will talk with the concierge in the morning, then book accommodation and tours. From there, they plan to fly to Cape Town to finish the book.

C.J. envisages the book will take at least another four to six weeks to write. 'I know we have a book to write, an important book, but you would also be aware that my father said "to stop and smell the roses." That could also be interpreted as "stop and see the animals",' remarks C.J. with a smile.

'You leave all the travel details to me, Mr. Stroheim.'

C.J. and Emma wake at 3:30 a.m.

'Damn jetlag,' mutters C.J., before taking the opportunity to cuddle Emma.

He starts to write as the sun rises.

Returning to the room after breakfast, Emma says to C.J., 'I've organized a rental car from this afternoon. In the morning, we've a four or five-hour drive into the mountains to Bongani, which borders Kruger National Park. The concierge said it was a 'unique experience in the African bush' – and they have safaris. I booked a week there, then a week nearby in a town called Malelane, just outside Kruger. I figured we could do a day in the national park, then you could spend the rest of the week writing. The hotel I booked has a deck overlooking a river filled with crocs and hippos, so it should make for an interesting backdrop to write. It also has Internet coverage.'

'Sounds great.'

'Now, tell me how I help research for the book, then I'll leave you in peace.'

'There is something you can do for me, please. Both you and I know that I am not a spy, yet seeing my name plastered all over the papers as a spy is a more than a bit unsettling. I am going to write this book regardless, but as my lawyer, Emma Burgess, could you look into the legal angle of having the book published?'

'So that time on the beach at Boat Harbour when you said you needed legal advice down the track, you weren't lying?'

'I lied to you once, Emma, and I learned my lesson – I'll never lie to you again. So, as my lawyer, can you help me?'

'Sure. US law is different in some aspects to Australian law. I'll do some research and see what I can find. It might take me a few days.'

'We're not in a race.' He leans across to kiss her on the cheek.

Emma investigates past whistleblowers pursued by the US legal system.

As a lawyer, she contemplated whether C.J. was liable under American law for revealing Max Stroheim's classified information. Many people have been prosecuted under what is called The Patriot Act, as well as The Espionage Act. Emma describes this to C.J. as 'an archaic piece of law instated in the US constitution in 1917.' It was originally in the US War Code introduced during World War I; however, has been amended numerous times since.

'C.J., it would seem that every time the US Government wants to prosecute someone, they add another amendment to the Act. Remember when we were in Surfers Paradise and I was telling you about that couple in the 1950s who were alleged to be Russian spies? Well their names were Julius and Ethel Rosenberg. They were both prosecuted and executed under the Espionage Act. From what I read, there was little evidence against them – at best speculation, yet they were sentenced to death.'

C.J. jests, 'Do you think that, if I went back to the States, they'd send me to the electric chair?'

Emma stops to look into C.J.'s eyes. She is serious. 'That's what I've been looking into.'

C.J.'s jaw drops. 'Is it possible I could be prosecuted under the Espionage Act?'

'It's a question I've been asking myself. I've researched many people prosecuted under the Act over the years. In most cases, these people were not just prosecuted legally, but also persecuted by the media. I don't mean to be an alarmist, but the media in Australia has already published a story alleging you are a spy – with no proof and no explanations.

'Those previously prosecuted under the Espionage Act had all been employees or subcontractors of Government military divisions or agencies, or they were caught in possession of leaked Government files. I looked case by case at each of those prosecuted under the Act. There is good and bad news.'

'What's the bad news?'

'Those who were jailed or executed were pursued with venom. The full might of the US legal system was at the Government's disposal – and was used.'

'So what's the good news?'

'Not everyone of interest was able to be charged or was found guilty. Even before the likes of Edward Snowden went public, several former NSA employees had turned to the media to voice their concerns about the agency's agenda. These men were not charged, although they told stories of having their houses raided and ransacked by the FBI – and material such as computers were seized. They had guns pointed at their heads, before being taken away for interrogation. From each separate account, the ordeals were terrifying.

'What I find extraordinary is that these men could be subjected to such intimidation, have their private property taken from them, and yet no charges were ever laid. I thought that the American legal system was above reproach. The US is the land of what I call 'litigation culture,' where if someone or some establishment had done the wrong thing by another, the other party sues. I guess that doesn't apply if the likes of the FBI, the CIA, or the NSA are the ones being sued.'

'So, as my lawyer, do you think I have a case to answer?'

Emma says ominously, 'I pray to God that we never have to go down that path. But to answer your question, no.'

C.J. looks relieved.

Emma explains her rationale. 'You are not an employee of the NSA and you never have been. Yes, your father was, but that was well over thirty years ago. Max Stroheim told you nothing. There is no proof that while he was alive he said anything to you. I've read your father's memoirs – and can tell you that, although there is plenty of damning information contained in his notes, there is nothing copied directly from secret files or any other documentation. NOTHING. There is no theft of Government property and no hint of such.

'Even so, I wouldn't let anyone see your father's memoirs. Even if someone did see them, they are just the jumbled thoughts of an old man. Of course, you and I know that is not the case, however it would be almost impossible to prove otherwise in court. Even when the book is published, you can publish it as non-fiction because much of the information is based on his notes or is speculative – and we are allowed to speculate. Speculation is not against the law.'

C.J. leans in to kiss her. 'Well, Emma Burgess, it is more than just speculation that you are a very clever woman. I love you.'

Shortly after sunrise, they drive through the outskirts of Jo-burg, heading north east toward Bongani.

C.J. reveals what he has written thus far. 'I still have a long way to go, and down the track I'd like your help with the editing process, but it's starting to take shape. The information Dad gave me is incredible, yet it is factual and regimented. My father did not write with much emotion. I've been trying to place myself in his shoes, trying to make the stories and events in the book more personal.'

'He saw things most of us would fail to grasp. You more than anyone else now know what your father went through.'

'For more than sixty years he kept secrets that he would have loved to share. Share with my mum, other colleagues, his golf buddies – and me. I spent many hours talking with Dad about the universe and how it might work. I think I even told him that I believed other species had to live on other planets. We can't be the only intelligent life in a universe that contains billions upon billions of other planets. He nodded, yet never elaborated. He encouraged me to research thoroughly then to make up my own mind based on learning, instinct, and curiosity.

'My father quoted Albert Einstein: "The important thing is not to stop questioning. Curiosity has its own reason for existing."'

Driving through sprawling high-plateau savannah, Emma encourages C.J. to talk more about his relationship with his father.

Learning so much about his father in the last few months, C.J. always had the greatest respect for his father. 'Being an only child had its drawbacks – Dad was older and retired when I was born, but I never saw that as a negative. Dad was home every day. I'd see him before I went to school, and he was there every night went I went to bed. He was for the most part serious but he had a playful side.

'There's some lines from *The Hitchhiker's Guide to the Galaxy*. My father often repeated one adage about dolphins' intelligence:

> On the planet Earth, man had always assumed that he was more intelligent than dolphins because he had achieved so much – the wheel, New York, wars and so on – while all the dolphins had ever done was muck about in the water having a good time. But conversely, the dolphins had always believed that they were far more intelligent than man – for precisely the same reasons.

Emma laughs, 'I have a feeling there was more to these lines than you first thought. Your father was giving you advice.'

'To stop and smell the roses?'

'Or to spend more time mucking around in water!'

Driving further, the landscape becomes more mountainous, the vegetation more lush.

C.J. continues, 'He did not say much, but when he did speak it was always worth listening to. After Dad left S-4 he was handed Project Red Book. He never once said that Red Book was a NSA project. He said he was at S-4 from time-to-time, but was also given clearances and access to enter other facilities. Not all those other facilities were NSA controlled. My father was in a rare position of having access to different agencies and bases, as well as top-secret classified information – information that was also kept from the Government.'

'That's one of the key things I learned from your father. The Government funded most of these projects, yet knew very little about them. And it would seem that as time went on, the Government, as a collective, was completely shut out.'

'So individual Government officials may have known some things, but that would have been through their association with these think-tank organizations or MJ-12. Am I right?'

'Absolutely.'

CHAPTER THIRTY-EIGHT

At the gates to Bongani Mountain Lodge, they park the car to be picked up by a driver and tracker in an open-topped jeep. The tracker has a rifle. C.J. and Emma soon finding out why. The gates open, the jeep drives through, and the gates close quickly behind.

'You are now in the wild,' says the driver.

He explains that South Africa has what is called 'the big five' game. These are animals big-game hunters (and now safari tour operators) refer to as the five most difficult animals in Africa to hunt on foot: the lion, elephant, Cape buffalo, leopard, and the rhinoceros.

C.J. and Emma fail to see any of the big five on the ride to the lodge, but catch glimpses of impala, zebras, and giraffes.

Their accommodation is a freestanding stone and thatched-roof hut perched on a cliff overlooking the lush valleys, rocky outcrops, and savannah of Kruger National Park. After absorbing the majestic views, they join other guests for a late afternoon safari.

The open-topped jeep takes them on a sightseeing adventure. Leaving the dirt tracks, the jeep knocks down small bushes in pursuit of local wildlife. At one stage, C.J. and Emma were only a few paces from a pride lions. By the time the sun begins to set, they have seen four of the big five: only the leopard to go.

Returning from safari, C.J. and Emma are treated to a traditional South Africa banquet, eating a variety of game meats and boerewors sausages, pap (maize porridge), stews, and chakalaka, a spicy relish.

'I'm not sure I could eat this every night,' says Emma, 'but wow, what an experience.'

• • •

Over the coming days, while C.J. writes, Emma delves into the backgrounds of some of the MJ-12 members Max Stroheim talks of. She finds little of interest until reaching Bill Nedersham. What she discovers makes her jaw drop.

She looks across to C.J. and composes herself. She will reveal all to C.J. at sunset.

The sun sets behind the distant mountains; the mist-covered valley below is bathed in an eerie, golden glow. Checking her computer periodically, Emma tells C.J. about Bill Nedersham.

'Firstly, we know that Frank Reiner was likely murdered. But your father never mentioned the later career of Bill Nedersham. We know Nedersham was one of the best communications experts and code-breakers in America, with cryptology his forte.

'Nedersham left the NSA to head up a new department, called the Department of Defense Intelligence Command Control. This is now known as the CIIS (Center for Integrated Intelligence Systems). CIIS is part of the National Security Engineering Center, and its function is: "Supporting all elements of the intelligence community, including the military services, national agencies, and unified and specified commands."

'You'll never guess who all of these divisions, including CIIS, are controlled by? I'll give you a hint …'

'Not MITRE Corporation?'

'Yes, bravo! And there's more. The NSA was originally set up as a cryptology agency, that's why they recruited Nedersham.'

'And when Nedersham left to work for MITRE, I'm guessing the

NSA would have had to agree to that?'

'You'd think so,' answers Emma.

'Did Bill Nedersham go anywhere after MITRE?'

'No, he worked at MITRE until his retirement. If you thought he had a long and happy retirement, think again. Not long after leaving MITRE, he was admitted into a mental institution and was never released. He died there some years later.'

'So he went insane?'

'That's the question in debate,' replies a bewildered Emma. 'Nedersham had no family and few friends; however, just after he retired he apparently talked briefly about some of the things he learnt in his NSA and MITRE career. For some reason, he chose to talk with a radio broadcaster. The conversation in question was only brief, but straight after the broadcast Nedersham was whisked away by officials of some sort and institutionalized. Do you know who that broadcaster was?'

C.J. shakes his head.

'It was William Cooper!'

C.J. is speechless.

'The same William Cooper you researched and read his book. And Cooper was killed only a short while after talking with Nedersham.'

C.J. is flabbergasted. Max Stroheim voiced his skepticism regarding the reported suicide of Frank Reiner so, had he known about Nedersham, he would have said so.

How C.J. will write about these events is difficult, as much of the information is conjecture. He asks Emma, tongue-in-cheek, for 'a lawyer's opinion.'

Emma explains that the word *speculation* is used regularly in the legal profession. 'Most legal cases are not black and white. There is a certain amount of assumption and guesswork. Even the judge pauses for 'deliberation.' This means that most of the legal profession is based on speculation. If you speculate that it is reasonable to assume someone like Bill Nedersham was deliberately institutionalized without his consent or proper analysis, then say so but don't say something's definite that isn't. A legal threat is the last of our worries.'

Emma changes the conversation to discuss the next leg of their journey: Malelane.

Their new accommodation is on the river that forms part of the Kruger National Park border, the aptly named Crocodile River. Offering a spectacular viewing deck and bar perched over the river that teams with hippos and crocodiles, it's perfect for the local drink of choice: gin and tonic.

Several G&Ts later, C.J. returns to their room to write. Emma chats with the concierge.

Joining C.J., she relays that parts of the park are open for driving. 'We've just had a number of guided safaris, so I thought we might drive.'

C.J. agrees.

'We're not allowed to take the car off the road, so sometimes the animals are quite some distance away. The concierge suggested we ask at the gate where the lions or elephants were seen the afternoon before. I have a map already. He also recommended following tour buses as they often know where the larger groups of animals are.'

The next morning C.J. and Emma eat breakfast on the deck overlooking the river, before driving to Kruger National Park. Emma asks the gate attendant where the prides of lions and the herds of elephants have been recently sighted. The attendant marks the locations on Emma's map.

A large herd of elephants were sighted the day before, not far from the Malelane gate. As C.J. drives, Emma navigates. Elephants are nowhere to be seen, yet evidence of their movement is everywhere, including larger trees stripped of bark and smaller trees knocked down.

Kruger is mostly savannah, crisscrossed with a series of smaller and larger roads. Emma navigates toward where a pride of lions was recently spotted, around a raised rocky outcrop, which C.J. and Emma can see in the distance. Two other cars have followed them.

They are nearing the turnoff to the road where the sighting of lions was reported. As C.J.'s car turns off the main road, the vehicle immediately behind continues on. The second car follows C.J and Emma. C.J. drives slowly in the hope of seeing animals. The car behind edges closer.

BANG.

C.J.'s car pulls to the right – slowing down. The rear driver's-side tire has blown.

C.J. looks instinctively into the rear-vision mirror. A man is holding a gun out the window of the trialing car. C.J. recognizes the man. It is Ben Hamermesh.

'Duck down!' C.J. yells, placing his foot hard on the accelerator. The car swerves across the narrow road – wheels spinning in the red dirt either side of the bitumen – the metal rims scraping on the asphalt.

Bullets fly – the rear window explodes – shards of glass and bullets spray inside. The front windscreen also shatters. C.J. swerves the car instinctively, although the shattered windscreen obscures his vision. He pulls his shirtsleeve over his hands to smash out the broken glass.

With a blown tire, C.J. can't outrun Hamermesh. It's only be a matter of time before one of his bullets hit its target. C.J. has no choice. He leaves the road.

'Hold on – we're going bush!' he shouts.

The car cuts a path through the sparse trees; it fishtails through the grass, low shrubs, and thorn bushes. C.J. has no option but to drive as fast as he can. Ben Hamermesh holds all the cards – a gun in-hand and a fully functional car.

Hamermesh follows at a distance, following the path through the scrub. He stalks his prey.

C.J.'s eyes dart forward and sideways, searching for a path, for any opportunity to avoid the inevitable gunfire. A zebra appears from behind the bushes in front of C.J.'s car. C.J. narrowly misses the large animal, as he turns sharply toward the rocky outcrop with his pedal to the floor,

Another zebra races in front of Hamermesh's car. He brakes heavily to avoid hitting the animal. C.J. is able to open a gap between the cars. He drives toward the outcrop as fast as he can.

Ben Hamermesh sees C.J.'s car fly around the rocks. It won't be long before he can deliver that final blow. He follows the trail of bent grass and shrubs that winds around the rocky outcrop. C.J.'s car has stopped in long grass, hard up against a pile of rocks – nowhere to go. The engine is still running; the car doors are open – C.J. and Emma have fled.

Hamermesh pulls up behind the bullet-ridden car. C.J. won't have a weapon. He nudges up to the car's rear bumper, making certain it is blocked in. He turns off the ignition, placing the keys in his pocket. Stepping out of the car slowly, his pistol is poised and ready to fire. He takes a few tentative steps through the knee-high grass toward C.J.'s car. Although the inside cabin appears empty, he keeps his gun trained on the car.

A large rock smashes into Hamermesh's shin with force. The pain makes Hamermesh reel. C.J. releases his grip on the rock to roll out from under the car, swinging his right boot at Hamermesh. He connects with the other leg, bringing Hamermesh to the ground. C.J. scrambles to his feet, he unleashes unleash a well-timed kick into the hand holding the gun. The pistol flies free and falls into the thick grass – out of sight.

Hamermesh dives into the grass to retrieve the gun. C.J. charges him. They roll around in the grass –a flurry of fists and flailing body parts. Hamermesh's leg bleeds profusely but, for now, he remains strong and agile. C.J. manages to land several weighted blows. Hamermesh is able to break free. Scrambling backwards, he struggles to his feet. C.J.'s attack is relentless. Unseen by Hamermesh, Emma rolls clear from under the car.

The injured Hamermesh is no physical match for C.J. Movement in the grass distracts C.J.. Hamermesh breaks free once more. He draws another pistol from his trouser pocket and aims it at C.J.'s head. C.J. has never seen a gun like it – very small, with a short, stumpy barrel.

'GET IN THE CAR!' C.J. yells to Emma.

'DON'T MOVE!' Hamermesh shouts, with the gun now trained on Emma.

'Don't listen to him, Emma. Get back in the car!'

'I'll shoot,' threatens Hamermesh.

C.J. says to Emma, 'The gun only has a single shot. He can't shoot both of us and he'll shoot me first. Trust me.' C.J. makes eye contact with Ben Hamermesh. 'You can shoot me, but Emma will run you down with the car.'

Eyes peer through the long grass, just behind Hamermesh. He fails to notice, busy challenging C.J.'s logic.

'I am surprised you knew this is a single-shot gun. You've researched well, Stroheim.'

C.J. had only guessed it was a single-shot gun. He sees the grass blades behind Ben twitch.

'The bullet has an explosive head and will blow you to smithereens. I don't need a perfect shot to get perfect results. And even if your girlfriend manages to get the car out, I'll catch her easily. And I will kill her with my bare hands.' He takes aim at C.J.'s chest. 'Farewell, Mr. Stroheim—'

Just then, two lionesses spring from the grass. One smacks Ben Hamermesh in the back with ferocious force. He's knocked to the ground. The other clamps her powerful jaws around Hamermesh's neck.

Emma jumps inside the car, leaving the door open for C.J. He turns and dives into the car, slamming the door behind. A third lion, a large male, emerges from the grass to join his pride. The struggling man thrashes and screams. The lions savage Hamermesh. The knee-high grass obscures his body, but his blood-curdling screams are chillingly clear. Jaws on his throat, the lioness's whole bodyweight crushes down on his head. Hamermesh does not stand a chance – his body becomes limp – the screaming ceases.

CHAPTER THIRTY-NINE

Blood drips from the lion's mouth. His head rises from the grass, eyes looking directly at C.J. and Emma in the car. Although the doors are closed, the windows have been shot out, including the windscreen. One or all of the lions could easily jump up onto the hood and reach C.J. and Emma.

Hamermesh's car is undamaged but blocking them in. C.J. climbs into the backseat to open the rear passenger-side door, the side away from the lions. He sneaks the few paces to Hamermesh's car. It's unlocked. Eyes locked on the lions, he opens the door to slip inside. *No car keys.* C.J. suspects where the keys are. *Well, the keys can stay right there.*

Searching the car for any weapons or clues to Hamermesh's associates or identity, the only thing he finds is a cell phone sitting in the console. It is turned on.

He releases the handbrake and moves the gearstick to neutral. The lions are still preoccupied. He sneaks back to his car, handing the phone to Emma. C.J. climbs into the driver's seat and reverses against Hamermesh's car, pushing it backwards. He swings the car away from the rocks and away from the feasting lions.

C.J. and Emma discuss phoning the Kruger National Park authorities using Hamermesh's phone, but the risks of being traced are too great. C.J. places the phone in his pocket.

Nursing the car back to the main road, they hail a passing tour bus. Emma's concocted their cover story. They tell the bus driver they were chased by an agitated elephant. As they sped along the road, a tire blew, the car careened off the road and into the scrub. Fearing being caught by the elephant, they continued at speed until they could make it back onto the road. Some small tree branches shattered the windows and pierced the body.

Emma says they managed to control the car and make it back to the main road. 'We didn't see the elephant again.'

Surprisingly, their story is not questioned.

Returned to the park gates, C.J. and Emma arrange for the rental car to be picked up by a tow-truck.

They scroll through Ben Hamermesh's phone. Emma checks the recent calls. The last five phone calls are to the same number – the initials M.R. – the same initials on Ellis Buckman's recent call list. Scrolling through her photos, Emma finds Ellis Buckman's phone lists. The 'M.R.' on Buckman's phone has the same number.

'It's the same person.'

She takes photos of Ben Hamermesh's contacts and messages. She then shuts it down and throws it into a rubbish bin. If Ben Hamermesh knew where they were, others may know as well. *Who is M.R?*

At the hotel C.J. packs, while Emma checks flights leaving the nearest airport, in the city of Nelspruit. A flight is leaving for Nairobi, Kenya in just over two hours. Emma books it

C.J. finds the Buckman's injection device in his suitcase. He won't risk taking the device through security at the airport, so for now he'll leave it in the suitcase. He vows to Emma that, outside of airports, he won't be caught without it again.

How did Ben Hamermesh track them to Kruger National Park?

C.J. and Emma think it may have been through the rental car company, or maybe someone spotted them leaving Australia – and Hamermesh somehow traced them to South Africa. Either way, they must flee.

'Nelspruit Airport, please' they instruct the taxi driver.

On board their flight, Emma asks, 'Where do we go after Nairobi?'

'We can't fly back to Australia,' says C.J., 'so I guess we keep heading north.'

'As in northern Africa, the Middle East, or Europe?'

'Let's see what flights are available when we get to Nairobi.'

'Good idea.'

The four-hour flight allows time for discussion. The inflight magazine highlights a host of European destinations from Nairobi.

'Where would you go, if you had a choice?' asks C.J.

'We need to get to England at some point, but you haven't finished writing the book yet. We need time. It's not the wisest option, many of these global think tanks have roots in England – and close ties with the US.'

After walking off the plane in Nairobi, C.J. and Emma stand under the departures board. There is a flight leaving for Paris in fifty minutes.

'How's Paris sound?' asks C.J.

'What girl would say no to going to Paris?'

Just then the board changes; the flight to Paris is delayed.

After retrieving their luggage, C.J. and Emma approach the airline's sales counter to learn snow storms and blizzards in Paris have caused the delay. Alternatively, a flight leaves to Nice in an hour.

'Nice is in the south of France, right? So how's that sound?' C.J. asks Emma.

Her instant approval has C.J. purchasing tickets without hesitation.

While waiting at the boarding gate, Emma researches accommodation options in and around Nice.

'Look at this C.J., there's a cute, little villa available in a town near Nice; just inland, in the hills.'

Looking over her shoulder to see the villa, featuring a beautiful patio with flowering bushes and distant views of the Mediterranean Sea, C.J. says 'That looks perfect.'

Outside Nice Airport, C.J. and Emma catch a cab. As the taxi meanders up the hills towards the village of Biot, Emma looks at C.J. to smile affectionately, 'I know we've had some challenging times, but who would have thought we'd end-up in the south of France?'

He kisses her on the cheek.

Driving through the village of Biot, they see cafés and restaurants, shops and markets. The village is beautiful, with an old-world charm rarely experienced by C.J. and Emma. Their villa is only a short walk from the main street. Pulling up outside, Emma hugs C.J. She is truly excited.

The villa is small and basic inside, yet charming. The outside patio offers views back to the coastline. This is going to be the perfect location for C.J. to write and Emma to assist.

If the village looked beautiful from the taxi, it is even more appealing walking through the history-soaked streets, with ancient architecture and immaculately maintained buildings. Biot was a pottery center from the 16th to 18th centuries. In the middle of the 20th century, the village once again became famous for its decorative pottery and glasswork.

C.J. and Emma find a small supermarket, buying as many groceries as they can carry. At the top of the shopping list are bottles of French wine, baguettes, and Camembert.

An afternoon of writing and research leads to sunset on the patio, sipping Bordeaux wine and devouring local cheese.

'*Magnifique*.'

The setting sun chills the air. Attempting to light an old potbelly stove frustrates C.J. He is unceremoniously dismissed by the far more proficient Emma. She grew up in Tasmania, starting and stoking a log fire was a daily winter affair.

'I think I've had a tad more experience with these things than a city boy from LA.'

She is right.

Cuddled in front of the stove, C.J. reveals a change of direction for the book, 'Not wholesale changes, but a more personalized touch. I think we should be part of the story.'

'Oh?'

'Our journey to find out the truth behind my father's career will not only make good reading, but demonstrate just what lengths people will go to keep the truth hidden. We've been shot at on two continents, chased in cars, seen two men die, and we are still on the run. What do you think? Are you comfortable being written into the book?'

'I have no problems with that. I think it's a great idea. I'll help with whatever I can.'

• • •

Over the coming days and weeks, C.J. writes and Emma researches. They want the book to be as accurate as possible.

On a beautiful, clear Côte d'Azur evening, they stroll down to the village to a chic little café. Both are thoroughly enjoying the regional cuisine. C.J. has dined in French restaurants in the US but finds little similarity between the local provincial food, which is simple yet tasty, and the gastronomically complexities of LA's French dining experiences. He prefers simplicity; so does Emma.

In the intimate surrounds, they are wary not to talk too much about the book. The other diners are mostly locals and speaking French; however, C.J. and Emma realize the need to be discreet. Whoever has been able to track them halfway around the world must have arms spreading far and wide. Their security is more important than anything else.

Returning to the villa, they sit by the warmth of the potbelly stove to turn on computers. After an hour, Emma mutters something under her breath. C.J. looks up to see confusion on Emma's face.

'What's up?' he asks.

Emma's been blocked from entering several websites. This has never happened before. She was looking into MITRE Corporation and their ties when she was blocked from entering Wikipedia. Wikipedia is a public information site; it is for everyone to use, not a suspicious or dangerous site. She repeatedly tries to enter different sites featuring MITRE Corporation and is blocked on each occasion.

'Look at this,' she shows him the computer screen.

'What on earth is going on?'

'I have no idea.'

'I've just researched RAND – and I had no problems. Let me try again.'

This time she's blocked from that, too, with the same icon appearing on the screen.

Any key words relevant to the secret projects or organizations result in the same result. Everything else on the computer appears to function normally, albeit it seems to be running slower than normal.

C.J. has not been online with his computer for a number of days, writing offline. He goes online to visit the same sites Emma is blocked from. He is not blocked. Both are using the same Internet provider and yet he can access certain sites while Emma cannot.

'This is weird,' says C.J. 'Have you been on any sites where you may have picked up a virus or a cookie or something?'

'I've been basically using Wikipedia. They are a public website. I'm not blocked from all of Wikipedia, just certain subjects. How is it possible to blocked from one subject and not another – all on the one website? The other strange thing is that MITRE and RAND are private corporations. I can access their own websites, but not Wikipedia. It's bizarre.'

C.J. and Emma can't find a logical explanation. They decide to sleep on the problem to try again in the morning.

The next morning the patio is bathed in sunshine. They eat breakfast with the calm Mediterranean water sparkling in the distance.

Emma turns her computer on to discover she is still blocked from viewing the Wikipedia pages for RAND and MITRE Corporations. She notes that, whenever she attempts to enter these blocked sites, the computer is markedly slower responding afterwards. When visiting non-blocked sites, the computer functions normally.

'It's perplexing. It's though I'm being monitored.' This statement makes her eyes open wide. 'Surely my computer, working from a public site in a country area of France, can't be hacked into? Can it?'

It's a sobering question. Max Stroheim wrote about the surveillance culture of the NSA, particularly in recent years. He even mentioned Edward Snowden's revelations. For all the research into the NSA's past, it finally dawns on C.J. they haven't investigated Snowden's claims of the NSA monitoring phone and Internet traffic, not only in the USA, but the world. They were so focused on the past they've ignored the present.

Emma sits in silence, sick to the stomach. C.J. Googles *Edward Snowden.*

CHAPTER FORTY

C.J. and Emma learn that Snowden's disclosures revealed numerous global surveillance programs. Many were run by the NSA and the Five Eyes Intelligence Alliance, comprising Australia, Canada, New Zealand, the UK, and the USA. Five Eyes developed the ECHELON surveillance system, initially to monitor the communications of the former Soviet Union and Eastern Bloc. It is now used to monitor billions of private communications worldwide, and includes the cooperation of telecommunication companies and European governments.

'European governments and telecommunication companies?' Emma mutters under her breath, before C.J. types: *Can my computer IP address be traced?*

The first response reads:

> Yes your IP can be traced, when you post or log in online, your IP is logged by the server, from that they can trace what country you are from and your ISP's details, including the general region you are logging on.

C.J. immediately closes the computer. 'God, they know we're here. Come on Emma, let's get out of here!'

They throw clothes into their bags and wheel the suitcases down the hill toward Biot's main street. They duck inside a café and ask the staff to call for a cab.

Outside, a black car travels at speed, passing outside the café on its way up the hill – toward the villa.

'Stay here. I won't be long,' orders C.J. He sneaks out the door to see the black car turn into the villa's driveway. He slinks along the road in the direction of the villa, using trees and bushes as coverage. Sighting the black car through some bushes, he is confident he cannot be seen.

Two men in dark suits exit the car. C.J. can see they both have guns – raised to eye level. One man approaches the villa's front door; the other sneaks around the side of the building.

With the man at the side of the villa out of sight and the other with his back turned to road, C.J. sprints back down the road to the café.

'They'll see everything gone and think we've left to catch a plane or something,' says C.J. to Emma. 'Let's just wait it out here, then order a taxi after they're gone.'

Emma agrees.

Minutes later, the black car races back past the café.

Seeing C.J. and Emma's bags, the café owner asks, 'Are you leaving us, mademoiselle and monsieur?'

'Yes,' replies Emma. 'We've had the most beautiful stay here, but sadly it's time to go. We were thinking of going to Lyon, but we're a bit sick of planes. We thought we might see more of the countryside in a bus or a train.'

'I'm not sure about ze buses, but I do know ze trains leave Nice for Lyon.'

Arriving at the Nice Train Station, C.J. asks Emma 'So, would you like to go to Lyon?'

'I think we are better off in a bustling city like Paris. I said 'Lyon' just in case anyone does some snooping around.'

'You're a sneaky woman, Emma Burgess. So if we're going to Paris, we might need some warm clothes.'

Nice Train Station is a majestic old building, but a fashion retail center it is not. The only retail outlet selling clothing is a gift shop. C.J. and Emma buy scarfs, woolen beanies, and hooded jackets emblazoned with emblems of the local soccer team, OGN Nice.

The train ride from Nice to Paris is six hours. For now, at least, they are safe.

C.J. has no problem using his computer to write, as he can do that offline, however further researching may be an obstacle. Both have information and files on USB memory sticks. Emma revisits some of that information, while C.J. writes.

Halfway to Paris, Emma suggests they eat lunch in the train's diner.

They sit at a table next to a couple in their early twenties. The young lady is using her computer tablet; he texting on his phone. Emma leans across to talk to them.

'Excuse me, sorry to interrupt, do you speak English?' Emma asks politely.

They do, being English.

Emma introduces herself, then C.J., explaining they haven't booked accommodation in Paris and her computer is playing up. 'Later, and only after you have finished what you're doing, would it be possible to use your computer to find out what hotels are near the Paris train terminal?'

The girl can see that Emma is genuine. 'Yes, of course,' she says.

The couple are Thomas and Cilla. Thomas and Cilla reveal they are both students at the University of Cambridge, on their end-of-year-holiday and returning to the UK via Paris.

Emma asks, 'What are you studying?'

'History and Politics, with the view of either getting a job in the media or continuing studying, possibly Journalism at Nottingham Trent University or a summer course at Cambridge.'

C.J. is in two minds whether to tell Thomas and Cilla his true occupation. Realistically, telling them is not going to jeopardize or compromise their situation. C.J. looks at Emma and sees her subtle smile.

C.J. says, 'What a small world; I'm a journalist.'

While Emma uses Cilla's computer to search hotels in Paris, Thomas and Cilla talk to C.J. Both have only a year to graduation and are interested in any advice C.J. can give.

C.J.'s view of the journalistic world has changed immeasurably in the past months. The words of Ellis Buckman run through his mind: *How do you think I made it to the top of my profession? Do you think it was luck? The world does not run on chance. It is run by those who make it run.*

C.J. says, 'The old saying goes: It is not what you know, but who you know.'

'How so?' Thomas asks.

'Journalism at its core is about research and getting to the bottom of a story, but the big picture is about contacts. You need contacts. If you want to make a difference you need to be in the right position to do so. You can't get to that position without contacts.'

Thomas and Cilla hang on C.J.'s every word.

Emma has found a beautiful hotel in Paris. She apologizes for interrupting, explaining to C.J. 'It's a boutique hotel only a hundred meters from Liège Metro Station. The area is full of shops and cafés and also by the metro. The Champs Elysées and the Opéra Garnier are only fifteen minutes away.'

'Sounds perfect.'

Emma returns the computer to Cilla, thanking her. Thomas and Cilla are staying three nights in a backpacker hostel not far from the Champs Elysées. C.J. and Emma agree to catch up with the young couple on their last night in Paris. Cilla has heard rave reviews about the Buddha Bar near the Champs Elysées. Emma has also heard of the bar.

They bid farewell, returning to their respective cabins. They will see each other in Paris.

C.J. noted the students live in Cambridge. From his wallet he removes one of the business cards his father left for him in Bangkok. The publisher is Mark Dalgleish; his business is in Cambridge. C.J. wonders if Thomas or Cilla might know of him. He might ask them when they meet at the Buddha Bar.

C.J. planned to write the book to its completion at the Biot villa. That idea has been thrown out the window, so they discuss other options. In light of the possible hacking and tracing of their details when online,

C.J. will forgo Internet use. Emma will use public library computers to tie up any loose ends. She wants to find out as much information as possible about the NSA's abilities to hack into and trace privately operated computers.

'How long do you think you need to finish the book?' she asks.

C.J. smiles, ignoring the question. 'You know, I'd like to see the Eifel Tower, too.' He composes himself to answer. 'Two weeks. Three tops.'

Emma says, 'If we like the accommodation, then why don't we book it for three weeks?'

'Sounds good to me.'

Stepping from the train station and feeling the chill in the Parisian air, C.J. and Emma wrap their newly purchased red and black scarves tightly over the matching hoodies, featuring a gold eagle crest. Handing a Emma a beanie to wear, C.J. quips 'I know we look like we should be going to soccer game, but at least we won't freeze to death.'

'I think you look cute.'

Seeing their accommodation, and its location, Emma immediately goes to the reception to book additional time. 'Three weeks, *merci*.'

The weather is overcast and bitterly cold. Being a Tassie girl, Emma thought she knew what cold was. She reassesses. According to C.J., the first thing on their agenda is for Emma to buy warm clothes.

Emma looks at C.J. 'Well, that's a girl's dream come true.' She adds, 'As sexy as you look in your soccer scarf and beanie, I think you could do with some new clothes, too.'

They explore the shops near the hotel. C.J. quickly buys a jumper and a jacket, keen to return to the hotel to write. He leaves Emma to continue shopping. She jokes that she may never return.

C.J. had time on the train to think about the book and its direction. He has even given the book a name. Inspired, his fingers hit the computer keys in a flurry.

Emma returns from her 'Paris shopping expedition' wearing most of her new purchases. C.J. admires her new wardrobe, commenting on 'how beautifully French' she looks, kissing her on the cheek.

Emma located a public library only a short walk from the hotel and heads off to research.

In her absence, C.J. immerses himself in his father's story.

Max Stroheim was passionate about his scientific discoveries, yet equally perturbed at the deception in keeping that information secret.

Max was specific when he wrote: 'I want you to write the book to educate the general public about the truth of events.'

The key words to C.J. are: *truth* and *events*. The events in question are clear. Max Stroheim wanted the world to know about all the secret projects pertaining to alien contact, information, and technology. This is the core of the story; the reason he was employed by the NSA. The cover-ups, the deception, and the lies are peripheral to the big picture.

Max Stroheim met two, possibly three, different types of intelligent species. To most, the term *extraterrestrials* conjures images of little green men flying in from some other planet. C.J. is determined to steer clear of stereotypes; his father would insist on it. Max thought the likely origin of the Tall Greys was another planet, but was unconvinced the smaller Roswell Greys were from other worldly origins. He surmised they were created, or more specifically – cloned, here on Earth. He knew the Greys had underground bases – and that those bases had existed for possibly thousands of years. But he gave no indication to advocate the small Roswell Greys had such a heritage. Everything suggested that they were only a recently manufactured species, with little to no evidence suggesting the Roswell Greys and their craft were around much prior to WWII.

The information provided by Krll confused Max Stroheim. The EBE was deceptive and deliberate. Max thought the Roswell Greys were part of a collective think tank, with Krll manipulated. Max was highly skeptical the truth had been given and even more cynical for the reasons behind the lies.

Describing the Nordic aliens is a challenge for C.J. Max Stroheim was present at the top-secret meeting with two of these incredible beings; even so, he learned little. C.J. researched the Nordics from other's experiences, including some claiming contact. Descriptions varied, although many reports echo a striking resemblance to those accounts by his father. The Nordics' physical features were defined as similar to ours. Max Stroheim theorized that the Nordics look similar to us because they may indeed be DNA-based entities like humans.

'They may even share a genetic heritage with mankind,' Max deduced.

Max rarely guessed. This statement has made C.J. think.

When C.J. was thirteen, his father helped him with a school assignment. The subject was Evolution. At the time, C.J. had not given his father's past career a great deal of thought. This particular assignment asked the students to give examples of Darwin's Theory of Evolution. C.J. chose the evolution of man, questioning his father on the subject.

At one point Max Stroheim said 'Son, you are talking about the evolution of ape to man as though it is a fact. Remember that the assignment is on Darwin's *Theory* of Evolution. The key word is *theory*.'

The way his father said the words prompted C.J. to ask, 'So we didn't come from apes?'

Max Stroheim replied, 'I didn't say that, son. All I'm saying is what may look correct in theory may not always be the fact. Your assignment asks you to report on Darwin's theories. Do as the assignment asks.'

That was the only time C.J. and his father talked on the subject, but C.J. now feels there was more to that conversation than he'd thought at the time.

Did Max Stroheim believe we came from apes or did he think we were more closely related to the Nordic aliens?

It is an intriguing hypothesis.

CHAPTER FORTY-ONE

Emma returns from the library, smiling from ear to ear. It has just begun snowing outside. She should be tired, cold, and scared. In the past few months she's been shot at, involved in high-speed car chases, seen two men die, and just yesterday two men in black suits with guns were poised to kill them. They missed C.J. and Emma by mere minutes, yet she is still upbeat.

'It's snowing and I'm in Paris!'

C.J. turns off the computer and looks out the window. It is dark outside, the snow falling heavily. He puts on his new jacket and wraps a scarf around his neck.

Emma watches curiously, asking, 'What are you doing?'

C.J. smiles. 'Come on – let's go walking in the snow.'

They walk hand in hand along the beautiful Parisian streets, the streetlights illuminating the falling snowflakes before they nestle on the ground.

Emma talks of her research at the library. She had looked into whistleblower Edward Snowden's revelations of NSA's hacking of civilian computers.

'And it wasn't just the NSA with the access to the files of private individuals, companies, and governments. In fact, Edward Snowden didn't even work for the NSA, but the private contractor Booz Allen

Hamilton. This is true. So all the Internet information, including our personal information, is available to a private company. That's scary stuff. Tomorrow I'll research more about Booz Allen Hamilton, as well as follow up on some of Snowden's allegations. How'd your writing go?'

'Good. It's starting to take shape.'

Emma spends most of the next day at a library, only one train stop from their hotel. She learns that Booz Allen Hamilton is one of America's biggest security contractors and a significant part of the constantly revolving doormob between the US intelligence establishment and the private sector. Booz Allen Hamilton's board is littered with former CIA management and bosses. The company has contracts awarded (not bid for) by not only the NSA, but also the IRS and the Department of Homeland Security. Emma then learns that Booz Allen Hamilton is owned by the Carlyle Group conglomerate. Another corporation with links to MJ-12.

Why is Emma not surprised?

She shakes her in disbelief, a smug grin on her face.

Returning to the hotel, Emma reveals what she learned about Booz Allen Hamilton, as well as Edward Snowden's disclosures.

'From what I can gather, each time anyone goes online or uses a mobile phone, the information is tracked and sent via a series of relay stations and satellites to the NSA and other global agencies and contractors, such as Booz Allen Hamilton. And it doesn't matter what antivirus or security software you have, the telecommunication companies and the search engines, the email companies, Facebook, Instagram, Twitter, the lot have agreed for the usage to be monitored. The NSA uses the guise of "national security" as an umbrella to justify the saturating monitoring, yet everything is monitored. Sure, the US Government justifies the "national security" tag because of terrorist organizations like al-Qaeda or ISIS; however, the vast majority of Internet or telephone users aren't terrorists.

'Although about twenty thousand work at the NSA's headquarters in Maryland, the NSA has also outsourced much of their work to Booz

Hamilton Allen. Edward Snowden was stationed in Hawaii, so there are affiliated stations all over the United States, as well as the world. It's saturating, yet it's impossible to personally monitor every Internet and phone call on the planet. From what I read, the NSA and the like use the latest in computer programing software to screen and generically profile users.

'I guess, in the case of what happened to my computer, I looked at a series of certain sites repeatedly, which triggered a response. The NSA's computer software has deemed me a risk of some sort; however, I'm certainly not a terrorist risk. Either way, they've blocked me from certain sites. What is even more frightening is they can access personal files and even trace a computer's location.'

'So they can access files as well?'

'They can even watch you. Edward Snowden told that laptops, desktop computers, tablets, and mobile phones are all at risk of being hacked – and they can access the built-in cameras to take pictures and videos while you are connected to the Internet. Edward Snowden urged every computer user to cover their webcam with a sticker.'

'So every time you or I were online, they could not only view what we were researching, but they could potentially see us as well?'

'Yes. That means they can spy on the location you are in, as well as trace your movements via the Internet Provider location. I read varying theories about how effective IP tracking is. Quite frankly, no one knows. I would guess that whoever is monitoring you – and that could be a number of sources – they seem to have accurate GPS map location of mobile phones, yet computers are harder to pinpoint. It seems they can locate the general area, but an exact location is more difficult to obtain. It might be why whoever was monitoring us took a while each time to find us. The bottom line is, we need to be extremely careful.'

C.J. and Emma need to get ready, as they're meeting the young couple from Cambridge at the Buddha Bar.

The Buddha Bar is spectacular. C.J. and Emma's dining table is in front of a gigantic, imposing gold Buddha statue. The main room is full of tables and diners. Above is a mezzanine floor with balconies and a bar. After dinner the dining tables are removed and the ground floor becomes a pulsating nightclub.

C.J. and Emma are meeting with Thomas and Cilla later in the night. The restaurant may be too expensive for the limited budget of students. When Thomas and Cilla do arrive, C.J. buys everyone drinks, moving to a balcony booth on the mezzanine. All are suitably impressed by the luxurious backdrop.

Thomas and Cilla talk about their sightseeing around Paris, tinged with disappointment at leaving the next morning. C.J. mentions he will be traveling to Cambridge himself in about three weeks' time.

'I am meeting with a publisher. I know Cambridge is quite a big city, but have either of you heard of Mark Dalgleish?'

Cilla gushes, 'Stella Dalgleish is in our college course. She's one of my best friends. Her father is Mark Dalgleish.'

'Wow, what a small world,' says C.J. 'I've never actually met Mark, but he comes highly recommended.'

With C.J.'s subtle questioning, Cilla divulges that Mark Dalgleish's father was an American who moved to Cambridge to set up the publishing business Dalgleish Publishing. Stella Dalgleish's grandfather had passed away several years ago, with Mark taking over the business. She conveys that Mark Dalgleish is an ethical man and a 'straight shooter.' Many of the books he'd published were controversial and political. 'Where other publishers may shy away from contentious subject matter, Mark Dalgleish relishes the opportunity. I know I'm making it sound like it's a small, independent publishing house, but it's not. Mark has the contacts and the professionalism to make any author successful.'

'Dear, oh dear, Cill, are you working on commission?' jokes Thomas.

'Mark Dalgleish's father was a good friend of my father,' says C.J. He thinks momentarily, before asking Cilla 'I wonder if you could do me a favor Cilla? When you get back home, could you tell Mark Dalgleish that Max Stroheim's son will be calling in to say hello in just under three weeks' time?'

C.J. picks up a coaster from the table. Emma removes a pen from her handbag.

C.J. writes: *Max Stroheim's son coming in three weeks. I'll call into the office* on the coaster, then gives it to Cilla.

Before leaving the Buddha Bar, Thomas and Cilla ask if Emma will also be going to Cambridge. It is something C.J. and Emma had yet to fully discuss.

'I am not sure at this point, but I'd like to,' says Emma.

Cilla says, 'Well, if you have the time, we'd love to see you both. I'll give you our number. We're at college weekdays, but we're usually finished by three or four in the afternoon.'

During conversations, Cilla reveals that the University of Cambridge is massive. She and Thomas study at one of the eight faculty buildings, the Faculty of History, referred by Cilla as the 'History Faculty Building'.

With snow falling, C.J. and Emma walk to the nearby train station to catch the train back to their hotel. They discuss the upcoming trip to Cambridge. Emma is a strong-willed woman, not hesitating to announce she is going to England with him.

C.J. is equally forthright, explaining, 'England and the US have very close ties – not just with Governments, but also many of these secret organizations. I think it could be dangerous for one of us to go, let alone two.'

Emma pleads, 'We're a team.'

'Yes, we are, but let's think this through. We have three weeks to decide.'

C.J. is right to not make rash decisions. The men in black suits with guns found their villa in the tiny village of Biot. The chances of being traced in England could be much greater.

The next morning C.J. and Emma awake to find beautiful clear skies over a thick blanket of snow-covered ground. It is with great excitement they hail a cab, to instruct 'Tower de Eiffel, *merci*.'

The view from the top of the Eiffel Tower is stunning, the visibility crystal clear. C.J. and Emma overhear another English couple comment they'd been to the top of the tower a dozen times, with this the clearest day they'd had. C.J. drapes his arm over Emma's shoulder to pull her in closer. She looks at C.J. and smiles.

C.J. and Emma have the most amazing day; walking hand in hand along the river Seine, lunch at Café de la Rotonde, and later coffee at Montmartre outside Basilique du Sacré-Cœur. Over the coming days they will visit the Louvre, Musée d'Orsay, Notre Dame, Arc de Triomphe, Tuilleries Gardens, and Place de la Concorde. They have a job to do; however being in a romantic city such as Paris is too good an opportunity to miss.

'*Stop and smell the roses*' Max Stroheim urged.

Although C.J. uses his computer, offline, to write, the Edward Snowden revelations have spooked both he and Emma. He has rebooted his computer, covered the camera with tape, and perused all previous files and settings thoroughly.

While C.J.'s been writing, Emma has made a habit of visiting a local patisserie, to return with steaming coffees and delicious pastries.

Sipping coffee and nibbling on the freshest croissants they've ever eaten, Emma says, 'I've been thinking about Ellis Buckman and Ben Hamermesh – and this person with the initials M.R. may be the link we're looking for. I know it might be looking for a needle in a haystack but I have a few ideas – and I have M.R's phone number. At some point, we could ring the number.'

'That's too risky.'

'Yes, at this point. Maybe we can revisit the thought down the track. For now I'll see what I can find out on the Internet.'

Emma returns from the library late in the afternoon, looking a little glum.

C.J. pauses from writing to ask 'Are you okay?'

'I'm fine. I'm silly, but I'm fine.' She holds up her handbag. It has a large rip on the side. 'I caught the bag on a chair at the library and look.'

'Don't worry about it; it's only a cheap knock off.'

'It's not the point. I love the bag. It's such a good size and my computer fits perfectly inside.'

'We can get it fixed.'

Emma shakes her head. 'I don't think so.'

'We'll buy another one. Hell, this is Paris – isn't it the handbag capital of the world?'

'You'd think so, but believe it or not, this handbag is a British design.'

It is not the end of the world, she'll stick tape over the rip. 'I'm making a habit of taping-up rips in my bags; it's no big deal – there are more pressing issues.'

C.J. closes his laptop. 'Did you find out who this M.R is?'

She shakes her head. 'I searched every relevant corporation, company, and agency to find who this M.R. may be. I assumed it is a man, as few women seem to be involved at the higher end of these businesses. M.R., at a glance, refers to someone with the initials M.R., but it's possible that the 'M' in M.R. could mean 'Mr.' If that's the case, then it's someone with their last name beginning with 'R.' I found many very influential people who fit the bill. It could be any one of them – or it could be someone else. I'm no closer to having an answer.'

C.J. invites Emma to sit down beside him. 'I've been thinking about some of these individuals and families who my father urged me not to mention in the book – for obvious reasons. I have a proposition for you.'

'I'm intrigued, Mr. Stroheim. What's your proposition?'

'I'd like you to do the opposite to what my father instructed me to do.'

'What?'

'I want you to name names – to list the board members of private corporations who are involved with Government contracts and Federally Funded Research Center grants; to mention the families controlling banking, oil, and military supplies and infrastructures; to find out who this M.R. is; and to gather as much evidence as you can to link Ellis Buckman and Ben Hamermesh to these organizations.'

'Are you serious, C.J.?'

'Absolutely.'

'So you're going to include this information in the book?'

'No.'

'No?'

'We'll mention that we have the information in the book, without actually naming names.'

'Oh, you are devious, Mr. Stroheim. So we will hold onto this information, with the promise of releasing it if we're threatened.'

'Call it insurance if you will.'

'I'd prefer to call it *blackmail*. I love it.'

CHAPTER FORTY-TWO

Over the ensuing days Emma visits an array of libraries researching for what C.J. now refers as Emma's 'special project,' while C.J. makes vast inroads into the script. He is only a day or two away from completing the initial draft, also knowing it will take a number of days to edit. He would like Emma to not only read the book at that point, but also help with the editing process.

Emma, carrying coffees and croissants, returns from yet another library to discover fresh flowers on the table and two bottles of Bordeaux wine.

'I can see someone has been out and about,' she comments.

For all her teasing ways, she's very appreciative. She kisses him on the cheek.

'Are you ready for me to talk about my "special project" now?'

'I was ready days ago.'

'Okay, you wanted me to name names. I know that means individuals, as well as corporations. Most of the information that I have found you already know; most, but not all. The key to your father's involvement with all these secret projects and the like is MJ-12. The original members are all well and truly gone now but it seems that, as one member died or retired, they were replaced by another, sometimes more. What is certain that as time went on, more and more influence was exerted by the private sector and individual businessmen.

'I have most of those names.'

Over the next two hours, and several glasses of wine, Emma divulges those names and corporations.

'And these people have access to all sorts of intelligence material. We know about the CIA, the DIA, the FBI, and the NSA; however, I counted more than thirty different American intelligence agencies or divisions just within government circles. This doesn't even include secret agencies and projects attached to corporations like MITRE and RAND, as well as MJ-12's MAJI. God, the list goes on and on.'

'You've certainly been a busy girl,' says C.J., filling up Emma's wine glass.

'What did you think I did for all those hours at the libraries, read romance novels?' she jokes. 'Some of these agencies and intelligence-gathering departments are purely governmental, some are run by private enterprise, and some, well, let's just say that the lines are blurred. Agencies such as the NSA and the CIA are funded by the Government, but are not controlled by the Government. They are listed as "independent." It begs the question: *Who does control them?*'

'MJ-12.'

'Of course. Firstly, I want to talk about the media and their role with some of these intelligence agencies. Your father wrote about the CIA's Operation Mockingbird and how they manipulated the media to push a certain viewpoint. That was in the fifties and sixties. You're a journalist and you now know so much more than you did just a few months ago. My question to you is: *Do you think that in today's world, the media is still being manipulated?*'

'Without a doubt,' he answers in a heartbeat.

'Do you mind if I make a speculative observation about the media business?'

'Please, be my guest.'

'The owners and decision-makers of the largest media companies in the US belong to many of the top-tier organizations such as The Trilateral Commission, the CFR, and the Bilderbergs. These are the people making the big decisions. Some of the journalists, like Ellis Buckman, belong to secret societies like the Freemasons and The Bohemian Club. These also have close ties with some of the intelligence-gathering agencies. One thing I've learnt more than anything else is that nothing is black and white. Often the lines are blurred and one organization or agency has close associations with many.'

'My father mentioned the same thing.'

'What I am saying is that the media has close ties with all these groups and very rarely is there news published about these groups. The Bilderberg Group have meetings each year that go for three or four days. They include the world's richest people, members of royal families, and current and past prime ministers and presidents. These are the most powerful people on the planet, yet the media doesn't say "boo." If there were a meeting between the head of Iran and the president of North Korea, it would be front-page news, but these people meet every year and it doesn't rate a mention.

'These think tank organizations have members within government but little to nothing to do with the Government as a collective. Your father talked about a revolving door policy existing in the US. I find it extraordinary that conflicts of interest like that could exist. In Australia, a politician is not even allowed to own an investment property and lease it to a government employee without it being deemed a conflict of interest. Yet in America you can be the CEO of the world's biggest oil company or the States' largest construction and engineering conglomerate and be made the secretary of state.'

'Oh my, Emma Burgess, do I detect a political dig?'

'Absolutely. Almost every US secretary of state or secretary of defense, and many vice presidents and senior security advisors since Harry Truman's presidency have come from these corporations we've researched – and they've also been members of these think tanks.'

'And many have been MJ-12 members?'

'I would presume so. Can I share my views on MJ-12?'

'Please do.'

'We know how and why the group was formed. Yes, the Government effectively set up MJ-12, however the Government lost control. From what I can gather, documents using the MJ-12 name were deliberately destroyed, so it is obvious that they wanted to remain secretive. Your father referred to them simply as 'The Group.' Whatever they're named, it's clear that their power-base grew – and they became even more powerful.

'I'm fascinated how cleverly they've manipulated government funding to run much of their operations. I have some figures I'll share with you later; however, you already know about the Federally Funded Research Center grants, and we know many of the MJ-12 members had their own companies also. When you add their involvement with the NSA, the CIA, and a host of other government funded projects, then you can understand just how powerful MJ-12 became.

'Forgive my philosophical analogies, but from what I have read, that power and control come from two things: either money or information – with information being knowledge. Groups like the Bilderbergs, the CFR, The Trilateral Commission, and so on are primarily money-based power groups. The world banking systems are at the core of most, along with oil – and often the individuals are involved in both. MJ-12 is primarily information or knowledge based. In many ways that's more powerful.'

'And if you combine knowledge with money …?'

'Exactly. A large part of the knowledge and information is protecting that knowledge. Power is nothing if you give that power away. That is why MJ-12 has been so protective. That is why they set up so many intelligence agencies, not only using the Government's money and land, but also private enterprise's resources. And somehow having the likes of NSA and CIA was not enough for MJ-12, so they created their very own intelligence support group, MAJI.

'Your father kept saying "If no one talks, then no one dies." Processes were put in place to stop people talking.'

'And if they did talk, they were dealt with.'

'Both you and I know that many people died in the pursuit of the truth. It's hard for me to definitively say they were all murdered but, off the record, it looks mightily suspicious. Unfortunately without proper autopsy reports and case files it is hard for me to legally accuse an organization of first-degree murder. What I can say though is that we know firsthand someone is prepared for people to die to keep secrets.

'I've been thinking about how we're fed certain points-of-view in the media. I remember reading about Saddam Hussein and his weapons of mass destruction (WMDs). And, at the time, the public believed it. We now know otherwise.

'On the other side of the coin, all the media reports of UFOs and alien abductions – or should I say "lack of reports" are treated with contempt. It would seem that there's been a concerted effort by the media to ridicule or discredit any UFO witnesses or abductees. Mention the word *extraterrestrial* and most people immediately go on the defensive. We're conditioned. It's hard to accept something new and credible when, for years, you've been told it's false and unlikely.'

C.J. loves hearing Emma talk with passion.

'We know that in 1947 Albert Einstein and Robert Oppenheimer warned the Government about taking measures to address extraterrestrial issues. This was only weeks before the Roswell crash; however, that document was not forwarded to President Truman – or James Forrestal. After the death of Forrestal it was determined that all information about UFOs and ETs were to remain secret, to be kept and controlled by MJ-12. A line had been drawn in the sand, so a complex web of deceit was initiated – and then evolved.

'Allen Dulles was instrumental within the CIA and, when he became the Director in the early 1950's, he expanded MJ-12 and the CIA's influence on the media. They no doubt instructed the media that any reports of UFO sightings or alien abductions should be treated with contempt. I'm sure some of the really bizarre stories were concocted, and other UFO sightings could be explained by natural phenomena. Your father wrote that Donald Menzel did this sort of thing. He called it *disinformation*.'

'But, just in case the truth got out, MJ-12 created so-called 'top-secret' projects like Blue Book, which would be released to the press or the Government should they need to be.'

'It also appears that snippets of UFO information – or disinformation – were leaked to the media over a number of decades through farcical projects like Blue Book, with the goal of proving that UFOs were not real. Particularly through the fifties and sixties, the media were relentless in their denial and quick to mock anything with ET overtones – an attitude swaying several generations. I know it swayed me. If the words *UFO* or *alien* were used, I'd automatically cringe or be skeptical. I now know why.'

'I know our book, when published, will be met with skepticism from most,' notes C.J.

'Yes. A few words of truth will be difficult to erase decades of lies.'

'Wow, Emma Burgess, that is very profound. Can I use that quote in the book?'

'Absolutely.'

C.J. jots down: *A few words of truth will be difficult to erase decades of lies.*

Emma reviews her notes on the computer, while C.J. orders room service and tops up their glasses.

Emma sips her wine and continues. 'To be honest, I could spend months researching these massive corporations and the people who run them, and still feel like I've only just scratched the surface. I did note some trends, so rather than talk about individual companies, which could keep us talking for days, I'll be generic. But just to let you know, I did look into many individual companies, particularly those with military contracts from the US Government. Firstly, nearly all of these companies have headquarters in the same area; only a stones-throw from each other in the states of Virginia and Maryland. And where are the NSA and the CIA headquarters?'

'Virginia and Maryland?'

'Bingo. Also, they're strategically placed near Washington DC. It will come as no surprise that the larger military supply companies have many lobbyists – one has more than fifty fulltime lobbyists on their payroll. These people are specifically employed to lobby the Government for funds and contracts –most of the Lobbyists are recruited straight from the Government, some from the current Administration, and others from the previous Government. It's a blatant, yet effective way of the companies maintaining or increasing their military contracts – and obviously, we are talking a lot of money. There are trillions of dollars at stake.

'On the boards of these companies sit former CIA Directors, former vice presidents, former secretaries of state, defense secretaries, national security advisors and personnel ... you know the drill. It's the old "revolving door policy." And most of the top-line government jobs are given to CEOs or board members from the very same companies we've been talking about.

'The other thing that blew me away is the amount of money the Government allocated to these private companies, in the form of research funding. We've discussed the Federally Funded Research and Development Center grants but there's so much more. Some military supply corporations receive additional direct funding, as too do private institutes and universities. Some of these 'institutes' are institutes by name only – and they're affiliated with or subdivisions of massive military supply companies, as well as sometimes working in joint partnerships with other private corporations.

'C.J., the amounts of money involved are ridiculous. The US Government, like all democratically elected governments, has budget allocations, so by and large they need to be accountable for the money they hand out. Well, sort of. They fund all these secret projects and organizations under what's called the *Black Budget* – nothing is itemized or accountable, being considered 'not in the interest of national security' to disclose.'

'How convenient.'

'Exactly. And we are not talking a few dollars here and a few dollars there. Some reports I read suggest that as much as a quarter of the US Government's budget is spent on Black Budget allocations. A quarter!'

'It's no wonder America is in debt for trillions of dollars,' comments C.J. with sarcasm.

'Finding out how much money is spent on Federally Funded Research and Development outlays wasn't easy. I read that around one hundred and fifty billion dollars a year is spent in this area alone – and from what I understand, this money isn't even included in this "Black Budget" spending. Then you've got the additional budgets for the NSA, the CIA, and those other thirty or so intelligence agencies the Government fund. Add this to the military contracts the Government allot and we get some sort of idea how much money is at stake. It's a sobering thought.'

CHAPTER FORTY-THREE

With room service delivered and the food savored, the couple finishes the last of the wine. Emma is a little drunk – and flirtatious.

'Why Emma Burgess, I haven't seen you quite this provocative.'

'It's the wine,' she blurts, before sitting on C.J.'s knee to talk seriously. 'You're a good man, C.J. Stroheim. Your father would be very proud of how you've handled yourself. I know my mother would have loved you.'

'Thanks for sharing that,' he replies, while Emma runs her fingers through his hair. 'I have a question I've been wanting to ask.'

'Fire away.'

'I know you're proud of your family – and I love calling you Emma Burgess.'

'I know.'

'If, one day, you were to ever marry, would you keep the name *Burgess*?'

'Why Mr. Stroheim, that's a serious question. To answer it: No. I'm a traditionalist. I believe if you marry someone, then you become part of that someone, name and all. Now stop being so serious and kiss me ...'

Over the coming days, while C.J. works on the last chapter, Emma thinks about their next destination. Somewhere to hide out while the book is being edited and printed. She would love to have seen London, although she now agrees with C.J. that it's too risky for them both to go. She thinks to herself, *What girl wouldn't dream of spending time in London, Paris, or Rome?* Pausing for a moment – 'Rome?'

Rome as a destination has merit. They can catch a train to Italy from Paris. 'It'll be easy blending in with all the other tourists in a big city like Rome.'

C.J. is confident he and Emma can begin editing his work the next afternoon. Allowing for editing and his trip to Cambridge and back, they can now plan for the next leg of their adventure: Rome. The thought of going to Italy has both excited.

Emma visits yet another library to make the travel arrangements online. She's also 'further researching a few little details' in regards to her 'special project.'

The last chapter of the book is the hardest to write. The whole project's been daunting, yet the information enlightening. C.J. was always a confident man. It is not in his nature to suffer anxiety attacks. Any self-doubt is eradicated when he reads his father's words again, being the last words Max Stroheim wrote:

> I can only imagine how you are dealing with all this information and the consequent effect it is having on your life. I have entrusted you with a huge responsibility. I was not prepared to gamble on my family's wellbeing while I was alive. It is with a heavy heart that I involve you, but I am sure you have come to realize the importance of sharing the truth with the world.
>
> I will always be with you. Always.

C.J. types the last words of the book on his computer. With satisfaction, he looks over to where Emma normally sits. Many hours of hard work have led to this point. He would have loved to share the moment with her. C.J., however, has other plans.

He steps outside.

When Emma returns to the hotel room she sees fresh flowers, a bottle of champagne, and the beaming smile of C.J.

'Take a seat, Emma. I want to share this with you. The book is finished and has a title.'

'A title? I can't wait to see,' she exclaims, sitting in front of the computer.

The opening page of the book appears as Emma slides the chair in closer. She notices C.J. moving in her periphery. He appears to be kneeling down to pick up something.

Although distracted, her eyes are glued to the opening lines on the front page:

THE SIX SECRETS:
The Max Stroheim Story
By C.J. and Emma Stroheim

Emma sees the name *Emma Stroheim*. She is momentary confused, turning to look at C.J. He's on one knee, holding a ring box in his hand. Before she has the chance to say anything, C.J. reveals a dazzling diamond ring.

He looks her in the eyes. 'Emma Burgess, I told you I fell in love with you the moment I met you and have fallen more in love with you every day since. I know we're in unusual circumstances and I didn't think it was possible to love you more …'

He does not finish the sentence, as she wraps her arms around him.

'Yes!'

There was no indecision from Emma in agreeing to become *Mrs. Emma Stroheim* – that was easy. What she feels uncomfortable about is having her name on the book. 'This is your father's life. This is his legacy – and will become your legacy. It is *your* book. I had very little to do—'

C.J. interrupts, 'I wish my father was still alive so he could meet you. He would have loved you – and I can tell you, from the bottom of my heart, he'd want your name on the cover of the book.' Although she is unconvinced, C.J. continues. 'You've become as important to not only my life, but the story as well. When you read it, you'll understand.'

The opening page reads:

> My name is C.J. Stroheim. I am an American journalist. My wife Emma is an Australian lawyer. Neither of us has worked for any government-affiliated agency or organization. My father, Dr. Max Stroheim, did. He spent thirty-four years as an employee of the NSA, or working under the umbrella of the NSA, operating

within the inner core, often deep underground within Nevada's top-secret base, Area 51. This was under the management and control of a group called MJ-12. They had a motto of secrecy: If no one talks, then no one dies.

Consequently, very few talked. Those who did, talked no more.

My father never mentioned a word of his secret career until near his death. Even then, he only gave instructions for me to research, to unlock certain codes and keys. This eventually led me to his written memoirs, which I discovered some fifteen weeks after his passing. I must stress that these were his thoughts, his words. There were no documents. There were no files.

During this period, Emma and I were pursued across three continents by a host of men trying to kill us. At the time, we had little idea what we were actually looking for, yet we had assassins firing bullets at us, so we knew that what we were pursuing was obviously important.

Someone did not want us to find the truth.

We somehow managed to avoid being shot, leaving a trail of bullet-ridden cars and two dead assassins behind us. We realized early just how important this journey was to become.

But this is not our story. This is the life work of an incredible man, Max Stroheim, and the truth behind not only his world, but the world around us. Sit back and prepare to learn the truth.

My father once said, 'One can only understand the truth if at first they have a concept of deception.'

You'll need to ignore most things you have read in the past. What we are told as true is not always necessarily so. The cover-ups and deceptions enforced on recent generations are ingrained, orchestrated, and saturating.

A few words of truth will be difficult to erase decades of lies; however, join us in taking the first few steps toward the truth.

Emma glances momentarily at her dazzling engagement ring, as the streaming light through the hotel window catches the angular edges of the impressive diamond perched over a gleaming gold band.

She returns her eyes to the manuscript, before turning to C.J. 'I love it!'

'What, the manuscript or the ring?'

'Both.'

Editing the book, Emma discovers she is referred to as *C.J.'s wife*. She likes it. C.J. has woven their experiences and research into the fabric of Max Stroheim's career. Much of the book is based on Max Stroheim's memoirs. Emma notes that Max's words can be quoted as fact, but much of the research both she and C.J. have done is based on 'speculation.' C.J. is fortunate to have a legal expert as his fiancée. The last thing he wants is to face legal repercussions from the book. Emma is confident that will not occur.

It takes almost a week to read and edit *The Six Secrets: The Max Stroheim Story*. For all the stress and distractions during the writing process, C.J. made surprisingly few errors. The publisher's editor will rectify grammatical and format mistakes to showcase the facts in the best possible way. Both C.J. and Emma realize those facts are mind-blowing – and will be controversial.

C.J. has a clear picture of Max Stroheim's working career in an era that shaped the fabric of American Government and how the country runs to this day. The years of cover-ups and deceptions have left a trail of destruction. C.J. relays to the reader some of those lies and why they were told. Within the last pages of the book, he writes about the personal costs he and Emma have endured:

> Max Stroheim had warned of the dangers in pursuing the truth contained within this book. He was right. Someone does not want this book to be published. We know who that someone is, but have not named names. Those were my father's instructions.
>
> This book is about letting the public know the truth. We do not want to face any more danger. We will not pursue matters further. This is our protection. We have completed what we set out to do, so having us killed now would not achieve anything. Even so, we have insurance:
>
> Emma is a lawyer. She has documented, with proof, the murder

attempts and incidences that happened to us while researching and writing this book. She has named names.

This was Emma's 'special project.'

We have enough evidence under US and Australian laws to prosecute; however, we know many of the agencies and networks operate under their own laws. It is a path we would prefer not to tread. Regardless, we've taken meticulous care in gathering material should it be required.

We have enclosed all this information, including hard evidence and substantiated allegations, into sealed packages. Emma has used her lawyer associates and I my journalist and media contacts. Should anything suspicious or threatening occur to either of us, then our lawyers are under instruction to send each of those sealed packages to the addressed media personnel. Some sections of the media are corrupt, but not all. The information, the legal charges, and the names would then be revealed in entirety to the public and the authorities.

We are confident that the attempts on our life will cease. If not, the story you are reading will become so much bigger.

My father, Max Stroheim, was not only an incredible scientist, he was an incredible man. I once read there is only one thing better than being a good man – and that is being a good father. Max Stroheim was that good father. He taught me patience, persistence, and honesty. My mother instilled in me to always tell the truth. This book is the truth the world needs to hear. I have faith that you will be a little wiser for our effort.

We should not be forced to live in a world where phone calls are tapped, computers hacked into, and the information read in the media contrived. We should be encouraged to speak openly and honestly on subjects such as UFOs and extraterrestrials – and not ridiculed for that discussion. We should be given the truth at all times. It is the least we should demand.

Some of the wisest scientists in modern history, the likes of Einstein and Oppenheimer, von Braun, and Teller, to name a few,

> wanted this information made public. It should have been made public, yet it wasn't. Worse still, it was buried under a sea of lies. Harry S. Truman once told my father, 'Sometimes it is best to disregard what you thought was true until you know it is true.' You now know what is true.

While the book is being published and distributed, Emma's task is to complete gathering all the evidence C.J. has written about – to present it in the correct format. C.J. has vowed to help; it's something they can work on in Italy. For now, the priority is for C.J. to take the completed book, downloaded to USB memory sticks, to Cambridge, England. He'll catch a train to England first thing in the morning.

Reading and editing the book has been all-consuming. They hadn't even truly celebrated their engagement yet. That changes tonight.

C.J. and Emma walk hand in hand along the left bank of the river Seine to Montparnasse. They are dining at La Coupole, a restaurant frequented by artists such as Picasso, Dali, Leger, and Matisse. It's famous for its artwork and a magnificent painted dome above the diner's heads.

Drinking champagne and eating fine French cuisine, they discuss C.J.'s upcoming visit to England. Emma is understandably concerned for C.J.'s safety. He will only be gone twenty-four hours or less, yet they still need to plan thoroughly. When C.J. returns to Paris they'll leave immediately.

After dinner they walk along the Seine to enjoy what will be their last night together in Paris.

Henry Miller once wrote, 'So quietly flows the Seine that one hardly notices its presence. It is always there, quiet and unobtrusive, like a great artery running through the human body.'

Enjoying the serenity in the heart of a pulsating city, C.J. and Emma stop to reflect. Not to talk, but to soak in the surrounds – to appreciate not only Paris's rich past, but their own future.

CHAPTER FORTY-FOUR

C.J. is traveling light, only carrying his backpack with some toiletries, a change of underwear and a spare shirt, a digital voice recorder purchased in Paris, and a USB memory stick containing the '*The Six Secrets*' manuscript. In his jacket pocket is a backup USB stick and the injection device.

C.J. exits the Cambridge Station to walk the handful of blocks to Dalgleish Publishing's office. Passing quaint shop-fronts, some with designer clothes and bags, a handbag on display grabs his attention. It is the same handbag brand and design that C.J. bought Emma in Bangkok, now ripped. He dashes inside the shop to buy the bag, placing it in his backpack.

It is lunchtime in Cambridge, with the local eateries and pubs bustling with patrons. Turning the corner to enter the street of Dalgleish Publishing's office, he notices a typically English corner pub – the chatter infectious – fish and chips – sausages and mash – pints of beer. C.J. peers momentarily through the open doorway. Had he more time he would have loved to stop.

He can see the publisher's office building.

Without warning, a man wearing a long, black jacket steps from a shop doorway. He rushes behind C.J. Hand inside his jacket, he pushes the jacket into C.J.'s back.

The first thing a shocked C.J. can feel is the hard barrel of a gun pressing into his lower back.

'Don't make a move, Stroheim,' instructs the man in a gruff cockney accent. 'If I have to shoot you here in the street, I will. Keep walking – slowly – we are going to cross the road and walk to that car over there.'

A black car is parked on the other side of the road; a sinister-looking man opens the car door.

C.J. barely has time to think. He must act – and act quickly. Before crossing the road, they stop momentarily for a passing car. C.J. slips his hand inside his jacket pocket to flip off the cap from the injection device – he's practiced this maneuver many times. As the car passes, C.J. slides the device from his pocket. In one motion, he swings it around his body, jabbing the device into the man's arm holding the gun.

The man lowers the gun almost immediately. His arm twitches – becomes limp – his hand convulses – the gun falls from his waning grip. He collapses to the ground, writhing in pain.

C.J. looks across the road. The other man steps from the car, gun in hand. Sliding the device back into his pocket, he runs as fast as he can in the direction from which he came.

Sprinting around the corner, he discovers a long open street in front of him. He stops, doubles back, and enters the pub he admired earlier.

C.J. strides slowly past the patrons to walk to the toilets. Looking over his shoulder to make sure no one is watching, he enters the women's toilets. Inside are four cubicles, the type with a three-quarter door. None are occupied. C.J. ducks into the last cubicle, closing the door to lock it.

The man from the black car runs to his colleague slumped on the sidewalk, thrashing in agony. The man looks around to see if anyone is watching. A shop-owner is looking in his direction. He blocks the onlooker's view of the scene, bending over to check his colleague, discreetly picking up the spilt gun to slip inside his own pocket.

As his colleague takes his last breath, the man yells to the nearby onlookers, 'Quick, don't just stand there, call an ambulance.'

The man then takes off in pursuit of C.J., turning the corner to look up and down the street. There is no sign of C.J., so he enters the pub.

After looking all around the bar, he walks into the men's toilets.

There is no sign of C.J. there, so he enters the ladies toilets. He looks inside each empty cubicle before looking under the door of the one cubicle in use. He sees a pair of smooth legs, with a handbag resting in front.

He leaves the toilet and the pub to search the next premises on the street.

The moment C.J. entered the cubicle, he removed his toiletry pack and Emma's new handbag from his backpack. Taking off his socks and shoes, he rolled up his pants, and shaved his lower legs. He then placed Emma's new handbag over his feet and everything else on his lap. When the man looked under the cubicle door, he saw freshly shaved legs and a woman's handbag sitting over what he would have assumed to be women's shoes.

C.J. allows a few minutes to pass before leaving the toilet. He can hear the siren of an ambulance approaching. Some of the pub patrons look outside to see what is going on. C.J. uses the distraction to slip out the door. He spots the man from the black car entering a shop three doors down. C.J. sprints in the opposite direction, crossing the street to hail a passing cab.

'Take me to Cambridge University, the Faculty History Building, thank you.'

With the publisher's office under surveillance, he has to find the students met in Paris, Thomas and Cilla.

Inside the Faculty of History, C.J., using his press-pass credentials to obtain access to the building. He inquires as to which lecture room Stella Dalgleish is attending, knowing Cilla and Thomas should also be there. He waits until the lecture is finished before greeting the surprised couple. C.J. asks to talk in private, with Thomas and Cilla taking him into a quiet corner of a communal area. 'I'm sorry to barge in like this, but I need your help. I need to get a message to Mark Dalgleish. I can't go into detail at the moment, but I promise you, I will. I have written a book; Mark is going to publish it. Hopefully you'll get to read it and everything will become clear. For now I need to get that message to Mark Dalgleish.'

'Do you want me to phone him?' offers Cilla, taking her phone from her handbag.

'Not yet' replies C.J. 'Is it possible to get Stella?'

'Yes,' answers Thomas, 'We were going to have a snack at the Tea Room with Stella anyway.'

'It's in Seeley Library, which is next door' says Cilla. 'Follow us.'

Cilla introduces C.J. to Stella Dalgleish. After a quick explanation of C.J.'s plight, a plan to get Mark Dalgleish to the university is implemented.

Stella calls her father. Mark Dalgleish is sociable with several of Stella's lecturers, calling in to the Seeley Library and the Tea Room from time to time anyway. Stella asks if her father is able to meet her for afternoon tea. Stella rarely asks to see her father so Mark Dalgleish obliges.

'It's all organized,' she tells C.J

'Excellent,' he replies. 'Good work, Stella. Can I ask, do you know what your father was wearing this morning?'

'Yes; a tan pair of pants and a brown jacket. Like that fellow over there. That's Professor Braithwaite, one of our lecturers. Why do you ask?'

C.J. tells the three students Mark Dalgleish will probably be followed. They formulate a strategy to take both Mark Dalgleish and C.J. to another place away from the university.

Mark Dalgleish is indeed tailed. The same sinister-looking man who chased C.J. in the streets earlier has followed Mark Dalgleish to the university. From a distance, in his black car, he keeps Mark Dalgleish under surveillance. Mark has planned to meet his daughter in the Tea Room, however when he arrives, Cilla and Thomas are waiting to quickly usher him away.

Cilla says 'Sorry to startle you Mr. Dalgleish, but walk this way; hurry please. We are taking you to see C.J. Stroheim. He says it is urgent.'

Stella stayed in the Tea Room She is now sitting with Professor Braithwaite, in his brown jacket, seated with his back to the door. From behind, he looks like Mark Dalgleish.

When the man following Mark Dalgleish enters, all he sees is Dalgleish and his daughter chatting.

CHAPTER FORTY-FOUR

Thomas and Cilla drive Mark Dalgleish and C.J. to a coffee shop close to a train station in the nearby town of Ely. C.J. takes note of a public phone box outside the station.

He hugs Thomas and Cilla and says his goodbyes. Thomas takes Mark Dalgleish's car keys, before he and Cilla drive back to the university. They will give the keys to Stella, so she can pick her father up at Ely later that afternoon.

C.J. and Mark discuss the book in a private corner of the coffee shop.

Mark Dalgleish met Max Stroheim just the once, in the States, with Mark's father. Before Mark's father passed away, he adamantly stated that anything that Max Stroheim or his son C.J. writes should be published. Mark knew Dr. Stroheim spent thirty-four years with the NSA, but the tone of his father's words left no doubt that a book by either of the Stroheims would be provocative.

Mark realizes the dangers associated with publishing a book like C.J. has written but, without hesitation, confirms his willingness to take risks.

C.J. tells of the threats to his and Emma's lives. 'Even today, I had a gun pulled on me while I was on my way to see you.'

'Was it anything to do with that chap who had a heart attack on the street outside my office an hour or so ago?'

'He was the one who pulled the gun on me. Mark, can I talk open and honestly?'

Mark nods. He is sincere.

C.J. instantly likes and trusts him. 'I've already seen two other men die. They were accidents and both incidents are mentioned in the book, but today I killed a man. Yes, I had a gun stuck in my back, but I was responsible for the death of another human being. It does not sit well with me.' C.J. reaches into his pocket to show Mark the injection device. 'I think this is what killed him. Emma and I were in Australia when an assassin came after us. This was a man I had known in the US for years. His name was Ellis Buckman. I mention him by name in the book. He was used by some organization to monitor me, to make sure the information my father knew would be kept a secret. Ellis Buckman followed me to Australia and tried to kill Emma and me – not just once, but twice.

'Cutting a long story short: Buckman and I fought and he fell. He died instantly and this injection device was in his pocket.' C.J. hands the device for Mark Dalgleish to inspect. 'The device injects some sort of toxin that evidently brings on a heart attack.'

'So this Buckman character was going to kill you with this?'

'No, the device was a backup. He had a gun, but I'm sure this type of device was used for many years as a weapon. God knows how many people over the years, who supposedly died of heart attacks, were actually murdered.'

'So you are saying many people were killed?'

'In many different ways, including with devices like this. I'd be interested to find out exactly what the liquid inside is.'

'I have contacts at the University labs. I can have the liquid analyzed if you like. No one needs to know where it came from.'

'That would be great. Can you keep the device in safe hiding? We might need it down the track as evidence. I haven't written about the device in the book, nor will I mention it, so this is just between you and me, okay?'

'As far as the world knows, that man in the street had a heart attack.'

C.J. hands Mark Dalgleish the USB memory stick containing the manuscript, as well as Emma's 'special project.' C.J. explains that Emma is a lawyer, so they prudently isolated the facts from speculation. 'I don't think we'll be facing any legal challenges – and Emma is confident we can't be pursued under some of the antiquated American anti-spy laws.'

'You sound like you've taken lots of precautions.'

'We've had to.'

'Once the book is published it will be too late,' says C.J. 'They will go into damage control. At that point, it would be senseless threatening Emma and me – or yourself, for that matter.'

'You said "they." Who are you talking about?'

'That is the question Emma and I are still researching. At the end the book we talk about this. No names are mentioned; however, we outline Emma's 'special project.' She has compiled legal information and named names – and we have that information, or most of that information. We will send it to you also, in two to three weeks' time. We're also sending copies to a number of legal firms that Emma knows. Should anything happen to us, the law firms will be instructed to release the information to a host of designated media outlets.'

'So you have essentially blackmailed those who might threaten you?'

'Exactly.'

'That's very clever.'

'It's our insurance policy.'

Mark Dalgleish recognizes the quicker the book can be published, the quicker C.J. and Emma can attempt to live a normal life. From what C.J. has said about the manuscript, Dalgleish knows it will make a spectacular book. He can't wait to read it. 'I have several editors who work for me, but this I will edit myself. I understand the secrecy. I'll start tonight.'

C.J. warns Mark to read the manuscript offline. He explains what happened to Emma's computer and the ramifications of the information revealed by Edward Snowden, 'Any computer on the planet can be hacked into. I'd be surprised if your phones aren't tapped and monitored.'

Mark knows a man died on the street today – a man who had a gun in C.J.'s back. He has every reason to take the situation seriously.

C.J. discusses how best they can keep in contact. Their computers may be monitored, so Mark suggests for C.J. to set up a new email address and send any correspondence to his daughter Stella. 'You can talk cryptically. I'll work it out. Maybe you could pretend to be one of her friends.'

As Mark writes down his daughter's email address, C.J. thinks of a name. 'Okay, I'll be *Nicole Josephs*.' C.J. took Emma's mother's first name and added an 'S' to his uncle's name, Joseph.

The two men shake hands.

Mark asks, 'By the way, what is the name of the book?'

C.J. tells him. '*The Six Secrets*, with the sub-heading *The Max Stroheim Story*.'

'So there are six secrets?'

'There actually many more, but my father was always one to categorize everything. He listed six major secrets. You'll find out what they are when you read the book.'

'I can't wait. I'll start tonight. I have an old laptop, which can't even connect to the Internet. It will be perfect.

The train station is diagonally opposite the coffee shop. C.J. purchases his ticket from Ely to London, before stepping back outside to enter the public phone box. Removing the voice recorder from his backpack, he retrieves M.R.'s phone number written on a piece of paper in his pocket. He dials the number, holding the voice recorder to the phone's earpiece.

'Who is this?' answers a man, his American accent strong and abrupt. 'Who is this and what do you want?'

There is a momentary pause. The man hangs up. C.J. turns off the recorder, steps away from the phone box, and walks to the platform.

CHAPTER FORTY-FIVE

Arriving back in Paris, C.J. walks into the hotel room. Emma rushes him, hugging him so hard his breath is momentarily taken away.

She's sensed something may have gone wrong in England. Between cuddles and kisses, she asks a series of questions about the publisher and their meeting.

'Mark Dalgleish is a great guy and extremely interested in the book,' says C.J. 'He's going to edit it personally, then publish it as quick as he possibly can.'

C.J. is unsure how to broach the subject of having a gun in his back and the subsequent death of the man at C.J.'s hand. The death is justifiable, but C.J.'s concern is how Emma will react to the news. One of the strongest aspects of their relationship is their ability to be honest and accept the ramifications of that honesty.

C.J. tells Emma the truth.

C.J. tells of the man with the gun and how C.J. had used the injection device. 'He slumped to the ground. I later found out he died of a heart attack.'

Concerned and shocked, Emma goes straight into lawyer-mode. 'Maybe the authorities won't do an autopsy. Even if they do, they probably won't find out anything. I'm sure a heart attack will be the official cause of death. Were there any witnesses?'

'I don't think so.'

'Where's the injection device now?'

'I gave it to Mark Dalgleish. He'll tell no one and he has contacts within the university to have the toxin inside the device tested. He promised to keep the device in safe-keeping, should we ever need it as evidence.'

Emma is impressed with C.J.'s actions, yet troubled by the traumatic set of events he experienced.

He tells of hiding in the ladies' toilet, rolling up his pants to show her his shaved legs.

'Very sexy,' Emma snickers.

'By the way, I have a little present for you,' says C.J.

He removes the new handbag from his backpack to present to Emma. She is mightily impressed.

'Sorry it's not wrapped, but I used it to cover my big masculine feet in the cubicle.'

The train ride to Rome is more than twelve hours. In their own compartment, between brief naps, they discuss Emma's 'special project,' before perusing Emma's notes.

C.J. states, 'The book is in safe hands – and it's now out of our control. We still have a bit to do with your "special project," but we've time to play tourist.'

'I'm so excited – we're going to Rome,' she gushes, snuggling up to her fiancé.

The train arrives in Rome in the early morning.

Emma booked four nights at a classic hotel right outside the Colosseum, centrally located, within walking distance to many of Rome's tourist attractions. The hotel is not busy and, with Emma's negotiating skills, they've been upgraded to a deluxe suite.

They open the curtains to reveal the Colosseum in all its glory.

Rome is one of the world's best cities to walk around. Although the cobblestone streets are hard, and at times uneven, C.J. and Emma explore almost every nook and cranny of central Rome in the coming days. Emma manages a few hours of research at a nearby library, however the excitement of being in Rome has momentarily overshadowed almost everything else. They tour the Colosseum, visit the Pantheon, the Trevi Fountain, the Vatican's Sistine Chapel, The Roman Forum, the Spanish Steps, and walk through countless piazzas and squares. They eat traditional pizza and pasta and drink Chianti:

'*Eccellente.*'

Knowing C.J.'s and Emma's lives are in danger until the book is released, Mark Dalgleish gave C.J. a speedy three to four weeks for *The Six Secrets* to be edited, copies printed in the UK, and then distributed in England. Copies will be shipped to Europe and then Asia in the following weeks. He would confirm this via email. C.J. sets up a new email address under the name *Nicole Josephs*.

C.J. asks Emma's advice on how a twenty-one-year-old girl might write an email.

'How the hell would I know?' she cheekily replies.

C.J. writes to Mark Dalgleish, via Stella Dalgleish:

> Hiya Stell, great catching up the other day. Hope u liked the book I gave u. Let us know when u have read it & if u think its cool. LOL Nic x

A short time later, Stella responds:

> Hey Nic, book awesome. Have exams at uni next week, so might take another three weeks to finish, but will let u know ASAP. X Stell

The book should be ready in three weeks. Emma's 'special project' needs to be finished by then, too. There is much to do. The first thing C.J. wants to investigate is the voice of M.R. He has a recording on the voice recorder. Emma compiles a list of all the M.R.s and family names beginning with 'R' who might be connected with one or more of the organizations and people researched. Some of the names on the list are well-known identities.

C.J. and Emma trawl the Internet, using YouTube.

Can we match the voice on the phone recording with any of these people on YouTube?

After much trial and error, they find a video clip of a business speech by one of the men on Emma's list. 'Bingo – that's him – that's M.R.'

C.J. transfers all the information Emma has collected to his computer. He downloads the voice recording of M.R. from the voice recorder, as well as the YouTube clip. Emma knows that, in a court of law, the recordings would need to be taken to an expert or may not be allowed as evidence. But for now they have tangible proof M.R. is connected with both Ellis Buckman and Ben Hamermesh, including proof of each man's phone history. It is the break they had been looking for. If this is indeed the same M.R., then he is truly a powerful man, involved in numerous organizations and companies C.J. and Emma have researched.

• • •

C.J. and Emma spend the coming weeks further researching Emma's 'special project,' as well as taking the time to 'play tourists.'

They travel north to Tuscany, spending time in Florence and Sienna, before heading toward Venice. The weather is not obliging in northern Italy, so they stay only briefly, before turning around and catching a train south again.

Emma had heard that Positano, and the Amalfi Coast region south of Naples, is spectacular. With the change of direction, comes a change of weather. Basing themselves in Sorrento for several days, they spend a day at the Pompeii ruins and another at the Isle of Capri, before moving to Positano.

The weather is now idyllic. Positano is everything Emma thought it would be. The hotel's balcony has sweeping views across the Mediterranean, only a ten-minute walk from the main, pebbled beach. C.J. and Emma may be fugitives hiding from assassins with powerful allies, but they've certainly stayed in some stunning places.

C.J. receives several emails from Mark Dalgleish, continuing to use his daughter's email address. Mark Dalgleish obtained the results of the toxin used in the injection device. Mark writes about getting food poisoning as a cryptic analogy:

> I only had 2 oysters and a few mussels, but felt like I'd been bitten by a cobra snake & then injected with over half a dozen chemicals, I was so ill. I think it was the oysters. It could have been the mussels. Sometimes small doses of something bad can be worse than a larger single dose.

C.J. interprets this message as being the contaminant had a number of different poisons in the mixture, including shellfish toxin, chemicals, and cobra venom.

'The usage of small doses of various toxins is ingenious. Even if a victim had an autopsy, each individual poison would be in small enough quantities not to register within a toxicity report. In all the cases of journalists, writers, and whistleblowers having sudden heart attacks, there was never any mention of toxicity reports. Even if one was ordered, I doubt whether it would have made a difference anyway.'

In Mark Dalgleish's cryptic email he further indicated reading the book:

> I read that book u recommended – loved it! Will c u in 2 weeks in London. I have a friend in town who's in the UK, then a few stops in Europe, then she's off to Asia. Hope u can meet her if u r around?

C.J. interprets this as meaning the book will be published in a fortnight, with the first publications released in the UK, then Asia..

C.J. and Emma must finalize Emma's 'special project.' They still have more research, with Emma desiring to get all her notes in order.

A week in Positano has revitalized C.J. and Emma. They've discussed what the next leg of their journey will be: Thailand. His father gave C.J. his uncle's lawyer's details. That lawyer is in Bangkok. C.J.'s instructions were to visit the lawyer, Wichit, after the book is written. That time is now.

In Bangkok they'll package and send the additional information from Emma's 'special project.' C.J. is reluctant to return there directly for safety reasons. Ellis Buckman knew C.J. had been to Bangkok – and Ben Hamermesh and others probably knew as well. They may guess he'll be returning.

After discussing and researching alternate routes to Bangkok, Emma books tickets to one of Thailand's bordering countries, Laos. A visa is required for entry, but can be issued at the airport. It's a simple procedure of showing passports and paying money. A direct flight is booked from Rome to Savannakhet in Laos, on the Thai border.

For the past few months, C.J. and Emma have traveled luxuriously. That is about to change. After landing in Savannakhet, they catch a bus across the Mekong River border to the town Mukdahan, before transferring to another bus that takes them to Ubon, then transferring to yet another bus. Emma's been incredibly well organized with their travel plans to date. After five hours on the WWII relic of a bus, she admits she's made a big mistake – they are only halfway to Bangkok.

The bus constantly stops. As the bus's suspension system is virtually nonexistent, the stops are the only respite from the pounding of worn tires on uneven roads. The only thing outnumbering the stops is the amount of potholes the bus hits.

Viewed through rattling windows, some of the scenery is exquisite. Much of the journey is along winding roads, through thick rainforest surrounded by lushly forested mountains. They pass through (and stop in) many small villages, seeing beautiful temples, children playing on the streets, and even elephants being ridden. This is a part of Thailand C.J. has not seen before.

On arrival in Bangkok, they catch a cab to the same hotel C.J. stayed on his last visit, just around the corner from his Uncle Joe's and his father's lawyer's office. But before visiting the lawyer, C.J. suggests he should go alone and in disguise.

'You never know, the building might be under surveillance. Why don't we go to Khao San Road first? I can probably buy a wig or something.'

They leave Khao San Road with a tacky backpack, khaki shorts, flowing batik shirt, and a cap resplendent with braided dreadlocks.

Donning his 'disguise,' C.J. slings the new backpack over his shoulder.

Emma comments, 'You look like a European backpacker.'

'I thought I looked more like a white Bob Marley.'

Although the lawyer's offices are only around the corner, C.J. catches a *tuk-tuk*, a motorized rickshaw. He instructs the driver to take the vehicle past the lawyer's offices, drive around the block, then return from a different direction.

Driving slowly past the office block, C.J. sees there is only one entry to the multi-level building. No cars are parked outside and no one seems to be monitoring the building, apart from a security guard just inside the glass doors.

C.J. exits the tuk-tuk to slip into the building, past the security guard, and into the elevator.

Only when he leaves the elevator does he remove the sunglasses and wigged cap.

He meets with the man stated on the business card Wichit.

Wichit is genuinely pleased to see C.J. 'Please, take a seat. I met your father and your Uncle Joe on many occasions,' he relays in fluent English, with a slight American twang. 'They were both fine men. I am sorry for your loss, but I've been expecting you. I have documentation waiting. I'll will return with it in a moment.'

Wichit leaves the room to return with a file.

'I already know what is in here. First, let me say that your father transferred most of his assets to Thailand before he passed away. Your uncle already had his assets here. Both men were meticulous in preparing their wills, especially your father. He spent many hours with me. I think your Uncle Joe only updated his will and financial assets because of your father. Needless to say, both wills are legally sound and binding.

'I have good news and bad news. I will start with the bad news. We have been informed by your late father's lawyers in America that the Internal Revenue Service has frozen your father's assets in the United States. As I said, most of his assets were transferred here; however, your father's home in Palm Springs was impounded.'

'Impounded?'

'The reason for this is an allegation that Mr. Stroheim owed taxes, but there have been no official charges laid. It is something we will need to fight in court but, I must say, that could be costly and take time.'

C.J. is disappointed and annoyed. His father's house, in a retirement village, was state of the art – and now it is impounded.

'I thought the IRS may pull a stunt like this,' C.J. says. 'So all my father's personal items in California are also impounded?'

'I'm afraid so, Mr. Stroheim; everything that was not taken out of the USA.'

C.J. is further enraged.

Wichit continues to speak. 'But there is good news for you, Mr. Stroheim, because your father managed to transfer much to Thailand. His bank accounts, bonds, and shares are with us here in Bangkok. I'll show you the breakdown of your father's assets shortly, but there is more.' Wichit opens the file. 'As you would know, your Uncle passed away only recently. He had no heirs, so you have been named as the sole beneficiary, apart from one of his assets, a small building containing a business in Jomtien Beach. This is to be left to a woman by the name of Ploy Wongsawat.'

'I've met Ploy. She's lovely.'

'Your uncle had other properties, as well as cash and business assets; so too your father.' Wichit slides a piece of paper across the table. 'This groups your total inheritance from both your father and your uncle.'

The paper has lists of properties, plus shares, bonds, and bank accounts listed separately under the names of Max Stroheim and Joseph Stroheim. At the bottom of the page is a combined figure – a very large figure.

Wichit says, 'This is only an approximate estimate of your inheritance to date, excluding, of course, your father's property and cash still in the United States.'

At first glance, C.J. can see the number 42 and a whole string of numbers. He thinks it might be 42,000 or 420,000 but then he focuses on the figure: it is more than 42 million.

C.J. has a lump in his throat. 'Is this in baht?'

Even in Thai baht it is approximately US$2 million.

Wichit calmly replies, 'No. It is in US dollars.'

C.J. nearly falls off his chair.

CHAPTER FORTY-SIX

C.J. knew his father was financially savvy and that his uncle was a successful businessman, but never in his wildest dreams did he think he would inherit more than a million dollars, let alone US$42 million. Much of his father's wealth came from shares. In a sweet irony, most of the shares are in the company Raytheon. Max Stroheim paid only a handful of cents per share back in the 1950s but, today, shares are worth almost US$70 each. Max Stroheim has tens of thousands of these shares.

Max Stroheim may have been shielded from much of the corporate world's goings on, but he knew a good investment when he saw one.

C.J. walks into the hotel room with the biggest smile on his face. 'I think you better sit down, Emma Burgess. I have some news that is going to knock your socks off …'

On the hotel concierge's recommendation, they book a table at the Issaya Siamese Club. Set in a renovated 1920s house with striking tropical gardens, it is only a few minutes away by taxi. Over mouthwatering Thai cuisine, they discuss their next move. Emma is reluctant to talk about the money.

First priority is to package and send the information of Emma's 'special project,' their insurance policy.

The next morning, C.J. buys 80 USB memory sticks and pre-paid envelopes.

Back at their hotel, they set up a production line. C.J. downloads all the data from Emma's 'special project' onto 72 memory sticks, which Emma places into addressed envelopes. Emma has chosen six Australian lawyers she knows well, including her friend Anna. Inside each parcel are a covering letter instructing the lawyers that, in the event of anything untoward or suspicious happening to C.J. or Emma, each will send the enclosed twelve envelopes (each with covering letter and USB stick) to a team of journalists in the US. C.J. had selected the dozen journalists he thought might have the independence and the means to publish Emma's 'special project' if required.

Additionally, they have covering letters and USB sticks (containing the unedited book manuscript) for six of Emma's family and friends, including her father and Sarah from the Boat Harbour Beach café. With Emma's 'special project' included, in the event of anything 'untoward' happening to C.J. and herself, they are also instructed to contact as many media organizations as possible.

Emma says, 'We really only need to let Sarah know down at Boat Harbour Beach; it won't take long before everyone else finds out! I'm sure the local community will keep an eye out for us. If these people try to mess with us in any way, shape, or form – they are going down.'

Emma has told of their engagement in the letters.

'I'm not sure how your dad will react,' says C.J., 'but, after the book is released, we'll buy phones and I'll have a chat with him.'

The next morning, C.J. receives another coded email from Mark Dalgleish. *The Six Secrets: The Max Stroheim Story* will be released the next day in the UK. The timing is perfect. C.J. and Emma complete the remaining memory stick packages, taking them to the local post office.

Sending the packages is a poignant moment. C.J. and Emma are aware their whereabouts will soon be traceable to Bangkok. Bags already packed, they head straight to Bangkok's International Airport to board a flight to Singapore.

Arriving in Singapore, they catch a cab to the city and buy new computers. They then take a ferry on a 45-minute boat ride to the Indonesian island of Bintan.

Emma has booked accommodation at a luxury waterfront golf resort. Their plan is to lay low for a few days while the book is released. Using their new computers, they'll monitor the publicity of and public reaction to the book, confident they'll be safe.

Their beachfront villa is spectacular: magnificent ocean views in front and golf course behind.

'Not a bad place to be a fugitive, hey?' remarks Emma.

They monitor *The Six Secrets*' release in the UK, with the book receiving little initial fanfare.

Using the resort's business center to check emails from Mark Dalgleish, C.J. still writes cryptically. He ascertains Mark has deliberately kept a low-key book launch. Mark hints that copies will be sent to distributers all over Europe in the coming days, accompanied by a major press release.

Looking over the golf course, Emma says, 'I know you play golf.'

'Yes, I play, badly. What about you?'

'I played a few rounds in Tassie as a kid, but it's been a while.'

'So are you interested in a game?'

'Why not? We can't control what's going to happen with the book. It's all in Mark's hands now. A game of golf sounds perfect.'

On the first tee, C.J. hits his ball with a severe slice. There's no need to curse; it's what he expected.

Emma approaches the tee, confidently takes a rhythmical practice swing, then hits her ball straight down the middle of the fairway.

'So there's another thing I didn't know about the future Mrs. Stroheim. Are there any more hidden talents I should know about?'

'It was a lucky shot,' is her nonchalant reply.

Emma has many more 'lucky shots' over ensuing holes, as they enjoy the magnificent golfing surrounds.

By the end of the round, even C.J. hits the ball better.

Walking toward the eighteenth green, Emma asks, 'Do you know what would top-off a fantastic day?'

'Why, Emma Burgess!'

'I was going to say "a two-hour massage," however …'

Over the coming days they play golf daily. C.J. remarks that five hours of golf followed by 'two hours of massages' is a lifestyle he could well and truly become accustomed to. Emma wholeheartedly concurs.

Comments about *The Six Secrets* begin appearing online – and in a flurry. The book is causing quite a stir. Mark Dalgleish hints that, since the press release and distribution throughout major European centers, sales have boomed. Media coverage is starting to surge.

C.J. and Emma know they have passed the point of no return. It's been a gamble – their lives in constant danger while writing and researching. Now, the book is out.

Will their lives still be in danger?

This is yet to be determined.

While in Bangkok, C.J. set up several bank accounts to access some of his inheritance monies. Cash is not an issue; should they need to stay in hiding, they can. They've come too far to jeopardize their safety now.

The 'special project' packages should have reached their destinations by now. Emma's family and friends would have learned that C.J. and Emma are safe, are engaged, have written a book, with that book published. They have entrusted her family and friends to contact a designated lawyer should anything 'suspicious' happen.

'Tongues will be wagging in Wynyard and Boat Harbour Beach, no doubt,' she quips.

The small Tasmanian towns of Wynyard and Boat Harbour Beach are not the only areas learning about the death-defying months C.J. and Emma have spent – and the incredible information they uncovered. Over coming days, C.J. and Emma read countless Internet articles about the book. It has really set the cat among the pigeons.

Then appears the headline: 'NEW BOOK A LIE!'

The Six Secrets was released in Europe and, just today, it was released in Asia. Although not released in the US yet, the book is starting to make waves. The interest is such that the United States Government has issued a statement about the book. C.J. and Emma read the brief press release statement together:

> The recently released book entitled *The Six Secrets – The Max Stroheim Story* has been classified as non-fiction. The reality is that it is far from factual. The book is based on the claims and invented memoirs of the late Max Stroheim who, while alive, claimed to have spent thirty-four years as an employee of the National Security Agency.
>
> Max Stroheim was never an employee of the NSA.
>
> Official government documents clearly show that Mr. Max Stroheim was, at no stage, employed by the NSA or any other government agency or department. He had on several occasions been subcontracted through his employment within the public sector to advise on several minor, yet confidential military projects.

Both C.J. and Emma note that even though the article refers to 'official government documents,' no substantiation is included. Whoever wrote this press release would forge documents anyhow. They read on:

> Although there appears to be no evidence of Max Stroheim's alleged memoirs, it must be noted that Mr. Stroheim's son, a journalist of dubious repute, wrote the book and admits the so-called memoirs were written just before Mr. Stroheim's death. Max Stroheim was in his nineties when he died. Medical records confirm that Mr. Stroheim suffered from bouts of 'delusional and psychological behavioral anxieties consistent with mental health issues.'

C.J. knows such medical records do not exist. Even if they did, they would have been falsified. They read on:

> Mr. Stroheim's fantastical claims are baseless, contrived, and untrue. The United States Government condemns them as such. This book is a work of fiction.
>
> The authors of the book will not be pursued under the Patriot Act for divulging classified information, as the claims in the book are not based on fact. It is the United States Government's strong recommendation to the publishers and distributors of this book that the book be reclassified as a work of fiction.
>
> We trust the general public will see the book for what it really is.

C.J. wears a huge smile. Emma is shocked. This article has ridiculed his father, accusing him of being a liar and mentally unfit. They have also attacked C.J., calling him 'a journalist of dubious repute.' C.J. should be furious.

'Is that the best they can come up with? They insinuate that my father was nuts and accuse me of being a poor journo?' With a grin from ear-to-ear, he declares, 'We've won, Emma, we're safe!

'It will be difficult not being able to respond to the lies and accusations, but so be it. The book is out. Nobody can stop that. People will judge the facts for themselves. I'm confident that, if we keep quiet and let the book do the speaking, we'll be left alone.

'My father was right. He was always right.'

With Indonesian food and the best champagne the resort can offer, C.J. and Emma celebrate in style. Each time their eyes lock, they can't help but smile.

Waiting for dessert, C.J. says, 'I once read "difficult roads often lead to beautiful destinations." This is one beautiful destination.'

'I agree. It's a tropical paradise.'

'I wasn't referring to here. I was referring to you, Emma.'

The next morning they sleep in. Emma makes online plans to return to Tasmania.

'Everything is booked,' she tells C.J. 'We leave tonight. We have a few hours shopping in Singapore before we need to go to the airport.'

'Sounds like a plan.'

CHAPTER FORTY-SEVEN

C.J. and Emma are excited beyond words. Having bought phones in Singapore, Emma contacted her father to inform of their arrival in Tasmania the next day. C.J. then talked with Gary Burgess privately. Assuming it was something about C.J.'s supposed guilt in placing her in danger or approval to marrying his daughter, Emma didn't ask questions.

Arriving in Launceston Airport, C.J. and Emma are surprised to find dozens of well-wishers, from Wynyard and Boat Harbour Beach. At the front of the group are Gary Burgess and Craig Hope.

Gary rushes to his daughter, hugging her tightly, tears streaming down both their faces.

C.J. watches on, delighted that Emma is reunited with her father, but unsure of what Gary Burgess's reaction to him might be.

The big, burly policeman unwraps his arms from around Emma to turn and face C.J. With more tears welling, Gary looks C.J. in the eye, and pushes forward to hug C.J. tightly.

'You kept your promise. Thank you for returning her to me. Thank you. Thank you,' Gary blubbers.

Craig Hope drove Gary to the airport in Craig's large all-wheel drive vehicle, suspecting C.J. and Emma to have huge amounts of luggage.

He guessed wrong; they have only have a suitcase each, two shopping bags, and filled backpacks.

On the drive, Gary and Craig reveal reading *The Six Secrets* and all the other information on the USB stick. Prior to fleeing Boat Harbour Beach, C.J. had explained what he knew to date. Gary and Craig did their own online investigations pertinent to C.J.'s initial revelations.

Gary says, 'If my daughter is shot at and runs off with an American, I want to know why.'

When his daughter's photo appeared in the local paper, linking her with 'a suspected American spy,' he had an inkling the story was falsified. He trusted his daughter and trusted C.J. It was a major show of faith for an innately skeptical man.

In recent days, Gary has become aware of the denial and defamatory statements posted by the US Government about the book. Gary saw right through the statements.

'The US Government are retaliating, aren't they Emma. As I understand it, those intelligence agencies, NSA and the CIA, are not government departments anyway. How the hell would the Government know what was really going on?'

'Wow Dad, you *did* read the book.'

'And I read that additional information, your "special project." If they pursue you, all that information will go public. That's very clever, Em.'

'That was all C.J.'s idea,' says Emma.

Gary asks his daughter how long she and C.J. expected to stay in Tasmania.

'We don't intend to go anywhere for a while. I might need to dust off my old golf clubs!'

Gary asks C.J., 'I guess she told you she used to be the local ladies' junior champion?'

'No, she chose not to tell me that little bit of information,' he comments, looking at Emma. '"Lucky shots" hey? You are a mischievous woman.'

Emma assumed she and C.J. would be staying at her father's house in Wynyard. Craig Hope drives past the Wynyard turnoff and heads toward Boat Harbour Beach.

'Where are we going?' she asks.

'You'll see,' replies Gary, with a smile.

They pull up outside the beach house. A perplexed Emma turns to C.J. But Gary does the talking.

'C.J. rang me from Singapore. He asked for a favor regarding the beach house. He wanted to buy it, so I contacted the owners. There was a little bit of to and froing … anyway, to cut a long story short, the owners accepted C.J.'s offer and, although there is still the paperwork to sign and six weeks before settlement – the place is yours.'

'Mine? what do you mean *mine*?' Emma is astonished.

'Technically, not yours – *ours*,' corrects C.J., with a beaming smile. 'There are a couple of holiday bookings over the next few weeks or so, but the owners are trying to move those to other beach houses. We can move in now – and yes, the house is *ours*.'

Emma could not be more excited, wrapping her arms tightly around her fiancé.

Unloading their bags to their new home, Gary suggests that, as it's almost dinnertime, they should eat at the café. 'I'm sure Sarah will be pleased to see you both. Why don't you freshen up and walk along the beach in half an hour or so. While we wait, Hopesy and I might have a cold beer …'

'… or three,' adds Craig.

C.J. bought some copies of the book in Singapore, for Vince and Steve Pomerel in Queensland, as well as the promised signed copy for Sarah at the café.

With the book in one of C.J.'s hands and Emma's hand in the other, they walk along the beach.

Walking up the sand to the café, they discover it is brimming with people. As they enter, the whole café erupts in unison:

'Welcome home!'

• • •

It is a glorious Boat Harbour Beach afternoon. Dozens of formally dressed people gather on the beach in front of C.J. and Emma's beach house, including Emma's friend Anna; Vince Pomerel and his son Steve; Sarah, Rob, Deb, and Tara from the café; Craig Hope, Mick Heath, and his wife; and from the UK are Mark Dalgleish, his daughter Stella, as well as Thomas and Cilla.

C.J. looks resplendent in a designer black suit. He grins with pride seeing Emma, dressed in white, being led down the beach house steps by her father. C.J. has never seen anyone look as beautiful as Emma does right now.

The sun sets, the glimmering hues reflecting on the tranquil water. One chapter of C.J. and Emma Stroheim's life may have concluded, but a new has just begun.

Taking a moment away from their guests, C.J. and Emma walk hand in hand by the water's edge, the moonlight dancing on the small waves.

C.J. turns to Emma. 'My father once quoted me this from Douglas Adams: "I may not have gone where I intended to go, but I think I have ended up where I needed to be."' He places his arms around her. 'I came here not really knowing what I was looking for. I've discovered so much more than I ever could have imagined. I found the most important things in life: Understanding, truth, and love.'

She kisses him.

William Cooper wrote: 'Like it or not, everything is changing. The result will be the most wonderful experience in the history of man or the most horrible enslavement you can imagine. Be active or abdicate. The future is in your hands.'

C.J. and Emma Stroheim have opened the doors for past lies to be explored – to be reasoned – to be evaluated.

Edward Snowden wrote: 'Truth is coming and it cannot be stopped.'

So let the truth reveal the lies of the past and, more importantly, let it inspire the events of the future.

AUTHOR'S NOTES

Congratulations on not only reading what I hope was an entertaining story, but for also learning about the processes, structures, and hidden secrets that have shaped the way America, and much of the world, runs. You would no doubt realize that the events, projects, and organizations portrayed in the book are real. I encourage you to ask further questions, trusting this will be the beginning of your own investigative journey.

Of the characters in the book, I've been asked who are real and who are not? Naturally, famous scientists, such as Einstein, Oppenheimer, Teller, von Neumann, and Von Braun are real, as too are their revelations and documents. Additionally, Dr. Guillermo Mendoza was a real botanist, as too were the careers and ensuing deaths of William Cooper, Jack Wheeler, Dr. William Reich and Captain Edward Ruppelt. All of the MJ-12 members mentioned, including scientists and administrators Vannevar Bush, Detlev Bronk, Lloyd Berkner, and Donald Menzel, are also real.

The Oppenheimer–Einstein document 'Relationships with Inhabitants of Celestial Bodies' was only declassified recently. Combing through genuine documents from both these famous scientists, I found no indications to suggest that the document is anything but authentic. The note at the end of their paper, with the initialed signature of Dr. Vannevar Bush, provided further proof that this is historically accurate. Had this document been given to President Truman, with Einstein and Oppenheimer's recommendations implemented, much of the subject matter in my book may have become public knowledge already, yet it was not.

Politicians such as Presidents Truman and Eisenhower, and Secretary of Defense James Forrestal, were portrayed as truly as possible; the events and projects of the era were thoroughly investigated, and their quotes and much of their dialogue were genuine.

During thousands of hours of Internet research, my computer was monitored and files copied. I was often blocked from entering certain sites, including Wikipedia. Some of these real 'issues' are written into the manuscript. In many ways, the intrusive monitoring by the NSA, and probably others, guided the direction of my research. I'd take note of those blocked sites to later research on public computers, much the same as Emma did. Sites that were not blocked made me somewhat suspicious of the content's authenticity.

Edward Snowden was aided, and subsequently was helped to escape the USA, by WikiLeaks; however, many whistleblowers brave enough to divulge some of the NSA's secrets died prematurely. Secretary of Defense James Forrestal did fall to his death, William Cooper was shot dead, and Jack Wheeler was murdered then thrown in a dumpster.

The characters Ellis Buckman and Ben Hamermesh are fictional, yet their associated companies and organizations are real. Their weaponry, including the injection device with the deadly toxins, are based on genuine CIA armaments, uncovered during various government investigations and raids over a number of decades.

Most of the legal stories and interpretations within the book are factual, as I did seek legal guidance. An example of this is the story told by Emma about the Australian importing an America car, only to discover that local importation taxes were furtively sent to the US. I was told of this account directly, with further investigation confirming the story.

Emma's 'special project' was also my 'special project.' I took precautions similar to those mentioned within the manuscript. You can appreciate why I did not name names and why I chose the path of writing a 'fiction' book. The dangers are very real.

The story of Emma as a child seeing 'lights in the sky,' alerting her grandmother then watching the lights 'take off at speed' is something I witnessed when I was eight, at my grandmother's house. It was an event that helped spark my interest in some of the topics within this book.

I'd like to take this opportunity to thank my family for their support throughout years of researching and writing, as well as the editorial guidance of 'my personal editor,' Elke Madison, as well as the stellar editorial work and meticulous attention to detail by editor Jessica Cox. Few stones were left unturned in our efforts to present the facts and the locations as accurately as possible.

All of the locations C.J. and Emma visit during their adventures are places I've been – and know well. Some of my favorite global settings were incorporated into the story-line.

If I could give one piece of advice to aspiring novelists, it is to write about what you know and what you believe in. Writing this book did take many years of exhaustive researching and writing, yet throughout the whole process I was totally enthralled, as I hope you were.

Is this the end of my, and C.J.'s and Emma's, journey?

No. It is only the beginning.

I hope you'll continue to share the journey with me.

Sincerely
Daniel Springfield

First published in 2018 by New Holland Publishers
London • Sydney • Auckland

131-151 Great Titchfield Street, London WIW 5BB, United Kingdom
1/66 Gibbes Street, Chatswood, NSW 2067, Australia
5/39 Woodside Ave, Northcote, Auckland 0627, New Zealand

newhollandpublishers.com

A record of this book is held at the British Library and the National Library of Australia.

ISBN 9781921024771

Group Managing Director: Fiona Schultz
Publisher: Alan Whiticker
Project Editor: Jess Cox
Designer: Catherine Meachen
Production Director: James Mills-Hicks
Printer: Hang Tai Printing Company Limited

10 9 8 7 6 5 4 3 2 1

UK £14.99
US $24.99